QUEENS

OF

SPELLS

AND

STONE

VESSELS OF THE GODS

I

KATERINA STEVENS

First Paperback Edition April 2025

Cover art by Tina @tcdesigns271 [Instagram]

Interior art by Katerina Stevens

[Canva Pro & Inkarnate Commercial License]

Editing by Rattle the Stars PR

ISBN Paperback: 979-8-9985657-0-0

ISBN E-book: 979-8-9985657-1-7

To my husband—I will forever be truly yours.

Thank you for believing in me from the very beginning of this crazy dream of mine, and for loving and supporting me every step of the way.

I could not have done this without you.

Queens of Spells and Stone is a thrillingly epic romantasy filled with morally grey characters, friendly-*ish* beasties, and a kingdom in peril. As such, this story includes elements that might not be suitable for all readers. Violence, gore, bodily injury, blood, murder, death (including the death of parents and siblings), imprisonment, dealing with loss and grief, seizures, perilous situations, alcohol, graphic language, manipulation, sexual activities, mentions of domestic violence, and mentions of war are depicted. Readers who may be sensitive to these elements– please take note and prepare to uncover secrets that can destroy a kingdom...

OBSIDIAN KINGDOM
OPAL KINGDOM
IRRIDESSEN
LARIMAR ISLANDS
SLATE KINGDOM
THE SEVEN KINGDOMS OF
TERRAMERE

INGOTHERIA
JADE KINGDOM
TOPAZ KINGDOM
RUBY KINGDOM

PROLOGUE

Long ago, when the Bramberry Forest was nothing but saplings and the Zircon Mountains were only just learning to carve their rivers through the earth, two sister goddesses awoke surrounded by the quiet beginnings of life.

Alone, with only gurgling streams and the whispers of breezes to greet them, the goddesses tried desperately to find a way back to their home realm, Aurramere, with no luck. But they had each other, immortal lives, and their magic that sang through this strange new realm.

The first goddess, Faune, radiant and beautiful, quickly grew to love the lands she now inhabited. Divine magic thrummed through her veins, begging to release light upon this new realm. She wanted to bestow loveliness upon it, wanted her power to bloom into creation itself.

Phades, the second goddess, never forgave Aurramere for her unexpected exile. Draped in shadows and distrust, she spent years scouring the landscape with the intent to rip through its peaceful illusions and find the secrets contained beneath its surface. She knew this realm must connect to Aurramere and she was determined to tear the veil apart until she found another way home.

The decades passed as the sisters experimented with their magic, slowly drawing further and further apart, lost to their own restless minds. Faune marked the land with a surge of omnipotent power and creation *burst forth—unending and unyielding. Pleased with her contribution, Faune named this new realm Terramere—the realm for the living.*

Phades used her power on every corner of the realm, hunting where the veil between realms thinned, still seeking a way to return to Aurramere. Instead, she uncovered an empty god realm burrowed deep in the heart of a mountain. After exploring every groove and hollow it contained and finding no way home, Phades named the realm Minmere and returned earthside to reunite with Faune.

She found Faune agonizing over one of her poor creations, a being with now-withered skin and soft brown eyes. Faune cried as her first creation took their last breath. Guilt over leaving Faune alone for so long had Phades gently carrying the being's body into the depths of Minmere to rest forevermore in peace.

Phades loved Faune and was hesitant to leave her again, knowing her sister needed her now more than ever. So, the Goddess of Life created and nurtured new beings into existence, and the Goddess of Death carried them into the soft embrace of Minmere once their decades on Terramere waned.

This worked until it didn't. As the years passed, Faune became frustrated over losing her creations to mortality, and began imbuing bits of her magic into each one so they would live longer. Phades warned Faune of the dangers of this, stating they should keep their magic to themselves, fearing what these creations would do if they became too powerful.

But Faune did not heed her sister, determined to create a being time could not take from her so quickly. One night, when the moon was full and Phades carried another creation into Minmere, Faune snapped, torn apart by grief over death, and recklessly imbued a being with so much of her god magic that the creation rivaled the goddesses themselves. Faune called her newest creation Vessel, a companion time could not so callously erase.

When Phades returned from Minmere, she grew angry, demanding Faune take her gift of magic back from the Vessel. Faune refused, and Phades struck the creation down, stating the Vessel was too dangerous to keep alive.

The sister goddesses fought, branding Terramere with their fury. Their battle scorched forests, leaving wastelands of glittering sand in their wake, barreled across the seas and shattered massive islands apart, leaving marks on this realm forevermore.

Faune claimed their magic should be shared, and Phades argued it should be protected.

Compromise did not come, and when neither reached an agreement, Phades stormed off into the depths of Minmere, leaving Faune alone on Terramere, swearing to never return to her sister's side.

And though Faune never again created an equal to her Vessel, she did bring forth a new race of beings imbued with small bits of magic, and Faune named them Fae.

DEEP, RHYTHMIC BREATHING ALERTED the Queen that the Princesses were fast asleep. Through the room's large, gilded window, stars peeked out from behind wispy purple clouds, illuminating the Royal Gardens below.

The Queen softly closed the book of fables, murmuring prayers to the goddesses above and below to watch over the two small, blanket covered bundles as she slipped from the bedroom, finding the King standing alone outside the door.

"What is the point of a bedtime tale if they fall asleep before the ending?" the Queen asked as the King extended his arm to her. "They didn't even get to the part where the sister goddesses reconcile. I swear, Scottrell, they *never* hear the moral of the story."

"They are ten years old, Elera," the King chuckled in response, guiding his Queen down a hallway lined with glittering opal columns. "Even if our daughters listened to the ending, I doubt they'll be spouting introspective musings anytime soon."

"The story this evening was of Faune and Phades," Queen Elera said as they traipsed down the hall.

King Scottrell shot his Queen a tight smile as he replied, "Phades and Faune, sister goddesses with their own strengths and weaknesses—who fought over power, forgave out of love, and ultimately ruled their realms together." He paused, pressing a kiss to his Queen's forehead between the slim opal horns that protruded from her head. "Esmeray and Adara *will* learn the moral of that story one day, my Queen."

CHAPTER ONE

LENNA

Eighty - Eight Years Later

THE AFTERNOON'S RAINSTORM LEFT humidity and muck in its wake. Lenna trudged through the puddles, the wicker basket in her arms growing heavier with each step as she tried to ignore the creeping pain forming behind her eyes. Keeping her head up, she rolled her shoulders back, attempting to relieve some tension, while praying the grime would easily wash from the hem of her dress.

Rounding the corner of the narrow dirt path, the tall stone wall surrounding the brick Manor came into view, its arched roof jutting out above the embankment. Heavy fog clung to the branches of the silent trees leading up to the Doortan Estate. It was as if the untamed forest appreciated the recent winds and rain and now slumbered until the sun once again warmed their bark. The only sounds left were the heavy swish of Lenna's mud laden skirts and her labored breathing as she ascended the small hill to the front gate.

Ivy covered the stonework–broken up only by the twisting metal archway of the gate itself. Passing through the yawning mouth of the entryway, dirt and puddles gave way to pebbled white gravel. It was a vast and well-manicured difference from the wildness of the path leading back from town.

Overhead, the sky reflected Lenna's mood.

Gloomy, dreary, dull, *grey*.

Chewing her lip, Lenna looked longingly to the side of the Manor where she could sneak in through the servant's entrance without being fussed over. Ultimately, she didn't want to chance running into her husband. This time of day he would be hunkered down in his study right across the hall from the less used entrance–either pouring over the latest shipping reports or drowning himself in brandy. With a sigh, Lenna trekked on towards the arched front door. She knew he would throw a proper fit if he saw her disheveled and muddy after walking back from the town's bakery alone.

By the time her boots hit the first stone step, the grand doors swung open with a groaning creak. The entrance hall was a flurry of movement as servants dressed in the dark colors of the Doortan Manor surrounded her, taking the basket of baked goods to the kitchen for dinner service, tsk-ing at the mire coating Lenna's dress and boots, and calling for a bath to be drawn.

In hindsight, she should have taken the private side entrance after all.

Less bustle, less notoriety, less acknowledgement.

She extended a small smile to the servants as she relinquished the basket and allowed herself to be steered from the front door to her chambers. Once inside her bedroom, muck dripping onto the cool tiled floor, Lenna's head twinged with fresh pain. A heartbeat later, her handmatron, Olivera, strode into the room, took one look at Lenna's sodden appearance, and disappeared into the connecting washroom with a huff. Lenna heard the splash of water filling the tub, accentuated by Olivera's veiled grumbling. Too exhausted to decide if she should apologize for her disheveled state or dismiss the woman, Lenna mutely stripped off her mud-soaked coat, followed by her dress skirts and undergarments, before standing in front of her bedroom mirror. Though the edges of the silver rimmed glass had long ago begun to tarnish, she paid them no mind.

Her hair, usually well maintained, lay frizzy and matted beneath the light green scarf she wore for her walk. The reddish gold curls were dull, reflecting the weather and the now consistent head pain thudding across the front of her skull. Ripping off the scarf, Lenna shook out the curls with her fingers and locked eyes with the reflection staring back at her. Her hands smoothed down soft stomach, where no trace of abs or muscle definition remained from when she was younger, when she lived on horseback, racing, hunting. When she had been so full of life. Soft lines marred loosening skin below honey-brown eyes now perpetually rimmed in purple from lack of sleep and sun. A woman of fifty-one. Though she loved the lush curves that graced her hips, she missed the strength and tenacity of youth, where a walk to town wouldn't tire her out so completely. Her body felt too weak, as if it was unable to keep up with the march of time itself. Lenna couldn't tell if the tears welling up in her eyes were from drifting thoughts or the persistent throbbing in her temples.

Lenna tugged her robe from the hook next to the mirror and belted it tightly, screwing her lids shut against a particularly sharp burst of pain. Half-staggering into the washroom, she shuffled across the ice-cold floor to sit on the bench next to the tub. With her head in her hands, she waited on Olivera to finish filling the tub with warm water.

"Is there any peppermint oil left?" Lenna asked as she rubbed tautness from her shoulder. It lessened the onslaught of the violent throb that radiated from her head down into her jaw for a single, blissful moment.

"Another headache, my Lady?" Olivera questioned—but without waiting for an answer, she pulled a small vial from the shelf next to the tub and added some drops into the now steaming water. Lenna groaned in confirmation with her eyes closed. She rubbed her face with her fingers, trying something, *anything*, to chase that sliver of relief. Olivera shut off the squeaky tap before taking her leave. "I'll give you privacy and check on you in a bit."

Lenna raised her head just enough to watch Olivera depart through pain-slitted eyelids.

The headaches started their merciless assault last month.

At first, they were short pangs of discomfort that blurred her vision and made her dizzy. But as the days progressed, the headaches increased in agony and length, and her husband, Leon, called upon the town's healer to request any concoction of salve or oils that could bring Lenna comfort.

Neither the recommended peppermint oil nor the crushed herbs and increased water intake lessened the pain at all. The healer also recommended shoulder massages to pull tension out of Lenna's head and neck muscles. Of course, Leon made a snide comment of how Lenna had zero stress on her shoulders and the headaches were probably some *"womanly"* problem from getting older. The healer had pointedly ignored that since Leon paid handsomely for house calls and usually let him leave with some rare bottle of brandy.

Some nights, Lenna would lay in bed, curled up in a ball, quietly sobbing until sleep dragged her into a deep slumber where agony was replaced with disorienting nightmares of winged demons and monsters with red eyes lurking in the shadows.

As the water in the tub grew cold, and the sickly-sweet aroma of peppermint dissipated, Lenna gingerly made her way out of the washroom and back into her robe.

Sleep. Darkness. Quiet.

All she wanted was to lay down and beg the gods to allow the pounding in her head to subside before morning. Olivera greeted her once she stepped back into the bedroom. The handmatron had closed the curtains, making the room as dark as possible. Lenna would have considered that sweet if it wasn't for the fact both women knew Leon was currently entertaining Olivera's daughter in his study, and Olivera had been told to let Lenna "*rest*" until morning.

Which was a very polite way of saying "*keep Lenna out of Leon's balding hair for the night.*"

The newest affair had started months ago. It was not the first affair, and it certainly wouldn't be the last. She felt nothing for her husband or any of the young woman he became enamored with. Honestly, Lenna couldn't remember the last time she "*felt*" anything. She was desensitized to the affairs that had gone on for years. By the time the third woman had come and gone, Lenna found herself wishing Leon would hurry up and find another. She knew it was selfish, but she despised the man her husband had become. He was quick to anger and had used his fists to convey that rage onto Lenna on a few occasions.

But life went on, and the abuse happened further and further apart. Lenna wasn't by any means happy, but divorce was out of the question in Doortan. No holy folk would grant one and no court would accept Leon's infidelity as an excuse. So, Lenna went on, confined to the doldrums of hiring servants, running the domestic chores the Estate demanded, and gardening.

Gone were the days of riding swift horses through the woods, hunting the sure-footed bucks bedded down in the lush forest, *adventuring*. Gone were the days where Lenna's heart would pump fire into her blood as she embarked on mighty ships and sailed the coast of the Slate Kingdom. Gone was any other life purpose aside from being an obedient wife and Lady of Doortan Estate.

"Is there anything else I can get you, some tea perhaps?" Olivera offered, interrupting Lenna's brooding and pulling extra blankets from the cedar chest by the bedroom door.

"Tea would be lovely, thank you." The small talk made Lenna want to crawl out of her bones. She could deal with the fact her husband only enjoyed two things–alcohol and young woman. She could even deal with the headaches–to a degree. But nothing got under Lenna's skin more than the fake concern slipping out of the handmatron's mouth.

Olivera left the room to fetch tea as Lenna sank into bed. The weight of the extra blankets sucked her down as sleep beckoned from the edges of her fuzzing vision. The velvet curtains blocked the sinking sun, casting the room in dancing hues of dark reds and purples.

Almost thirty years of marriage, yet it became apparent after the first six months that Leon had no intention of sharing his bed with her. Which was fine by Lenna. The ache to feel loved dulled over time–from a razor-sharp dagger between her lungs to a blunt dinner knife. Lenna felt the years slog by, the times of revelry and excitement far behind her.

Thirty years and still Lenna felt like a guest in the Doortan Estate. Leon refused her pleas to change any of the visceral décor of the Manor, where his disturbing paintings of the gods' monster-like protectors lined the shadowy halls, dismembering non-believers and carrying away wicked women who forsook their marriage vows.

Lenna only wanted to replace the painted gargoyles ripping apart immodestly dressed women with something a bit more tasteful. The grotesque postures and snarling faces did little to calm her mind, reminding her of the stories her mother would recant of gargoyles snatching disobedient wives from their homes if they did not heed their husbands and their faith. Leon had been raised with the same ideals, though his lackluster attempts at swaying the temple priests into believing he was a spiritual man were only slightly more convincing than stories of demonic gargoyles crawling up from the ground to swallow one whole for not paying the tithe on time.

Even the dark colors of the fabrics and upholstery were off-limits to change. Lenna wished for just one room, one corner, to call her own. But to Leon, the request alone deemed her an unruly wife trying to interfere with the integrity of his iron will.

This Manor would never feel like home.

Lenna had learned to accept that.

Pulling herself from the haze of memories, she focused on her breathing, willing her body to calm. Even the short walk to and from the bakery had worn her out and made her legs sore. In and out, relaxing her muscles, in and out, deep breaths. She shoved down any thoughts of what her husband was doing. Pushed it away and breathed. The banging in her head quieted. The blankets were warm, the room silent.

By the time the tea was delivered, Lenna was already asleep.

CHAPTER TWO
LENNA

THE GOLDEN STONE GLOWED unnaturally, throwing disorienting shadows against the craggy walls. It was the sole light source in the dark room, yet it gave off no heat. Lenna shivered. If anything, the stone made the room seem colder, sucking into it any warmth that remained.

A crumpled figure in the corner groaned as death approached. Leathery wings rustled out of eyesight. "Esmeray..." The old man weakly lifted his head. A flash of gold illuminated the crone's crumpled body. Chains clanked together. A dungeon.

In the fracture of light, Lenna could see sunken eyes, dirt caked into his matted white hair. Dried blood from some old wound remained on his face. "Esmeray...please..."

Another flash of gold.

Then—total darkness.

A feminine voice broke the silence, otherworldly and smooth, "I'm sorry, old friend... This is the only way." A gurgling noise...then...nothing.

The light shone closer to the crone and death stared back. A gloved hand came into Lenna's view, closing eyes that would never see again. Another whisper of wings pierced the thrumming silence.

The gold light faded, leaving the unmoving body in shadow. The last thing Lenna could make out was a small, peaceful smile on the old man's face.

LENNA BOLTED UPRIGHT IN bed, sweat pouring down her back. It took a moment for her eyes to adjust to the morning light creeping into the room. Her heart raced. *Just a dream,* she told herself over and over, willing her erratic heartbeat to slow.

Shoving the nightmare from her mind, Lenna stretched her arms above her head, rolling her neck between her shoulder blades. She felt–*good.* For the first time in a month, no lingering soreness remained behind her eyes, no tension knotted in her back.

Elation itself was a rare occurrence, but the alleviation of mind numbing pain allowed Lenna to get out of bed and draw open the curtains with a renewed flourish. The main reason she chose this room lay right outside the tall window. Sprawling flower gardens dotted the Estate's fields, a colorful and lively contrast to the gloom of the Manor's interior. Needle straight hedges pushed out from circular, well-groomed beds exploding with color after the recent rains. Past the garden, tilled plots bustled with servants busy harvesting vegetables and herbs for the kitchen. In the distance, smoke from the town's chimneys wafted lazily towards the clouds, no bigger than the tendrils that puffed from Leon's expensive cigars.

Leon.

As Lenna picked her discarded robe off the floor, she wondered how he fared this morning. After drinking, Leon typically awoke with a nasty hangover and an even fouler mood. Sliding her feet into soft slippers, Lenna aimed for the dining hall in the center of the house to find out how miserable the Lord was feeling. Though she ignored the vicious paintings that lined the walls, dread followed each of her footsteps.

Leon already sat at the long wood table that had been a wedding gift from her late father. Since most of the Doortan socialites moved south years ago, the grand table was rarely set for more than two. As Lenna entered the room, the smell of alcohol and a sticky, musky odor met her nose.

"Good morning, husband. I prayed to the gods in hopes you had a restful sleep," Lenna exhaled, failing to clear her nose of the stale stench and plastering a vapidly cheery disposition on her face in response. She pulled out a chair across from Leon and sat down. Even with the bright morning outside, the shadows pooling in the corners of the dining room seemed permanent, as if they refuted the sun's claim to shine in here. The Lord of Doortan Estate was nearly invisible behind the large newspaper that held his attention—not even deigning to look up. Lenna smoothed the wrinkles from her robe, reminding herself to take a calming breath as Leon grunted an answer and continued reading.

The silence pressed in, sullen and bottomless. Lenna busied herself with a biscuit that had been set on the table prior to her arrival. Cutting it in half and generously buttering both sides, Lenna scowled at the back of the newspaper. The quiet was suffocating. Lenna searched for some sort of words for her husband. Anything to break up the crypt-like atmosphere in the dining room. "How did you sleep?"

Leon slammed the paper down so hard the plates rattled, causing Lenna to startle and revealing the blotchy start of a black eye on the right side of his face. "What the fuck, Lenna. Are you blind? I'm reading the godsdamned newspaper. *Why* are you so chatty this morning?"

"Leon." Lenna pursed her lips against the retort that bubbled up, searching his face for any sign of the smart, kind man she met at the tender age of twenty-one when they married. That man had changed–years of anger and alcoholism irrevocably warped his features. Eyes that used to be shining indigo were replaced with cold hues of grey and blue. The dark brown hair that she used to love running her fingers through at night as they lay in their marital bed was barely still there. Thinning as much as his patience with her was. "Would you like me to get something for your eye?"

"It's fine," Leon growled, bits of spit landing on his plate. "I fell in the study. Don't worry about it." He snapped the newspaper back up, blocking her view of him. Lenna shook her head, focusing on her breathing as her hands trembled.

Servants filed into the room, smiling at Lenna while giving Leon a wide berth, setting tea, fruits, and eggs on the table. Lenna took a sip of her tea, still staring at the newspaper concealing her husband. Part of Lenna wanted to leave it alone, finish her breakfast, and get out of the room. The other part, something reckless and dark inside her, wanted to push–to push until Leon exploded. To push until she felt something, *anything*.

"You fell? Did anyone help you up?" The feigned innocence of the question held a sting of venom. That was no fall. Falls didn't make a perfect circle around one's eye. A small circle–like a fist. A fist that was probably connected to a certain servant that was glaringly absent from breakfast service.

Without moving his newspaper, Leon reached for his own tea. Half of his scowling face appeared as he glanced down into the white cup.

"Brandy," he snapped at the servant hastily placing sugar and honey on the table–a young man named Marlo Asrar that Lenna hired last spring. Marlo was very sweet and very quiet around Leon, but was a ruthless gossip when Leon was out of sight. He knew everything about every servant currently employed at the Manor. She'd ask him later what *really* happened.

Marlo disappeared from the dining room, returning a beat later with a bottle of brandy. He poured a few mouthfuls into Leon's tea while glancing over the Lord's head, giving Lenna a little wink.

Oh, he definitely knows, Lenna thought to herself. She crinkled her nose at Marlo behind her teacup and he gave her a quick bow of his head before slipping from the room.

Ignoring the possibility of another outburst of Leon's temper, Lenna cleared her throat, sitting up straighter against the hard backed wooden chair. "I'm going to take one of the horses out today and check the plots in the gardens that started yielding carrots." As much as Lenna hated small talk, this at least broke up the unending silence, and now that the help was around, she didn't want whispers of her as a sullen Lady of the Manor scaring off any potential servants she'd hire for the coming months. "I'll have Marlo come with me. You know, he's overseeing his first plot of vegetables for the season. And I'll speak with our gardeners about the rotation of herb beds."

All she got in return was a dismissive hand wave that appeared to the side of the newspaper. The rest of the meal was eaten in silence. Lenna, chewing thoughtfully, let her mind wander back to the nightmare. The dead crone, the rustling wings, the odd golden light. She dismissed it as a weird dream. Maybe she would tell Marlo about it. He was always interested in dreams and what they could signify.

Marlo claimed his ancestors descended from roving bands of wanderers that explored far off lands and charged small amounts of coin to interpret dreams and read one's future. It was one of the reasons she liked him. He brimmed with life, always telling grand stories that were rarely, if ever, true. She knew for fact the only family he knew had passed away.

After breakfast, Lenna wandered the halls to seek out Marlo, who appeared carrying a tray of tea and oatmeal for the servants working in the main hall. His short blond hair was trimmed neatly, cut close to his head, per the requirements of working in the Estate. When she first met him, it had been down to his shoulders and peppered with dirt from living on the street.

"Do you have time to take a ride over to the vegetable plots and the greenhouse today?" Lenna questioned, her lips quirking up as the servant came into view.

Marlo laughed, his blue eyes lighting up as he noticed she cornered him. "I absolutely do. I'll get the stable hands to saddle up two horses for us." He winked before breezing past her to deliver the contents of the tray. Lenna knew Marlo would tell her all about Leon, as Marlo was the only servant Leon trusted to get expensive brandy out of his locked cabinets. And the only servant bold enough to spy on him during his drunken stupors.

Lenna smiled at the young man's back. Marlo was tall and lanky with the same arrogance and invincibility as every other twenty-four-year-old man she'd ever met. She hired him last year after finding him begging on the streets. It didn't take long for Lenna to learn all about Marlo's upbringing–the father who left before he was born, the mother who passed when he was a small child, the elder uncle who raised him as his own. The trauma of watching his uncle go mad and drink himself to death before being sent to the streets to beg for coins to feed himself through the winter hit Lenna in the heart, and she offered him a position at the Manor before even learning his name.

Even though there was an almost thirty-year age gap, he was the closest thing she had to a friend here. She hoped one day he would find a sweet girl, get married, and travel far away from this wretched house.

Lenna hurried back to her rooms where Olivera was busy making her bed.

"M'lady," Olivera greeted her, "How is your head feeling this morning?"

"Much better. Thank you, Olivera," Lenna replied politely, crossing the room to her wardrobe and shuffling through the drawers for anything she could wear riding. "Didn't there used to be a set of breeches in here? I'm riding over to the vegetable plots."

"I packed them away with the light linens. Let me retrieve them." Olivera fluffed the pillow she was holding. setting it back down on the bed, before pivoting to the cedar chest where Lenna stored clothes she rarely wore.

Lenna chose a white button up, quarter sleeved blouse and fished socks from the bottom drawer. Olivera came back with the breeches–a pretty chestnut color–and tall, black boots that were perfect for riding. The handmatron frowned, rubbing her hand across the toe as she brought them to Lenna.

"These haven't been polished in a while, I'll get oil."

"No need, Olivera. I won't be gone long, and the boots will simply get dirtier anyway," Lenna replied hastily, squeezing into the breeches and noting they were now slightly uncomfortable, the buttons digging into her skin. Lenna huffed out her frustration before trying and failing to suck in the soft pudge below her belly. Just a month since she last went riding–before the headaches began controlling her waking moments and the nightmares her sleeping–and it was clear her body had grown stiff and soft with the lack of movement. Lenna shook her head. She hadn't done much at all this past month, forgoing her usual activities in favor of laying in bed to rest. Hopefully, the headaches would subside for a long while, and she could get back to walking, riding her horses around the property, and working in the flower gardens she had diligently maintained since she was newly married.

Lenna straightened off the bed, shoving her heel down into the last boot before walking up to her mirror and ruffling her hair. The springy red curls puffed up with the humidity in the air, and no amount of smoothing was going to control the flyaways. Olivera appeared at her side, holding a small bottle of glistening hair oil and a pearl comb Lenna found during one of her walks into town that the shopkeep swore would do wonders for her curls. It was too pretty to not purchase, and the shopkeep had thanked Lenna about one hundred times before she left.

Life in the small township of Doortan was hard. There were few inhabited Estates left in Doortan after a particularly snowy winter concluded with an exodus of socialites yearning for warmer weather and a more vibrant city. Since Leon's Lordship passed down from his late father, along with the deed to the largest Manor in Doortan, he refused to move.

With the remoteness of the town, the only lucrative work was found during the summer when ships came back from sea. Captains came looking for new sailors, sailors came looking for a good bottle of rum, and any man with two coins to rub together looked for a few women to warm their hostel bed. Sailors would spend their pay in brothels and bars before dropping small amounts on the counters of the shop folk. Unfortunately, this negatively affected Doortan's social standing as well—with more than one not-so-friendly street Lenna avoided at all costs.

Leon's inheritance also included a fleet of merchant ships and a large abundance of wealth with the Lordship and Estate. Leon knew very little about trading, and even less about how much the captains ripped him off to sail Doortan lumber to Bardon, a larger port situated to the south. Lenna had been to Bardon only once, early into their marriage, and felt very out of place there, too. It was a much livelier town with an abundance of glittering shops, plenty of wealth, and enough sin to keep the temples packed on service days. The social crowd consisted of many Lords and Ladies, most much younger, who received their money through inheritances and barely lifted a finger to do any sort of work.

"Have you seen Orla today?" Lenna asked Olivera, keeping her face neutral. She might as well push and see if Olivera knew anything about the black eye Leon was sporting. Orla was a newer servant to the Estate, hired due to Olivera's status in the Manor, though Lenna had only spoken to the young woman on a few occasions. "She wasn't at breakfast service–was she pulled to help elsewhere?"

"She...isn't feeling well this morning, M'lady. I told her to stay in bed." Olivera's thinning lips confirmed for Lenna that she struck a nerve.

"Goodness, I hope she's alright. Is there anything I can bring her back from the gardens? We have cabbage ready to harvest and potatoes we can add to a stew for her dinner." Lenna kept the bite out of her words, taking the olive-green head scarf Olivera brought over from the vanity. Wrapping her hair up and out of her face, Lenna watched Olivera's reaction in the mirror.

"That won't be necessary, my Lady. I'm sure she'll be feeling better tomorrow." The handmatron gave Lenna's shirt a brisk sweep down her back, removing a few pieces of dust while dutifully avoiding Lenna's hardened gaze.

Expressing her wishes for Orla's speedy recovery, Lenna hustled down to the stables. She couldn't wait to hear what ripe piece of gossip Marlo had for her.

CHAPTER THREE
LENNA

LENNA GALLOPED ACROSS THE perfectly manicured lawns, kicking up that atrocious white gravel, feeling the power of the beautiful brown mare's muscles shifting underneath her. As they neared the first vegetable plot, she gently pulled against the reins, slowing to a trot before easing into a walk. Marlo, on the grey dapple next to her, mimicked her movements.

"I'm going to assume you don't truly care to hear about vegetable yields," Marlo drawled, removing his worn riding gloves. "You want to know about Leon's latest nightly activities."

"Was the black eye a gift from Orla?" Lenna asked quietly, scanning the area to make sure they weren't overheard. A smattering of servants worked at the next plot over, their baskets bowing under the weight of the leafy produce they picked, far enough away that they couldn't hear the quiet conversation.

Marlo rolled his eyes at Lenna and nodded. "I fetched Leon a new drink and was leaving the study as she was walking in."

"Leon was drunk?"

"When isn't he?" Marlo pursed his lips, throwing Lenna a knowing look. "After I dropped off his glass, I hung around the hall. I heard him start yelling at her, and then I heard a glass break–which made Orla cry.

He started laughing but I think Orla hit him right after because he started cursing at her." Marlo rubbed his eyes with the back of his hand. "Orla left the room a few moments later, her shirt was ripped, and she was cradling her face in her hands–scurrying back to the servants' quarters to cry to her wretched mother."

Lenna gingerly dismounted the mare and led her over to a wooden fence dividing plots of vegetables. "Olivera never seemed very motherly to me," Lenna mused, expertly tying the horse's reins to the squat post. Wrapping her arms around herself, she meandered down the line of planted carrots, her boots shuffling through the soft soil at the edge of the raised earth. Soothing aromas of dirt and herbs wafted through her nose as she put her hands on her hips and took a deep breath, committing the delectable smells to memory in case her headaches came back with a vengeance and kept her bed bound for another month. "Some sick part of me wishes Orla hit him harder–maybe knock some sense into that balding head of his."

"The day Leon sees sense, I swear to the gods and goddesses above and below, I will quit this job and run all the way to Bardon. I don't want him finding out I swap his expensive brandy with the cheap stuff," Marlo laughed. "It's my little satisfying '*fuck you*' for how shitty he treats you."

Lenna gaped at Marlo. "You do not. Do you really?" Leon was extremely picky about the alcohol he put down his throat nightly. She had witnessed him hurl half full bottles that didn't meet his expectations into the fireplace in rage. One time, he narrowly missed her head as he threw a subpar bottle to the flames after one of their more harrowing fights.

Marlo grinned, his blue eyes twinkling with barely leashed mirth. "Oh, I absolutely do. He's none the wiser, and I don't feel bad that the good stuff is warming my belly at night instead of his."

Linking arms, the two wandered the gardens and greenhouses, the conversation veering from Leon to the other servants and their debauchery.

Marlo knew so much in the little time he had been at the Manor–who was sleeping with who, what drama was going down with the laundry staff, which servants seemed awkward around each other insinuating there were secrets being kept. Lenna drank it all in greedily, giddy as a sense of happiness flooded her. Being stuck in the Manor for a month drained so much of her cheer. Talking and laughing with Marlo truly brought color back to her cheeks.

Stopping at a line of blooming pink flowers, the conversation ebbed, and they stood in comfortable silence–so different from the heavy, tension-filled quiet the Manor demanded. Lenna breathed in the summer air, the tickling perfume of flora washing over her. She closed her eyes, turning her face towards the sun. When she looked at Marlo, he was staring at her with a concerned look on his handsome face.

"How are you feeling? Are you having any more of those terrible nightmares?" Marlo's brows knitted together as he surveyed her. "I haven't seen you lately and...I've been worried. The house seems emptier without you around–like it lost its only sparkle."

Lenna smiled tightly, squeezing his arm. "You're a sweetheart to worry about me. I'm sure the healer's right, and the headaches are merely a side effect of getting older." She sighed, fiddling with her scarf. The heat was turning her curls into a sweaty mess atop her head, and the thick fabric did little to allow small breezes to cool her neck. "I did want to talk through my latest nightmare with you. I had one last night, but it was...different. Like I was there–instead of past ones where I just saw flickers of images. This was closer. More...real." It was hard to explain. How could she tell Marlo she had nightmares so ominous she woke up more exhausted than when she went to bed? How the terrors from her dreams brought so much stress and discontentment into her waking moments?

Since the headaches started, she avoided everyone in the house. Weeks passed with Lenna confined to her room, trying to rest, forsaking meals in the dining hall, preferring the solitude of eating alone. The loneliness had encapsulated her. She rarely left the bed to do anything since the fatigue lasted longer than the migraines themselves. The walk to the bakery yesterday taxed her, and the frustration that she was not getting better was beginning to frighten her.

She dove into the elements of the nightmare, describing the frigid dungeon, the wings, the flashes of light. How that coldness stayed in her bones even after she woke. The dead eyes of the old man with the dirty white hair still haunted her, and she left that detail out as she recanted the rest. Marlo hung on to every word, his eyes widening as Lenna rehashed the dream.

"Gods above," Marlo breathed after she finished, "I don't know where to begin interpreting any of that. It's no surprise you're having a tough time getting rest. Those nightmares would keep even a hardened soldier of King Dalen's court awake at night."

"They *are* just dreams, but they show places I've never seen. I don't know how my mind conjured up those images." Lenna picked at the scarf on her head as she settled down into the grass before absentmindedly digging her fingers through the dark soil. Marlo plopped down next to her, stretching out his long legs and crossing them at the ankles. Lenna murmured, more to herself than Marlo, as she pulled a stray weed from the bed, "I just felt good this morning and wanted to get out of the house. I don't know when I'll feel able to do this again, and it's nice to have someone to talk to."

Marlo leaned back in the grass. Lenna propped her hands on her knees and stared up at the sky. Neither of them spoke as dark clouds rolled in, pushing away the beautiful summer weather and the calming sun.

"Another storm's going to break soon," she stated. "Let's get back to the Manor. As much as I love being outside, I don't want to get stuck in the rain." Marlo groaned in agreement as he stood, extending a hand to help Lenna get back on her feet. They untied the horses, galloping to the stables just as the first threatening booms of thunder filled the sky above.

After turning over the horses to the stable hand, Lenna and Marlo bolted through fat rain drops to the servant's entrance, earning a reproachful glare from a passing laundress, her hands filled with neatly folded linens. She took one look at their clothes, soaked and dripping on the floor, and muttered a prayer to the gods below before stomping off. Lenna and Marlo exchanged a sheepish smile before parting ways, both returning to their own, very different, worlds to prepare for dinner service.

Captains that already completed the run from Bardon and offloaded their wares were coming to speak with Leon tonight. They would collect their wages from their last shipment, work through budgets, and plot future shipping routes.

And drink–a lot.

Lenna knew she was expected to join, though Leon never asked directly. As the *"Lady of the Manor"* she was to dress modestly, welcome the men to her home, and play the role of Leon's subservient and gracious wife. She had hosted these dinners numerous times over the years, growing quieter and more invisible with each one.

Reaching the doors to her bedroom, Lenna found Olivera filling the tub with warm, soapy water. As Lenna began undressing, Olivera wrinkled her nose in distaste, her narrow eyes tracking Lenna's every move.

"You smell like horses," the housematron grumbled disapprovingly, shaking sweet smelling oils into the steaming tub. "And you have to be presentable in less than an hour." The scents of jasmine and mint hit Lenna's nose–so powerfully fragrant that the first warning pulses of a headache threatened. Her stomach sank. *Was another migraine on its way already?*

"I'll be fast," Lenna swore, ignoring the slight pang in her temples. For emphasis, she made a show of shucking off her boots quickly. But as she wrestled with the too-small breeches, an errant movement caused her to trip slightly over the discarded shoes.

Olivera sighed harshly through her nose as she watched Lenna stumble, crossing the room and throwing open the rickety doors of the wardrobe. The handmatron turned shrewd eyes to the paltry array of dresses Lenna owned, exhaling dramatically once more. Lenna loathed choosing what to wear for social occasions and had deferred that task to Olivera years ago. For the Captain's dinner, Olivera's selection was a dove grey, long-sleeved dress with small frills around the neck. The silhouette was billowy and simple at the bottom. A modest choice for a modest woman.

Lenna hated it.

It didn't hug any of her curves and made her feel like she was wearing a frumpy potato sack.

Knowing this wasn't a fight she would win, and cursing herself for skipping her last appointment with the only seamstress in town, Lenna dismissed Olivera to finish setting up the dining hall before the guests arrived, waiting until the handmatron had departed before easing into the tub.

The hot water did wonders for her aching thighs. Getting back onto a horse felt great at the time, but it left her sore in muscles she hadn't used for the last month. The ride tuckered her out, and the news Marlo relayed about Orla saddened her now that the elation of getting out of the Manor had worn away.

It had been years since she felt any love towards her husband. Lenna's worry was directed towards Orla, who was playing a very dangerous game with an ill-tempered man. Lenna leaned her head back in the tub, the water swirling around her breasts and knees as she adjusted her feet against the porcelain. She could close her eyes for a second... Then she would get dressed... Then she would play the role of the sweet little wife who had no twisted thoughts to be otherwise.

Lenna stood outside the ruined temple that lay half-buried in snow.

Bone cold.

Eerily silent.

The temple's pillars were arranged in a semi-circle, leaning into each other. Some already succumbed to time, while others sat crumbling or broken in half. The stones encompassing her were chalk white, with only a few unbroken pillars reaching haphazardly towards the sky—a sky that Lenna squinted up at...

A sky that shifted—replaced with a swirling vortex of darkness...

Lenna reached out her hand in wonder as ashes swirled down, landing against her bare skin.

A rustle out of the corner of her eye startled her enough to drop her arm, turning to find the source of the noise. A black stone gargoyle, larger than a horse and more terrifying than the rendered paintings in the Manor, stalked towards her on all fours. Lenna tried to scream. No sound came from her throat.

Closer...its huge wings tucked tight at its side, its depthless eyes fixated on her...

Lenna tried to move, tried to run, but her legs burned and locked up. The gargoyle neared...stopping three feet shy of Lenna.

"I am looking for you..." the gargoyle spoke around a mouth filled with jagged, black teeth, its voice both gravelly and smooth as silk.

"I am looking for you..." it raised a stone finger, sharp talons pointing at Lenna's heart as it beat wildly against her ribcage.

Crouching, the gargoyle sprung towards her–

CHAPTER FOUR
LENNA

"M'LADY!" OLIVERA'S CURT SHOUT jarred through her subconscious. Lenna jolted back into reality a millisecond before the stone gargoyle's maw would have wrapped around her throat.

Water surrounded her.

Cold water.

"Did you fall asleep? The captains are already *here*, Leon is *asking for you,*" the handmatron hissed, grabbing a towel as Lenna stood up from the tub on shaky legs. Reeling from the nightmare, she chanced a dazed look around the room, but no giant beasts came into sight. "You need to get dressed *now.*"

Lenna couldn't form a single word as she snatched the towel from Olivera and scrambled out of the water. Another nightmare. *How had she drifted off? How long had she slept?* She hastily dried her body, squeezing out the water from the ends of her curls.

"Shit," Lenna gasped, expertly conveying the gravity of the situation. Wrapping the towel around herself, she bolted towards the dress and undergarments neatly laid on the bed while Olivera waylaid two younger housemaids from the hall, snapping at them to start working in sections to dry Lenna's hair and to put light make up on her.

"Just use the comb and towel to dry, and your fingers to twist the ends of the curls. Thankfully, her whole head isn't wet." Olivera instructed the first maid, a scrawny dark-haired girl no older than sixteen. The maid threw an insolent look in Lenna's direction. "You," Olivera snarled, pointing at the older maid, "light rouge, *light* powder, on the Lady's face. Grab the sapphire necklace from the jewelry box *and don't even think of pocketing any of it.* I am watching you."

Olivera was in her element. Lenna sat stiffly as the two maids blanched in front of the snarling matron before rushing around the room, starting their assigned tasks and not daring to utter a word.

The two girls did well considering the pressure of Olivera constantly breathing down their necks while they worked. Lenna stayed quiet the entire time, as if Olivera's sharp tongue would snap at her if she moved or opened her mouth, but she kept replaying the words the gargoyle whispered to her. *"I am looking for you."*

It was not real. A bad dream, she reassured herself firmly, as Olivera flitted across the room, unbuckling straps on low heels for Lenna to slide her feet into. Gargoyles were a symbol of the gods' protection. Besides the ostentatious paintings Leon revered, gargoyles were carved and chiseled on temples by master stoneworkers, their likeness pressed reverently upon the spiritual books Lenna emotionlessly chanted from at service each week. Some shopkeepers even purchased statues of the horrendous beasts to keep the sea birds from roosting on their roofs. And the only monsters Lenna knew were very much human.

After the maids were finished, and Olivera appraised Lenna up and down, clicking her tongue with approval, Lenna hurried to the dining hall to begin her act of dutiful wife.

"Ah, there she is. Finally," Leon slurred, as she opened the wooden door to the dining hall and gave him a small curtsy as an apology.

Leon and the captains lounged at the table, heaps of pheasant and roasted vegetables neatly spread out around them. Even with the delicious smells coming from the large platters, the men were more interested in the three bottles of rum illuminated by candlelight. Seeing as Leon's poison of choice was brandy, Lenna speculated the captains provided the rum to get him good and drunk before talking salary expectations for upcoming travel.

"Many apologies, husband," Lenna mumbled as she slid meekly into the seat to the right of Leon, who leaned back in his chair at the head of the table and ignored her in favor of the rum. Three of the captains barely looked up or acknowledged her presence as well. However, the fourth burped loudly as his eyes roved Lenna's body, surveying her ample hips, her hair, gently curling from the bath, and pausing to stare at her supple breasts. He was easily the oldest captain, all white-haired and fat, with a huge grey mustache and soulless eyes. The captain grinned hungrily, revealing teeth missing from his top gums, making Lenna recoil. Lenna was suddenly very grateful to Olivera for choosing such a modest outfit. It was apparent in the man's demeanor that she was no more than property to claim. She shrunk back into her chair, trying to make herself smaller, to disappear completely from his leering view.

Four captains had come to talk with Leon, all bigger, louder, and hairier than the last. With Leon's slicked back hair trying desperately to cover bald spots, and a thin frame from many nights of alcohol instead of dinner, these men looked beastly by comparison. Thankfully, the conversation of shipping vessels and route timelines snared the white-haired captain's attention, breaking his predatory stare from Lenna.

He roared with laughter after Leon uttered a dirty joke on timing the tides and how they compared to women, pouring himself a hearty swig of rum.

A twinge of pain shot though Lenna's temples, causing her to grit her teeth. She hoped it was due to the din of Leon and the captains talking over each other and not the start of *another* headache that would end in a nightmare. Contemplating ways she could excuse herself, she stared down at her hands neatly folded in her lap. Nothing came to mind that wouldn't pique interest or divert all eyes her way.

It took all her willpower to not stand up and leave, excuses be damned. Frustration reared through her before she tamped it down swiftly, resulting in another jab of head pain.

She hated this.

Hated the man her husband had become.

Hated these disgusting captains with their raucous voices all trying to vie for Leon's favor.

She hated that she had nothing to contribute, no voice to express any thought or conversation. Besides the short visits to town to politely chat with shopkeepers, and the few and far between conversations with Marlo, Lenna couldn't remember the last time she felt *heard*. The crushing realization made her screw her eyes shut, forcing out a short breath. Which in turn, made her head throb again.

Lenna's thoughts subsided as Marlo appeared, silent as a ghost. He placed a plate in front of her that held a good helping of pheasant meat that had been set aside, avoiding the groping and ripping by the captains and Leon, who were now passing around the platters, wolfing down the pheasant with their fingers, snapping the bones and sucking the small remaining fragments of meat off. With a sympathetic look, Marlo slid out of the dining room.

The rest of the meal went by without a single word from Lenna.

After the pheasant was rendered down to its bones, and the rum bottles lay empty, Leon suggested they take this "meeting" to the study while boasting about his prestigious brandy collection, earning boisterous approval from the captains, who all stood when he did. A couple swayed a little–as if they were still on a boat and readjusting their limbs to land.

Drunks, the lot of them, Lenna thought, biting down on her lip to keep disgust from showing on her face. As they all stumbled out of the dining hall, not even one turned back to look her way.

The voices grew distant, and Lenna did not dare breathe until she heard the satisfying thud of the study door shutting, muting out the rowdy group. Lenna forced herself to relax, unclenching her jaw, loosening her hunched shoulders. Servants were not in the room yet to clear dinner, so gathering her wits back about her, Lenna began collecting the platters. The dinner had been so delicious, and she wanted to personally thank the kitchen staff for all their hard work.

Leon wouldn't.

As Lenna carried dirty cutlery and empty bottles to the cart in the corner, the door to the kitchen creaked open. She looked up, expecting to see Marlo peeking into the room.

She was not expecting to come face to face with a bruised Orla.

Lenna gasped, dropping one of the bottles in her hands. It clattered to the floor, the noise causing the woman in the doorway to flinch. Orla's face was a mottled mess of bruises, her stormy grey eyes bloodshot and puffy. Her black hair was slicked back and tied in a low bun against the nape of her neck, where ringed bruises that looked like handprints marred her throat. Orla lowered her eyes, embarrassment heating her golden-brown cheeks.

"Orla," Lenna breathed, all thoughts eddying out of her mind as she beheld the woman in front of her, "did Leon do this to you?" Heart pounding, she reached her hand out. Orla did not meet her gaze or take her hand.

Olivera had lied.

The thudding in Lenna's head grew into a roar. Orla hadn't been sick. She'd been hiding out of Lenna's sight so Lenna wouldn't see the damage her husband did. Lenna's blood turned to ice in her veins, her ears rang as she took in the wraith-like young woman in front of her. Lowering her voice, Lenna slowly took a step towards Orla. "Tell me what happened. You won't get in trouble. I just... I need to know." Without any fuss, Orla allowed Lenna to steer her over to the table where Lenna quickly pulled out a chair. Orla took it, grimacing when she sat, still not meeting Lenna's worried expression. Lenna took the seat next to her, clasping her hands in her lap.

Olivera's daughter was roughly the same age as Marlo. But where Marlo had vibrance and life behind his eyes, Orla's eyes held nothing but pain. "Orla, look at me. Whatever is going on with Leon, I can stop it. I can help you. I need you to be honest with me. Did he do this to you?"

Tears welled up in Orla's pain-wracked eyes, streaking down the purple marring her cheeks. Orla lifted her head slightly, cringing at the movement. "At first, everything was fine, but when he started getting drunker and screaming at me, I wanted out. Lord Leon threatened my mother's position, and mine, if I didn't do what he wanted. He said if I stayed, he would double both our wages, but my pay never changed, only my mother's did. And if I tried to run..." Another wave of tears streamed down her face. "I don't have anywhere else to go, and the little money I have... It's not enough to book passage to Bardon. Besides, mother said she'd never allow me to leave. I tried to, but she stopped me. She said I needed to stay and do my duty for this house. For her. No matter what." A strangled half-sob escaped, choked back by Orla's gritted teeth.

Lenna sat in shocked silence as the small sense of balance she felt in this world kicked up and off its axis. There was no doubt in her mind that Orla spoke the truth and Leon was a bigger monster than Lenna ever surmised. And Olivera… The woman fed her daughter to the wolf for extra salary.

Extra salary that she spent on what? Lenna mulled the thought around as her anger towards her husband grew. None of the extra money went to Orla.

With some gentle prodding and reassurance from Lenna, Orla poured out the whole sordid story. She spoke of late nights where Olivera forced her to work in Leon's study when he was already drunk to bring him more drinks and stay for the aftermath. She spoke of the abuse she was told she had to endure, forced to stay silent by her cruel mother. Olivera served Orla up on a silver platter–just to gain footing above the other servants in the house and better pay from Leon.

"Olivera knows all of this," Lenna stated slowly, her blood pumping loudly in her ears, her voice flat. "Olivera *encouraged* this." Orla nodded once, twisting the hem of her white apron in her tawny, trembling, hands. Guilt wracked through Lenna as she realized this had escalated drastically while she hid away in her room. Even though it was due to the unbearable migraines, Lenna hated that she had no idea what was going on just a few hallways away. "Do any of the other servants know what happened?" Orla shook her head. Lenna stood up, the woman in front of her scrambling to her feet, a flash of fear shooting across her bruised face. "Come with me." Seeing the panic on Orla's face, Lenna added gently, *"Please."*

Lenna stormed into the kitchen, a hesitant Orla in tow. Shouting for Marlo, Lenna ushered Orla forward, weaving between the low preparation tables. Against the back wall, Marlo stuck his head up from the pot he was washing in the sink. His face paled when he took in Lenna and Orla. Quickly drying his hands on a rag tucked into his belt, Marlo hurried over. "What *happened*?" he asked in a strangled tone, gaping at Orla's busted face, before quickly shaking his head and steering both women into a large walk-in pantry where none of the other servants could overhear.

"Leon's been doing more than just slapping her, Marlo. And Olivera knows. He's *paying* Olivera to keep quiet about it. Do you have any idea why Olivera would stoop so low for extra money?" Lenna hissed, quieting her voice to a mere whisper. Orla averted her eyes, scuffing her worn leather flats against the tiled floor of the pantry. "Why wouldn't she just come to me?"

Marlo searched Lenna's face before glancing back at Orla, his lips tightening into a thin line. Lowering his voice, he leaned closer to the women, the seriousness in his normally carefree tone giving Lenna pause. "Olivera owes money to someone. I don't know all the details, but apparently she had very dangerous friends in the past, and they collect from some sort of debt she owes them." Marlo sighed and shrugged his shoulders, shoving his hands in the pocket of his trousers. "Olivera doesn't talk about it, and I daresay she wouldn't have opened up to you, either. I saw her when I was picking up an order from the butcher. She was arguing with a tall man dressed in some sort of mercenary armor in an alley. She handed him a bag of what I assume was payment for something, and I heard him say it wasn't enough." Lenna watched Orla carefully as Marlo's brows knitted together. "The armor stood out to me. I have never seen the design around Doortan before. It was copper with an odd sun symbol engraved on the chest plate. I don't think that the man was from *here*."

Lenna closed her eyes, pinching the skin at the nape of her neck. Her headache was pounding now. There was so much deceit, right under her nose, and she knew nothing about it until now.

"Did Olivera see you?" Lenna prodded. Orla stayed silent, monitoring Marlo like a hawk from under her thick lashes. Lenna knew that look–it was the look deer gave as they froze in a field after hearing a branch snap–one wrong word and Orla would dart off.

"No," Marlo breathed, holding up his hands, "The man left, and she went into a bar at the end of the alley. I tailed her there but couldn't find her again. It was weird, but I couldn't stay and do more digging. I had to pick up the meat order before the butcher closed for the evening."

"When was this?"

"A couple months ago." Marlo cocked his head, his blond hair gleaming in the dim light from the crack in the pantry door. "Right before Orla got pulled from kitchen duty and moved to Leon's personal maid."

"*Fuck.*" Lenna rubbed her eyes, a string of harsher curses followed.

This could not continue. Lenna knew that. She felt sick. She failed the woman in front of her who stood broken and alone. Marlo furrowed his brows, concern laced through his soft features. They deserved better than this life. This life that Lenna had gotten sucked into and stuck in. This life where she felt so trapped and alone.

How fast the perspective of time changed. Lenna contemplated that thought amidst the warring feelings inside her of sadness and anger. One moment she was happily married, moving into a bright, big mansion with a rich husband who doted on her, with all the luxuries money could buy. The next, she was nearing fifty-two, in a loveless marriage to a cruel man, stuck in a pantry with her husband's mistress, and Marlo - who she could honestly say was her only friend.

And suddenly a wild, insane, completely nuts plan formed between the thrums of her headache.

CHAPTER FIVE
LENNA

"YOU NEED TO LEAVE," Lenna said slowly, the idea forming rapidly in her mind. "You *both* need to leave. Get out of this house, get to Bardon or a different town far away from here. Start your lives. If you go together, you can secure passage on a ship and watch out for each other. Orla—you know some of the sailors who are coming into town this week, would any of them help you and Marlo get to Bardon?"

Orla and Marlo stared at her, dumbfounded.

Finally, "We…couldn't leave even if we wanted to," Marlo sputtered, a hint of defeat in his voice. "We have no money, nowhere to go."

Lenna shook her head, talking faster, her hands waving as she pieced together the plan. "I have jewelry—gold. You can have it all. It will sell well. Especially in Bardon. Leon will never notice any of it gone. And, if you sail to Bardon, there's a small township two days' travel west of there—Wilfur. My dear friend, Diana—she's Lady of the Wilfur Estate. She would absolutely give you both positions in her Manor, or see to it that you're secured with other jobs in town." Lenna looked at Orla, noting the wariness in her eyes. Gently, Lenna added, "Lady Diana is a kind woman who would help you." Lenna squeezed her hands together trying to calm her heartbeat.

This had to work. She had to help them live a life absent of terror and abuse. "I can write a letter, asking her to give you both work. Diana was my childhood friend and lived in Doortan until she married her late husband, who passed ten years ago. Take the letter to her."

Though Lenna had neither spoken to or seen Diana in a decade, the generosity the woman always displayed was a gift time could not warp. Lenna felt a pang of sorrow as she reminisced on the friendship that grew stale and dusty over time, but the questions that Diana would undoubtedly ask were not questions Lenna felt she could answer honestly. Her marriage to Leon left an embarrassing stain on her heart, and curling up into a state of isolation was easier over the distance and years than admitting to her old friend that she was unhappy.

Marlo gave Orla a shrug, silently deferring the decision to her. Orla's eyes filled with tears again. Lenna realized it was probably the first time in her life the woman could make any choice about her own path.

"It's...too much, why would you do this for us, my Lady?" Orla choked, wringing her apron in her hands with such ferocity, Lenna waited for the garment to unravel and fall to the floor in threads. Marlo hovered between the two women, shifting his weight from one foot to the other.

Lenna knew right then and there they would go. "Please, Orla, call me Lenna. I cannot leave, but you can. You have your whole life ahead of you. Marlo, you are my dearest friend here, you are strong and kind. *You* can leave, make a name for yourself, live to your heart's desire. Orla, what my husband was doing to you, what your mother did to you, is unacceptable. You are in a bad situation. I can help. I *will* help."

Orla looked up slowly, the first glimmer of light returning to those storm grey eyes. Setting her jaw, determination growing on her bruised features, Orla said, "I want to go. I want to get away from this place, from my mother, and *Leon,*" she spat, forsaking his title, as if he did not deserve to be the Lord of Doortan. "I will owe you for the rest of my life if you help me." Orla turned her attention to Marlo, "Help *us*." Marlo met her eyes for a moment, searching, before he nodded.

"We will go, Lenna. We will go, and never forget this kindness you've shown us."

"Then we must prepare." Lenna breathed a sigh of relief. She thought it would be harder to convince them, but seeing how Marlo looked at Orla, like he was finally *seeing her* for the first time, Lenna knew he would go–for Orla's sake, and for his own shot at freedom.

Preparations were made right there in the cramped pantry closet, surrounded by the dwindle of servants coming in and out of the kitchen. Lenna would retire to her room, write the letter to Diana, and collect jewelry and gold for them to sell when they reached Bardon. Orla would return to the servant's quarters, get some rest, and slip food into a pack in the morning before the other servants awoke. Marlo would notify the stable hands that Lenna wanted to ride into town, and to get three horses ready for first light by using the cover story that Lenna wanted to bring two of the servants with her to town to purchase more seeds for the garden. A lie that would sell. And Leon would be too hungover from the captains' dinner to keep tabs on any of this.

When Lenna came back home, with two extra horses riderless, Lenna would use the excuse the servants stayed behind to enjoy a night at the tavern in town as reward for their excellent dinner service the evening prior.

Any excuses afterwards would be on Lenna to create. Lenna knew the biggest issue would be Olivera, who would be furious to learn her daughter disappeared. Furious the extra money would be gone–with no actual concern for Orla's wellbeing. Leon would be a different story, but Lenna knew he would cut his losses and say two less servants meant two less salaries to pay. He didn't care for Orla, not in a way where he would miss her.

He will find some new woman to torment, Lenna thought with a flash of hatred. But at least Orla would be safely out of his reach.

Lenna, Marlo, and Orla hurried out of the pantry once the sounds of servants disappeared and only anticipatory silence filled the kitchen, all three eager for this plan to work. Orla gave Marlo a swift peck on the cheek as she departed. Marlo watched her go, hand touching where her lips met, as if the ghost of the kiss remained.

Leaving the kitchen, Lenna kept her head low, slipping through the back halls and keeping to the shadows the night cast across the somber Manor. She slid into her room, closing and locking the door behind her, a signal that she would not need assistance getting ready for bed. Lenna didn't know what she would do if she ran into Olivera. Part of her wanted to grab that scrawny bitch by the throat and give her the same bruising Leon gave Orla.

The fierce need to protect and help the less fortunate was a moral Lenna held onto dearly. As a young woman, before her marriage, she would hunt extra doves and rabbits to bring to the poorest in town so they could enjoy a nice meal for the night.

With no children of her own, Lenna adored helping the town's orphans who weren't taken care of. She did whatever she could to help make their lives easier through charity work and large donations that Leon would never notice on his ledgers.

Her migraines may have inhibited her from helping Orla prior to this, but now that she knew help was needed, Lenna would stop at nothing to see to it that Orla was safe and could begin making her own decisions in her life, and that Marlo could have a true shot at making a name for himself outside of this dead end town.

The letter to Diana was written quickly, giving detailed explanation with an added little lie that Marlo and Orla were moving to Wilfur due to family circumstances. The letter asked if Diana had room for them, or if she could set them up with a job in town.

Lenna carefully worded the letter, keeping out any hints that they would be safer in Wilfur, or that they could not come back to Doortan. Diana shared the same soft spot Lenna held for the impoverished. Their pasts linked through an easy friendship that blossomed from raising funds and donating coats in the winter to help the people who needed it most. Lenna knew her old friend would see Orla and Marlo as two souls in need and would help in any way she could.

Wistfully, she added a line in the letter asking if they could meet next time she was in Wilfur, dreading the reality that it would likely never happen. Leon kept her locked up in this town of nothing, not caring to allow her the freedom to explore or go anywhere other than to town or to walk the outskirts of the forest surrounding the Manor.

After the letter was finished, and Lenna successfully raided her jewelry drawer for the biggest and most expensive pieces she owned, she lay down, her mind buzzing. Her headache had subsided. As if it sensed she was too busy to be down for the count right now. She hoped it stayed away.

Tossing and turning, Lenna pondered over the conversations from the captains' dinner. One of them made mention of a ship from a rival trading company leaving tomorrow for Bardon, and Lenna prayed Orla and Marlo would be able to secure passage easily on a boat that had no connections to the monster she married.

CHAPTER SIX
LENNA

LENNA CRACKED OPEN HER eyes, staring down at the hooded figure tread-ing slowly through the woods. The colors of the dream distorted, throwing the world into soft hues of black and white. As the figure moved through the trees, a pale hand extended from beneath the black cloak, gripping a branch and ducking under it wearing...wearing Lenna's own wedding band. With a jolt, Lenna realized she was staring at the top of her own head, out of her body and above the ground, as if she stood amongst the treetops. Lenna watched herself pick carefully through the woods, going deeper and deeper into the foliage. Lenna kept pace, not letting the dream Lenna out of sight.

A cluster of thick branches came into view, and she lost sight of the figure below. As she pushed through, a rustle of wings sounded behind her. But as if she had no control over what her eyes saw, or where her eyes went, the branches parted, and she found herself peering over a large tree limb.

A shudder of anticipation ran through her bones when the cloaked Lenna came back into view...standing over a...over a...a swirl of grey and white smoke that stretched out between two trees, twirling faster and faster. The Lenna below glided forward, as if in a trance.

There was no fog, no mist anywhere else on the forest floor... Only the wisps in front of the Lenna below curling, fighting, darting between its other colors, *knitting tighter and tighter into a ball that begun glowing pure white and growing–longer, taller, brighter.*

It pulsed, throwing shadows against the forest floor, as if inviting the dream Lenna into its depths. The light grew to her silhouette, causing the outlines of trees surrounding it to be thrown into darkness. Only one glimmer of light was left...behind the hooded Lenna. The brightness morphed into two unfurling wings... Wings that grew larger and larger as Lenna's disembodied sight came closer and closer...

A LOW KNOCK AT her bedroom door startled Lenna awake. Her eyes darted to the curtains, where the first tendrils of morning peeked over the horizon, to the door, still locked from the night before. As Lenna's eyes adjusted to the dimness of dawn, the low knock came again. Lenna rolled out of bed, quickly throwing a robe over her undergarments, and unlocked the door.

Marlo and Orla stood awkwardly holding small burlap packs, huddled together in the threshold. Both wore dark brown pants–Orla's were baggy, the waist cinched tight with a thick leather belt–black, long-sleeve, cotton shirts, and heavy maroon coats with a hood that would make it much easier to achieve the necessary anonymity needed to slip out of the Manor undetected. Lenna bet the clothes dwarfing Orla were a spare set from Marlo, since the female servants exclusively wore bland shift dresses in Doortan Manor.

Marlo's eyes shone as he gave Lenna a hesitant smile. Orla ducked her head in a polite bow, her dark hair slicked down and back into two braids. Lenna moved aside, ushering them both into her bedroom.

"The horses will be ready in ten minutes," Marlo started, speaking low, "Orla got some bread, cheese, and dried fruit from the kitchens for us to eat on the ship, so I think we have everything we need." The packs on both their shoulders were small. Lenna winced at the thought that all their worldly possessions fit into two little bags.

"Here is the letter for Lady Diana," Lenna whispered, handing the rolled-up note to Orla who gripped it tight and packed it reverently in her bag—the one thing that would bring her freedom. "And here," Lenna moved to the dresser where she stuffed the jewelry into two thick wool socks, tied tight with ribbons, "are your jewels. This sock," she explained, hefting one grey sock in her hand slightly above the other, "has a bunch of loose stones in it. Use this once you get to Bardon. They should fetch a nice price. Change them all out for gold little by little so no one thinks you stole them. If anyone asks, tell them they were your inheritance."

She handed the heavy sock to Marlo, still holding the smaller sock in her hand. Offering the smaller to Orla, Lenna murmured, "*This* sock holds jewelry and gold coins. Use these if you need to bribe sailors for any supplies or food before you land." She had given the larger to Marlo to better protect their monetary supply. Orla was tiny and bruised, and Lenna hated the thought of someone trying to rob her of the jewels as they traveled thinking Orla would be an easy target. Marlo would hold his own. She noted the thin dagger strapped to his waist, and knew she made the right choice, though how he got the weapon was beyond her.

Marlo and Orla shuffled their bags open, pushing their socks to the bottom. Once secured, Orla hefted her bag higher on her shoulder with a fierce expression.

"Thank you," Orla said tightly—as if waiting for Lenna to take it all back, to rip away this shot at salvation for her. "Thank you for helping us."

Lenna waved her hand. "I would do it for anyone."

And she meant it.

Selecting a hooded, midnight blue cloak for herself, Lenna pulled on riding breeches and a loose cotton top to mimic the dark color palette Orla and Marlo wore, stuffing her feet into the boots Olivera had thankfully not yet taken to get shined. She felt like she was flying by whim alone, the recklessness of this plan making her heart thrum and her legs shaky.

The halls were silent as they hustled to the stables, taking the longer route through the main hall to avoid passing Leon's study and the servants' quarters. A few maids were already preparing for the day, but no one looked twice at the three hooded figures as they opened one of the ornamental front doors and stepped outside, down the steps, and towards the stables, crunching the small white pebbles under their feet as they walked.

Marlo slipped his hood off as they spied two horses saddled and ready to go, and the last getting the harness attached by a young stable hand. Orla kept her hood up as instructed by Lenna. She didn't want word getting back to Leon that Orla was with her, nor any follow up questions to that statement.

"Thank you," Lenna said, keeping her voice light, as if this was another day where nothing was amiss. "We'll be back before dinner service."

The stable hand gave the reins over to Lenna with a bow as she hoisted herself up into the saddle. Orla and Marlo followed suit. Marlo gave the stable hand a broad grin as he situated himself in his seat. Orla stayed quiet as she clumsily mounted a white gelding and gripped the reins stiffly, visually uncomfortable.

"There's nothing to be afraid of—this beastie is a very sweet and gentle ride. He won't let you fall," Marlo assured her, seemingly noticing the same thing.

"I've never been on a horse before," Orla muttered quietly, knuckles paling with her vice grip on the reins.

Lenna reached over, squeezing her shoulder. "It's okay to be afraid, but we will not let anything hurt you. Hold your head high, and remember—this is the beginning of the rest of your life."

With that, Orla took a deep, shuddering breath, and sat up straighter, rolling her shoulders back, and looking determinedly out to the gate the stable hand left open for them.

As they casually trotted onto the dirt road beyond the Manor, as nonchalant as they could manage, Lenna glanced back towards the house only once to be sure they weren't drawing the attention of anyone around, seeing Marlo also twist in his seat to watch the Estate fade in the distance. Lenna noticed Orla didn't spare a look back. Focused determination played across her face and Orla stared forward, a bit stiff-backed, as she left her old life behind.

The ride into town was blissfully uneventful. Lenna led the way, with Orla behind her, Marlo bringing up the rear. The silence only broken by the occasional advice Lenna threw out as she thought of it.

They made it to town within an hour, right as shops began opening for the day, and townsfolk began their morning bustle. The trio passed the town square where two priestesses were singing the chorus of a song celebrating the gods, surrounded by a small gaggle of Doortan's residents bowing their heads and softly singing along.

The harbor was a fifteen-minute ride past the town's square, the voices from the ethereal singing growing faint as they rounded the corner of the last shop. Blinking against the sunlight glinting off the water, the port sprawled before them. Ships of all lengths moored in the water, bobbing as waves threw themselves to the stone walls of the docks. Gulls screamed above, circling the vast masts and flags decorating the two largest ships, the colorful fabric snapping in the gusts wafting off the sea. The smell of rotting fish and salt filled the air, mixing with the unmistakable odor of unwashed sailors, and a twinge of sweet rum. Orla crinkled her nose in disgust but made no comment.

Approaching the narrow rampway down to the wood-paneled docks, Lenna dismounted, tying her horse to the thin railing to the side of the cobblestone path down to the ships. "Orla, do you recognize any of the sailors working on either of those two large ships?" Lenna pointed them out, chewing her lip, a small sliver of doubt rearing its ugly head. Trying to get them both on a manifest–without too many questions asked–was going to take luck and a prayer. Lenna hoped none of the captains from last night were here. A chill ran down her spine. *What if they recognized her? Would they go running straight back to Leon?* Lenna tucked her bright, noticeable hair further into her hood–hoping that the gods would take mercy on her and her two wayward companions.

Orla peeled back her hood, squinting her eyes against the sun. Still on her horse, she fought a wobble to rise higher in the stirrups, trying to make out individual faces of the figures shouting, moving crates, laboring to get the ships out to sea as quickly as possible.

By some divine miracle, she didn't have to look long.

A voice shouted above the din of port. "*Orla!*"

Orla whirled around and squealed with glee, quickly clambering off her horse to rush towards the squat young man in a sailor's cap that spotted her as he came out of the shop closest to them.

Lenna shot a quizzical, almost disbelieving look over to Marlo, who merely shrugged, his eyes fixated on Orla as she clasped her hands into the sunburnt grasp of the sailor who looked to be a few years younger than her. Lenna saw the young man cup her face and ask a question, most likely about the bruises on her cheeks, but Orla shook her head and laughed as if she was dismissing the question. They spoke a few more minutes, Orla talking quickly and gesturing to the ships behind them, the sailor nodding along, interjecting here and there. They were too far away for Lenna to make out what they were saying. But then, Orla turned to pull the sailor back to where Marlo and Lenna waited. Marlo slid off his horse, pulling his pack off the saddle, before collecting Orla's as well.

"Lenna, Marlo," Orla said breathlessly, "this is my cousin, Dollin. He was just telling me that he got a job out of Bardon on that ship." She pointed to the largest vessel with pale-yellow sails. Lenna breathed a sigh of relief. Yellow sails meant the ship was owned by someone from Bardon–not affiliated with Leon's fleet. The gods were really looking their way today as Orla confirmed with Dollin that he could *absolutely* get them passage to Bardon, and that he had just been in the shop to grab last minute documents for his captain before they boarded to sail.

Marlo strode forward, grasping hands with Dollin, and the two exchanged pleasantries. Lenna stayed back, letting Orla and Marlo have a moment of privacy with Orla's cousin.

Dollin gave Orla a quick kiss on the cheek and squeezed her hand, motioning over to the ship with the yellow sails. "We are leaving in about an hour. If you are ready to go, there is a gangway set up and the crates have just finished being loaded–there's a bit of a line for people boarding, but tell the man stationed at the bottom there that I approved your travel." Dollin puffed up his chest. For him to have that type of pull, he must be one of the captain's trusted mates. Lenna felt relief wash over her–another man to keep an eye out for her wayward friends.

Another blessing.

Orla and Marlo exchanged a glance as Dollin strode off. Marlo wordlessly handed Orla her pack and she slipped it over her shoulders, securing it to her body. They both turned to Lenna. Orla opened her mouth to say something, but Lenna pulled her into a gentle hug. "Take care," Lenna said quietly. She clasped Orla between her outstretched arms and smiled tightly, before turning her attention to Marlo.

"Marlo," Lenna choked, saying goodbye to her only friend in this town, "take care of her and take care of yourself. I am so proud of the man you have become, and thank you for being my friend." Marlo looked close to tears, but he grabbed Lenna in a tight embrace, conveying the emotion that swam in his eyes.

She was shorter than him, her head reaching only to his chest, but Marlo curled his torso down until his body covered hers. Lenna felt her throat constrict, as she realized just how important Marlo had become to her—the son she never had. "Thank you, Lenna," Marlo whispered, "I owe you a debt. Please come to Wilfur when you can." Marlo squeezed Lenna one last time and let go, reaching over for Orla's hand. Lenna felt a couple stray tears spring from her eyes, and hastily wiped them away with a sniff.

Lenna stood with the horses as she watched Marlo guide Orla to the ship, watched as they boarded, as the gangway was raised, as the vessel began pulling away from the harbor, as the wind filled the sails, pulling into open sea.

Lenna stood there.

Watching until the ship, and the last friend she had in her life, disappeared into the horizon.

CHAPTER SEVEN
LENNA

THE SUN WAS BOLDLY overhead as Lenna finally ripped her eyes away from the shimmering inlet. Her legs wobbled with relief that Orla and Marlo made it onto the ship. The gods and goddesses were truly looking out for them. Maybe they noticed the desperation or the kindred spirit of a helping hand. Whatever it was, Lenna felt a weight lift from her chest, and she whispered a prayer of thanks skyward.

A pang of disappointment followed immediately by guilt hit hard. For one tiny moment, she wished she could get onto that ship, sail into the unknown, begin anew. Skirt her responsibilities as Lady of Doortan, cast away on one last adventure. But that wasn't the life fate chose for her. Lenna pushed away the awful feeling that crashed over her like a wave, and started to slowly walk back to the horses that were still tied up and waiting to be taken back home.

Out of the corner of her eye, she saw a flutter of wings that made her heart skip a beat. On top of the shop that Dollin had come out of, a large gargoyle statue stood, ostentatious in size compared to the narrow roof. The statue's wings tightly curled into its sides, mouth open, showing stone teeth frozen in a silent roar. She gave the statue that was used to repel birds from landing on the roof a glower, the nightmares still fresh in her mind.

The wings she saw flapping by must have been some dejected gull, now looking for a new, less occupied, place to perch.

Nearing the horses, she began unfastening their ropes and tied off the extra leads to the small clips at the base of her saddle. Once secured, Lenna hoisted herself up onto her seat, but she couldn't help shooting a glance back at the gargoyle. Her mind must still be playing tricks on her because for a split second, she could have sworn she saw the statue's stone grin widen.

THE RETURNING RIDE TO the Manor was slow with two extra horses trailing behind. Lenna was exhausted and couldn't wait to scurry into her bedroom and lock the door. She didn't want to see anyone–especially Olivera and Leon. As she made her way slowly through the last leg of the dirt trail and through a sparse alcove, she contemplated her dream about the odd fog in the forest.

Completely lost in thought, she didn't notice the lead of the third horse slip from the anchor point she had tied. The horse, sensing its chance to meander into the woods and find a snack, was already past the tree line by the time she realized.

"Hey!" Lenna yelled, a little louder than intended. The mare didn't look back as it traipsed through more brambles, looking for delicious clover. *"Get back here."*

Lenna scrambled off her horse, forgetting, for a second, to secure the other two. Frantically lunging back to the lead line, Lenna growled a curse under her breath as her eyes darted around for a place to tie the two horses.

Thankfully, the Doortan fields were on the other side of the trail, the wooden slats bordering the farmland easier to tie off to. She hastily secured the ropes before trudging over to the trees after the wandering horse.

She peered into the forest, pulling her coat around her as she shivered. The temperature was falling, a sure sign another summer storm was on its way.

"Shit, shit, *shit*," Lenna hissed, pulling her hood up as the first fat raindrop plopped on her shoulder. She couldn't leave the horse to wander, gods knew where it would end up, and she didn't want to think of the reprimanding she would get from Leon if one of the expensive horses, *plus* two servants, went missing in the same afternoon.

Slowly and awkwardly, she shuffled through the brush, trying to be quiet and not scare the loose horse into running. She could barely see in front of her as mist started forming, ready to receive the afternoon's rain. Lenna wove deeper and deeper into the trees, scanning ahead of her, trying to track the horse by the hoof prints on the ground–praying she found the damned thing before the rain washed away her only source of direction.

Lenna clicked her tongue, trying to call the horse back. As a young huntress, she had been great at tracking game, but this was all the shittiest variables with the shittiest timing for someone who let those skills rust over the decades. She pushed a fallen tree branch out of the way, ducking under it and proceeding on.

She almost gave up when she finally heard a faint rustle. Picking up the pace, Lenna hurried towards the noise, straining her ears to any other indications she was heading the right way. "C'mon you damn beastie, give me some direction here," Lenna muttered. She came to a stop, held her breath and closed her eyes–trying desperately to confirm where she needed to go.

Another rustle—but this time it came from above her. *Probably a squirrel getting out of the way of the storm,* she thought to herself, even as nerves jittered along her spine. The forest around her seemed to billow and grow as mist built up. Lenna pushed on, but as the woods grew thicker, her hope of finding the horse waned, and her patience thinned. The clouds opened, dumping an icy onslaught of rain. Thunder boomed overhead, cracking through the trees. Lenna looked up, swearing she saw large wings above her, illuminated only for a blink by a second flash of lightning. She closed her eyes, took a deep breath to calm her nerves, opened her eyes...

And gasped.

Three tendrils of mist snaked their way into the air, just as they had in her dream. As they wove together, thrashing, fighting, curling into each other, she took a step back, almost tripping over a tree branch behind her. The vapor and smoke knotted itself tighter and brighter, until a small orb of pure white light grew out of the fog. The rain stopped—or at least parted—away from the unnatural sight.

"Hello, Oracle," a gravelly voice behind her whispered.

Lenna whirled around and screeched. The gargoyle from her nightmare, no—from the *harbor,* leapt out of the trees and landed ten feet away, walking towards her on all fours—larger than a horse, but not by much. The beast smiled and stretched its grey wings out. Lenna squeezed her eyes shut.

Not real, not real, she chanted to herself.

But when she opened her eyes, the gargoyle remained in front of her. The beast sat on the ground, giving her a feral grin, its spiked tail wrapping around its legs. It was taller than Lenna, looking at her through curiously glittering pupils that were slitted like a snake. Up close, Lenna realized the gargoyle was not actually stone, but covered in a thick, leathery grey hide.

Wide wings mimicked its skin, the thin membranes connected to the boning a soft matte shade. She could see muscles rippling through the beast's sides and haunches as it settled on the ground, head tilted. The teeth were more concerning. Razor sharp grey canines came into view, and Lenna was confident those jagged fangs would be ripping her to shreds in just a few moments.

"You *do* speak, right? Gods–this is going to be so much harder if all you do is scream." The gargoyle shook its head, waiting.

"You...*you* speak?" Lenna gasped. "Are...are you going to eat me?" She nervously held a hand to her throat.

The gargoyle laughed, the sound croaky. "*Eat* you? No. Gross. I don't eat *humans*. I'm just here to collect you. You *are* the Oracle, right?"

Lenna rapidly shook her head, still in utter disbelief.

The gargoyle rolled its eyes. "You have headaches–right? See things? Probably saw something that looks like me at least once. Weird dreams you cannot explain–*right*?"

Lenna let out a squeak, quickly clapping a hand over her mouth. Apparently, all the confirmation the gargoyle needed. It huffed, mist rolling out of its maw. "It's been a long time since I came to your land. In mine, this is all common knowledge. You get the headaches–the visions, and you get activated once the visions start manifesting. Then, you serve the Seven Kingdoms of Terramere, their Kings and Queens. Well, serve *someone*, not positive on *who* at the moment," it grumbled.

"I am not an oracle, "Lenna whispered, thinking back to the tales she was told as a child of witches and seers–oracles, who read fortunes at carnivals or brewed little love potions for the young adults who swore they needed the concoction for their first love's tea. Theatrics, stories of grand lands and magic and...monsters. Like the one sitting in front of her. "I'm just..." She paused. What exactly was she? Lady of Doortan? Lady of a loveless marriage? Those dreams had seemed so real but...the gargoyle couldn't be real. She couldn't be an oracle.

"There's only one. Not *an oracle–the* Oracle.*"* It stretched out its wings, tail lashing impatiently against the ground. "You have the dreams–visions. You were activated. The last Oracle died, so the magic was passed on. It gets passed on randomly by the God of Sight. Apparently, he had a sense of humor and picked someone from the Slate Kingdom to make my day difficult."

"But magic is not real," Lenna said slowly, and not all the way convincedly.

"This is the Slate Kingdom, the land where magic is *stifled*. Where you humans are the majority species and where this," the beast motioned to itself, "is the only version I can be here. I am much lovelier in my land where magic is in abundance."

Lenna knitted her brows. The dreams–visions. Could this be true? The gargoyle stood very real in front of her, though she was still skeptical if this was all a hallucination. She wasn't sure of the intentions of the gargoyle, but she was not gargoyle meat yet.

A small blessing.

The orb of light began thrumming like a heartbeat, drawing the gargoyle's attention. "We have got to get going, not much time left before that portal starts disappearing."

"I am *not* an oracle–the Oracle. And I am not going anywhere. This is my home." Even saying the word *home* made her wince. This place hadn't felt like home in decades. The gargoyle shook its head sadly, as if it felt bad for her.

"This isn't your home. I've been watching you for weeks. It's *miserable* here. These beings are more monster than me–especially that balding one. But well... We can do this the easy way where you walk through the portal with me and I explain more, or the hard way where I drag you through." The gargoyle picked up its front paw, inspecting the large talons at the tips.

Lenna paled. "What about the horses? I must get them back. They can't stay out here in the storm."

"Already back at the house. Yes–all three of them. Right after you strolled into the woods, that third horse came back with one of those skinny stable hands. He took all three with him. Oh, and no one is looking for you by the way–if that helps your decision. I think the only person who cared about you in this boringly dreadful town is on that big ship sailing gods know where. Any more questions?"

Lenna swallowed against the lump forming in her throat. No one was coming to look for her. No one cared enough to investigate three riderless horses and no Lady of Doortan in sight. Steeling her resolve, with a tidal wave of recklessness that overrode any lingering sense of caution, Lenna narrowed her eyes at the gargoyle. "Lead the way."

CHAPTER EIGHT

LENNA

THE GARGOYLE STRAIGHTENED AND stretched out its wings, motioning for Lenna to walk into the portal. Lenna took two steps towards the pulsing light and paused, opening her mouth to speak–the gargoyle's paw shot out, gently shoving her through. There was a brilliant flash, and Lenna braced, screamed, and closed her eyes against the unknown. Next to her the gargoyle chucked. "Open your eyes, Oracle. We have arrived in the Opal Kingdom."

Lenna warily opened one eye, taking in the scenery around her. She was curled in the fetal position, summer air and a beautiful cloudless day greeting her. The forest of dense trees she was in just a moment ago was gone, with no evidence of rain or lingering mist. The field of grass she lay on was soft and warm under her, brushing gently in the breeze. She exhaled, her gaze bouncing around her surroundings, until she looked back for the stone-like monster from the forest, and surprise dropped her jaw.

Where the gargoyle had been seconds before now sat a tall and very muscular man. He wore all black from his pants to his loose cotton shirt, save for the broad grey belt wrapped around his middle, showing off a large sword sheath. Lenna could barely make out a set of small wings crested in blue stones at the top of the pommel. She scrambled up and away, instinct taking over. The man let out a rough laugh, his dark brown eyes cautious but pleasant. Lenna's gaze shot to the large grey wings protruding from his back, and the slate hued horns that swept out above his shaggy brown hair. "I told you I looked much better in a land with magic." He was sitting next to her in the grass, arms wrapped casually around his knee, watching her with wicked amusement as she backed away.

His tanned skin shone almost bronze in the sun, and five thick, black, tattooed bands wrapped around his right forearm. Standing with a grunt, ignoring the fear in Lenna's face, the man stretched. "After being a Sentry for weeks, it's weird being back on two legs." He dusted off his pants and extended a hand to Lenna. "Merrick," he said as a way of greeting. A grin was flashed, his teeth, now pearly white, and much less pointy, save for two sharp looking canines, made Lenna relax a fraction of an inch.

Lenna gingerly slid her fingers against his callused palm. He towered over her by a foot. "Lenna," she breathed as Merrick shook her hand, practically holding her up. She may not have been the best judge of character in Doortan, but as she appraised the man in front of her, it was his kind eyes that she focused on, reminded her tensed body of.

"Well, Lenna, it's nice to formally meet you." Merrick released her hand, stretching his wings out. They looked similar to the wings on the gargoyle from the forest. Grey, leathery, yes–but with intricate scales like a snake. The membranes of the wings caught the sun and seemed to almost glow.

"What are you?" Lenna asked cautiously.

Merrick smirked, another good sign to Lenna that he was not reconsidering eating her. "A gargoyle," he admitted. "That part is true. But in your land with stifled magic, humans can only see me when I am in my Sentry form. The stoney-looking beast that you had the pleasure of meeting is what I shift into when I enter the Slate Kingdom. In the Opal Kingdom, this is my true form, since there is magic in these lands. I must say, I prefer it here." Merrick looked around, taking in the surroundings. "Well, it looks like we made it to Spinella. Let's go, much to do."

Lenna stayed where she was. Crossing her arms, her red hair glistened like fire under the summer sun, the curls starting to frizz as they dried from the rain she left behind in Doortan. Not even bothering to ask where or what a Spinella was, she faced the man. "You said you would explain more if I went with you. I went with you—so, explain."

She watched a muscle jump in Merrick's jaw, and he sighed roughly, pushing his dark hair out of his face. If she was now truly annoying him, she didn't care. She just uprooted everything she knew in life on a wild whim and wasn't sure yet what else to do but stay with this towering man and hopefully get some answers.

Answers from a mythical creature.

Lenna still had half a mind that she may have gone mad.

Doortan felt a million miles away in her brain, and this new mysterious land called to her soul in a wicked and wild manner. It may have been the overwhelming emotional toll, or the easing of her mind that she was someplace *new*, that caused the delirious giggle to escape from her throat as a tingling sensation spread from the tips of her fingers, up her arms, until her body erupted into goosebumps and she doubled over, gasping for air as she laughed at the absolute absurdity of this entire situation.

Merrick pursed his lips, staring down at Lenna as she coughed, her fit of hysteria subsiding. "I'm going to give you the gist of it—when we get someplace safe." He scanned the horizon. "We need to get into town. I have a friend there that is waiting on us." Dryly, Merrick added, "He won't eat you either, before you ask. Unfortunately, he's *much* more refined in a lot of ways."

"How is this place not safe?" Lenna questioned, throwing her arms out wide, fascinated with the nature around her. There wasn't a soul to be seen in the field of tall, green grass. It was serene. So peaceful. But under the surface, her heartbeat hammered in her chest. The breeze blew gently, wafting the scent of freedom through her. Her giddiness overwhelmed any sort of common sense.

Free.

Overwhelmed, nervous, unsure, but *free*. She stared in wonder at the gargoyle, so still and rigid next to her.

Her small jolt of joy crumbled at his fierce expression, leaving unease to grip her tight, a whiplash of emotions churning through Lenna as she blew out a shaky breath. Deciding on a course of action, she settled on the path to obtain solid answers.

A growl reverberated out of Merrick's throat, and Lenna knew she was getting under that bronzed skin, but though she surreptitiously relaxed her shoulders, she noted her own irritation growing and coiling in her belly with his half-truths and the *later* talk.

Maybe she hadn't made the right decision to go through the portal–the portal that conveniently disappeared the moment Merrick had introduced himself.

No way back now.

The thought rang through her. There was no room for indecisiveness. Merrick interrupted her contemplation. "Let's put it this way–the previous Oracle didn't just *die*, he was murdered. Every royal with half a brain cell or a fraction of skin in the hunt for power wants *you* on their side. Oracles win wars, more than any sword or magic. You have the one thing all royals desire–the ability to see the past. The one who controls the Oracle, controls the view of history."

A tidal wave of fear crashed over her. With every sentence, Lenna had more and more questions, more uneasiness. "Did you just bring me into a war?" Lenna blanched. Her thoughts turned dark. The portal was gone. Did she leave Doortan willingly? Yes.

So, why did she now feel trapped?

"It's not that cut and dry yet... But maybe?" He shook his head, a muscle in his jaw feathering. "Again—we have got to *go*." Merrick shot his eyes skyward, his features unreadable as he scanned their surroundings again. "I swear I will explain more soon, but we are *very vulnerable* out here, and there are certain fights I cannot win."

With that, and the fear Lenna heard in Merrick's gruff voice, she relented. Once again crossing her arms, she trailed behind the gargoyle as he stalked through the field, looking to the horizon and the sky as he went, his hand never straying from the pommel of his sheathed sword. Even though she had no idea what he was watching out for, she found herself doing the same.

AFTER HOURS OF WALKING, with Merrick slowing only when Lenna lagged to let her catch a breath, a small cluster of cottages came into view beneath the last of the rolling green fields. Lenna's legs burned with every step further from Doortan. Every step reminded her she had no clothes, no money, nothing but the cloak on her back. She didn't let her mind go past that. Didn't want to think of what was happening in Doortan, where Marlo and Orla were, what Leon probably thought.

Lenna gleaned little as they walked. Merrick explained that they headed towards the town of Spinella, how it was the safest place for her to be right now, and that his friend also had her best interests in mind. Lenna tried reading between the lines, but Merrick said with no uncertainty that he still was not sure about *her*, and he did not want to give her more information until he could trust her better.

So, Lenna, between gasping breaths from their hike, filled the silence with her life's story. If Merrick cared or was even listening, was hard to say. No responses or follow-up questions were aimed in her direction. He seemed to miss a step and stumble slightly when Lenna told him about the black gargoyle from her dream that tried to attack her, but with no other reaction, Lenna chalked it up to him tripping on one of the scattered rocks in their path.

Their feet met with the crunch of dirt, leading them to a road large enough for a carriage to meander down. They followed the well-worn trail for another half hour before reaching the first of the cottages.

From certain angles, Lenna could make out a sheen of *something* covering the homes. When she asked her quiet companion, he grunted out that it was protection magic the townsfolks had recently enacted since they lived outside the hustle and bustle of the city limits itself. And then reminded her to keep walking.

Lenna didn't see any of the cottages' inhabitants, save for a few cows grazing in wooden pens. And one very large rooster. The beastie would have come up to her hips if she stood near it. Between feathers of reddish brown, bright gold plumes dotted down its back, mirroring its curved golden beak. And almost as if the rooster could feel her stare, it turned and scowled at her. Lenna quickened her pace, almost tripping on Merrick's heels to put as much distance as possible between her and the unnaturally large bird.

"It won't eat you either," Merrick chuckled tightly, as the massive beastie hopped over to the slatted wood fence, giving Lenna a defensive glare. "Fire Chickens only eat fleas, grass, and the occasional rabbit. No taste for Oracle flesh."

Before Lenna could ask why it was called a Fire Chicken, the beastie let out a hoarse croak and a spurt of flame shot out of its beak. Lenna did collide with Merrick this time, but it didn't knock him off kilter an inch. Merrick shot Lenna a bemused look as she struggled to righten herself. "I've seen your scrawny roosters in the Slate Kingdom, and honestly, I can't believe you *eat* those things."

"You don't eat Fire Chickens?" Lenna asked, as the beastie and its yard disappeared around a bend in the road.

"No, Fire Chickens are the best guards for a house to have. If you raise them from chicks, they will defend your home until their last breath. That one's been there for decades. Sometimes, it will even follow its owner into town and hiss at people who get too close."

"You live in Spinella?" Lenna looked around. The peaceful cottages had ivy curling up their stones, wooden doors that showcased intricate carvings of plants, vines, and animals, carefully painted in vivid hues. Colorful ceramic pots filled with budding flowers nestled between garden patches, and eruptions of well-maintained foliage were planted lovingly in yards next to the dirt path. It was very much the quaint country life. She couldn't imagine the hulking man with grey horns, deadly looking wings, and the muscled body of a warrior fitting into this place.

Merrick sighed, "I did, a very, *very* long time ago. I like to come back and visit now when I can. It's peaceful here usually, and I have friends that still live in town. It's definitely not as big as where you came from, but still has always been a home for me."

It was Lenna's turn to give him a chuckle back. "A very, *very* long time? You don't look older than twenty-five."

White teeth flashed in another wicked grin. "Thank you. I'm actually one hundred and twelve."

Lenna almost sat down in the dirt. "You're joking with me," she said flatly, looking him over again. The tanned skin, the lush brown hair, the beard just long enough to begin curling–no flecks of grey, no wrinkles–just muscle on every inch of his body and youth in his dark brown eyes.

"Nope." Merrick shrugged. "In your land, humans age differently because there's no magic. Here, once we hit a certain age, we don't age past it for centuries. I've looked more or less the same since I *was* about twenty-five." He raised his eyebrows and side-eyed Lenna. "It'll be the same for you, if you stay in a land of magic. I've seen humans reach five hundred. Granted, they're wrinkly old crones once they reach three hundred, but it's just the way the magic works. And magic affects everyone differently. With you being the new Oracle, too, who knows. The last Oracle was over eight hundred years old before his untimely death."

Lenna's knees did give out at that, and she did end up plopping down in the dirt. "Eight hundred," she whispered, "I could live that long?" Merrick glanced down the road and then back at Lenna. Her hair had come unbound, and her curls framed her face. Gripping the edges of her cloak tighter to her body, she fought through her panicked emotions. Lenna wasn't sure whether it was pain, or grief, or something...disbelieving, hoping. "I'll be fifty-two in a month," she finally said. Her eyes locked on Merrick as he stood over her.

Merrick snorted out a laugh, offering her his hand. "Then I'd say you are a very young lady."

Chapter Nine
Lenna

Getting her legs working again was difficult. As Merrick waited on Lenna to take his hand, she noticed a thin, delicate golden ring on his finger.

It seemed such a jarringly odd piece of jewelry for the rugged gargoyle to have, that Lenna focused on it a beat longer, until her mind buzzed her back to the present with the knowledge that she was irrevocably changed. Down to her core. From magic imbued in these lands. Now, her life stretched out in front of her–seemingly endless and overwhelming.

With one last glance at the bright gold ring, Lenna reached up and gripped his hand. He hoisted her out of the dirt easily, before resuming his silent walk towards where-ever-he-said they were going.

As she brushed herself off, Lenna mulled over everything Merrick revealed, ruminating most on his comment about her new lifespan in a land of magic. If she was unhappy with how the last thirty years of her life played out... How was she supposed to fill the next seven hundred?

Merrick seemed quieter after their short conversation, the uneasy silence prompting Lenna to continue her monologue about her past life. She wasn't going to walk for gods knew how long and be alone with her jumbled-up thoughts. As they trotted down the road, jovial music began trickling towards them. Lenna could make out tall, dark stone walls in the distance, an obvious confirmation that they were nearing some sort of civilized town.

As a thought niggled to the forefront of her restless mind, Lenna caught up to Merrick, hurrying her steps as she fell into place beside his brisk walk. "How long were you watching me in Doortan?"

Merrick raised an eyebrow, his brown hair swinging into his face with the movement. He met her eyes briefly before replying, "A while."

"Days? Weeks?" Lenna pushed, continuing to match Merrick's long strides.

Merrick sighed, looking back towards the city sprawled in front of them, before admitting, "About a month."

Lenna slowed. *A month*. Her headaches had started a month ago, right when Merrick began watching her. Merrick, realizing she had once again fallen behind, slowed his steps. "Why'd you stop?"

Shaking her head, Lenna plastered a fake smile on her face. "Nothing. I just feel like you could've saved us both some trouble by announcing your presence sooner, rather than later." It was an uneasy feeling, knowing that Merrick had been in Doortan for a month. She wondered if the gargoyle had been privy to the tears that she shed, the sadness she had been encapsulated in, the nights she woke in a cold sweat from her nightmares. She wondered why, now, he bought her here.

Was it a test?

Did she pass?

She felt guilty, as if she let him down by being bedridden for so long. Had he waited for her to begin feeling better before taking her here?

Merrick grunted, averting his eyes from hers. Lenna watched him fiddle with the golden ring on his finger, but he provided no more information. Lenna fell silent as they walked the last few miles towards Spinella.

As she crossed through the town's gates, she felt the transition from dirt path to slick cobblestone under her boots, the city alive and thrumming in front of her. She had a quick moment to drink in the bustle, the bursts of new sights, music and color, before Merrick stepped into her field of vision.

"Keep your hood up and your head down," Merrick advised quietly, gently tugging her hood over her hair. "We don't need to draw any attention to ourselves here."

Lenna swallowed. "I thought you said Spinella was safe?"

Merrick bent down, adjusting her cloak so her curls stayed put behind the heavy fabric. "We are going to meet my friend. *He* is safe, and there are protection wards around our meeting place, which is very secure. I just want to make sure there is no trouble getting there."

Lenna took one more longing-filled look at the city alive around her. Colorful flags dipped and danced from two-story stone and wood buildings, merchants shouted above the din of musicians and shoppers, naming their wares and prices. The overlapping chatter sunk into Lenna, and she shrunk closer to Merrick as they hurriedly wove through the shopping district. Merrick's large body half covered hers as they made their way past carts of oddly smelling meats and cheeses, weird fruits that Lenna peeked at from under her hood, and garments ranging from silk robes to shirts with holes in the backs for wings. A merchant shouted near her, and Lenna quickly averted her eyes, panic rising, as she suddenly felt very small.

Her mind wanted to ask why they were avoiding the townsfolk, why Merrick was so guarded and on edge, but she wasn't sure she was yet ready to face those answers. Merrick had said he would tell her. A small piece of her trusted that.

They passed through the shopping district quickly, and she breathed a sigh of relief as they entered a less occupied part of Spinella. Lenna raised her head a fraction as the voices and noise dimmed behind them. They were on a side street with sleepy looking shops lining the cobblestone path.

A bell tinkered, and before Lenna could look away, her breath hitched.

"Fae," Merrick said under his breath catching Lenna's reaction to the svelte body, the almost feline eyes, the delicately pointed ears of the strange woman that exited the bookshop in front of them. "These lands, on the continent of Irridessen, are home to humans, gargoyles, and the fae."

"I've never seen a woman so beautiful," Lenna whispered as Merrick half-dragged her past the store.

Merrick dipped his head. "Female–not woman. With the motley of beings who live here, we go by female, male or just species name if one does not identify to one or the other. And the fae have excellent hearing," he muttered as the female giggled in their direction. "And are always annoyingly beautiful."

"Oh." Lenna paused, blush creeping up her neck as she realized the fae female heard her compliment. Merrick steered her away as the fae smiled again before disappearing in a flash of blue light. Lenna stopped dead in her tracks, gaping at the place where the fae had stood a split second before.

"They also have magic. Some fae can disappear from one spot and reappear a half second later someplace else, like that fae just did–it's called waning," Merrick continued, pulling Lenna with him. When Lenna didn't so much as turn her head to acknowledge she heard him, Merrick stopped and put his hands on either side of her shoulders. She jumped out of her trance and stared up at him with wide eyes.

Merrick seemed to stare at her for a long moment. Then, he took a deep breath and rubbed his beard with his hand. "I'm sorry, this is all so new to you, and I truly keep forgetting how much of these lands are not spoken about in the Slate Kingdom."

Lenna stayed quiet, chewing her lip until Merrick began walking again, slightly slower than before as they wound their way through alleyways and buildings. As they left the rest of the shops behind, Merrick quietly explained the basics to Lenna, in a voice barely above a whisper.

Merrick spoke of gargoyles first, not to Lenna's surprise. He described how the horns of a gargoyle were typically passed down through heritage, how gargoyles were blessed by Alke, the God of War, who gave them gifts of agility and strength. He explained how he could use his wings in this form as well as his sentry form.

Then he went into fae. Glossing over the ridiculous beauty and the pointed ears, their superb hearing, and their physical strengths–*less* than that of a gargoyle, he noted as a smug smile tugged at the corners of his lips. Lenna tried to follow the flurry of information, grateful that Merrick had begun to open up as he explained the complex history of the fae–noting that even he didn't fully understand how gods chose to bless different lineages with differing powers. Some gods and goddesses could grant fae the ability to bend elements to their will, conjure up a storm of rain to water their fields, start a small fire to light kindling for cooking. Some fae could wane from one side of the continent to the other, others could only manage a few miles.

Other gods could gift unique, more deadly magics, though those were few and far between. The God of Water, Beyos, could bless you with a trickle of control over water, or the ability to influence the tides. The Goddess of Destruction, Aella, could give you the power to start a forest fire or to shape lightning to your will.

He noted that all fae had some type of magic, though there was only a small percentage that held anything extraordinary. And some gods did not bless anyone, preferring to keep their magic to themselves, never to be shared with those who walked the land. He grumbled under his breath that there were darker gods, like Phades, the Goddess of Death, who preferred to keep their powers under wraps, not trusting any beings with their unknown gifts. He made a small gesture of reverence, that Lenna mirrored, as he spoke of the Goddess of Death who ruled the afterlife from the god realm, Minmere.

Lenna was relieved learning they all worshipped the same gods and goddesses—at least that didn't feel foreign. As Merrick trailed off in his explanation, her thoughts turned to her own knowledge of the gods. She had prayed to Alke in the temple in Doortan to give her the strength to be a good wife. Now, she realized Alke had been too busy gifting all these gargoyles incredible prowess. She had begged Beyos to water her crop fields during the dry spells that seemed to plague the soil once every few years. Lenna had even prayed to Phades, asking her to keep watch over the souls of those she loved that had passed, and Faune, the Goddess of Life, giving thanks when a new babe came into the world, wriggly and screeching.

But knowing that the beings in these lands had received gifted magic from the gods left a sour taste in her mouth.

"Why don't the gods grant magic to the people in the Slate Kingdom?" Lenna asked before truly thinking the question through, hoping, as the words were spoken, that the gargoyle did not take offense.

Thankfully, Merrick seemed lost in thoughts of his own, again fiddling with the ring on his finger. "There was a great war a long time ago, when the Slate Kingdom was under the rule of Ingotheria. Long story short, the Kingdoms of Ingotheria were defeated by the Larimar Islands and the Kingdoms of Irridessen–the Obsidian and Opal Kingdoms. The treaty that was drawn up took the Slate Kingdom from the clutches of Ingotheria and gifted the land of the Slate Kingdom to the humans who fought and for the families of the humans that died in the ruthless and bloody war." Around them, the cityscape changed, and they now walked down what looked to be the housing district. Short rows of colorfully painted homes connected with each other, weaving on both sides of the path like snakes through the cobblestone.

Merrick continued, "It was one of the major points written into the treaty after the war that Irridessen forced Ingotheria to sign. After the ink dried, one hundred fae constructed a magical dome around the lands of the Slate Kingdom, keeping out magic, keeping out fae. It gave the humans their own land to prosper without the threat of magic. It's what affected your lifespans, since there was no magic left in the land to extend them. There was another loophole, where gargoyles could still access the Slate Kingdom in Sentry form, but that wasn't discovered until years later. The gods and goddesses still bless the beings in the Slate Kingdom, but fae magic itself is not compatible with full-blooded humans. The only magic humans can be blessed with comes from Moirai, the God of Sight, who creates seers and the Oracle. But seers can be fae or human. The Oracle can only ever be human."

"Why?" The question was out before Lenna could stop herself.

"I don't know–ask the gods," Merrick muttered, his wings tightening to his back as they passed another group of fae chatting and walking together in the opposite direction. Lenna ducked her head, shrinking into Merrick's shadow.

As the sun began to set, they passed a noisy neighborhood bar that stood on the corner, beginning another row of the curiously linked houses. Merrick drew Lenna onto the opposite side of the street, tucking her into his side. "Even in these lands, humans cannot have magic. If humans breed with gargoyles or fae, their offspring have the chance to gain magic, but the only full-blooded human that will ever receive magic is the Oracle."

Lenna felt the tips of her rounded, boringly human ears heat at the implication of Merrick's statement. "Gargoyles, fae, and humans can reproduce together?"

Merrick chuckled wickedly, "Oh yes, they can. Though sometimes they fuck just for the sake of fucking." Lenna flicked her eyes up, taking in the bar scene through her lashes. Her blush deepened as she noticed there was indeed a female gargoyle lip locked with a fae male, as if they were the only two beings in the world, completely ignoring the rest of the tavern's patrons around them.

An abrupt turn towards the homes ripped Lenna's eyes from the bar to a dully painted yellow house in the middle of its row. Merrick turned his head, looking up and down the street. They stepped up to the door, the lock softly clicking open. Lenna glanced over to Merrick, whose face was set in a hard line. He quickly pushed open the door, ushering Lenna inside and into a dark and cramped living room.

A roaring fire burned in the stone fireplace, a small lumpy brown couch and two wooden chairs squeezed haphazardly into the sitting area. A threadbare green rug, coupled with the worn-looking furniture, showed evidence of years and years of use. But Lenna's attention was solely focused on the tall fae male standing by the fire, staring at them with an intensity burning as hot as the coals behind him.

CHAPTER TEN
MERRICK

"Lenna, meet Laurent," Merrick said quietly, closing the door behind him until the lock caught and clicked, the protection magic Laurent crafted snapping around the home once more.

Laurent bowed his head in greeting as Lenna sized him up, her honey-gold eyes widening and narrowing as she assessed the fae in front of her. Laurent's skin was the richest shade of black, and his chiseled features, broad shoulders, and shaved head made his already powerful presence even more so. Emerald green eyes tracked Lenna's every breath, near glowing in the dimly lit room. Small silver studs traveled up his lobes–up to the sharp points of his ears. Slightly taller than Merrick, Laurent stood impossibly still, the fabric of his purple robe not even sounding a whisper. Merrick watched as Laurent, in turn, appraised the short, curvy, red-headed Oracle, her pale cheeks flushed pink, with amusement. Merrick held his breath as he waited for Lenna to break the silence.

And to Merrick's chagrin, Lenna strode up to the fae, stuck out her hand, and declared, "Merrick was right, you seem *much* more refined than him." Laurent's solemn face broke into a bright grin as he grasped her hand in his.

"Oh dear, that's because I am," Laurent chucked, shaking her hand once before looking over the top of her head to Merrick. "How much have you told her?"

"Just enough. She knows she's the Oracle, and that the last Oracle died–"

"Absolutely not enough information." Lenna cut him off with a wave of her hand, turning pleading eyes up to Laurent. Merrick felt irritation begin creeping back in, but Laurent shot him a sharp look, telling him to stand down. "Can you please tell me what's going on? The full story–since Merrick is still deciding if he can trust me. Even though he uprooted my entire life and threw me into a portal to get here." Lenna seemed to reconsider her stance as she added, "Merrick *did* tell me about the god's magical gifts, and the differences between gargoyles and fae, though. So, he's got that going for him."

Laurent gave Lenna a warm smile, and Merrick realized Lenna was trying to play them against each other. Trying to get as much information as possible–not knowing they had been battle hardened and court managed together since they were both in their twenties. Laurent fiddled with the gold ring on his finger, and Merrick touched the sibling ring on his own hand.

"Have you told her of the Oracle's circumstances of death?" Laurent spoke into Merrick's mind, his smooth voice a relief in itself. They'd made it, where Laurent's magic and the protection wards around the house meant the difference in winning or losing any fight that came for the Oracle.

Getting the Oracle here safely. At least he hadn't fucked that up.

"I told her he was murdered–not by whom or why it was important." Merrick responded dully.

The rings, a gift from a lifetime ago, allowed them to speak directly to the other's mind. As long as both wearers touched the golden band, they could speak silently without alerting any nearby ears. Excellent for long distances, and for private conversations while navigating the intricacies of court life.

Lenna looked from one to the other but confusion at the silence was the only expression on her face. Turning his eyes back to her, Laurent cleared his throat.

"This is a long story. Can I get you a drink? Something to eat? You must be half starved." Laurent didn't wait for an answer, striding past Merrick and Lenna with his purple robes snapping around his ankles, disappearing into the connected kitchen and returning a moment later with a bowl of stew and a glass of water.

"Oh–thank you," Lenna said, taken aback by the swift delivery of food. She took the bowl offered, looking around the living room nervously. Laurent gestured over to the wooden chairs.

"Why don't you sit and eat. Merrick and I will do our best to tell you everything we know."

Merrick hid his smirk at seeing Laurent in his element, always processing information, always two steps ahead mentally of whomever he had to survey. All those years working closely with the late King of Irridessen had created a silver-tongued mercenary. Laurent was adept in a fight, but even more deadly utilized as a spy.

Laurent turned towards the fire, his hands clasped behind his back, and stared into the depth of the glowing embers before he began.

"The reason you are here, my dear Lenna, is because this is the safest place for you," Laurent began, speaking directly to the fire. Behind him, Lenna chewed her first bite of stew slowly, never taking her eyes off the back of Laurent's closely shaved head. "We've warded the doors from any outside ears–fae or otherwise. We are taking every precaution as we navigate these new waters, so to speak. You see... This whole conflict started a year ago, and we are finally poised to begin fighting back now that we have you. We need your help as the newly activated Oracle."

Laurent began his story with the flair that Merrick had grown accustomed to from nine decades of listening to Laurent's tales.

"Well, this all *truly* started two *hundred* years ago, when the Fae King of the Opal Kingdom found his mate–the Gargoyle Queen of the Obsidian Kingdom."

Realizing that Laurent was going *all* the way back to the beginning, Merrick got up to get his own dinner from the dusty kitchen. Laurent had a knack for dramatic story-weaving, and in all the years of Merrick knowing him, Laurent never made a long story short–preferring to make a long story...even longer.

"Mate?" Lenna questioned, looking from Laurent's back to Merrick, as he plopped onto the worn couch with his meal. Merrick dug in, shoving food in his mouth as fast as possible to avoid speaking.

"You didn't tell her about mates?" Laurent demanded, turning, and fixing a twinkling stare at Merrick.

"I didn't have a chance," Merrick growled, mouth full of food. He waved his fork in the air, gesturing towards Lenna. "She had a full-blown breakdown just talking about our lifespan."

Lenna glared at Merrick.

"*Excuse me* for being shocked that my lifespan just went from *maybe* seventy-five years to *over eight hundred*," she hissed.

Merrick groaned. He was trying to be patient, but how long would it take to break down *every part* of their lands to explain to a newcomer? "*Okay*, mates are the other half of your soul. Your soul tie. The being that becomes so closely linked to your own self that if they die, you do, too. It's the truest form of love, something most beings desire more than anything. To be with that one soul that understands their own completely." He took another heaping bite of stew, silently thanking the gods that Laurent cooked because he always made the most delicious food.

"To find your mate is not easy since it can be anyone, any species. Some beings refuse to settle down until they find their mate. Others don't wait for a soul tie, opting to just spend their lives with a partner instead, similar to the marriages you have in the Slate Kingdom."

Laurent went on, throwing a scathing look in Merrick's direction. "When the moon is full above us, it is the closest we are in this existence to the Goddess of Soul Ties, Carra. The legends say she was born from the moon to gift love to the beings who prayed for salvation. Now, we gather to honor her gift to us—the soul tie. Parties in every town are thrown on the night of each full moon. Everyone who is looking for a mate comes together celebrating Carra, and a lucky few might find their fated companion at the celebration."

Merrick felt his heart ache for that sort of love. But the life of a warrior, destined for battlefields, did little to entice lovers. He usually spent the full moon belly up to a tavern bar, avoiding any of the beings that approached him, only returning their attention *after* the full moon began to sink lower in the sky, taking the magic of soul ties with it.

Laurent continued, "Soul ties bloom once you make eye contact with your destined mate. Once both beings of the new soul tie touch each other, their souls fuse together irrevocably, and the soul tie is complete."

"Eyes are the window to the soul, the key to forming a tie to another being. Touching is the lock—showing the other that you will walk this life with them until you breathe your last breath together. Beings who have found love take their partner to the festivities, to see if Carra blesses their union with a soul tie. But it can be months, years, *decades*, before they get a soul tie—if they get one at all."

Lenna hummed, slowly processing the information as she took another bite of stew. "Have either of you found your mate?"

Merrick shook his head, ice slithering through his veins, as Laurent answered, "No. We've been to many full moon gatherings, but neither of us have a soul tie."

"Three species of beings in Terramere—fae, gargoyle, and human—are susceptible to soul ties in lands of magic. But it could take hundreds of years before you meet the one Carra chose for you. The only beings that cannot gain a soul tie are the witches in the Jade Kingdom," Laurent huffed in disgust. Merrick grunted in agreement.

Known for their ruthlessness, cruelty, and backwards views of the world, it had been a blessing in itself that anyone with witch blood was forced to live in the Jade Kingdom after the last war, and the fact that they couldn't be blessed with a soul tie prompted whispered discussions wondering if witches even had souls to begin with.

"So...the Fae King and the Gargoyle Queen had this soul tie," Lenna stated, bringing the conversation back to the story she obviously was desperate to hear.

Laurent nodded. "It was the first time in history that a King and a Queen were mates. They joined the lands and their people together. And for almost two hundred years we have, more or less, had peace throughout Irridessen."

"What broke the peace? The last Oracle?" Lenna asked.

Merrick shook his head, taking over the story telling from Laurent. "Tht is not what broke the peace, no. The King and Queen had twin daughters. Half fae, half gargoyle. Adara, the eldest by only a few minutes, and Esmeray."

Lenna started at the name of the latter, but kept her mouth shut. Merrick noted her knee jerk reaction but continued, "For the first time, the

King and Queen changed the rules for the line of succession when the twins were born to give thanks to Carra for their soul tie. They changed it from the typical rule that the elder takes the throne to whomever meets their mate first wins the Opal Kingdom, and the latter would rule in the Obsidian Kingdom. Whoever won would be the Queen on High, ruling out of the Opal Palace. The other twin would oversee the Obsidian Palace with the title Lesser Queen–still a Queen, but not as influential and powerful for Irridessen as Queen on High."

"What's the difference between the Obsidian and Opal Kingdoms?" Lenna asked. Merrick was proud of how well she was holding up with all of this. She definitely showed signs of shock at the soul ties, but seemed to want to find out about her role as the Oracle. *It was a good sign*, Merrick reassured himself. She wasn't running for the hills, demanding to go back to the Slate Kingdom.

Laurent stepped forward. "Once you see both Palaces, you'll understand. But the main difference is that the Opal Palace holds most of Irridessen's army, almost the entire court, and has riches that exceed even the wildest of imaginations. The Obsidian Palace is now more of a...stronghold...for times of war. It's used primarily to train soldiers, and only a small court is assembled there." He cocked his head, choosing each word carefully. "The Opal Palace offered a potential shot at the throne. Families fought over the honor of being invited to even *one* of the Opal Palace's full moon celebrations. Every month, a fortune was spent on the parties, and eligible males and females would queue for hours to see if they were the mate of either twin. The Obsidian Palace hasn't held a gathering since Queen Absolute Elera received her soul tie to King Absolute Scottrell. The Obsidian Palace also has...a pretty severe punishment system and an underground dungeon that breeds fear into even the most hardened prisoners. Not the best place to raise a family, rule from, or even just *live* in."

"Both of the twins wanted to rule as Queen on High," Lenna said quietly.

Merrick finished his stew, rising from the couch with a groan. His voice rose as he continued the story from the kitchen, above the clinking of the ladle against the chipped ceramic bowl, helping himself to seconds.

"At first, yes. But a rift formed between them. Adara obsessively made it her life's purpose to find her mate, lock in a soul tie, and grab the succession from her sister. Esmeray never cared about royal duties in the slightest. At least that's how it seemed from an...outside perspective," Merrick finished lamely. He didn't know how else to describe the circumstances. "Esmeray never *really* showed interest in wanting to rule–but she didn't want her sister to be Queen on High if it meant she had to answer to Adara. In a way, I guess Esmeray *wanted* to be Queen on High, just without the responsibility of ruling. The twins were close when they were young, but things escalated drastically over the last couple years. They've gotten competitive–ruthless, really–neither wanting the other to win."

Laurent cleared his throat. "Esmeray is a very powerful being with magic these lands have never seen before. And she is as deadly as she is reckless. Adara hated the fact she was half gargoyle, with less powerful fae magic. Adara could never beat Esmeray in a duel for power if it came down to it. To secure her reign, we believe Adara has been learning forbidden spells, how to cast just enough magic from them to be more in league with her sister's power. The spells *do* amplify her magic–but at a steep cost. It takes a lot of energy to perform even one spell. The price is bits of a being's life force for each spell cast, and it's because of that the Fae outlawed spell work centuries ago. Adara found an ancient book that taught her spells these lands haven't seen in thousands of years."

"To secure herself as Queen on High once she found her mate, to protect herself from her sister," Lenna breathed. Merrick grunted his confirmation, scooping more stew into his mouth. "Did Adara or Esmeray find their soul tie?"

The grief Merrick knew colored his features must have been more vivid than he thought, since Lenna put her fork down and leaned in closer, her forehead crinkling as she wrung her hands together, her anxious focus making it harder for him to get the words out around the lump forming in his throat.

"Last year, at the Opal Palace's first full moon gathering of summer, we, the King's Guard, were present. Typically, the King kept us from the full moon gatherings, allowing us the night off to celebrate amongst ourselves in town. But there was a threat of rogue fae making trouble on the outskirts of the border, and he wanted his top soldiers at court to guard the party." He swallowed, taking a steadying breath. "Well, we received notice that the situation was dealt with. Our commander, Keerian, went up to King Scottrell on the dais to confirm that the issue had been handled. And...the moment Keerian looked at Esmeray, a soul tie bloomed."

Lenna's eyes widened again at the mention of Esmeray, and Merrick made another mental note of it. Laurent finally moved away from the fire, taking a seat on the couch next to Merrick.

"It was...pandemonium. The King was upset because he wanted his daughters with a mate that came from a line of royalty. Adara was also...angry. Understandably," Laurent said, unable to sit still. With a sigh, he got up from the couch again, going over to the small window and peering outside.

"What did Esmeray do?" Lenna whispered, fork hovering in the air, frozen on the way to her mouth.

Merrick pressed his head against the thin pillows lining the back of the couch. A year later, it was all still raw, fresh, in his mind. The night that royally fucked up his entire life. "Princess Esmeray *grabbed* Keerian's hand, immediately solidifying their soul tie, and waned them out of the throne room." He closed his eyes, the memory of the chaos driving him to instinctively touch his ring.

Keerian had looked into Esmeray's eyes, and the entire court witnessed the shimmering magic that began veiling the pair. The soul tie had bloomed, and Esmeray, seeing her shot at the throne, lunged for Keerian as Keerian stood there, stupefied. The magic hit its crescendo and the entire throne room had been bathed in white light. The brightest soul tie he'd ever seen activate. And then—they disappeared into the unknown, Esmeray's flash of golden magic smothering the pure light of the soul tie.

"We will figure this out." Merrick heard Laurent through their rings. He looked over at his oldest friend and smiled grimly.

"Woah." Lenna slumped back in her seat. "She just...took him and disappeared?"

Laurent nodded slowly. Merrick knew Laurent was watching him, analyzing his mental state. It irritated Merrick more than he cared to admit.

The next hour was spent filling Lenna in on more of that fateful night, Laurent taking over most of the talking, patiently going through the details—as detailed as if he was explaining the happenings of a battle to the King.

Merrick was grateful for it. His mind was still storming over the look on the King and Queen's faces as they realized what happened. Adara's frozen rage, her beautiful face twisted with loathing, *hatred*, for the sister that ultimately won everything she'd wanted for the last ninety-eight years.

Queen on High.

But Keerian was his friend.

He'd practically grown up with Keerian and Laurent. They'd met in their twenties when they began training, each growing into soldiers in their own right over the years–their strengths and weaknesses balanced between them. Keerian was also a full-fledged, pureblooded gargoyle with the strength and brutality to go along with it, and they had Laurent, defending their backs with magic while they fought their way through any foe that dared cross them.

Laurent had just finished detailing the scenes of the evening after Esmeray waned away with Keerian, and how no one knew where they disappeared to. He described the guests, the royals in attendance, their reactions. Lenna held on to every word.

Knowing what Laurent would say next, Merrick stretched out his legs, crossing them at the ankles, and closed his eyes.

"The next morning, the King Absolute and Queen Absolute, albeit begrudgingly, acknowledged the soul tie to the assembled court, and declared Esmeray as the rightful Queen on High. A celebration was supposed to be held a week later, but Princess Esmeray and Keerian were still nowhere to be found." Laurent rubbed his face and smoothed his hand across his bald head. "Two days before the celebration was to be held, Esmeray and Keerian showed back up at the Palace and went straight into a secret meeting with the King and Queen. They did not speak to anyone else, not even us, which was odd. Keerian has been our closest friend for almost one hundred years, but he passed us, unseeing, not even stopping to tell us where he had been." Laurent looked at Lenna solemnly. Merrick sent his own steadying words through his ring to Laurent.

"Esmeray didn't ask to speak with her twin–and no one could confirm Adara knew Esmeray was back. We were all concerned the sisters would fight it out, so every housed warrior at court was told to guard Adara in case Esmeray wanted to take out the competition and be crowned Queen Absolute of Irridessen–ruling both Obsidian and Opal–or in case Adara tried to rebuke Esmeray's succession."

Laurent sighed, shaking his head, his silver earrings gleaming in the light cast from the fire. "We both personally warned the King to take precautions against Esmeray's return. The King's Guard worried Esmeray would want to be crowned immediately and take out her parents and sister to make sure her reign wasn't challenged after the celebration. On our continent, Irridessen, Kings and Queens only rule for three hundred years, and then they must name a successor or heir. Esmeray and Keerian were set to be crowned as the successors once the King and Queen's reign was up. We are as close to immortal as we can get so putting a limit on how long royals can rule is the only way to keep them from killing each other for a throne.

Esmeray only had *one hundred years* to wait to be crowned Queen on High. But the next morning, the King and Queen were found dead. Murdered."

Chapter Eleven
MERRICK

"Esmeray and Keerian *killed* the King and Queen? Her own parents?" Lenna's brows shot up in surprise. With a grimace, Merrick plopped heavily onto the wooden chair across from her, kneading his sternum with a fist, wings drooping to settle against the floor. He'd been hunting Lenna for a month and now she was here and he was just...tired. Tired down to the very marrow in his bones. Recanting the night when his life went to shit wasn't helping the tightness ease in his chest, either.

Wasn't talking about your problems supposed to help?

Laurent growled, his tone at odds with the impeccable demeanor he normally displayed. "Keerian would *never* murder his own King and Queen. He served them faithfully and loyally his entire life. The *facts* are that Esmeray was the only other being the King and Queen saw the day before their deaths. And she's more than powerful enough to kill them. It was *most likely* her, wanting to secure her Queenship as fast as possible. She tried to murder her sister in front of the entire court in response to Adara's summons."

"Princess Esmeray tried to kill Princess Adara?" Lenna looked over at Merrick, and to Merrick's surprise, she pulled her hand out of her lap, reaching over to grip his own. Merrick squeezed her fingers gently, surprised she looked at *him* in a way to comfort *him*—though his facial expressions were enough of a giveaway to his feelings.

"Adara called the Opal Court to the throne room before requesting Esmeray and Keerian meet us. We were all there—numb. In shock. Grieving." Laurent's agitation grew palpable. Behind him, the fire hissed and flared brighter, the edges of the flames burning blue and licking up the mantle with the magic Laurent struggled to contain.

"*Calm down with the crazy fire shit,*" Merrick snapped through their rings, before he continued aloud, "Keerian swore his innocence—as did Esmeray—but Adara didn't believe them. She demanded to know about their last meeting with the late King and Queen, yet Esmeray and Keerian refused to divulge anything. Esmeray just kept loudly repeating that she did not kill her parents. Some of the Lords in court believed Adara should sentence Esmeray to death without a trial. Adara refused, stating she didn't want to see her twin die when there was not a clear verdict. Instead, Adara exiled Esmeray to the Obsidian Palace while the investigations were ongoing. Esmeray accepted the temporary exile...until Adara forbade Keerian from going with her."

Laurent looked over at Merrick, hand in hand with Lenna. "Adara then crowned herself Queen Absolute, stating Irridessen needed a strong ruler that wasn't on trial for murder. Someone the court and the council could trust without fear. She stripped Esmeray of her titles, calling her the Queen of Nothingand Esmeray...went crazy. She challenged Adara to duel to the death right there for the title of Queen Absolute, the title their mother held over both the Opal and Obsidian Kingdoms. The whole court watched in terror. We were the strongest warriors of Irridessen, sworn to protect the crown, but no one could take on Esmeray and live. She's too powerful. Her fae magic is...strange. It's magic we don't know how to contend with. But before it came to a battle, Adara used a spell to forcibly wane Esmeray out of the Opal Kingdom, and warded the Opal Palace against Esmeray's return. Queen Adara also arrested Keerian, warding him *in* the Opal Palace until his innocence is confirmed."

"Adara's spells protected her from Esmeray after all," Lenna mused.

Merrick's horns glimmered in the firelight as he nodded, tracking the glint of light that shadowed the wall with his movement. He spoke in a half-daze as he moved his head side to side slowly, the small fracture off his horns reflecting the motion. "We attempted to gain an audience with Queen Adara to speak on Keerian's behalf—to swear to his character and loyalty—but Queen Adara dismissed the entire King's Guard under Keerian without honor. Without our honors, we were disgraced from court, our word and influence reduced to ash." With a sigh, Merrick shrugged, pretending the sting of dishonor wasn't as brutal as a dagger to the heart. "No one at court would listen, neither would the Royal Council. They all turned their backs on us instead. Laurent and I fled the Palace and banded together here, trying to figure out how to help Keerian on our own."

Laurent seemed to be half listening himself as he wrangled his magic under control. Merrick spared a glance in his direction before shuffling his wings and turning back to Lenna.

"Princess Esmeray disappeared without a trace until a month ago, when she resurfaced and captured the previous Oracle. She tortured him, *killed* him, as a message to her sister to release Keerian. Which activated...*you*. Adara refused to grant Keerian freedom, and since Esmeray ruthlessly murdered the Oracle in cold blood, Adara gave the order to capture and kill Esmeray by any means necessary to protect Irridessen from Esmeray's growing madness."

"Did you speak to the previous Oracle before Esmeray murdered him?" Lenna questioned, her voice pitching around the last two words.

Merrick shook his head, Laurent cleared his throat. "We tried to seek out the Oracle after we were dismissed from the Palace to see if he could peer into the past and confirm who killed King Scottrell and Queen Elera. I–*we*–could not find him."

The fear in Lenna's eyes grew, and Merrick felt like he needed to comfort her now. To be thrown into their world *this morning* and finding out her predecessor was murdered... It was a big ask they were coming to her with.

"The facts are *we don't know* who killed the King and Queen, and well... That's where you come in, Oracle." Merrick patted her hand and let go, leaning back in the chair again. Gods, he wanted more of that damn stew. Or a drink. Or a mindless fuck with some stranger from the bar. Or a good night's rest.

"What can I do?" Lenna asked a bit breathlessly, her honey eyes as large as saucers.

The fire had calmed, and Laurent was once again cool and collected. "The Obsidian Palace is home to many artifacts with magical power. One of these items is the Prism of the Oracle. The Oracle can use it to peer through time to recover memories from the past."

Merrick stood, stretching out his wings. "We need to collect the Prism and have you look into it to see what *really* happened to the late King and Queen. If it confirms what we think–what Queen Adara and the rest of the court thinks–that Esmeray is the killer of the King, Queen, and Oracle, we need to bring it to Queen Absolute Adara and the Royal Council."

"Are you still loyal to Queen Adara since she dismissed you?"

"We're loyal to *Keerian*–our commander and closest friend. We *know* he would never do this, and Esmeray admitted she was responsible for the death of the Oracle. If she can kill the Oracle, a death sentence in itself, Esmeray could've acted alone in the killing of her parents," Merrick clarified. Laurent agreed with a grunt.

"The Prism would potentially clear Keerian's name, but if he's soul tied to Esmeray, it would mean a death sentence for him too, right? If Queen Adara kills Esmeray?" Lenna's red curls bobbed as she looked from the fae to the gargoyle. Merrick could almost see the wheels turning in Lenna's head as she pondered all the new information they had given her.

"And that is another reason why we *need* to find the Prism, why we were so urgently looking for you. We need you to clear our friend's name so we can beg Queen Adara to not deliver a death sentence, and instead, use her spell book to bind Esmeray into the darkest dungeon in the Obsidian Palace and throw away the key. If Esmeray was locked up, Keerian would live." Merrick said.

"An army of two." Lenna chewed on her lip, deep in thought.

Merrick gave her a small smile. "Hopefully, an army of three–if you'll help us."

CHAPTER TWELVE
LENNA

THEY WERE RIGHT. THIS was a big ask.

"Isn't Esmeray in the Obsidian Kingdom? Wouldn't she be there when we went looking for the Prism?" The combination of the long day and the world altering information made her head spin. Lenna rubbed her temples, eyelids drooping with exhaustion as she fought to stay awake and alert. Her body was up against her mind, and her mind was balking, slowing to a sluggish pace.

"Queen Adara moved their uncle to the Obsidian Palace to rule as Regent. Esmeray isn't there. We aren't sure where she is, but with Queen Adara's command to capture and kill by any means necessary, coupled with the uptick of fae guards hunting her, Esmeray wouldn't dare show her face in the Obsidian Palace. The death of the Oracle changed everything." Laurent looked at Merrick, and Lenna noted the weird thing they did again–like a silent conversation.

Merrick stood up and clasped his hands together. "Right. Lenna, you must be exhausted." He picked up his empty bowl and collected hers from the small table. "There's a bed down the hall to the right. If you want to wash up, there is a washroom adjoining. Get changed, get some rest."

Lenna awkwardly stood up. Her legs, tired from the day of adventure, wobbled a bit. Her thighs burned. She looked down at her clothes, and before she could say she didn't have anything to change into, Laurent spoke, more to the fire than to her.

"We have some things for you to change into. They aren't the best quality, but they're clean." He frowned–almost as if in apology. "Before we head to the Obsidian Palace, one of us will go into town and get you some new clothes if that is alright with you."

Lenna smiled at the fae. He was trying so hard to make her comfortable here. It was the nicest thing anyone had done for her in a while. She held a hand to her heart. "Thank you, Laurent, that would be lovely."

Laurent bowed his head slightly, a ghost of a smile flitting across his face. Lenna took that as her dismissal, making her way down the hall to the small bedroom. The door creaked open, revealing a narrow bed wrapped in thin burgundy sheets, a set of wooden dresser drawers that had seen better days, and a tiny washroom that Lenna made a beeline for first. She didn't realize how long she'd held her bladder until her eyes fell on the toilet in the corner. Then, making her way to the sink, she washed her hands, splashed water on her face, and stared at her reflection in the cracked mirror.

Her hair was crazy. She tried patting down the wayward red curls that frizzed out of control, finally giving up and wetting her fingers under the cool water in the sink, finger curling each section until the frizz lessened and the curls were damp enough for her to braid down her back, the length trailing past her shoulder blades. She secured the braid with a small strip of leather she found on the counter. Lenna wondered if the band had been Merrick's–if this was the childhood home he'd briefly mentioned.

Stepping back into the bedroom, Lenna searched the dresser in the corner. Some of the clothing was much too small for her, but she finally found a thin set of tan linen pants and a loose matching shirt to wear. The pants were much too long, and she figured these could've been Merrick's as well. Turning to the bed, she pulled the scratchy sheets back and scooted into the middle, the frame creaking with the movement. Her head rested against a pillow that was somehow both flat and lumpy.

But she didn't care.

Free. She was *free*.

Today had been the wildest day, and half of her wondered, once she closed her eyes, if she would wake up back in the Doortan Manor, confirming this had all been a dream.

Chapter Thirteen
MERRICK

After Lenna had gone to bed, Laurent perched on the edge of the chair the Oracle vacated and ate a single bowl of stew. Merrick sat with the fae in total silence and growing darkness as the fire died down, the pair lost to their own thoughts. It didn't take long before those very thoughts drove Merrick into the kitchen to find whatever alcohol still remained in this dwelling after his lengthy absence.

Merrick unearthed a dusty bottle of red wine from the back of a cabinet as Laurent joined him, moving around Merrick's wings with languid ease to put his bowl in the sink to soak. The stuffy kitchen seemed even smaller than Merrick remembered as he tightened his wings to his side. Of course, he hadn't been back here and stayed for longer than a few days since he was a child. Any trips he took to Spinella over the past ninety years were short. He'd either end the night in a stranger's bed or be so drunk that he didn't make it past the misshapen couch in the living room, only to be up and out of Spinella the moment the sun rose above the horizon the next morning.

His family home. To be back here, with Laurent, weirded him out, but also settled something deep in his gut. Two different sides of his world he never thought would cross paths. He pushed down the feeling of embarrassment at Laurent seeing how he grew up. There had been many late nights at the Opal Palace talking with Laurent and Keerian about their completely different upbringings, but seeing Laurent, dressed in his least expensive robe, trying to assimilate into the poverty Merrick was so accustomed to was an odd sight.

"Lenna seems to be absorbing all of this well enough," Laurent said, gently taking the wine from Merrick and using his magic to heat the top of the glass bottle until the cork shot out.

"Thanks." Merrick pulled two glasses from the shelf over the sink, wiping the dust off with a threadbare dish rag before handing one to Laurent. "Is it crazy to believe we could get Keerian's name cleared quickly?"

The tight grimace Laurent returned had Merrick's stomach dropping. Laurent knew the probability was slim. Gods, Merrick did, too. But for Keerian, they had to try.

Not ready to delve into a heavy conversation until the alcohol chased away some of his anxiety, Merrick swiftly changed the subject. "I know we've been off on our own journeys this past month but...I'm glad you're here," he admitted.

Laurent chuckled, taking the offered wine glass from Merrick and breaking the gloomy tension. "It's definitely a change from our usual haunts, but I'm glad your search went well."

"Thanks for putting the portal so far away, by the way. Spending half a day trudging through fields with a very slow human was fun." Rolling his eyes at the fae, Merrick swirled the wine around in the glass with a smirk. This was the most normal exchange they'd had in months, and it was all thanks to their success in finding Lenna.

Sarcastically, Laurent bowed deep–keeping his now-filled wine glass above his head. "I couldn't very well put it slap ass in the middle of the street. Anyone could have walked through it."

Laurent's portal conjuring was a rare fae ability. It came in handy for Merrick since gargoyles couldn't wane, and using a portal was much faster than flying. Laurent couldn't wane either–but the portals were efficient. Albeit slow to create due to the magic exerted. Laurent built the portal from the Opal Kingdom to the Slate Kingdom and back to land Lenna here.

Thinking of the walk to Spinella, Merrick's mind snagged on a particular part of Lenna's rambled story–the black gargoyle Lenna admitted to seeing in her dream. "What do you know about seers?"

Laurent cocked his head, dark brows furrowed. "Not much. They're blessed by Moirai, like the Oracle. But where the Oracle *sees* the past, seers get visions of the future. And seers rarely follow a bloodline. It's more of a one-off blessing from Moirai. Why?"

Shaking his head, Merrick sighed, "Lenna mentioned some dreams she had in Doortan, and they sounded more like prophecy. I didn't want to alarm her, but I think there may be more to her than just being the Oracle."

Laurent snorted, and the sound was so out of character that Merrick choked on his wine, coughing out a laugh before adding, "Moirai is the only god that blesses humans. What if he made her both?"

"Human seers are rare. I'll bet you ten silver coins that she is not."

Merrick raised his chin. "Ten *gold* coins and you have a deal."

Laurent hummed, amusement crossing his features, illuminating those brilliantly bright emerald eyes. "Deal."

They headed back into the living room, Laurent taking up post at the window to peer through the tattered yellow curtains. Merrick could make out a sliver of the street from the position he took up on the couch. The bar across the street was slowly emptying–the fae patrons waning while gargoyles flapped up into the night sky. Some of the drunker ones walked arm in arm, wings drooped, singing bawdy tunes as they wove through the rows of connected homes, the songs fading as they disappeared. After a minute of silence, Merrick knew Laurent was collecting his thoughts and keeping a tight leash on his magic.

Glancing at the tamed fire, Merrick frowned. The heavy conversations needed to happen, and the wine gave him a slight edge to be bold, the apprehension from bringing his fears up earlier gone. They needed to talk, and those nagging questions did no good hiding and festering in the back of his mind. Merrick gritted his jaw, rubbing his beard with a hand. Tomorrow was going to be a long day.

The clock on the mantle of the fireplace read three in the morning. Merrick swallowed a grumbled curse. Tomorrow had already arrived.

With a rough breath, Merrick averted his eyes from the fae and asked the question he'd been afraid to bring up earlier. "What if Keerian did do it?"

"Stop," Laurent sighed, the word curt but tired.

"No, seriously, Laurent. I mean…neither of us have a soul tie. How do we know it doesn't fuck with your head? What if Esmeray asked him to, and he couldn't say no?"

The tension in the room grew suffocating as the question settled into the dust of Merrick's childhood home.

Laurent finally turned from the window, a coolness in his green eyes. He leveled a stare at Merrick that had been used to break traitors and gain information from Laurent's days as Spy Master. "I refuse to believe the male who almost sacrificed his life multiple times in service of King Scottrell and Queen Elera would stoop to commit such an atrocious act. I want to believe if Esmeray asked Keerian to kill her parents, that Keerian would have chosen to drive a sword through his own heart instead."

"Keerian was always the best of us," Merrick conceded, those quiet fears dissipating with Laurent's declaration, "to the point of annoyance."

With the slip of a smile on his face, Laurent raised his glass. "To the point of annoyance."

Merrick chuckled hollowly, raising his own and taking a sip.

Laurent downed his wine before turning back to the window. "Get some rest. I'll keep watch."

Not needing to be told twice, Merrick put his empty glass on the side table next to the couch. His wings felt heavy, the horns on his head felt heavy. He just felt overall...heavy. A breeze filled the room, stifling the dying fire. Merrick glanced at Laurent but the fae didn't move from the window.

The room without the fire was cool, dark. Merrick closed his eyes and drifted off to grab a few hours of rest before the sun rose on another day in an uncertain world.

Chapter Fourteen
LAURENT

STAYING AWAKE AND VIGILANT at his post, overlooking the sleepy rows of homes in Spinella's housing district, Laurent didn't tear his gaze from the window until the sun finally crested over the horizon. It was only then that he allowed himself to move. Glancing over at the heap of gargoyle who had his legs dangling off the couch, wings draped over the sides, snoring lightly, Laurent snickered.

Gargoyles were so noisy—even when sleeping.

The first signs of Spinella's residents waking and starting their days began. Muffled sounds of rustling wings, hushed voices trying to avoid waking loved ones, and clinks of mugs being filled drifted through the thin walls on either side of him.

Until this crucial trip, Laurent had never stepped foot in Spinella, and he knew the people here were not well off, though they seemed happy. Laurent thought back to the stories Merrick used to narrate about playing in the streets as a young gargoyle with sticks that became legendary swords, the victor winning pieces of twine threaded through small stones to wear on their heads as an imagined crown.

Hearing about it was one thing, but seeing Merrick's childhood home, imagining Merrick's late mother cooking meals and choosing the curtains, made Laurent's heart hurt for what his friend had lost. He knew it was difficult for Merrick to be back here, but they had desperately needed a safe place to gather their bearings after being relieved of duty from the King's Guard. A place for Laurent to track the hint of magic that flared from the Slate Kingdom and concoct this hairbrained plan to save Keerian from death. Merrick had offered his house without a second thought.

His fae hearing confirmed Lenna was stirring in the bedroom, and Laurent smiled grimly as he allowed a flicker of hope to flash through his chest that they very well might pull this together.

The Oracle had survived her first night in their world.

An accomplishment.

And she seemed to want to help them.

A blessing.

Laurent made his way to the small kitchen, joining the noise of the neighbors as he checked the cabinets looking for some ground coffee—or even a tea bag.

Lenna padded into the kitchen, bleary-eyed and yawning. Laurent gave her a warm grin when she came into view. Her beautiful red curls had been tamed back into a braid, though sleeping allowed some smaller ringlets to escape the confines of the leather band. The linen shirt she wore fell to her knees, and the pant legs were so long the extra fabric pooled around her feet. Laurent could only assume they were Merrick's old nightclothes.

"Good morning," Laurent greeted her, "I was just about to give up looking for any type of coffee—seems there's none in the house."

"Good morning," Lenna gave the fae a sleepy smile before looking down at her clothes and cringing. Laurent watched her face redden, a creeping blush that started around her throat and worked its way across her plump cheeks in a delightfully charming way that had his smile growing. Merrick stomped into the kitchen with a grumble, heading straight to the cabinet closest to the sink. His face cracked into a wide smirk as he beheld Lenna's outfit.

"I'm glad someone's getting use out of those clothes. My mother always found fae hand me downs but never had the time to adjust them for, you know, wings." He winked at Lenna, stretching his arms above his head. "Probably why I sleep naked now." Lenna blushed wildly at that, averting her eyes from the gargoyle.

"Thank the gods you didn't sleep in the nude last night," Laurent replied, his tone clipped, "I would've had a much harder time keeping watch."

Merrick threw his head back and roared with laughter. His morning hair was tousled, sticking straight out in the places closest to his horns. "Laurent is notorious for having an affinity for gargoyle males *and* any female he comes across."

Lenna looked dumbstruck, but Laurent merely rolled his eyes. "The horns get me every time," he deadpanned, turning to the gargoyle. "Merrick, there's no coffee in this house."

"There's a coffee shop two rows down. I'll go over there before I get Lenna some essentials." Merrick had come to the same conclusion on the coffee. The lack of it.

Lenna arched a brow. "I'm assuming I'm staying here?"

Merrick grunted in acknowledgement, "You assume correctly. It's too dangerous to parade you around town. If anyone finds out who you really are, Lenna, it would cause a lot of unwanted attention. Laurent and I can only fight so many. Gods help us if word gets to Queen Adara and she waylays us because she doesn't like our plan. Or Esmeray shows up to kill you and take another Oracle out of play. I'll go, grab you some clothes, and be back before you know it."

Lenna muttered her understanding, though she did not seem too pleased with the conclusion.

"When are we going to the Obsidian Palace for the Prism?" With deft fingers, she began undoing the leather band that was struggling to contain her curls.

Merrick looked sideways at Laurent, rubbing his golden ring gently. Laurent felt his own ring heat slightly—the sign Merrick was going to mind speak with him to avoid Lenna overhearing.

"Should we let her rest one more day and leave tomorrow? One day for us to get her situated and packed? I don't think we'll come back to Spinella for a while once we depart."

Laurent rubbed his neck. *"I don't see the harm in one more day—it will give me time to build a portal powerful enough to take us directly to the entrance of the Obsidian Palace. If we left today, the furthest I could take us is still roughly a two day walk. By tomorrow afternoon, I will have it done."*

"You need to sleep anyway. Get some rest and I'll get us packed."

"I'll be fine, I just need some coffee."

"No. I'm serious. I need you to get some sleep—you stayed up all night. I don't want to waltz into the Obsidian Palace without you at full strength."

Laurent *was* exhausted. Purple bags rimmed his eyes, and his chest was heavy with the lack of deep rest. He had been pushing his magic past its normal, familiar, threshold for days, and the effects were running him ragged.

Holding open the portal for Merrick and Lenna, and then staying up watching for any potential trouble last night depleted his energy. The adrenaline was constant lately, but he knew his mind needed to rest for a few hours. The urge to do something, anything, to stay busy, hounded his heels. But Merrick was right. He needed to replenish his body and magic, owing it to his commander to be at his best physically and magically before venturing off into danger.

"Okay." Merrick clapped his hands together once, after Laurent dipped his head in a nod of forlorn agreement. "We will leave tomorrow afternoon and Laurent will start working on the portal," the gargoyle glared pointedly at the fae, "*after* he gets some rest. I will go get the supplies we need for the trip."

Lenna narrowed her eyes. The Oracle obviously figured out some silent conversation went on between them. They couldn't lose her allegiance now, not when the only thing going for them was that Lenna agreed to help clear Keerian's name. Getting in front of the potential trouble, Laurent extended a hand to Lenna. "See this ring?" Lenna peered at it with a healthy dose of apprehension. "It gives us the ability to speak directly into each other's minds."

"Woah." She gently grasped Laurent's hand, inspecting the plain, slim gold band on the fae's pointer finger. "So that's why you guys both get that weirdly vacant look sometimes. What do you talk about?"

Laurent shrugged. "Well, we were just talking about how I need to rest before working on the portal."

The Oracle made a small noise of surprise at the fae's admittance, and Laurent had no choice but to concede as she fussed at him once finding out he was tired. Lenna even demanded he sleep in the bed she slept in last night, as it was the only one in the house. She wouldn't take "*no*" for an answer, and Laurent found himself smiling slightly as she fretted over him, setting a glass of cold water on the small bedside table and fluffing the lumpy pillows.

After Lenna changed back into the clothes she wore yesterday, and Merrick departed the little home, Laurent yielded to the Oracle's pleading. Lenna stayed in the living room, leafing through a small collection of books Merrick pointed out before he departed. For the first time in a year, stretched out on the narrow bed, Laurent allowed himself to sleep soundly.

CHAPTER FIFTEEN
LAURENT

THE PORTAL WAS ALMOST finished. Laurent swayed slightly, steadying himself on instinct alone. Beads of sweat rolled down his face, silver rivulets from his forehead to his throat. The few hours of sleep had helped replenish some of his magic, but the strain of creating a portal still weighed down his muscles, pulled at his breath. Night had fallen over Spinella, but the tiny living room was bathed with light. Merrick had scrounged up some half-melted candles from the kitchen cabinets, and the glowing tendrils of the portal near the burning fireplace had been growing, bigger and brighter, over the course of the afternoon as Laurent fed the portal bits of his magic.

He did feel better after resting, more energized than he'd been in weeks. Of course, building and holding portals open for Merrick all over the Slate Kingdom had put a toll on him, but Laurent could feel the power under his skin building to a new threshold. Every portal he made pushed his magic to a new limit, tested him and grew with him. As a warrior, he was used to getting short sleeps and had long since trained his power to adjust.

Lenna was still curled up on the couch, skimming through a new book, a few other titles scattered at her feet, conquered. The titles ranged from children's stories of heroes and magical journeys to *Advanced Anatomy of Gargoyle Wings*—a book healers studied as they learned to navigate the intricacies of muscle and bone contained in the complex wing structures.

Her brow knotted as she sipped from a cracked pink and white mug Merrick filled with peppermint tea, the wares from shopping in town scattered around the room.

"Tell me again, Merrick, what the shopkeep said." Laurent struggled to keep the wheeze from his voice, not wanting Merrick to see how winded he was from filling the portal.

Merrick's face was set in a grim line. "Esmeray was spotted outside of Florra two nights ago. Queen Adara's warriors tried to capture her, and Esmeray killed them all. Every last one. Queen Adara is enraged, she's setting curfews for the towns in the Obsidian Kingdom to protect the citizens against Esmeray's wrath."

Lenna worriedly looked from gargoyle to fae. Laurent rubbed his face with his hands. "The city of Florra is not far from the Obsidian Palace. Esmeray could easily wane that distance and head us off."

"It's a risk we need to calculate," Merrick admitted carefully, glancing at the thrumming portal.

It was Lenna who spoke up, softly, as if she didn't want to interrupt. "Can Princess Esmeray tell if we are in the Obsidian Palace?"

Merrick shook his head. "Esmeray doesn't have any sort of tracking magic from what we know. If we can get in, get the Prism, and get out, we can hopefully avoid piquing her interest."

Laurent knew their chances of obtaining the Prism easily were slim, but to clear Keerian's name, if they could confirm Esmeray killed her parents and acted alone, Queen Adara would grant them protection...right? The Regent, Lord Magnamus, was loyal to Queen Adara. Would Lord Magnamus help them if they begged for sanctuary against Esmeray?

They fell into an uneasy silence—broken only by the quiet *scheck* of a dagger Merrick sharpened against a piece of whetstone. The hulking gargoyle glanced over to Laurent's portal every so often, as if he could gauge how far they'd travel just by peering through the swirling smoke.

"It should be ready by mid morning if I calculated correctly," Laurent murmured to them both. He closed his eyes, giving another morsel of magic over to the milky depths. The portal glowed in response. Laurent felt the magic being tugged out of him, and a few breaths later, replenishing through his bones, warming his soul.

Lenna clapped her hands together, briskly hopping off the couch. "I'll finish packing then." Abandoning her book, she started rifling through the shopping bags. Pulling out a new black pack, she filled it with the other items Merrick purchased.

Before Merrick left the house earlier, Lenna insisted she would figure out how to pay him back, but both Laurent and Merrick shushed her, agreeing that her helping them clear Keerian's name was payment enough.

Merrick finished with the dagger he had gotten wickedly sharp, tapping the blade against one of his horns before sliding it into the leather sheath at his waist.

The gargoyle's packing had only taken a few moments, as Merrick never truly unpacked after arriving yesterday. Laurent was packed as well, the deep brown leather bag sitting neatly next to Merrick's tan, worn, canvas one.

"We need to get you a new bag." Laurent sent down the ring.

Merrick, feeling the warmth on his finger, touched his back. *"Nah, it's fine—it still holds everything I need."*

"You got that pack second hand from the barrack's market twenty years ago."

"What can I say? I buy good quality shit." Merrick rolled his eyes, scratching his beard as he nodded admirably to his pack by the door.

Laurent chuckled, turning from the portal to the window, gazing out to the cobblestone streets that held the night's bustle. Across the row, a fae female with beautiful tawny skin and flowing skirts of deep red watered pots full of plants outside her front door.

Her magic poured from her hands, watering each stalk of multicolored flowers gently. She flicked her wrist, and the stream ebbed before she moved to the next pot filled with bright orange peonies, conjuring water to trickle from her fingers to the blooms, smiling serenely the entire time.

Another lifetime, Laurent thought to himself, he would have gone over to her, complimented her hard work, inhaled the sweet smells of flora. And fae. Maybe asked her to grab a drink with him down the street. Behind him, Merrick started loudly counting off on the packs and supplies they gathered, accentuating the counts with a deep burp every few seconds, causing Laurent to sigh audibly.

Just a little longer, and the portal would transport them to the entrance of the Obsidian Palace, where they'd request a meeting with the Regent, and Lenna would reveal herself as the new Oracle to secure the Prism.

Where they would stay was still up in the air, but with both Merrick's and Laurent's past training in the Obsidian Palace, he hoped Lord Magnamus would allow their stay as guests of the Queen Absolute. Without actually *having* the Queen Absolute's expressed approval, of course.

Lost in thought, Laurent felt the portal tug at him again, and he fed it another morsel of magic. The power in the room turned into a thrum, mirroring his heartbeat. Just a few more hours. Then, they could begin clearing Keerian's name to Queen Adara, and petition for Esmeray to be locked up instead of killed for her numerous crimes.

"I think we are all packed." Merrick surveyed the bags, patting his waist and the weapons attached. Laurent turned from watching the beautiful stranger to check their belongings.

A loud *boom* shook the house.

Laurent whirled back to the window, seeing the fae female's face whip up from her flowers and look down the street. She gasped, and in a flash of blue light, waned away.

Laurent had his short sword out in the span between seconds, bright sparks of blue and white flames flickering down the length. Behind him, he heard Merrick also draw, palming the newly sharpened dagger, and crouching into a defensive stance in front of Lenna. The Oracle whimpered and shrunk behind the grey wings Merrick flared out.

"Stay behind Merrick," Laurent hissed to Lenna. She visibly began trembling. Laurent slowly slid towards the window and peered out the side of the curtain. "*Fuck*," he cursed under his breath as the chaos unfolding in the narrow street came into view.

Outside, screams of fear began, the beings on the street flying, waning, and running away. The cacophony of wings and running footsteps faded a beat later–and an unnerving silence filled the air.

"What's going on?" Merrick hadn't moved from his defensive position in front of Lenna. He was perfectly still, living stone made flesh.

"Go through the portal. Now," Laurent breathed. His green eyes flashed with power, and the portal pulsed harder. He poured every remaining ounce of his magic at it, getting them as much distance as possible from the dark silhouette of the winged figure now standing alone in the middle of the cobblestone street, mere feet from their front door.

Chapter Sixteen
Lenna

Lenna felt fear—true undulating fear—as Laurent's magic filled the portal, the whine of power making her ears pop with the renewed rush of pressure.

She was tucked behind Merrick's outstretched wings, struggling to see what was happening outside the window. She knew without a shadow of a doubt that this had something to do with her. The thought terrified her, and Lenna's body reacted accordingly, her shaking increasing, her palms slick with sweat.

"Esmeray found us," Laurent rasped, slowly backing away from the window. Lenna's heart slammed into her throat. Her trembling was getting worse by the second. With a sweep of Laurent's hand, the candles and fireplace extinguished.

The only light in the house emitted from the portal behind her, illuminating the outlines of the fae and gargoyle standing between her and the killer of her predecessor.

With Laurent out of the way of the window, Lenna was able to catch a quick glimpse of the figure now pacing slowly outside the doorway. Black wings, black curled horns. Her breath caught. The fear of what Esmeray would do to her if she made it past Merrick and Laurent made Lenna's stomach roil.

"Oh, come on, Laurent. Wards...*really*?" The strangely familiar female voice purred. Laurent reported quietly that Esmeray was stopped at the threshold of wards, testing for weak spots. Merrick shifted his weight, keeping Lenna behind him. "You really think *these* are going to keep *me* out?"

Lenna shot a panicked glance at Merrick and Laurent. They were both touching their rings in a silent conversation that Lenna wished she was privy to.

Would they give her up in exchange for their own freedom?

Without a word, Laurent backed towards Merrick and Lenna, snagging their three packs as he went—never taking his eyes off the door.

Crack.

Wide eyed, Lenna startled and winced.

"Esmeray broke through the first ward," Merrick mumbled as he tucked his wings in, blindly reaching his tattooed arm out to Lenna.

"Lenna." Laurent turned to face her, his features cold, his eyes dull. "Take Merrick's hand."

Lenna reached forward shakily, gripping onto the gargoyle. Merrick's fingers laced through her own, squeezing tightly. Laurent gave Lenna a reassuring nod. Lenna took a deep breath, and before she had a chance to exhale, Merrick twisted around her body, his wings curling her into his chest, and launched them through the portal, Laurent a split second behind.

The last thing Lenna heard was Esmeray's shriek of frustration before the portal enveloped them in a flash of bright light, leaving the murderous Queen of Nothing and Spinella far behind.

CHAPTER SEVENTEEN
MERRICK

MERRICK ROLLED OUT OF the portal, meeting the hard stone beneath him with a grunt. Lenna let out a squeak as they crash landed, still nestled safely in his arms. His wings took the brunt of the force, protecting the Oracle from harm.

He gingerly unwrapped her from his wings, tentatively stretching them out to feel for sore spots. The jarring landing had knocked them against the rocky ground, but a quick assessment assured him no injuries would impact flight. Merrick slowly stood to face the silvery glow of the portal.

Lenna stayed curled up on the stony ground for a moment before letting out a curse and scrambling to her hands and knees, hefting herself up straight and dusting off her black pants with trembling hands.

Merrick didn't realize he'd been holding his breath until Laurent hurled through the portal a beat later, gracefully landing on his feet. He threw their packs on the ground before slashing his hands across the portal, cutting its power, and sealing them off from Spinella.

From Esmeray's rage.

The portal dimmed and disappeared, the smoke listlessly billowing away–taking with it their only source of light. Darkness clung to the three of them, scrambling Merrick's senses.

"How the fuck did she find us?" Merrick snarled, squinting his eyes against the night, grabbing his pack and Lenna's.

Laurent let out a low growl, staring at the spot the portal had been moments before. "Esmeray cannot track magic. She may have been tipped off by someone who saw you. Maybe a fae spy that can sense the Oracle's magical abilities? Or Esmeray isn't as alone as we originally assumed and has another being at her disposal that can track magic. If she has spies of her own, there's no telling what she does and does not already know."

Merrick felt his temper rise. All that work finding and preparing Lenna for this task, building those damn wards, and they'd been caught off guard within two days of bringing Lenna to Spinella. "She cracked that last ward *as we went through the portal*. Like it was *easy*."

Laurent's voice was icy compared to the heat and venom in Merrick's. "We knew they wouldn't hold forever. They gave us enough time to get here." He picked up his own pack before sheathing the short sword still in his hand. "I got us as close as possible–look."

Merrick whirled around. Darkness. The looming silence pressed in, causing a ringing to begin in Merrick's ears. "I can't see shit, Laurent."

Laurent clicked his tongue in response. "Well, I can, and we're a few miles deep in the canyon. I can see the tips of the Obsidian Palace. The portal got us all the way to the last stretch of Pyritee Pass."

Merrick bit out a string of curses. Fucking fae with their stupid enhanced eyesight. Gods below, he was in a bad mood. They weren't even lucky enough to have starlight on their side. He hated how vulnerable it made him feel not being able to see two feet in front of him.

"How long until we make it to the Palace?" Lenna asked from Merrick's right.

"Half a day–tops." Laurent opened his hand and held it at chest level. A small flame flickered to life in his palm, giving them enough light to make out each other's faces. "But I think we should wait for the sun to rise before making the journey. That way, Merrick can fly ahead and keep watch for any threats."

Merrick thought that was a shit idea before realizing why Laurent suggested they rest. Laurent had thrown a huge amount of his magic at the portal those last few minutes as Esmeray was cracking the wards to get them even this far, and his friend needed a bit of time to recharge.

"Can you see any place around here that has cover?" Merrick asked the fae.

"Yes, a couple hundred yards away, there is an overhang we can stay under." Laurent motioned in the direction, before taking a few steps. Merrick watched the flame sputter–but hold–as Laurent led the way.

It had been decades since Merrick last walked Pyritee Pass, the canyon threading through the mountains surrounding the Obsidian Palace. He usually flew in over it, or if he was with a fighting unit, rode in on horseback.

With barely enough light to see anything, save for Laurent's silhouette in front of him, Merrick steadied his breathing and slowly picked his way through the rocky path. The flat stones underneath his feet shifted haphazardly with each tentative step. Paranoia crept in, and Merrick kept a steady hand on his dagger, trying to breathe through the fear squeezing his lungs, vise-gripping his chest.

Merrick kept one eye on Lenna, who had ditched the hard-to-see-in-the-dark head scarf, her fluffy red curls reflecting the flame in Laurent's palm. At least now Merrick could make out a few feet in each direction, even though his eyes strained against the crushing blackness outside of the firelight.

Not that there was anything to see except walls of black stone that came into view every so often as the light hit it just right, and flat black rocks beneath their feet.

They walked in silence, until Merrick could make out the overhang Laurent had spied. Underneath, a small alcove was carved into the canyon wall, no larger than the kitchen they'd abandoned back in Spinella.

Laurent reached the covered cave first, releasing the small flame from his palm. It settled onto the ground, casting a ball of light off glittering stone walls.

Merrick ushered Lenna in before following. He dropped his and Lenna's packs to the floor and gestured to Laurent to do the same.

"I'll keep watch," Merrick grunted, nodding to Laurent and Lenna, the latter staring into the fire, twisting her pale hands. He knew that the visit from Esmeray had shaken her, but he hoped her resolve held firm to still help them.

"Get some rest." Merrick said through his ring. *"We need you at full power tomorrow."*

"I'm not going to argue that." Laurent sounded exhausted through their shared mind speak.

Merrick straightened, rolling his shoulders back. It was going to be a long night, but he owed it to Laurent to stay awake and keep an eye out for any sign of danger. He looked out into the darkness beyond and couldn't make out a damned thing.

Chapter Eighteen

Lenna

As the first signs of morning light shone down into the Pyritee Pass, Lenna breathed a small sigh of relief. During the night, she had a hard time distinguishing the black behind her eyelids from the surroundings in their alcove. Three walls of ebony stone cut off her view of the starless night sky, confuddling her own perception of depth and distance. Even widening her eyes, straining to make out a shape was pointless. The adrenaline in her veins had left her shaky and overstimulated, and when goosebumps had risen on her flesh, she felt a rolling nausea that seemed determined to get her to lose the meager contents in her stomach.

Lenna opted to curl up against the cool back wall and pray to whatever god happened to be listening for safety. She wondered if being the Oracle held any sway with the gods above, or if her prayers were merely added to the unending list of requests the gods received. It didn't help that as soon as Laurent closed his eyes, the flame that steadily grew weaker in the middle of their makeshift camp winked out.

Lenna spent the next few hours using her cloak as a pillow, laying on her back, her gaze unseeing. The pitch-black kept befuddling her senses every time she tried closing her eyes. With the hard ground below her, sleep came fitfully at best. Lenna's ears had strained to pick up any sounds, but only heard a few quiet curses following the *tink* of a loose stone shifting against another, confirming to Lenna that Merrick was also unable to see well, and was *also* tripping over the rocks littering the ground as he kept watch.

The events from Spinella weighed on her. She couldn't get the sound of Esmeray's shrill scream of rage out of her mind. Lenna kept replaying the nightmare of the old man–who she now assumed had been the previous Oracle–again and again.

How had Esmeray captured him?

How could she avoid the same fate?

Why was Esmeray hunting her?

The silent night pressing in around her provided no answers.

Apprehension plagued her thoughts. Thoughts that drifted towards Doortan. Lenna had felt so alone, unnecessary, nothing more than a servant disguised as a wife. She wondered if Leon notified the city guards of her disappearance.

She doubted it.

Gritting her teeth, Lenna warred with the emotions inside her. Their marriage had started out loving, but that love had been used up quickly, diminishing to nothing within a year. Lenna was still lost, though new fears slithered against her mind now. The idea of having a mate somewhere in this big new world was steadying, and she clung to that slim hope that there was a being out there who was designed to love her the way she needed to be loved.

The path forward was fraught with peril. But it was a path, and she *was* needed and acknowledged here, even confided in. Merrick and Laurent were kind and caring, and she held onto that feeling tightly, too.

When morning began slipping through the opening of the alcove, Lenna got to her feet, her back muscles tight after laying on the hard ground. She groaned as she stretched her arms over her head. Her hips hurt, her back hurt. She hurt all over. Lenna squeezed the muscles at the nape of her neck, trying to get the blood flowing.

Merrick appeared in front of her, flashing a tight grin, "I do apologize for the lack of luxury you've experienced since you arrived in Irridessen, M'lady."

Giving up on getting any relief to her sore muscles, Lenna worked on her hair, tying it out of her face with the grey scarf she used as a miniature blanket last night. She shot Merrick a bemused smile. "It's still more interesting here than Doortan. Even though my company keeps putting me in precarious situations."

Laurent appeared at her side, making her jump. He was so quiet she never heard him coming. *It must be a fae thing,* she thought to herself. Stealth. "Let's get moving." Was his only response before picking up his pack and sword.

Lenna glanced from gargoyle to fae. "Did you both start the new day on the wrong side of the rocks?" Their weird mood made her skin crawl and her nerves jumpy, but she kept her tone nonchalant.

"It's...weird. Being here," Merrick admitted. His wings rubbed against each other, as if it comforted him. "A lifetime ago we rode and flew through this Pass while we trained. Now, it doesn't feel familiar."

Lenna empathised, knowing the feeling he experienced. How her own home had become a stranger to her over the years. She wondered if she would ever see Doortan again—wondered if she would ever *want* to leave and go back to the Slate Kingdom. Even with the events of the night before, she couldn't see herself going back. *Was this land her home now?* She couldn't give herself an honest answer.

So many questions, but no answers looming around the corner. It was unsettling after a lifetime of knowing what was coming, everything cut and dried. Be a subservient wife, stay out of Leon's way when he was drunk, keep the house and servants running smoothly.

She was completely out of her element now.

Lenna took a deep breath, determined to see where this journey took her. Maybe once they cleared Keerian's name and Esmeray was locked up—maybe she would find a small town in Irridessen to call home or go back to Spinella. She wondered if Laurent or Merrick would come visit her, or even think about her again after she helped them. They very well could equate her with this terrible time in their life and want nothing to do with her after.

Lenna, Merrick, and Laurent made their way back to the openness of the canyon, and her jaw dropped. What she was unable to see last night was now bathed in morning light.

Surrounding her on both sides were towering walls of black stones, veins of silver glittering across their facets as the sun shone down. The Pyritee Pass was at least fifty feet high, wide enough for at least ten horses to stand side by side comfortably. It all felt very ancient. Lenna herself felt very small.

The canyon stretched in front of her, but the mountains that rose high above them were visible.

"The Obsidian Palace is located...there...on that mountain right ahead of us." Laurent pointed out to her. Lenna squinted, barely making out the black turrets built into the side of the mountain piercing the drifting clouds above.

Merrick wordlessly handed his pack to Laurent, before unfurling his wings and shooting into the blue sky. Lenna watched him fly ahead until he was no more than a speck between fluffy white clouds. Laurent followed her gaze, his face grim. "It's difficult for him to be back here. His father took him to the Obsidian Palace to learn how to be a warrior when he was eighteen. It was not the life Merrick would've chosen for himself."

In the sun, it was much easier to see the winding path ahead, and Lenna began slowly picking her way through the canyon. "Did he not have a good relationship with his father?"

Laurent shook his head, the silver studs in his pointed ears glimmering. "Merrick was raised by his mother in Spinella, hidden from his father once she became pregnant. But his father found out about him when Merrick turned eighteen, and took him from Spinella to train. He told Merrick's mother that no son of his would grow up to be weak."

"He sounds like a total dick," Lenna muttered.

"Oh, he was," Laurent huffed a dry laugh. "He was one of the commanders for the Queen's Guard in the Obsidian Palace. He didn't go easy on Merrick, as if it was Merrick's fault he was even born."

"Poor Merrick," Lenna breathed, more to herself than to Laurent. She was quiet for a moment before cocking her head to the fae beside her, "Does he ever see his mother?"

Laurent stopped walking and abruptly turned towards Lenna. "Merrick's mother was killed a few months after Merrick was taken by his father. If I were you, I wouldn't bring it up to him. There's still a lot of pain there."

Lenna looked down at her feet, and then back to the fae. "I understand," she said softly. Her heart hurt for the fierce and protective gargoyle that had been her companion for the last few days. "What about you? Did you train here?"

Laurent seemed appreciative of the conversation shift. "I did—for a short time. Once the commanders found out about my...usefulness...they moved me from here to complete my training at the Opal Palace."

"Your magic." Lenna nodded in agreement. She had seen small glimpses of his power over the last couple days and could confirm he had some sort of control over fire as well as the whole portal making thing.

"Yes." Laurent surveyed the path ahead, his dark skin beading sweat under the sun. Lenna thought he was one of the most handsome males she'd ever seen. "My individual skill set pushed me from training as a grunt to becoming part of the King's private circle of elite warriors. I met Keerian and Merrick in the Obsidian Palace–but did not see them again until they both finished their training and qualified to become part of the King's Guard as well."

Lenna mulled over the conversation as they picked their way through another hundred yards of rocks. Laurent kept circumventing any explanation of what exactly his magic could do. Lenna didn't know if he was just being humble, or because he didn't want to divulge the amount of power he so obviously held.

Chapter Nineteen
Lenna

The hours passed slowly as Lenna cut her eyes anxiously to the clouds for what felt like the hundreth time. Though the only creatures she saw were carrion birds and hawks, every time a flutter of wings caught her gaze or a crow called out with a screech, she got panicked and jumpy all over again.

The rocky terrain of the Pyritee Pass proved laborious for Lenna, making it hard to focus on anything else outside of tentatively putting one foot in front of the other. Her legs were significantly shorter than Laurent's, though he slowed his stride to keep pace with her own. Her body was too soft and the small amount of muscle mass she had did little. The leg and core muscles she hadn't used in years roared in protest as she hiked on. Heat sizzled against the rocks, throwing mirages of shimmering waves against the ground that disappeared as she neared. Lenna's pale skin was no match for the harsh sun's rays bouncing off the shiny black stone walls. She felt the burn through her clothing and prayed her skin wouldn't blister.

Laurent had no difficulty with the walk, even though he, too, poured sweat. Lenna felt the dripping perspiration coat her, rubbing her thighs raw as the slick skin chafed against the coarse material of her pants. She ripped off her head scarf as the sun reached its apex, opting instead to wrap her red curls in a tight bun on the top of her head. Laurent had not removed his flowing robe, even with the fabric growing damp and cumbersome.

The curve of the path provided a closer glimpse of the mountain range ahead, the peaks white-tipped with snow. Laurent told her once they rounded the bend she'd get her first full look at the Obsidian Palace.

He wasn't kidding. The last curve of Pyritee Pass brought the Palace into view for her human eyes. Ahead, the canyon opened to reveal the rest of the mountain range. Built into the front face of the tallest mountain, the Obsidian Palace loomed, seemingly growing out of the mountain itself.

Spiraling black towers touched the clouds, piercing and ripping them apart with quiet violence as they blew gently through the sky. Lenna tried counting the number of turrets, but lost count after she hit twenty. The overall design was haunting and spindly, as if the architects tore the mountain apart to reveal the skeleton beneath.

Below the dark towers, stark against the contrast of the snow above, levels of the Palace shone with an eerie gleam. The Palace secreted ancientness and didn't project a welcoming aura to those that ventured towards it. It was *huge*, Lenna thought to herself–completely blown away from the sheer size of the Obsidian Palace. As they got closer, she could make out the path towards the front gates. Twisting iron was built into a stone border, rising into arches tipped with sharp, talon like, spikes. Another notice for those who came forth to really make sure they knew what they were getting themselves into.

There were two long bridges leading to the front of the Palace gates, one right in front of them, one jutting off to the east, disappearing between two smaller mountains. Both bridges were mixtures of iron and stone, and the one they aimed for was as wide as the canyon they were so close to putting behind them. The peaks of iron on each side of the bridge rose and fell in waves, each apex tipped with the same dangerous looking spikes.

As Lenna and Laurent picked their way through the last quarter mile, the walls of the canyon sloped down before plateauing to the beginning of the bridge. Lenna looked behind her at Pyritee Pass and thought about their walk. The questions she hoped she'd find answers to were still completely out of reach. She knew one thing though, for certain. She never wanted to walk through the Pyritee Pass again.

Laurent stopped before the first steps of the bridge, holding up a finger to Lenna and fiddling with his mind speak ring before breaking the quiet. "Merrick requested a meeting with the Regent, Lord Magnamus, who refused to see us until this evening. But, if it's any consolation, the Regent allowed us to stay here for the night which gives us time to clean up." Laurent's nose crinkled a bit. She blushed.

Yeah, Lenna could smell herself. The sweat hadn't dried, and dark stains of perspiration coated the cotton shirt she had on.

"That will be a welcome relief." She smiled encouragingly to the fae who looked extremely uncomfortable in his slick-with-sweat robes. "I know I stink."

That coaxed a soft chuckle from Laurent, his green eyes looking down on her with care. "Just so you know, we will be with you every step of the way tonight. You won't have to worry. Remember, the Regent is loyal to Queen Adara."

Lenna's tight shoulders relaxed a fraction. It was a relief to hear. The uncertainty of the night swirled over her–but knowing these two males, who already protected her once, stood by her side did calm her.

Laurent touched the ring on his finger. "Merrick is on his way to us. He'll escort us to the Palace to get ready for tonight."

Within moments, a winged figure appeared from the top towers, making a beeline towards the bridge. Lenna and Laurent tracked the movement through the sky, until the gargoyle landed in front of them.

Merrick had already washed up and changed. His shaggy brown hair was tied back into two tight braids that met at the nape of his neck and merged into one braid down to his shoulders. His horns looked polished, gleaming brilliantly in the sun.

His casual clothes from the last two days were gone, replaced with a loose, black, long-sleeved shirt, and black pants—a much nicer quality than the ones he had worn that morning. His now familiar weapons belt also looked oiled and shiny. His long sword with the blue gem pommel was strapped to his back between his wings with a leather harness that crossed over his shoulders, holding it in place.

To Lenna, Merrick looked deadly. Epitomizing the image of a warrior primed and in his element. Standing before them both, he flashed his bright white teeth—and immediately began rolling the sleeves of his shirt up to his elbows. "Like the new digs?" Merrick asked cheerfully, finishing one sleeve and moving to the other, the black bands of his tattoos now visible.

Lenna raised her eyebrows at him. "You clean up well, Merrick. Were you getting pampered up there in your bird's nest while we trudged through this damn canyon all day?"

Laurent grinned as Merrick bristled. "Trust me, it was a lot less pampering and a lot more begging for an audience. After the first meeting I had with Lord Magnamus, he outright declined to host us." Merrick rolled his eyes. "I had to resort to court charm—hence the handsomeness before you." He bowed, a smug smirk on his face.

Next to Lenna, Laurent growled low and deep, as if this sort of thing happened before—with varying results. "Define '*court charm*' Merrick."

Merrick waved off his friend. "Well, the Regent said without Queen Adara's expressed permission, the Oracle wasn't welcome in the Obsidian Palace. So, I went to every servant, royal, and court guest I could find and started a bit of gossip that I heard the new Oracle was activated *and* she was coming here to claim her birthright of the Prism. Needless to say, the entire court is in a tizzy–they haven't had any action in a while. They're all scrambling to dress their finest and pay respect to Lenna. Oh, I *also* may have lied and said you could read their futures for them." A wicked gleam flashed in Merrick's eyes. "Once word got back to Lord Magnamus that his entire court was assembling to the throne room tonight to meet you, he made it sound like it was *his* idea to host you. I didn't correct him."

"Well, you have been busy," Laurent gritted out, loosening a harsh breath. He gestured towards the bridge, wiping a trickle of perspiration from his face with his other hand. "Let's not disappoint."

Lenna sidled between the gargoyle and the fae as the three took the first steps onto the bridge leading them to the Obsidian Palace and the Prism of the Oracle.

Chapter Twenty

Lenna

It was a whirlwind of motion once they stepped into the Obsidian Palace's massive entryway. Lenna didn't know where to look first.

Rough cut stone walls were lined with golden torches designed to resemble skeletal hands. Their flames lit an uncanny amount of space, throwing strange shadows against the interior of the Palace carved from the mountain. Even the air felt charged with magic and power, as if it emitted from deep within the rocks itself. Lenna craned her neck up to the cavernous ceiling high above, where sharp cliffs jutted out at all angles, connected by narrow, golden bridges.

Gargoyles, disregarding the crossings all together, flew through the open air, and more than one dove closer to glimpse her and the company she kept. There were a few fae standing along those bridges, and she knew they could see her–probably hear her–even from that distance.

"This meeting may not be as smooth as we hoped," Merrick admitted quietly, "Lord Magnamus can be unpredictable. Keep your head on a swivel and don't let your guard down." Lenna knew that last part was meant for her to follow. "Don't mention Esmeray to Lord Magnamus either. If he knows she's stalking us, he may rescind his offer to allow us to stay here." Lenna chewed her lip as a side door into another dark corridor opened with a flourish.

Three servants appeared, dressed in dark blue tunics with flowy matching pants that cuffed at their ankles. In sync, the servants bowed, ushering each of them to a separate room down the same hall. Lenna had only a single moment to shoot a panicked glance back at her companions before she was escorted into a large bathing room by a female gargoyle as short as herself. The gargoyle pointed to an array of soaps and lotions, directing Lenna to wash up quickly and meet back in the adjoining bedroom to dress.

The bathing room walls were similar to the entryway, though the ceiling tapered only about fifteen feet up. A large tub that seemed more like a jagged pond took up the entire middle of the room. Lenna gingerly stepped down the first of three stone steps into the water. The tub was carved out of a lighter grey stone, as if it had been moved into the room instead of carved from it. More of the skeletal hands held torches in here, and Lenna marveled at the small magical flames that threw the entire room in light.

She stripped her dirty clothing off, and they vanished with a soft *poof* the second they hit the floor.

Gaping at the spot the clothes disappeared from, and acutely aware she was naked and alone in this strange, magical place, Lenna subconsciously covered herself.

Magic had taken her clothes.

That thought seemed so absurd to her that she snorted, shaking herself back to the task at hand. Edging closer to the lip of the tub, she took a deep breath and stepped into the waiting bath.

The water was much warmer than she anticipated, and she let out a tight breath as she focused her attention on scrubbing the dirt and crud off her body. Her pale skin held a brighter, pinkish hue from the formidable sun, and was covered with a fine layer of dust from the day's trek through the pass. Lenna winced as she felt the stringiness of her dry hair and dunked her head underwater to scrub at her scalp.

After she deemed herself clean, Lenna climbed gingerly out of the tub, careful not to scrape herself on any of the rock. Once both feet were firmly on the floor, a fluffy towel and robe appeared on the tub's rim. She snatched them before the magic could make anything else disappear, and dried herself off as she waddled into the adjoining room, her aching muscles humming.

The bedroom was decorated sparsely. Only two skeletal hands adorned the walls, the light a bit dimmer yet oddly cozy. A four-poster bed in the center of the room, expertly draped with rich maroon curtains, tugged alluringly at Lenna. She desperately wanted to crawl under the covers after spending a night sleeping on the ground. A dark red dress with golden embroidery lay upon the mattress, and Lenna took a tentative step closer, sliding her hand down the fabric in awe. It was thick, well made, and looked like it cost a small fortune. Lenna's hands trembled at the nasty thought that niggled through her brain.

What if it doesn't fit?

She knew it was a harsh thought the second it crossed her mind, but after years of having seamstresses fret over her measurements–wide through the bust, wide through the hips, slightly narrower at the waist–trepidation crept in whenever others picked out clothing for her.

She nervously slid the dress over her head and felt the fabric almost...come alive. It slithered down her body, contorting itself, sizing up and down, adjusting its own measurements until it perfectly fit her body–better than any seamstress could ever match. The creamy material caressed her skin, causing a whimper of shock to escape Lenna's hanging jaw.

Lenna realized her face showed more surprise than she anticipated as she walked over to the full-length mirror next to the bed and gaped at her reflection. Before, she'd hidden her plump curves and soft stomach under loose flowing smocks and dresses–per the request of Leon, and societal expectations throughout Doortan that focused on the importance of extreme modesty.

Modesty pleases the gods, her mother used to snap when Lenna tugged at the high necks, scratchy fabrics, and full skirts she wore before marriage. But those gods, who seemed so distant and cold in the Slate Kingdom, felt closer here, in Irridessen, where beings wore what they fancied, donning garments that didn't conceal or hide away their figures.

Now... *Now* she felt *beautiful* for the first time in decades. The red dress fit perfectly. Her breasts were still covered but a slight sight of cleavage rose above the vee neck of the gown. The fabric clung to her curves, through her waist, across her stomach and hips, before pooling at her feet. The golden threads glowed in the light of the torches in the room.

Flat golden slippers appeared next to her, and she slid them on with the same ease as the dress.

"You look lovely, Oracle." A soft voice with a rich accent spoke from the door of the bedroom. Lenna turned to see the same gargoyle female that had shown her to her room upon arrival. Lenna had been too enchanted with the Palace that she barely registered the being when they first arrived. The female's horns were a lighter grey than Merrick's and curved ever so gently from her head forward. They were only a few inches long with a smooth, pearlescent sheen. Her wings matched the horns, also smaller than Merrick's and more feminine. The talons at the tips less sharp and deadly, more rounded. Her short black hair waved down to her throat, her skin a deep bronze hue. But it was her eyes that caught Lenna's attention most of all–they were ruby red.

The gargoyle bowed. "My name is Ballah, and I will be escorting you to the throne room to meet the Regent."

"Thank you, Ballah." Lenna liked her already. She possessed an air of order and kindness that instantly put Lenna at ease.

Ballah inclined her head and gestured to the open door. "Captain Merrick and Spy Master Laurent are ready and waiting for you. They'll meet us before we enter the throne room."

The titles surprised Lenna since Merrick and Laurent were stripped of their positions by Queen Adara. Thoughts churning, she opened her mouth to ask Ballah, but the gargoyle turned on her heels, wings slightly flaring out, and led Lenna out of the room. Lenna hurried behind, holding the skirt of her dress to keep up with the clipped pace Ballah set.

Merrick and Laurent were waiting at the end of the corridor, resplendent in their individual outfits. Laurent stood tall and immaculate in a new satin robe, the same red as Lenna's dress, with golden stars embroidered along the wide sleeves and down the length that stopped at his knees. Black pants and boots finished off his outfit. He inclined his head in greeting and gave Lenna a tight-lipped smile as she appeared. "You look lovely, Lenna," he murmured. Laurent seemed much more at ease here than he'd been in Spinella.

"I *also* think this dress suits you much better than what you were wearing when I found you," Merrick chimed in, shooting Laurent a scathing look that made the fae chuckle. Merrick had changed again and was now dressed in more formal attire from head to toe, in a shade of grey slightly darker than his wings. Twin serpents were carved into the leather vest on both sides of his torso, their intricate scales flowing from the nape of his neck, down to the knife belt at his waist. Various bronze buckles adorned the top, also intricately carved. He looked every inch the warrior Lenna had heard about.

Truly the Spy Master and the Captain. Poised and deadly.

Lenna gave both males a grin as they simultaneously offered her their arm. She stepped in the middle of the two and looked from gargoyle to fae. "Let's go get this Prism."

CHAPTER TWENTY-ONE
LENNA

THE THRONE ROOM WAS the most terrifyingly enchanting place Lenna had ever seen. As they took their first steps in, Lenna looked up. There were no jagged stones above them, only openness stretching a hundred feet into the air. Ballah bowed to Lenna, Merrick, and Laurent before briskly turning around and disappearing back the way they came.

"The throne room is set right in the heart of the mountain," Laurent said quietly as Lenna stared. "It took years for stone wielders to carve out this room alone."

Wonder painted Lenna's face. There were about twenty gargoyles and a smattering of fae gathered in the throne room, the compilation of the small court assembled here. All seemed to watch her every move, her every step, silent and waiting. At the end of the room, a large stone dais sat, and atop it, completely opposite of all the other décor in the room, sat a white throne. The throne seemed to be carved out of opal with the way it shimmered in the dim torch light–very out of place with the jagged black stone rows of seating that lay before it.

"Lord Magnamus destroyed the obsidian and bone throne when he took up the Regency. He saw it as a symbol of evil. Needless to say, he grew up in the Opal Palace and highly favored Adara as Queen." Merrick followed

Lenna's sightline, but he steered her to the right side of the throne room. Laurent, hands behind his back, strode forward. Lenna watched him, the way he moved effortlessly over the...floor?

Lenna's heart hit her throat as she looked down...and down. And down. The floor was no more than transparent glass, and below it was a deep, dark cavern that tunneled far into the mountain itself. Her feet started to sweat in the silk slippers she wore. Merrick placed his hand on the small of her back, the touch grounding. Reassuring. "The glass has never broken." The words were uttered under his breath so only she could hear. Lenna reminded herself that Merrick had wings. And that it would be in his best interest to catch her if she somehow fell through. She *was* the all-special Oracle after all...right?

"What is down there?" Lenna whispered, trying to avoid looking into the depths below. A wave of vertigo threatened, and she breathed through it, focusing on staring straight ahead, the off-kilter head rush thankfully passing as quickly as it came on.

"It tunnels down into the dungeons, treasure troves, and dragon dens. Only those who have permission from the ruler of the Obsidian Palace are granted entry." Merrick slid a glance at her and winced as Lenna's head whipped to his face, her eyes growing wide, her blood running cold.

"Dragons?" she hissed, the words ending in a squeak that caused a few fae near her to throw curious glances in her direction. "Dragons are *real?*"

Merrick grunted his confirmation, before clearing his throat. "Shit, yes. Sorry. We probably should've mentioned that."

Lenna stared incredulously at him, her stomach rolled, and she felt as if she might puke. Her head was heavy and light at the same time, her fingers cold and tingling. "And treasure troves. Treasure troves like where the Prism would be?" Dragons were real. The creatures of myth that supposedly burned down towns and wrecked ships lost at sea. The creatures that would scoop you from your yard if you talked back to your parents. Creatures that were *made-up* by tired parents to scare young children into behaving.

Scrunching his nose, Merrick seemed slightly abashed as Lenna continued to glare at him. The gargoyle shuffled his feet. "Most likely it is but–"

He was cut off as trumpets began playing, three short blasts with a longer fourth note quivering through the room. The trumpets sounded again, and as if it were an order, the assembled court filed into the black stone pews, all standing and facing the dais. Merrick ushered Lenna to the middle of the room, closest to the entrance they had come through. Lenna looked around for Laurent, finding him standing at the foot of the dais, facing the assembled court.

A bright white light flared, and Lord Magnamus, Regent of the Obsidian Kingdom, waned into the throne room and stood before his court. He was fully fae, Lenna realized, which would make him the brother of the late King Scottrell. He looked no older than Lenna, but she mused with his fae lifespan, he must be hundreds of years into his life. His face was clean shaven, showing high cheekbones and elegantly curved, full, lips. He sported an icy white pallor, as if his royal skin never stepped directly into the sun. The Regent's black hair was cut short to his head, and a thin crown of silver studded with blue gems adorned it.

"Be seated." His voice, one of utmost authority, boomed through the room. The court sat. Only Laurent, Merrick and Lenna still stood. Laurent turned to face the Regent and bowed deep.

"Your Royal Highness, Regent Magnamus," Laurent began, "may I present Lady Lenna, the Oracle of Terramere."

Lord Magnamus took his seat upon his throne and leaned back. Without a reply to Laurent, he grunted, beckoning once towards where Lenna and Merrick stood.

Lenna's legs felt like jelly as she began walking towards the throne, the implication that dragons dwelled below her not settling in the slightest. Merrick stayed at her side, one hand resting on the sword that he now wore at his side. His wings were tucked in tight, his posture rigid. She stopped as she neared the throne, in line with the first row of seats closest to the Regent. She could feel the eyes of the court upon her, but she did not dare look as she curtsied deep. Merrick, a step behind, bowed.

"Rise, Oracle," Lord Magnamus ordered. "Tell us why you've come."

Lenna craned her neck up to look at the Regent, and when he scowled, as if her presence irked him, her tongue became tied. She hadn't planned what to say. Her heart hammered. "I–I came to retrieve the Prism, so that we can clear Keerian's–um...*Sir* Keerian's name, and...and...bring the news to Queen Adara." She trailed off, unsure what else to mention.

Lenna clasped her hands in front of her to try and alleviate their shaking. The Regent was far more intimidating up close. And she'd never been good at speaking in front of a crowd–even as Lady of Doortan. She always left the grand speeches to Leon. Had just stood to the side as the quiet wife. Now, here, before Lord Magnamus, she realized just how little she knew about politics. Her stomach sank.

Especially as Lord Magnamus leaned forward and *laughed* at her.

"Queen Absolute Adara already knows everything about the situation between her traitorous sister and *Sir Keerian*," the Regent retorted mockingly. Around her, the court murmured, some chucking as the Regent had. "She would not deign to be questioned on this matter–least of all by an Oracle so *untested* and from the *Slate Kingdom*."

Lenna reared back, face paling. She had messed up. She'd messed this *all up* so swiftly.

Laurent took a step towards Lenna, his hands still clasped behind his back, the symbol of fealty and subservience. But Lenna saw him rubbing the golden ring. "Your Highness, the laws of our lands state that the Prism of the Oracle can be claimed as any Oracle sees fit." He spoke so confidently, so sure of himself. Lenna wished she had the same grace about her.

"And yet, we see many rules being rewritten these days," Lord Magnamus crowed with a vicious grin, his too-sharp teeth glinting in the candlelight. He was playing with them, toying with them, before sending them out with nothing. "Her Majesty, Queen Absolute Adara, has closed the investigation into the tragic death of her parents—my brother, and his mate. To request the Prism, to *question* our good Queen's judgement, is an affront to the crown of Irridessen."

Laurent thinned his lips, though his demeanor stayed calm. "Lord Magnamus, we only request the Prism to clear the name of our commander, Sir Keerian—a loyal and brave soldier of the late King's Guard. As Princess Esmeray is his mate, a death sentence for her would result in his death as well."

Lord Magnamus cocked his head, weighing the words Laurent spoke. Merrick stayed silent but continued touching the ring on his finger. Lenna hoped whatever conversation was happening would work in their favor.

"If your commander aligned himself with the Queen of Nothing, then I hope he finds his peace in the afterlife," the Regent stated simply, baring his teeth in a grin that did not warm his steel blue eyes. Lenna loosened a breath. She had failed her new friends. She failed them because she didn't know the politics, the background, the centuries of history on a Kingdom she never knew existed until a few days ago.

Lenna opened her mouth to say something, *anything*, to fall to her knees and beg the Regent if she had to, when the doors of the throne room burst open with a now familiar flash of golden light.

CHAPTER TWENTY-TWO
LENNA

LENNA WHIRLED AROUND AS Merrick drew his sword and Laurent took up a defensive position between Lenna and Lord Magnamus. Guards standing at attention around the dais scrambled to formation around their Regent, weapons drawn.

Between the visions and the quick glimpse through the curtains in Spinella, Lenna had never fully set eyes on the exiled Princess. Until now.

Esmeray was the epitome of beauty and death. It took Lenna's breath away and made her blood run cold.

The dubbed *Queen of Nothing* strode down the aisle towards the dais. Her blue-black hair fell loosely to the middle of her back. Black wings, as dark as a moonless night, were open and out behind her, sporting deadly looking talons that curved slightly in at the apex. But it was her horns that made Lenna swallow, her throat suddenly bone dry. Thick onyx spirals, like a ram's horns, curled from the front of her head to the backs of her pointed ears. Fear freezing her in place, Lenna couldn't look away from the Princess. Esmeray's pale face showcased the same sharp cheekbones as her uncle. But where his eyes were icy blue, hers were glittering, serpentine green.

A long golden staff clacked loudly against the glass floor as Esmeray approached, fully ignoring the assembled court gathered. A few of the fae hissed as she drew near. One brave gargoyle spat, "Murdering whore," as she passed. Esmeray ignored him.

She was dressed in similar leathers that Merrick wore, but hers were deep, bloody red and sleeveless, showing off her fully tattooed arm.

Where Merrick's tattoos were five solid black bands around his forearm, Esmeray's entire limb from her shoulder to the tips of her fingers was tattooed black. Esmeray stopped abruptly ten feet away from Merrick, nostrils flaring delicately. She arched one perfectly manicured eyebrow at the sight of Merrick's sword.

Merrick snarled. Esmeray gave him a saccharine smile in return.

"Well, *this* is no way to welcome your Queen," she crooned, her wings folding in slightly as she tapped her staff against the glass again. "Uncle." Esmeray's gaze flicked from Merrick to the Regent, now standing before his throne, glaring at her. "Get out."

"I will do *no such thing* in *my* Palace," Lord Magnamus growled. "You have no Queenship here. Guards, arrest this murdering traitor immediately by order of our Queen Absolute, Adara."

"You forget, *Uncle*, that these males are not yours to command. My sister may call herself *Queen Absolute*, but we all know who really rules these lands, do we not?" Esmeray murmured, ice and venom lacing her soft words, her eyes sweeping over the warriors that crept around her, swords drawn. A small group pressed closer to Lord Magnamus, their blades at the ready, even as their faces revealed hints of fear. Lenna wondered if Esmeray could sense their terror because she turned her attention to the soldiers surrounding the Regent. "Bow."

One by one, they dropped to their knee, backs bent. Lenna covered her mouth against a gasp, realizing it was not sheer obedience that put these males down. It was magic. Esmeray's magic she wielded as half fae.

Esmeray's glee was palpable as she turned to the Regent, who looked as if he would smite her himself. "You too, *Regent*," she laughed, her green eyes pinning him in place as she tapped her golden staff once more. Lord Magnamus's face twisted with rage as her magic forced him down. Until he too was kneeling before her.

As the Regent knelt, the warriors flanking Esmeray from all sides also collapsed to one knee. Lenna watched a gargoyle warrior attempt to push himself up with no success. Disgust and panic clouded his eyes as he screwed his face into a silent snarl of defiance.

"Good." Esmeray smirked, nodded once, and the warriors and Regent regained control of their bodies, slumping forward before rightening, hastily getting to their feet. "Now that everyone here remembers what I can do–*get out*." Esmeray's sharp gaze landed on Lenna, and Lenna felt the blood rush out of her cheeks as she made eye contact with the fearsome Princess. "Except for you three," Esmeray snapped at Laurent, Merrick, and Lenna, pointing her staff directly at Merrick's chest. Merrick didn't flinch, but Lenna noted the knuckles gripping the pommel of his sword whitened. "We have private matters to discuss."

The staff rose above her head before she bought it down upon the glass floor. Spider webs of golden magic shot from the tip, revealing hidden orbs that bobbed around the circumference of the room. Another burst of light, and each orb of gold disappeared with a resounding *crack*. The hauntingly familiar sound echoed. Lenna flinched at the implication.

Wards.

The reason why none of the beings in the room fled at Esmeray's arrival. Why the soldiers and the Regent had not disappeared immediately. Esmeray played Lenna, Merrick, and Laurent at their own game, putting wards up to not allow anyone to wane in or out of the throne room–just as they'd done to her outside Merrick's home in Spinella.

At Esmeray's behest, colorful flashes of light erupted as fae that could wane grabbed gargoyles and disappeared. The few stragglers that couldn't wane ran, shrieking, out of the throne room. Soldiers once again surrounded their Regent as he waned out of the room, before they began backing out slowly, swords still drawn. Once the last one crossed the threshold of the throne room, Esmeray waved her tattooed hand in the air impatiently, and the doors slammed shut.

Lenna felt it now, in her blood and bones.

Death.

Her life felt so fragile, so insignificant. She was going to die. Did she regret leaving Doortan just to wind up murdered by a creature she hadn't even known existed outside of myth and legend? They'd run as fast as they could, and it was still not enough. The Princess that murdered her own parents, murdered the last Oracle, stood before Lenna as judge, jury, and executioner.

Laurent moved in front of Lenna, standing shoulder to shoulder with Merrick, blue flames crackling down his wrists and fingertips.

Holding the line.

Merrick and Laurent stood between Lenna and Esmeray. Lenna's whole body shook. Failing at getting the Prism was one thing. Dying on the other hand...

She couldn't talk, couldn't think, as panic set in.

Behind Laurent and Merrick, Lenna agonized over which one of her brave companions she'd have to watch die first, or if Esmeray could somehow kill all three of them simultaneously.

But a killing blow never landed. Instead, to Lenna's utter bewilderment, Esmeray merely stated, "I request an audience with the Oracle."

Chapter Twenty-Three
Lenna

"Not going to happen you fucking murderer," Merrick spat, flaring his wings out, taking up a defensive position in front of Esmeray. "Why don't you shift into *your* Sentry form–I'll do the same. We can make this battle beast versus beast."

He was goading her, trying to move Esmeray's focus off Lenna. But even as Merrick hissed out jeers, Esmeray stood her ground, a sheen of golden magic beginning to materialize around her closed fist. She appraised him with curiosity, but Lenna waited with bated breath for her to strike. So close, yet so far away–this first true adventure was coming to a brutal and bloody end alarmingly fast.

Esmeray cocked her head, her own horns vulgar in comparison to Merrick's much smaller set. Standing with predatory stillness, her black wings extended, Esmeray met the gargoyle's eyes, and whispered in a voice deathly quiet, and not without grief, "You are Merrick. Keerian told me so much about you... *Both* of you." Her green eyes took in Laurent–the blue flames wreathing his hands. "He told me you both are like brothers to him, and that if anything happened, I would need to find you."

Merrick growled but it was Laurent who spoke first, his tone guttural, "We were there, that day in the throne room, Princess. We watched as you stole Keerian away. We watched you challenge Queen Adara for the throne. We heard of your killing spree of the Oracle and Royal Guards. I couldn't save them, but I can save the new Oracle from the same fate as her predecessor. You will not kill today, Queen of Nothing."

Laurent took a step towards Esmeray, and Lenna noticed the slight touch of his ring. Almost instantly, Merrick shifted his stance and slipped behind him, circling Laurent's back, until he was right next to Lenna. Cold fear sliced over her. *Laurent* would challenge Esmeray and sacrifice himself for her–for the Oracle.

For the truth she needed to reveal.

Merrick was in position to grab Lenna and attempt a run to safety. With another step closer, Laurent raised his chin in defiance to Esmeray. "And if my last act on this realm of existence is to end you for your crimes, I pray Keerian understands it was in defense of the Oracle, of the truth, that you are so desperate to stifle."

The eloquent words were a challenge, hanging heavily in the air.

To Lenna's complete shock, Esmeray rolled her eyes at Laurent's violent declaration, popped out a hip and snapped at the fae, "Well, if *I* know anything about *my mate*, after meeting his friends, at least I can say you're all the same amount of stubborn. Keerian told me as much, but I knew I would have to see it to believe it. You want proof? Here." The golden staff vanished into thin air, and Esmeray reached into the bodice of her top to pull out a thin chain with a golden ring at the end, the sibling of the ones Merrick and Laurent wore.

Merrick lunged at her with a roar, sword ready to slash her throat. "You *stole–*" With a flippant wave of her slim hand, Merrick just...froze. He was locked in place, unable to move his wings, his body. Merrick's eyes darkened to pitch with wild rage. He struggled against the invisible bonds that held him, but Esmeray ignored him, her grim expression fixated on

Laurent. Lenna stayed completely still behind Merrick, warily assessing the interaction. She let out a breath before sucking in another shallow burst of air, doing her best not to pass out.

Laurent looked from Esmeray, to the ring, to Merrick, his brows pinching. The writhing flames that grew around his hands flickered out and dissipated into a few harmless sparks. Lenna's eyes shot up in surprise. She was completely confused and definitely lost in what all of this meant. But Laurent knew something.

Straightening, Laurent adjusted his robes, as if he hadn't almost sacrificed his life for Lenna's slim chance at survival. He was taller than Esmeray by a solid foot and now regarded her with a bemused expression on his face, as if he understood something that changed every facet of this situation.

"Keerian gave that to you." It wasn't a question.

"Yes. He gave it to me after we spoke to my parents, in the meeting that led to their death. But I cannot tell you any details here–the walls have ears and eyes. Keerian made me promise if anything happened, I'd use this ring to track you down." Esmeray winced, as if the memories bought up were too painful still. "I couldn't talk through it since I am not the one it was created for, but I could hear you two when you mind spoke to each other. It was how I confirmed you were in Spinella. Granted, you had the Oracle, which was a surprise, but you disappeared before I could explain anything." For the first time Lenna noticed the sadness in Esmeray's face as she held the ring out to Laurent, the gold chain sliding down her tattooed arm.

He took the chain and ring gently, inspecting it. "This is Keerian's ring," he murmured, sliding the ring across the chain. "There are only three of these sibling rings. One for myself, one for Merrick, and this one–for Keerian. A caveat of these rings is that they cannot be taken forcefully. If they are stolen against the wishes of the bearer, they self-destruct. They can only be freely given by the wearer to another without the threat of the ring simply destroying itself. But yes–you would not be able to speak to anyone, only hear."

Esmeray bobbed her head again, this time more agitated. "Yes, *yes*. Look, Keerian gave that to me. He said *you* would understand." Her throat bobbed as her wings lowered and folded in.

A long moment passed silently as Laurent closed his eyes, still holding the chain and ring in his large hand.

Finally–

"I understand," Laurent breathed.

At that, Esmeray's whole body relaxed. She snapped her fingers and the invisible force holding Merrick gave way. The gargoyle flared his wings to stop himself from smacking his face against the glass floor. Panting, he lowered his sword, sheathing it to the hilt, before narrowing his cooled brown eyes at his friend. "What *exactly* do you understand?" His tone was clipped, and although the sword was no longer in his hand, Lenna watched his fingers twitch, as if they were waiting for approval to jump into a fight.

"She didn't kill her parents," Laurent mused, handing the chain and ring back to Esmeray. "Esmeray did not kill the King and Queen."

Chapter Twenty-Four
Lenna

"Wait, what?" Lenna and Merrick asked simultaneously, staring at Laurent as if he'd gone mad. "How do you know for sure?" Merrick demanded, completely ignoring the beaming smile Esmeray shot his direction, as if she was preening "*I told you so*," at the gargoyle.

"Merrick, we know *Keerian*. Keerian would've never willingly given his mate his ring if he had any doubt in his mind, or even a fraction of a suspicion, that Esmeray murdered her parents." Laurent ducked his head to Esmeray in a half bow. "I will hear your story in full. We can go from there on the...specifics."

Relief flooded Esmeray's face and she sat down on the closest black stone row of seats the court had vacated, her wings drooping as if some of the tension came out of them, as well, with Laurent's declaration. "Thank you," she replied softly.

Lenna finally found her voice, it was croaky and filled with shake, but it worked well enough. "What about the Oracle? You killed him in cold blood."

Esmeray's grief flickered for a second before vanishing–replaced by a cool, stony expression. She twisted around in the pew until Lenna was fully in her sights. "Again. I cannot relay that here. Even with the few wards I left in place, anyone could hear us. And I don't have many friends here, as you may have noticed."

Lenna crossed her arms, blowing a loose curl out of her face. "Are you going to kill me?" Her blunt question made Esmeray rear back, before peering closer at Lenna, those cunning green eyes slitting as Esmeray studied her with interest. Lenna raised her chin, meeting the Esmeray's gaze with her own, daring her to find her lacking.

"I am not going to kill you–but I can understand the precarious situation you're in so, I'll do you one better." Esmeray let Lenna contemplate for a moment before following up with, "I will *give* you the Prism, take you to the safe house I've been staying at, and explain everything." Esmeray and Lenna stared at each other, a challenge, and a request.

Lenna weighed her words, the disbelief that she was still alive making her knees weaken under her gown now that the wave of nerves and adrenaline was fading. "How can you get the Prism? I don't know where it is, and the Regent outright refused to allow me to have it."

Esmeray grinned, the light returning to her scintillating eyes, and up close, Lenna could see small flecks of gold twined through the green, like a twinkling star that had fallen into a plush field of summer grass. Straightening in her seat and tucking her black wings tighter to her, the Princess remarked brightly, "Oh *we* won't be getting it. We're going to wait right here. I have someone collecting it as we speak. I may have taken some liberties with my plan on the off-chance I was able to speak with you, and figured you may need a..." Esmeray crinkled her pert nose as she searched for the word, cocking her horns to the ceiling, before snapping her fingers once it came to her. "A *peace* offering."

As if her words were a cue, a deep rumble filled the throne room, rattling the skeletal torches. Lenna noticed the golden hands seem to grip the flame tipped iron tighter in their bony fingers. Merrick swore as the glass floor under them shuddered. Lenna braced herself against the pew, looking down into the depths of the dark caverns in panic, though this time, a monstrous, moon-silver eye peered back up at her.

"Shit," Merrick said in awe, "I haven't seen a dragon in decades."

Laurent swallowed thickly, backing up until he was aligned with Lenna, his lips pursed together as he cautiously kept his emerald gaze focused on the floor, his hands bracketing Lenna to the pew as the room trembled violently again.

Behind the dais, the glass seemed to melt, ripples growing outward like the echo of a rock thrown into a pond. Lenna grabbed Laurent's arm to steady herself as the floor rocked again. But the creature that emerged made Lenna wish the floor would swallow her up and make her disappear.

A black dragon shot out from the caverns below, landing in front of the dais with a heavy *thud*. It was massive, with charcoal wings that unfurled with a heaving stretch and long, razor-sharp talons that scraped against the glass. Its armored scales illuminated silver hues in the faint glow from the skeletal hands protecting their fire. The floor sealed itself as the dragon passed through, its spiked tail curling around the dais as it ambled closer, each step of its considerable weight making the room shake again. The throne room was spacious, yet the beast easily took up the majority of the area in front of the pews. The dragon lowered its snout, one slitted pupil focusing on Esmeray, as it settled down on all fours, tucking its wings in.

Esmeray stood from her seat once the floor stopped quaking, her own wings folded tightly to her back, as she offered the beast her tattooed palm. The dragon lowered its head to smell her, and rumbled in contentment, the sound originating from deep within its belly. Her whole body, wings included, only came up to snout level, but she tilted her head up to the dragon with a cheerful smile. Merrick looked from beast to Princess, as if he could hear the words that no one spoke.

"Gargoyles are the only beings that can mind speak with dragons," Laurent explained, his arm protectively looped around Lenna, as he steered them down the aisle, giving the creature a wider berth. "It's one of the reasons the Regent here is not too fond of his new posting."

Lenna did not know what to say besides, "The dragon is mind speaking to Esmeray *and* Merrick?" Laurent shot her a bemused look but did not elaborate further.

Merrick stood behind Esmeray, his hand loosely gripping his sword in its sheath. The gargoyle bowed once to the dragon before turning and heading back to where Laurent and Lenna stood, waiting.

"That isn't just any dragon–that's Resso." Admiration filled his voice, his brown eyes wide. For Lenna's benefit Merrick elaborated, "Resso is the oldest and biggest dragon here. He guards the treasure troves in the caverns beneath the throne room, and only answers to the rightful ruler of the Obsidian Kingdom. Legends say Resso has lived inside the caverns since the first rulers began carving the Palace from the mountain, though Resso will never confirm nor deny that bit of lore." He shot a glance back to where Esmeray still stood before the dragon. She was stroking its massive maw and the dragon, Resso, had his eyes half closed as if Esmeray was petting a very lazy cat, and not a creature that could swallow her in one gulp.

A few moments passed, and Esmeray kissed the muzzle of the beast before Resso turned slowly around, careful not to knock into anything with his spiked tail, and slid back down beneath the floor. Lenna noticed how the glass parted, like the creature just swum up and swam back down. She braved a look below the floor right as Resso spread his wings out wide, gliding down into the depths, before disappearing into the darkness.

Esmeray met the group halfway and held out her tattooed hand to Lenna. "Here it is, but don't look into it right now. I want to get far away from this dreadful place before we peer into the past. I have some of my own suspicions I need to confirm."

She placed a blue silk bag the size of an apple into Lenna's hands. Lenna marveled at the weight of it. It was much heavier than it appeared. Lenna gripped it tightly against her body. Something deep inside her settled, as if holding the Prism clicked a part of her soul into its rightful place.

Esmeray directed her attention to Merrick, her wings flaring out ever so slightly in what Lenna concluded must be a dominance trait between gargoyles. "You heard our conversation–I hope it also confirms something for you. The dragons will only bring treasures from their trove to me. My parents named me Queen on High, and that title cannot be taken away as easily as Adara believes. Lord Magnamus couldn't give you the Prism even if he wanted to. Irridessen and its magic acknowledge *me* as its main ruler, my twin a secondary Queen as the succession dictated, and the dragons will refuse to affiliate with anyone except myself, which makes my uncle pretty testy. Adara can call herself whatever she wants–it does not change the fact she is *actually* Lesser Queen based on Irridessen's succession. And only I can change the titles now for future rulers."

Queen. Esmeray *was* the Queen on High–even if Adara rebuked her title.

Dragons and magical successions, hidden titles and secret royalty... Truly it all made Lenna very overwhelmed.

Merrick opened his mouth, closed it, and opened it again. "I will hear your story," he said a bit hoarsely.

Esmeray clasped his hand in hers. "Thank you. Even if you listen and still hate me after, we do have a common goal to save Keerian."

"Save Keerian from what?" Lenna heard herself ask, and she was surprised the words came out as steady as they had–especially since she just saw a *dragon* and now held an object that was currently humming in her hands with a type of magic that felt very ancient to Lenna's bones.

Esmeray growled, the bloodthirstiness in the Queen's eyes giving Lenna pause. Baring her teeth, exposing two sharp canines, Esmeray answered harshly, "From my sister."

CHAPTER TWENTY-FIVE
LAURENT

LAURENT WATCHED MERRICK APPREHENSIVELY. Their time serving King Scottrell had made it to where Laurent knew Merrick as well as he knew himself. While Laurent and Keerian preferred to deal with absolutes, Merrick never shied away from reveling in the grey areas of their duties. Merrick balanced them out as a fighting unit, but Keerian always groused that Merrick's temper would get him in trouble one day.

Esmeray's presence confirmed for Laurent, at least, that they should hear Esmeray out before deciding their next steps. Merrick looked ready to fight the Queen—yes, Esmeray was Queen on High after all, until his silent conversation with the great dragon and Esmeray. Now, he seemed too quiet, too subdued.

Seeing Resso had been a surprise since the dragons that lived below the Obsidian Palace typically avoided any interactions with the beings above them, and were prone to *"eat first, ask questions later"* when it came to beings stupid enough to venture into the treasure troves that tunneled through the caverns.

But Esmeray...

Laurent had seen both Adara and Esmeray in passing, though their words exchanged had been short and far between. No more than flat greetings on days where Esmeray deigned to even acknowledge her father's guard. Princess Esmeray always came across as the troublemaker, actively skipping Council Meetings her father would demand she attend, wane out of the Palace on a whim, returning days or weeks later with no explanation for where she was. She was cunning, aloof, larger than the box her parents begged her to fit into as Princess.

In comparison, Adara always sat prim and straight-backed in every Council Meeting, shaking hands with foreign nobility, giving small, approving smiles as laws were passed and new avenues of trade or other boring topics were presented. Adara encapsulated the perfect Princess that was presented to the beings in Irridessen as their next Queen—once Carra gifted Adara the soul tie. And now she had declared herself Queen Absolute.

Yet Carra had given the fateful soul tie to Esmeray, and now Laurent found himself in a very backwards situation.

"I'll do it." Lenna interrupted his thoughts, her bright red hair shimmering under the torchlight. "If it helps your um...mate. I can help. I want to help." Lenna ducked her flushed face as Esmeray focused on her, though the Queen seemed to relax at the admission.

Esmeray gave Lenna a tight smile, "Thank you, Oracle."

A feminine shout from the hall was their only warning before the throne room doors burst open. Esmeray whirled, her golden staff appearing out of thin air as Royal Guards flooded in, swords drawn and magic rallied around the fists of the fae fighters.

"Seems my warm welcome has officially run out," Esmeray noted sarcastically.

"Fuck," Merrick growled, his head pivoting from the Royal Guards to Esmeray, and Laurent watched the battle of the gargoyle's own morals play across his face.

Fight against the Crown and find yourself labeled a traitor.

Fight against Esmeray–find yourself dead.

With a prayer sent to the gods above, Laurent made the decision for him. Blue flame ignited at his fingertips as he took up a position of defense between Lenna and the guards, siding with Esmeray. Merrick cursed as he drew his sword, taking up a position on Lenna's other side.

"We're so fucked," Merrick commented as more fighters poured into the throne room.

"Laurent, can you wane?" Esmeray slashed her staff through the air, a gnarled mass of thorny vines appearing between them and the guards, the brambles thrashing on the ground like live snakes.

Laurent shook his head, directing a wall of fire to flank their sides, forcing the guards into a bottleneck against the thorns. The Royal Guards fought viciously as the vines pounced, the sharp points of the brambles piercing their metal armor effortlessly, yet the sheer amount of foes soon became overwhelming.

"I'll wane us," Esmeray shouted, throwing her hand out as Laurent's howling flames drowned out the yells of pain from the fighters ensnared by the magical plant, the bellows of those flying above them, hunting for a way to get closer. Merrick gripped Lenna's upper arm, propelling her towards Esmeray. Lenna screamed Laurent's name, fear strangling her voice, as she threw a hand out to him. Laurent hurdled towards it, grabbing ahold just as Esmeray caught Merrick by the lapel of his vest. Her staff blazed with magic, a wisp of golden light arching gracefully over the wall of flame before crashing into the opal throne on the dais, blasting it to rubble.

Laurent blinked in surprise. Esmeray shot him a sneaky smile before twisting, waning them out of the Obsidian Palace.

The golden flash of Esmeray's magic dissipated a moment later, depositing their group atop a grassy knoll. Esmeray staggered slightly as Merrick, Lenna, and Laurent landed in a jumbled heap of wings and limbs. Merrick groaned, heaving a ghost-white Lenna to her feet. Laurent squeezed Lenna's shoulder in reassurance, receiving flat glare in return. The Oracle did not seem adept to speak anytime soon, as if she left her voice in the throne room of the Obsidian Palace and needed a moment for it to catch back up.

In the distance, Laurent could make out the mountain peaks surrounding the Obsidian Palace, massive points that shot through the horizon, spearing into the twilight clouds. They were alone for miles in every direction under the night sky. A few stars had begun to illuminate their field of vision, a far cry from the pitch black of the Pyritee Pass.

"You destroyed the throne," Merrick directed at Esmeray, his bitter tone accusatory. "You blew the throne of the Obsidian Kingdom to bits. *That* is considered treason in itself."

"And *far* down my list of crimes," Esmeray spat back, rolling her slim shoulders as her wings flared. "I hated that throne." Esmeray sneered at Merrick, the budding comradery between gargoyles already crumbling. Esmeray was half fae, but Laurent mused there may be some jockeying for position between the two, even though the stubbornness gargoyles seemed to inherit was outright preposterous given their current situation. "The true throne of the Obsidian Palace was created for my *mother*, Queen Absolute Elera, crafted out of a piece of the mountain's summit, accommodating to my mother's gargoyle heritage. The throne *I* destroyed was too narrow explicitly so *my* wings would not fit. It was a symbol of my uncle's reign that I was happy to destroy."

Laurent stepped between the two, hands raised to bring the tension back down. "Where are we?" he asked calmly, prompting Esmeray to huff.

"It's a strain on my magic to wane you all so far. We'll need to wait for my magic to replenish and then we can go the rest of the way." Esmeray looked out to the horizon, and Laurent wondered where her mind went when her eyes became pin-pricked with tears for a moment. Lenna stood silently at his side, still clutching the Prism tightly to her chest as she, too, stared out into the distance, a soft presence opposed to Merrick's brooding.

The silence stretched, becoming thick with the weight of the treason they'd just openly declared against Queen Adara. The temperature grew colder, matching the chill in Laurent's bones that even his own fire couldn't heat away. Finally, Esmeray shook her head, blinking away from the dark landscape to glance over to them.

"Let's go," she muttered. Laurent raised his eyebrows as Lenna moved from her spot, firmly grasping Esmeray's hand. Esmeray's guarded demeanor seemed to melt as she offered a tentative smile to the Oracle. Merrick gripped Lenna's other hand, averting his eyes altogether from the Queen. Laurent gritted his teeth as he took Esmeray's other hand and prayed that Merrick would keep his shit together long enough for them to get the answers they needed.

Chapter Twenty-Six
MERRICK

MERRICK GLANCED AROUND AS they landed on a red-bricked walkway, the roaring in his ears dimmed from the travel. Taking in his surroundings, he could not for the life of him figure out the city in which they now resided. Chalking it up to the disorienting trip, he grumbled a curse under his breath. He hated waning–flying was his preferred method of getting around, but even Laurent's portals were less brutal than these jumps through space.

Lenna and Laurent released Esmeray the moment their feet touched down. The Oracle was doubled over, heaving as if she might throw up. Laurent halfheartedly patted her back before sliding a few feet away. Merrick knew it was to make sure no puke splattered his new robe.

"You get used to it–the waning." Esmeray looked apologetic as she tilted her horned head down to kick a piece of mulch off the bricks and back into its bed. "The first few times I waned, I almost passed out I was so nauseous."

"Goody," Lenna grumbled flatly, finally straightening to take in the sights, her hands on her hips and a worn, pinched, expression on her face.

They were in the middle of a circular courtyard, ringed with a low iron fence partially covered with vines that shot out orange and yellow fire flowers, vibrant plants that absorbed the sun's rays during the day, making them glow brightly at night.

A smattering of bird baths and feeders chaotically stuck out between dense bushes. In the center, a granite fountain of a dragon wrapped around a rose dribbled a faint stream of water from the beast's outstretched mouth to a filigreed basin. A path led from the fountain to a three-story yellow house with a pink front door. Stained glass windows adorned the cozy looking home, all portraying the theme of various birds and plants.

Lenna whispered a soft *woah*. Around them, more colorful houses lined the street. Some inhabitants were outside, working in their respective gardens, and a few gargoyles lay on various flat perches of their own homes, lounging in the moonlight.

Across the street, a gargoyle sprawled out on his second story roof cracked an eye open and waved to Esmeray, who gave the male a smile as she returned the gesture.

"See?" she bit out, the venom directed at Merrick, "Not everyone hates me."

"You live...*here*?" Merrick asked the Queen skeptically. It wasn't what he expected. This was a *neighborhood* for gods' sake.

With neighbors who weren't screaming and running away as she appeared.

"Not by myself," she answered cryptically as she turned on her heel from the garden and hopped up the front steps, black wings flaring out behind her.

She barely crossed the last step as the door swung open and a shrill screech filled the courtyard.

Merrick sucked in a breath at the fae that appeared in the doorway. She was the most beautiful female he ever lay eyes on. Golden blonde hair tumbled down past her shoulders, some locks swept into thin braids with pink flowers delicately placed between the strands. Her skin was the color of spring, a light tan that made her hair shine. Brilliant aquamarine eyes sparkled as she beheld Esmeray, and the slender cheekbones in her face only made her look more ethereal. The female's left arm looked as if it had been delicately dipped in black paint, the tattoo starting at the tips of her fingers and traveling up to her elbow before ebbing away, revealing more of that luscious, tanned skin on her upper arm.

The female threw her arms around Esmeray, who, to Merrick's chagrin, fiercely hugged the fae right back.

Merrick dumbly opened his mouth to introduce himself, as if he would just shout his name at her, when Laurent effortlessly slid past him and took the first two steps up to the front door. As he got to the top, he bowed deep to the female and asked for her name.

Merrick rolled his eyes.

Great. They were going to fight over this one.

He could already tell.

"Sparrow," the fae said a bit breathlessly, a faint flush creeping up her face. "My name is Sparrow."

The name clanged through Merrick, the most enchanting name he'd ever heard. Gods, he was in trouble.

Esmeray cleared her throat, breaking Merrick's trance before his inner thoughts got too scandalous. "Sparrow, meet Merrick and Laurent–and Lenna, the Oracle."

Sparrow's blue eyes danced over each of them as Esmeray rounded off introductions. It was a bit awkward seeing as Merrick tried to kill her an hour ago. He almost touched his ring to ask Laurent if he knew what the actual fuck was going on but remembered Esmeray held Keerian's ring and would also hear what he was saying.

That would be annoying.

Lenna clambered up the steps to shake Sparrow's hand, still half out of breath from waning, and Sparrow bowed to her–which made Lenna extremely uncomfortable by the shift in her body language. "Oracle." Sparrow reverently squeezed Lenna's hand. "Thank you so much for coming. It means the world to Esmeray." Struck silent by the customary welcome she had yet to truly experience, Lenna let out a squeaky *thank you* before shooting a warning glance at Merrick–he was the only one who had yet to move from their arrival point in Sparrow's garden.

"Let's get inside, we have lot to discuss," Esmeray said with a pointed look at the female. Sparrow rolled her big blue eyes before grabbing the Queen's hand and half dragging her through the threshold, gesturing for them to follow her.

Merrick looked from Lenna to Laurent who were both still warily standing on the small front porch. "Well, fuck, this will be interesting," he ground out as he stalked towards the bright pink door and the uncertainty beyond.

CHAPTER TWENTY-SEVEN
LENNA

THE INTERIOR OF SPARROW'S home was just as vividly eccentric as the front garden. Lenna only had a split second to take in the turquoise walls of the entryway, where paintings in mismatched frames depicted beasties frolicking through artsy landscapes, before Sparrow led them into a cozily lit living room. Lamps of varying shapes, colors, and sizes perched on small wooden tables or dangled across the ceiling with overlapping chains, all lit by a magic that bathed the room in a gloriously pure radiance–so unlike the haunting amber torches in the Obsidian Palace, or the somber, grey hued light of the Doortan Manor.

A large purple couch sprawled across one full wall of the living room, cornering up to a fireplace surrounded by a tiled mosaic of pink birds with long, stick-like legs. Inset shelves lined the walls around the mantle, filled to the brim with books and odd plants that snuggled up in a colorful array of ceramic pots.

Lenna soaked it all in. The house seemed so *cheery*. If she had her way in the Doortan Manor, Lenna believed she would've decorated it similarly to Sparrow's home. The Queen that plopped onto the plushy couch looked a bit out of place–even though she seemed to relax as Sparrow chattered animatedly to Merrick and Laurent, her hands waving around as she told them a lively story of how she procured certain rare plants and helped them grow and thrive with her magic.

Esmeray sat quietly, her eyes darting between the two males sitting precariously on small poufs by the intricate stained-glass window on the opposite wall of the couch. Merrick had his wings out slightly, his legs awkwardly crossed as he tried to figure out how to balance himself and the extra wing weight on the slowly sinking floor pillow. Laurent kept his regal, unruffled posture—as if he sat on poufs all the time—his legs straight out in front of him, crossed at the ankles, his red robe from the Obsidian Palace unwrinkled and smoothly tucked around his knees.

Esmeray delicately cleared her throat as Sparrow ended one story and launched into another without taking a breath. Sparrow twisted to the Queen and crinkled her nose as if to say *"whoops,"* remembering the reason Esmeray bought them all here. Declaring that she would go make everyone some tea, she stood quickly, the fabric of her silky pink dress swishing around her hips as she departed.

Esmeray sat up straighter, shifting her wings now that Sparrow wasn't sitting on the couch next to her. Her green eyes, bemused as she let Sparrow chat, were now glinting with determination.

"Let's talk about the obvious first," Esmeray started. Laurent and Merrick swapped a glance before the latter nodded.

Esmeray launched into a quick backstory that Lenna knew was more for her benefit than the two males that had been there the night Esmeray and Keerian became soul tied. "I knew, in a way, from the moment I met him, that Keerian was my mate. It was then that I realized fate may want me to be Queen on High, something I never considered before."

Lenna raised an eyebrow at that, and even Merrick and Laurent seemed taken aback by the unfurling story.

"I met Keerian a couple months before the first full moon celebration of summer last year. We kept running into each other around the Opal Palace." Esmeray swallowed. "Adara noticed, but didn't say much to me since our relationship had become so strained over the last couple years. She wanted to be Queen on High. Adara said it was her entire life's purpose. The night Keerian and I realized we were mates... I *knew* that she would wait until we cemented the soul tie to kill Keerian in order to take me out. I panicked...and grabbed him." Merrick grunted. Laurent only nodded.

Both males hung on to her every word.

Esmeray shifted in her seat, and Lenna again saw the look of torment flash in her eyes. But Esmeray continued, telling them how she waned Keerian here. How Sparrow, her childhood best friend and the only being she truly trusted, welcomed them in with open arms, demanded they stay here as Keerian and Esmeray navigated the first few days of being a newly mated couple.

"Sparrow has...well, let's call them acquaintances, that fed her information on what was going on back at the Opal Palace after Keerian and I escaped. The reports were that Adara was acting out of character, to the point where she was a danger to be around. She'd stopped going to council meetings, and was holed up in her chambers, refusing to eat and lashing out at any visitors. I feared this was an escalation towards volatile behaviors since she'd lost the title of Queen on High, and that she would begin plotting how to take it back. A couple years ago, she found a spell book that contained knowledge on forbidden fae spells, and she's been using them to the point that the spells are consuming her life."

"We were quietly notified of the spell book by your father," Laurent said carefully. "Though I do not believe the general public is aware of her fascination with spell work."

"They aren't," Esmeray growled. "My parents originally saw Adara's interest with the spell book as trivial–harmless. They never thought she'd actually *cast* any spells, so they never told their council, and the knowledge of what Adara was doing was hidden. I'm honestly surprised my father warned his King's Guard about it. But the small spells she's tried before are nothing compared to what she is attempting now. She's found a spell that can either break a soul tie, or transfer *my* soul tie with Keerian to *herself*."

"How can she do that?" Laurent questioned, his dark brows furrowed. In the light of the living room, his silver earrings glinted–as if they too were listening to the conversation.

Esmeray shrugged. "We don't know. There was only one instance when I was able to see the spell written down on a separate piece of parchment. But it's in a runic language from thousands of years ago. Sparrow only knew a few words from her studies of ancient history, but with the way the runes strung together, we concluded Adara was either trying to fully break my soul tie or transfer it."

Merrick shook his head. "I don't know anything about fae spells, but Adara is only half fae, how is she able to accurately cast any of them?"

"She *is* powerful, even though she's leagues below me, but I embraced my gargoyle side, leaned into it, and she tried her best to ignore hers. In some ways, I think her just *believing* she is a full blooded fae gave her a better ability to wield the spells in the book, but even that's a guess."

"So, you figured out Adara was trying to break your soul tie, or somehow transfer your soul tie so she could, what? Be mated to Keerian?"

Esmeray clenched her jaw. "Keerian and I knew we had to go back sooner, rather than later, to tell my parents what exactly Adara was trying to use those spells for. I thought that would be the end of it," the Queen admitted glumly. "Adara would be stopped before she could proceed with the spell, and my parents would punish her. Which would leave me to take up the crown with Keerian at my side after my parent's time on the throne was up in a hundred years. They would step down. I would step up." Her voice shook. Sparrow slid quietly back into the room, gently setting a pretty porcelain teacup on the low table in front of Esmeray, giving Merrick a venomous glare that seemed to say, "*play nice or else.*"

Esmeray's voice faded softly, as if she was talking only to herself, "Keerian and I were wary of Adara's lust for power, and after we left the meeting, my parents discreetly ordered Adara to be confined to her rooms while they found a translator for the spell book. They needed proof to condemn her for casting spells, though they still wanted to believe she was only interested from an academic standpoint–that she wasn't doing something illegal. To them, Adara was the daughter who never stepped a toe out of line, who always held herself to an impossibly high standard of right and wrong. This seemed out of character. So, for them to come to terms with the fact that she was planning on committing a heinous crime... It was tough."

Sparrow perched on the edge of the couch, rubbing Esmeray's back between the junction of her wings. Esmeray took a deep breath. "After we spoke with my parents and explained what Adara's fixation of spell work had come to, Keerian and I retired to our room–and that is when he gave me his ring and made me swear to find you both if anything went wrong. Well, everything from then on went wrong. When we woke up the next morning, Adara called the court to the throne room, and broke the news that my parents were dead. I had *no idea* before then. I was completely blindsided. The next couple minutes were a blur, but she sat on my mother's throne and put an invisible protection shield around herself." Esmeray bared her teeth, her eyes flashing a brighter, venomous green. "When she accused *me* of their murders, I lost it–my magic barreled through her shield and broke it. Unfortunately, *that* was tinder for her fire, and she exiled me right there. I played *right* into her hands."

Merrick nodded slowly, as if pieces of a puzzle he didn't know were missing were finally visible and clicking into place. Taking the small teacup Sparrow wordlessly handed to him, he took a long sip. Lenna accepted her own cup with thanks to the kind fae who had welcomed them into her home. The first taste shot through her, notes of honey, lemon, and something tart and citrus-y warming her belly instantly. A soothing blend after the news Esmeray was currently delivering them.

Laurent, his own tea in hand, hollowly murmured, "Adara banished you, but Keerian is trapped there. With Adara."

Sparrow looked at her friend, and when Esmeray didn't–or couldn't–answer, the fae, in a calm voice, continued where Esmeray left off. "We believe whatever spell she has needs a piece of Keerian to complete. It follows the notion that she isn't trying to destroy the soul tie. She's trying to transfer Esmeray's piece to herself."

Lenna addressed Sparrow, "Has the...soul tie been transferred?"

"No," Esmeray said hoarsely. "All the research Keerian, Sparrow and I did the week we were here noted that if it was transferred, or broken, I would endure a *pain so unbearable that you would wish yourself dead.*" And I can feel it–I can feel his soul is still entwined with mine." She put her tattooed left hand over her heart.

Sparrow gently picked up the teacup again and handed it to the Queen. Esmeray took a small sip of the offering, shooting Sparrow a grateful look. After swallowing, Esmeray added blankly, "The script had been written against me for far longer than I realized. And Adara fed into it, coating it with her own sweet poison. She already turned my parent's court against me, the Obsidian Palace's court against me, and named our uncle Regent while my...hoax of a trial was ongoing. When she exiled me to the Obsidian Kingdom, I landed in the throne room of the Palace. Eight soldiers were there, ready to drag me to the dungeon. They did not survive." She took another sip of tea, her fingers trembling ever so slightly.

"Esmeray waned here after." Sparrow picked up the story. "I heard through the grapevine that Adara crowned herself Queen Absolute and banished Esmeray. So, I waited for Esmeray to come back here. I built wards around my home, and layered as many protection magics as I knew so she'd be safe here while we figured this out."

The conversation fell into a lull, Merrick and Laurent both lost in thought. Not wanting to lose her nerve, Lenna blurted out the question she'd been afraid to mention since this story started, especially now that her heart mourned and sympathized with the Queen. "What about the Oracle?"

Chapter Twenty-Eight
Laurent

Esmeray's narrative had started in the late evening, but now, as it continued, the three-quarter moon arched closer to its apex in the night sky. The room began to cool, so Laurent politely asked Sparrow if he could light a fire in her fireplace, and she had beamed at him when he lit it with a snap of his fingers. He could light a fire with his eyes closed, but in the presence of this enchanting female, he couldn't help but show off–just a little.

They had all finally begun to relax a smidge around each other. Until Lenna bought up the one question that once again filled the room with a tang of distrust and unease. Even though Laurent knew for fact now that Esmeray and Keerian had not murdered the late King and Queen, Esmeray *had* killed Lenna's predecessor. She admitted as much.

Esmeray cut her eyes to Lenna, who seemed to shrink ever so slightly under the all-out attention Esmeray fixed on her.

"I will tell you this, Oracle," Esmeray's words were clipped, a slight bite tinting her tone, "If there had been any way, *any way at all* to save him, I would've done it. I searched for him for months after my exile–ask Sparrow. She's the one who ended up finding out his whereabouts. Adara locked him in the Soul Keeper's Cell inside the Obsidian Palace–the same place she tried to have those soldiers throw me."

Laurent sucked in a breath as he instantly understood the issue–and Esmeray's decision. Esmeray continued, spurred on as she noted the confusion in Lenna's face. "The Obsidian Palace has one unique caveat to the extensive dungeons in the lowest level of the cavern. There is a flat rock unnervingly named the Soul Keeper's Cell. There are no doors. The rock itself is keyed to the prisoner's soul. There's no escape, only death, once you are thrown onto it. And there is no way out once that hallowed ground marks your soul."

"Adara put the Oracle in the Soul Keeper's Cell." Laurent rubbed his temple with a single long finger. This whole situation was going from bad to worse with each reveal.

Lenna whipped her head to Laurent, her eyes questioning. "So, he couldn't get out?"

Esmeray answered, her words quickening, as if she wanted this conversation to be over as fast as possible. "Adara locked him down there before Keerian and I returned to the Opal Palace. She was the only one that knew where he was–and when Sparrow used her magic to find whispers of his location, that is where we found him. We also found no indication that any beings knew he was there. I couldn't get him out no matter what magic I tried. And I knew, going down there, that it was already a hopeless cause but…I had to try. In all the years I knew him, he was always honest and fair and kind. Adara put him in the Soul Keeper's Cell to slam another nail in my coffin. To frame me for his peril. To imprison an Oracle, a truth seeker, is asinine and fucked up. Not to mention *incredibly* illegal. Oracles are not tied to any specific Kingdom. They are regarded as living gods. Sparrow told me she found him, and I used my illusion magic to visit him without anyone knowing I was there."

Laurent glanced over at Lenna, who now looked half there half...elsewhere. Her eyes glazed over, the honey-brown becoming darker, muddled. Esmeray, still on the couch, didn't notice the subtle change in Lenna's posture. A slight swaying freed a few red curls Lenna had thrown over her shoulder.

Esmeray winced at her admission of magic, and turned to address Merrick and Laurent. "I have the ability to cast illusions, as real as if they were living, breathing beings. I've been honing it for years, as it is my own personal magic that has *never* manifested in any other being in existence. My illusions can ebb and flow, from smoke and mist to solid and unyielding. I channeled my illusion into the Oracle's cell. He was so far gone already, he'd been imprisoned for *months*. The soul bind to his cell was draining his life force at an accelerated rate. When my illusion entered his cell, he was half mad. But he begged me, he *begged me* to kill him. To release his soul from the bind so he could go to Minmere in peace."

Lenna stared blandly at Esmeray, *through* Esmeray, as she replied hollowly, distantly, "*Dead eyes, golden light, black wings. A death so merciful that the shell smiled as its soul was freed.*" A spilt second of silence—then Esmeray shot up, wings flaring wide. Laurent whipped his head to Lenna, mouth agape. Merrick shouted a warning, eyes locked on the Queen, his hand ripping free the dagger sheathed at his belt, pointing it at Esmeray's heart. Esmeray gave the weapon in Merrick's hand a miffed glare before plopping back down on the couch, horns cocked as she stared at the Oracle with intrigue.

"You..." Esmeray whispered, "you got activated that night, but you *saw* me kill him." The Queen looked, really *looked* at Lenna, still sitting, half-slumped, on the pouf. Lenna blinked, the lively, honey tint in her eyes becoming clearer, more focused.

"Lenna," Laurent questioned carefully, "do you know what you just said?"

Lenna started, realizing all eyes were on her.

"N-no?" Brows knitting in confusion, Lenna took in Esmeray's posture, Merrick's bright, proud expression. Laurent knew his own face showed the same shock mirrored on Esmeray's. Only Sparrow, still reclined on the gaudy purple couch, seemed unperturbed. Merrick puffed out his chest, a stupidly cheery grin on his face as he slipped his dagger back into its sheath and shot a gloating look towards Laurent.

"Well. That is unexpected," Sparrow mused, her voice lilting as she gracefully sipped from her cup, "Not only are you the *Oracle*, but you're also a seer."

Merrick cleared his throat, extending his hand towards Laurent as the words sunk in. Laurent shook his head, muttering indecencies under his breath as he reached into his robe, that smugness on the gargoyle's face reminding him of their bet from Spinella.

Laurent tossed a small felt bag to Merrick, the jingling of gold coins reminding the fae to never bet against the gods.

Or stubborn fucking gargoyles.

CHAPTER TWENTY-NINE
ESMERAY

"WHAT IS THE DIFFERENCE between an Oracle and a seer?" Lenna nervously wiped her hands on the fabric of her red dress. I felt it then, too wrapped up in my own shit before, but the magic coiled up inside me pulled towards Lenna.

To find out Lenna was not only the Oracle, but also a seer... It could change the world. Or damn it into the bowels of Minmere.

Sparrow, gods bless her, gracefully knelt at Lenna's side, her pink dress pooling around her knees as she took Lenna's shaking hands in her own steady ones.

"An Oracle has flashes of visions, and they may have started for you as violent headaches and grown from there. But once the Prism is claimed by the Oracle, the headaches should dissipate, as well as the choppy visions, since your power is now only able to be accessed by channeling the Prism. Before you claimed the Prism, your power was uncut–raw. Now it should settle since you claimed the Prism so quickly after being activated." Sparrow waved a hand, the flower buds blooming on the bookshelves closing up tight. I couldn't help but admire my dear friend. Her gifts were another I'd never seen before. Even my late father begged Sparrow to be part of his prestigious King's Guard, but she refused, saying her gifts were life–not death.

Like mine are.

My father, of course, never extended the offer to myself–from either fear of what unknown magic the gods had given to me, or because of my royal title and what it would look like to our realm if a Princess picked up a sword and learned how to use it.

Sparrow crossed the room, returning with a bottle of sweet, pink wine. "As the Oracle, there are limitations on what you can *see*. To use your gift as the Oracle, you hold the Prism and journey into it to *see* what others cannot." Sparrow handed Lenna a short glass filled with the pink liquid, gesturing for her to take a drink. Lenna puckered her lips at the first sip of alcohol, before raising the glass again, taking a second, longer, swallow of wine. "As a seer, you can *see* fate itself. Whether you want to or not." Sparrow squeezed Lenna's shoulder and gave her a kind smile. "Seers are rare, but their magic also comes from Moirai, who decides what information needs to be passed down to each individual seer and at what time."

My wings wrapped around my sides as I looked down into my own teacup. The events of the night weighed on me. I missed my mate. And explaining my actions made my heart ache, numbness slithering through my veins. I tightened my wings, feeling as if they were the only thing holding me together.

It was easier to believe another being infiltrated the Soul Keeper's Cell, another being made the hard decision to mercy kill the previous Oracle, another being was exiled and hunted for a crime they didn't commit.

But it was me. My life.

And I was so godsdamned tired.

"Sparrow." I wiggled my teacup, slipping on the mask I wore as a second skin these days to keep everyone from seeing how broken I truly was, recreating the gaudy teacup into a wine glass with my magic. It eased some of the strain that built up from not using my illusion gifts at full power. But my magic still thrummed, waiting impatiently for an outlet.

Finding the Oracle was my first stroke of good luck in almost a year. And I waited with bated breath to see if the gods would take this away, too.

Sparrow threw me and my wine glass a scathing look before laughing lightly. "I'll get a few bottles of red because you won't like this sweet stuff." I threw her an appreciative grin as Sparrow tugged Lenna up with her. "Lenna, can you help me down in the wine cellar? I have some old wines down there that I want Esmeray to try."

Lenna stood on shaky legs, still a little pale from the whole 'seer' thing, but she nodded and followed Sparrow's trailing skirts out of the room. Leaving Merrick and Laurent to both immediately turn their attention to me.

Great.

"Well, let's hear the verdict. But if you're still considering that it would be easier to kill me—let me tell you that Sparrow is *very* attached to this furniture, so we'll need to move the fight outside," I purred, locking eyes with Merrick. Gargoyles were territorial, and I'd seen enough of them go to blows over the stupidest things.

Merrick slouched further into the floor pouf before scowling at me, and I couldn't help but poke him a little more. "Can't get off the pouf?" I asked sweetly, pouting my lips at him, but it was Laurent who spoke first.

"Do you love Keerian?" Laurent asked, his expression unreadable aside from the hard glint in his emerald eyes. His power thrummed through the room, the flames in the fireplace turning from red and orange to ice blue. I leaned back further into the couch, sloshing the dregs of tea in my wine glass. If he was trying to intimidate me, he'd need to do a lot better than that. I knew all about the ferocious Spy Master, and he knew very little about me. I met his stare and held eye contact. I wouldn't back down. I was surprised at his question, but then again, I had one week with my mate before being forcibly separated for a year. Laurent and Merrick had known Keerian for almost a century.

Turning a horn towards Laurent, I debated opening myself up to him. I could recount events emotionlessly, but admitting my one weakness was Keerian...

I answered, albeit quietly, "Yes."

Merrick cut in, "Are you fighting for the integrity of the throne? Or for retribution against Adara?"

"Does it matter?" I snapped back to the gargoyle, before nodding to Laurent. "I love my mate, and I'd do anything to get him back, even if that includes taking the throne."

That seemed to be good enough for Laurent, because he rolled his shoulders back and grunted, "Why didn't Keerian tell us about you before?" I swore a flicker of hurt crossed his face and I couldn't help wishing that Keerian and I had more time... Time to meet his friends, build relationships, be together.

I missed my mate.

And I missed my parents. We rarely saw eye to eye, especially since I never embraced the lifestyle of a well-behaved Princess, but I loved them, and my heart ached from the void their deaths left.

Merrick added, after an unwieldy attempt at getting off the floor pillow–which I openly smirked at, knowing I got under his skin a little, "I want to know that too. He's our best friend, and you even said you had a feeling you were mates before Carra's ceremony."

I knew these questions were coming, and part of me was glad. If we were getting into the nuanced personal shit now, it meant they believed I didn't murder the King and Queen. But still—my heart hurt. My mate was out there, in my sister's clutches, and every second we wasted going over these stupid questions was another second that I was on edge, braced, waiting for the pain and agony of my soul tie breaking.

"We didn't tell anyone." I put the wine glass down gently on the wooden coffee table, aligning it so that the rim fit perfectly around a small painted flower petal I knew Sparrow added to the table after she found this rickety thing on the side of the street and announced she'd bring it back to life. Now, brightly painted plants decorated the tabletop, all painstakingly detailed by my friend.

I stood up, getting a small slice of satisfaction as both males scrambled to their feet and regarded me warily. "I had my suspicions of Adara since she told me she found that godsdamn spell book. She saw me as a threat." I blew out a rough breath. "So, she resorted to cheap shots and ugly tricks to get a foothold closer to my own power. When I met Keerian, I wanted to keep our infatuation with each other secret, and when the soul tie bloomed, I saw Adara's expression. I had no shields up—she very easily could've taken us both out in one shot."

"I hope you forgive me for all of the questions." Laurent rubbed his palms together, turning to face the warm fire in the fireplace. The flames had licked down to their natural hues, the wood popping and crackling. "But this morning, I woke up in a cave in the Pyritee Pass, with my fealty pledged to Queen Adara, and by dinner time...I am realizing just how blind I was. It's...hard to admit I—we—were so wrong."

I took a step forward, realizing what he was implying, as Laurent finished slowly, "I would still prefer Lenna use the Prism to look into some of the details herself—maybe she can see a better image of whatever spell Adara is working on. But I no longer feel as if you will slit my throat while I sleep."

I gave him a nod and a tight smile before slicing my eyes to the gargoyle standing to him. Merrick merely grumbled, "I hate to admit it, but I believed you the moment you allowed me to hear your conversation with Resso. I just wanted to know your side of the story." He extended his hand. I clasped his forearm as he mirrored the grip, the calluses on his palm rough against my skin. "Gargoyle loyalties are black and white. If Keerian likes you, that's good enough for me."

CHAPTER THIRTY
ESMERAY

I HAD TO ADMIT this all went *far* better than I anticipated. Sparrow breezed back into the living room, carrying a crate of red wine I knew was as old as myself. Lenna, trailing behind her, held a few more wine glasses for the rest of the group, seeming much more at ease around Sparrow.

Sparrow had that effect on every being she met. I didn't know if it was some part of her magic, or just the combination of her sweet face and bubbly personality, but it seemed a small trip down to her wine cellar had given her time to listen to Lenna's fears, and assuage any concerns the Oracle expressed.

Gods, Lenna was a seer, too.

Lenna had gone back to sit on her pouf after Sparrow poured each of us a glass of wine, but Sparrow patted the spot next to her and announced the couch was now females only, and the males could sit on the poufs. Lenna smiled at that, the fine lines around her eyes crinkling. Merrick told me she was fifty-one, which was apparently considered middle-aged in the Slate Kingdom.

I told him when I was fifty-one, I got in trouble with my father for using illusion magic to turn my hairbrush into a dagger because I wanted to learn how to wield one.

Before Lenna and Sparrow rejoined us, Merrick offered up brief snippets on how he found Lenna. I was surprised he'd been able to track her at all, but Merrick admitted that part was all Laurent. The ex-Spy Master hadn't looked particularly pleased Merrick offered up that tidbit, so I stored that kernel of knowledge away for later. Any being that could track magic was considered rare, and that was a fabulous quality to have in my corner.

The ease that we fell into conversation surprised me, but on more than one occasion, my pulse raced and my palms became sweaty. After ninety years of weighing every word and half-truth spoken and weaving through court politics, sitting on a purple couch with my dearest friend and Keerian's closest friends was...overstimulating.

I listened more than talked, my heart panging whenever Laurent or Merrick mentioned Keerian. My mate was out there, and our short time together could end at any moment if Adara figured out that transfer spell. I missed him, I needed him.

The week after our soul tie was cemented had been the happiest week of my life. We'd flown together through the forest, finding a secluded spot by a waterfall to land. I'd looked out at that beautiful view breathlessly before my mate kissed me deeply, our tongues exploring, his hands fisted in my hair, and I threw my arms around his tanned neck.

Keerian had hoisted me up, flown us to the top of the waterfall, and we consummated our soul tie right then and there, on the mossy bank overlooking the tumbling water.

That week we lived in Sparrow's house, gods bless her, she found many an excuse to stay away. Keerian and I hadn't been able to keep our hands off each other. The thought of him buried deep inside me, stroking me to that point where it felt like we were tumbling off that waterfall into bliss...

The edginess I felt was caused by the lack of him.

"Esmeray." Sparrow's sharp voice cut through my thoughts, and I raised an eyebrow at her. She probably knew exactly where my mind had wandered because her voice changed and she said softly, "We will get him back."

I averted my gaze, my throat tight. Merrick and Laurent exchanged a look as I stood up and announced I was going to fly. Sparrow nodded. I needed to blow off steam before I could even consider laying down.

"Lenna, I put some night clothes in the bedroom for you if you want to get some rest." Sparrow turned to me as Lenna departed the room, covering her mouth with a hand as a yawn overtook her. "I'm going to lay out some clothes for you too, Meer. I still have your bedroom ready."

I stretched out my wings. Flying was one of my favorite activities, and after the day I had, shit, after this whole year, I needed to launch into the sky and wear myself out. Plus, I had a hunch on what waited for me outside of this house, and wanted to confirm if my suspicions were correct. Or if I was being too paranoid for my own good.

I scooped up two bottles of wine, nonchalantly slipping them into the air next to me. My illusion magic had been difficult to learn when I first received my power–since no one in history had ever received the type of magic I did–but one perk I found early on was the ability to store things in a weird little pocket of space. To anyone who didn't have my type of magic, it would look like the bottles disappeared into thin air, but whenever I called upon it, I could see the pocket shimmering, and beyond it, a small rock alcove that was mine. It made it much easier to swipe Sparrow's good wine out from under her nose.

Merrick rolled awkwardly off the pouf, before hopping up and flaring out his grey scaled wings. "Mind if I join you? I need to get some fresh air, or I won't be able to sleep." I agreed, even though I felt like a small part of his request was due to me being Keerian's mate and he now felt the need to protect me. Or Merrick wanted to keep an eye on my behavior.

I grimaced internally. One night of me admitting my side of the story probably did not erase the years that I terrorized the Opal Palace with an array of pranks and complete dismissal of my duties as Princess. Still, I led him through the house and up the pink and purple painted stairs to the small patio on the roof.

This was my favorite spot in Sparrow's house. We decorated it together years ago after one of my more explosive fights with my mother about the training I'd, once again, been caught doing. I had promptly waned out of the Opal Palace and came straight here. Sparrow had been living by herself for over a decade at that point, and took one look at my face before deciding we needed to redecorate the patio.

Now, two low backed chairs leaned against a small half wall that Sparrow built flower beds into. Numerous days had been spent on those chairs–me sunning my wings, Sparrow sunning her body–while we shared the good, the bad, and the ugly dealings of court life.

Wooden slats painted a soft green lined the floor, save for two circular areas in opposite corners where Sparrow added bird baths. But my favorite part was the thin strings of lights we added to two posts above the half wall. At night, we would light them and sit out here for hours, sometimes in silence, sometimes with a bottle of wine, roaring in laughter, soaking in the view around us.

Sparrow's home was in a residential district in the city of Florra, one of the lesser known jewels of the Obsidian Kingdom. Although it was a smaller city than those closer to the Palace, its charm and color had always drawn a more eclectic type. Surrounding the city, waterfalls, lush forests, and a distant mountain range blended together.

Merrick whistled low as he surveyed our surroundings. He told me on the walk up the steps that he'd never been in Florra, but that if it was anything like Sparrow's home, he would love it. I smiled at that but said nothing—especially because I always thought of Florra as my home more than the Palaces I grew up in. Hearing him echo that sentiment... I knew that feeling, so similar to when Sparrow and I first came here—like anything was possible in this charmed, peaceful place that captured hearts.

I unfurled my wings, feeling the cool night breeze trail across them. Next to me, Merrick did the same, sighing, as he reveled in the chill. "Follow me," I said innocently before launching into the sky with a swift movement. He whooped and barreled over the ledge of the patio, reaching my altitude in two pumps. I leveled out, letting him catch up, as I lazily glided through a bolstered draft that rolled off the far away mountain range. Merrick shouted over the roar of the wind, "I'll go slow, sweetheart, so you can keep up."

Oh, no. Challenge on.

I shot him a wicked grin before lurching higher into the sky, rolling out into a straight nosedive as I searched for an updraft to ride. I heard him curse as I dropped low, and before he could collect himself enough to speed up, I found what I needed. As fast as a loosened arrow, I shot out straight towards Florra's dense forest with an exhilarated shriek, my black wings sleeker and more agile than his, giving me a massive advantage.

Merrick furiously tried to catch me, but I raced on, more nimble than a falcon, past the sleeping city, towards the twelve waterfalls churning mist into the air on the outskirts of the city.

As the largest finally came into view, its tumbling water crushing the sleek rocks below, I landed gracefully on the lip of the falls, perching precariously on a slick-with-moss stone that time and condensation warped flat, waiting on a defeated Merrick. My eyes traveled down to the base of the waterfall, where a winding river dumped into the sea beyond the coast.

He landed a few moments later, his chest rising and falling rapidly, though I watched him fight to keep his breathing even. I gave him a simpering look. "That's for calling me '*sweetheart.*'"

Merrick rolled his eyes, "Well, what should I call you then?"

"My Queen," I replied simply before leaning back, spreading my arms wide, and plummeting towards the river below.

CHAPTER THIRTY-ONE
MERRICK

MERRICK BARELY HAD A beat to catch his breath before Esmeray vaulted over the edge of the falls, her midnight wings tucked tight at her side. He yelled in panic, the stitch in his side causing it to come out more like a garbled gasp, as his best friend's mate plunged towards the sharp rock outcropping at the base of the waterfall. He scrambled to the lip, falling to his knees when his feet slipped dangerously against the moss, searching for Esmeray amongst the silvery mist. He watched her snap her wings out a second before she dashed against the stones, shooting up perfectly parallel to the barreling waterfall, landing lightly at his side.

"You are fucking *insane*," Merrick panted, leaning back and resting his palms on his knees as he fought to calm his racing heart.

She grinned at him, her bright eyes sparkling like the stars dotting the sky above them. "I had no one to teach me aerial maneuvers." Nonchalantly, she ran her fingers through the hair caught in the spiral of her horns, shaking the strands away from the curl until they cascaded down her back once more. "After a few tried and failed attempts, I learned that the air coming off a waterfall is a great training exercise to hone agility—especially with the pressure off the initial plummet. You should try it."

"I've trained as a soldier my entire life," Merrick retorted flatly, straightening and flexing his wings out. "I've outflown every other gargoyle in my legion. Why do you think your father chose me for his King's Guard? Because I'm pretty?"

"Then it should be easy for you, oh grand King's Guard," Esmeray goaded, showing off perfectly white teeth with those slightly lengthened fangs that fae possessed—just a tad longer and sharper than Merrick's own gargoyle canines. She gestured to the waterfall. "Just jump. And spread your wings to catch the wind at the last second. See if you can shoot straight up and land...here." She toed an "X" against the moss with her boot, making a target.

Merrick sighed roughly. He *was* being serious—the King had indeed seen Merrick's flying abilities as tactical, and Merrick trained countless other gargoyles to fly as well as he did.

And here was this saucy little Queen explaining to him the best way to leap off a waterfall. "Fine."

"*Fine.*"

Merrick advanced closer to the edge, swallowing down a snide remark, before backing up three paces. With a battle cry that woke half the birds nesting in the woods behind him, he took a running jump and free fell. The world tipped on its axis as Merrick was buffeted by the strong pressure of wind coming off the waterfall, and he swore as he flipped his wings up and launched skyward, nowhere near the straight trajectory Esmeray displayed annoyingly effortlessly. Backflapping hard to stop himself from careening into the tree branches on the opposite bank, knowing he'd never hear the end of it, he cursed again, filthier this time—a word he left for special occasions...like getting his King's Guard warrior ass handed to him. Still swearing, he glided back over to a ridiculously gleeful Esmeray.

"Show me again," he growled.

She obliged, thankfully, without saying a word of his failed attempt–even though she did add a degree more pomp to her "lesson" as she twirled over the edge.

He watched her fall, memorized the angle, the twist of her body, how she used her wings to fall faster–but as more of a counterweight. And finally–the way she snapped her wings open, riding the gust that rose over the rocks before she shot up again and landed right next to him on the "X" pressed into the thick moss.

She bowed.

Merrick felt a muscle jump in his jaw. "I'm going to figure out how you did that. I'm trying again."

It took him six more embarrassingly failed attempts before he managed a decently straight shot into the sky, and eight more after that to perfect it. Esmeray had taken the opportunity as he either crash landed next to her or disentangled himself out of various trees to sit on a rock and give him offhand pointers while using magic to grow and shape her nails.

"That one was much better." Esmeray gave him a look of approval as she tapped her now three-inch long, dagger-sharp, black fingernails against her horn, testing their strength.

"It's not as easy as it looks. I'll be the bigger male and admit you may have bested me at waterfall jumping," Merrick ground out, hands on his hips. With no proper flight training, she was already faster than him *and* more agile. Gods, why *hadn't* her father trained her as a warrior? She would have run circles around the gargoyles in the aerial legion.

His questions must have shown on his face because she climbed down off the rock she had been lounging on, the starlight above illuminating their surroundings gently. She moved to the grassy edge of the waterfall and sat, legs swinging over the rim. He stepped to her side and eased down next to her, still picking small pieces of bark and tree needles out of his hair.

"I know you were stationed at the Opal Palace, but the male that trained you, honed you as a weapon, and encouraged you as a warrior was not the same male I dealt with growing up. My father was...strict with me. Moreso than he was with Adara. When my magic began to show, he was ecstatic to continue his lineage—as any fae would be when their child was born to a gargoyle mother. But when he realized my gifts were given by a different god than his, he did not take the news well."

Merrick pulled blades of grass out of the earthy ground and let them drift over the waterfall, watching as they disappeared into the billowy mist below. "Your fae lineage had gifts from the God of Water, Beyos, right?"

Esmeray hummed, "I don't have a drop of water magic in me."

"Does Adara?"

"Yes, she does, and if we weren't twins...my mother's virtue would have been called into question." Esmeray waved her hand in the air, and two bottles of wine appeared with a soft thump in the grass between them. She took one and ripped the cork out with her sharp canine. Merrick stared at the wine bottle.

"Is that an illusionist thing? You can just conjure up alcohol?"

Esmeray smirked, "I can open pockets in our realm—I don't know any use for that other than a magical type of storage. But it takes the edge off the strain of me not wielding my full powers just carrying around a few invisible bottles of wine for a couple hours. I put them in there before we left Sparrow's house." Her pale skin seemed to glow under the stars as she tilted her head up, and Merrick began understanding why Keerian had fallen in love with her so quickly. She was stunningly gorgeous in a wicked and dark way, but much more complex than the roles she played at the Opal and Obsidian Palaces.

They sat in a comfortable silence as the minutes passed.

"I never spoke to you while you were Princess of the Opal Palace." Merrick hadn't ever said a word to her. All of the elite warriors–Keerian included–had been expressly ordered by their King to never associate with either Princess.

"I was a real peach back then," Esmeray said sarcastically, raising the bottle to her lips and taking a swig.

Merrick laughed, grabbing the bottle of wine from her as she let out a screech of indignation. He chugged it for a beat before handing it back.

"I was a spoiled Princess with no real friends except my sister for the first decade of my life. Honestly, I blame Sparrow–after her family came to court, she and I really started causing trouble."

"Sparrow was at court? I never saw her," Merrick stuttered. Esmeray must have caught how quickly the words tumbled out of his mouth because she gave him a smug grin.

"She was, but by the time my father put together the King's Guard you were on, she'd already moved to Florra. Court life wasn't the life she wanted to live." Esmeray sighed and leaned back, her tattooed arm bracing her as she took another generous swig of wine. "To be honest, it's not the life I wanted, either."

Merrick understood that all too well. His father had dumped him at the Obsidian Palace gates, leaving him to either pass the grueling training to become a warrior or die trying.

He turned to Esmeray to tell her that he sympathized, when Esmeray launched to her feet, the abrupt move making the wine bottle clatter and roll off the lip of the waterfall. Merrick paid no attention to the alcohol falling to the watery depths as Esmeray flared her wings and let out a snarl to the dark tree line at their backs.

CHAPTER THIRTY-TWO
ESMERAY

I wondered how long it would take Adara's cronies to track me down. I put on a grand enough performance at the Obsidian Palace to royally piss her off, and I was honestly a little disappointed it took this much time for her spies to catch up. Flying over Florra, I knew she would figure out where I was staying. She seemed to have eyes and ears in every city these days, tracking my every move.

"What's—*what's going on*?" Merrick hissed, narrowing his eyes and scrambling to his feet, unclipping two jagged daggers from his belt.

I could hear them now, slowly creeping through the trees. Their scent had wafted over me moments ago when I tasted the tang of arrogance—and something sharp and dark.

"Adara sent me a little present," I whispered to him, my fae senses counting the bodies as they began sliding between the trees into my enhanced sight.

Merrick cursed at my side, and his fingers must have touched the ring that connected him to Laurent, letting him know what was happening, because I felt Keerian's ring heat between my breasts. I only smiled as the first three gargoyles came into view.

This is only the beginning of my retribution for you—for us. I let Keerian's face enter my mind—his warm, moss-green eyes, his rough brown beard with those lightning bolts of red running through it, his square jaw...the way he smiled at me and kissed me, long and deep, on the patio of Sparrow's home. How he bent me over that rock and fucked me senseless—the same rock where I just finished fashioning my nails into throat slitting daggers.

I took a step closer.

Seven more gargoyles slinked out from the trees, confirmation I had chosen my spot well. They couldn't have flown in at us because the forest was too dense. The waterfall I chose was perfect for Adara's cronies thinking they caught us off guard with nowhere to flee. But unluckily for them, they discredited my fae senses—the roiling of the air being pushed off the waterfall alerted me to their presence far faster. And I had just taught Merrick a fun battle tactic they would never see coming.

The gargoyles formed a single line, shoulder to shoulder, drawing their swords in sync. The one in the middle stepped forward. "The Queen of Nothing—" he started.

I cut him off.

"Yuck. Did you know, I wasn't privy to the conversation where Adara decided my new title would be Queen of *Nothing*? If I had, I would've chosen a much cooler name for my exile. But, you know how she is...so uncreative." I cut Merrick a look that I hoped he read as '*stay out of my way.*'

The soldier ignored me. "Queen Adara has sent us to collect you to await judgement for the heinous murders of the Oracle, King Scottrell, and Queen Elera."

"Well, that's going to be a problem," I purred lightly, inspecting the gleam of my newly sharpened nails in the faint moonlight. "There's only ten of you."

Another gargoyle sneered, "Ten highly skilled soldiers dedicated to our Queen Absolute versus the Queen of Nothing and her traitorous sidekick? I like those odds."

Oh, I would rip his throat out first.

"I do too," I breathed, baring my teeth as I unleashed every ounce of my pent-up magic and rage at them.

CHAPTER THIRTY-THREE

MERRICK

One moment, Esmeray stood beside him, taunting ten highly trained gargoyle warriors. Merrick had been calculating the launch behind–down the waterfall. Questioning why she didn't just grab him and wane back to Sparrow's. The next moment, she struck as fast as a snake, launching a wave of golden light at their opponents. Three went down immediately as it blasted them apart limb by limb. While his mind had been focused on fleeing, the Queen was certainly not having that same thought.

She waned to Adara's warriors in the blink of an eye. Merrick caught another flash of gold as her staff appeared in her hand. With deadly accuracy, she whipped the staff towards two more soldiers, and they died where they stood. Her tattooed hand–ending in those deadly nails–slashed across the throat of the next male, his choking cut short as she blasted a hole through his face. Merrick stared, dumbfounded, by the lethal fluidity Esmeray fought with, and was almost caught off guard by two soldiers using the ensuing pandemonium to corner him with his back to the waterfall.

The closest one died first–with Merrick's dagger through his eye. The dying soldier lashed out, kicking at Merrick's shin, causing him to stumble back a step. The second gargoyle used the opportunity to slash his sword. Merrick dodged, parrying with his remaining dagger.

Fuck, why didn't he bring his sword with him?

Merrick's stance slipped, and he instantly realized how close to falling off the waterfall he was. But as he blocked the soldier's sword again, his foot landed on the "X" Esmeray had made in the moss. With a snarl, he realized exactly what Esmeray had been doing while he'd been perfecting waterfall jumping.

Bolstered with rage and wild abandon, Merrick allowed his opponent to push him closer to the edge, and Merrick fell–down, down, the spray of water now a familiar friend as he twisted, swept his wings up and around and launched skyward–perfectly straight. The warrior didn't even have time to process his impending death as Merrick drove the full length of his dagger into the gargoyle's skull.

CHAPTER THIRTY-FOUR
ESMERAY

I LEFT TWO FOR Merrick to finish off, and watched proudly as he shot up from the waterfall to kill the last of Adara's cronies. As the body slumped, wings crumpling, I slid my staff back into its pocket of space and crossed the trampled grass over to Merrick. The strain of magic I'd been carrying and building for the last couple days finally eased, and I already felt clearer headed, the incessant ache satiated.

Merrick didn't seem as relaxed as I was—I could tell by the glare.

"Did you *lure* those soldiers here as some sort of fucked up *bonding experience* for us?"

Oh yeah, he was fuming.

"No," I said truthfully, "I had a feeling Adara would send some band of assholes our way after I knocked our uncle's pride down several pegs, but I didn't know when or where they would show up. I smelled them coming, and gave you ample warning."

"You had a *feeling* they were tracking you here," Merrick's fuming turned to flat out pissed.

I nodded, wiping the soldier's blood off my nails onto my red leather top. "I'd much rather they try something here than at Sparrow's."

"What if Adara sends more?" Merrick rubbed his face, blood from his hands coating the sides of his cheeks. It took him a moment to register that he now had gore in his beard, and his expression scrunched in disgust.

I looked up at the moon, now fully risen above us, completely uncaring of the battle that was fought below it. I thought back to what Keerian said to me on the last night we had together–*the moon will always guide us back to each other*.

My sister knew she sent those males to their death, and *I* knew she wasn't losing any sleep over it. "She won't–for a while. If Adara really wanted to lock me up she would've sent way more than ten gargoyles. Did you notice how not a single fae was in that pack?"

Merrick blew out a long, rough breath, trudging over to the remaining wine bottle. The fight had pushed it against a tree, half hidden by the longer grasses around the edge of the forest. He ripped the cork out and drank deep before shaking his head in disbelief. "She's toying with you?"

"I think my uncle was displeased with the general lack of respect I showed his court earlier, and Adara sent those gargoyles as a halfhearted slap on my wrist to appease him." I reached for the wine bottle. Merrick scowled and took another drag before he handed it over. I tipped the bottle back, taking a swallow, the wine burning as it settled in my stomach.

"I will never understand court politics. Adara knew you could easily kill all ten of those males and sent them anyway. She saw them as disposable." The deadpan look in Merrick's eyes made my heart hurt for him.

"I don't think a single gargoyle life is disposable," I noted firmly, "and it's one of the hundreds of reasons I never wanted to rule. I don't want to hold beings' lives in my hands–gargoyle, fae or human. I don't want to explain to parents, friends, why their loved one died, why a mate dropped dead as their lover fought and died in someone else's war. But I will not take the fall for a crime I didn't commit, and I won't pull my punches and risk Keerian's rescue."

Merrick squeezed his eyes shut. "I've fought in many battles and it never gets easier."

"It's not supposed to." I handed the half empty bottle back to him. "But if I have to fight, I'd want you by my side since you nailed that waterfall jump."

Merrick looked at me incredulously for a beat before tipping his head back, roaring with laughter. "I can't believe I tried to kill you this morning."

I chuckled, one of the first times in months, finally understanding why my mate pushed me to find his friends if everything went to shit.

"Let's fly back to Sparrow's house." I nudged his wing with mine. "I think I can finally get some sleep now."

Merrick's brown eyes, which had been so heavy moments before, lit up. "I'll race you there."

And then he launched off the waterfall, disappearing from view. He let out a raucous whoop as he soared up in a perfectly straight line, shooting out of the trees and into the open sky.

I DIDN'T LET HIM win.

As I touched down on the patio, I came face to face with Laurent and a very pale Sparrow who took one look at my blood covered clothes and pursed her lips into a flat line of disapproval, eyes flaring.

"I thought we agreed no fighting in Florra."

"*Technically,*" Merrick corrected, landing behind me, "We were defending ourselves."

Sparrow appraised him with a '*look*' only she could give. I don't know how she mastered it. The slight raise of her brows, the narrowing of her blue eyes, the tightness in her mouth. It was the epitome of '*sit the fuck down and shut the fuck up.*' I had seen males cower before that look for years. Merrick gave her a wide grin–seemingly unaffected.

Interesting.

Merrick recanted our evening at the waterfall, and lucky Laurent and Sparrow even got a blow-by-blow summary of how Merrick waterfall jumped to land the final killing blow. Sparrow seemed to be half listening, more *tsk*-ing over Merrick and I dripping blood on her patio. With a sweep of her dainty wrist, the gore disappeared from the both of us. Merrick whistled, taking in his clean clothes. "Neat trick."

Sparrow bristled but addressed me. "I ran you *both* baths and laid out clothes for you–and don't even *think* of getting into bed before you wash up. I cleaned the blood off, but you both still smell like death." Her nose crinkled.

Laurent had stayed silent since our return, but his eyes kept straying to Sparrow standing there, arms crossed, in a baby blue fluffy robe cut right at mid-thigh–giving both males a view of her long, golden legs. She may have been miffed that I got into another fight, but she damn sure had her eyes on Laurent.

Or Merrick.

Or both.

And my antics wouldn't stop her from her hunt.

And with that cringing thought, I dismissed myself to the bathroom where I soaked in the tub for a long time.

CHAPTER THIRTY-FIVE
MERRICK

MERRICK WISTFULLY WATCHED ESMERAY slink off since Sparrow now blocked the door with her arms crossed and a snarl on her face. She waited until Esmeray's footsteps disappeared before whirling on him, speaking low and quickly about her house rules. Most of them revolved around a common theme of keeping Esmeray out of trouble, such as, *"Don't let Esmeray instigate any more fights,"* and, *"Never drip blood on the living room rugs,"* as if she already knew rule number one would be broken again.

So, Merrick stood there and took the verbal lashing the petite fae female launched on Laurent and himself. All the while imagining what Sparrow looked like under that delicious robe.

Laurent, hands clasped behind his back, concentrated intently on every word Sparrow spat at them. After Sparrow had run out of rules–deemed by her stuttering and just jabbing her finger at them over and over, Laurent smoothly held out his arm and asked if he could bother her for one more glass of wine, steering her towards the stairs and initiating a conversation that involved his burning questions regarding a particularly exotic plant he spied on the bookshelf in her living room.

"Kiss ass." Merrick shot through his ring as Laurent guided Sparrow away.

Laurent turned his head ever so slightly and shot a sly wink in Merrick's direction.

Once he was alone on the patio, Merrick took his leave to the bedroom Sparrow assigned him. The room was small, yet cozy, with a bed just large enough to fit a gargoyle. A smattering of plump pillows with floral patterns and the soft greens of the bed sheets beckoned. Merrick forced himself away, fearing the wrath of the beautiful fae that had expressly forbade him to lay down until he washed up. Merrick tucked his wings tight as he slid past a low dresser and into the bathroom. The tub steamed, aromas of jasmine and something woodsy filling the room.

Gods, help him.

She put oils in his bath.

Merrick made quick work of unbuckling his sword belt and shucking off his leathers. With a groan at the muscle-relaxing heat, he lowered his body into the tub and leaned his head back, trying to force his mind to slow down so he could process the day.

Esmeray was nothing like he expected. The wicked, traitorous, blood thirsty monster Adara led two Kingdoms of beings to believe lurked in every shadow waiting to make another kill was, in reality, one of the most fierce, badass, loyal females Merrick had ever met. It was apparent Esmeray didn't care how the world portrayed her, and would *lean into* the role of the villain if it meant it got her closer to getting Keerian back. She took him waterfall jumping for gods' sake. Esmeray had sat and listened to him express his feelings and didn't mock him for it, only supported him. And then took down eight of Adara's soldiers *easily*. There were so many similarities Merrick saw between her and Keerian that Merrick knew Carra made the perfect match.

If the world ever got to see it, King Keerian and Queen Esmeray had a nice ring to it.

CHAPTER THIRTY-SIX

LAURENT

THE SUN HAD JUST begun peeking over the horizon as Laurent stared out towards the city of Florra, sipping coffee on the patio at the top of Sparrow's eclectic home.

He had barely slept. The events from the last few days were culminating quickly, and Laurent worried that Lenna using the Prism would expedite whatever end they were careening towards. Laurent inhaled through his nose, reminding himself there was nothing he could do until Lenna awoke. Shifting his weight on his feet, he bit down on his inner cheek, trying to soothe the nerves fraying under his skin. Taking another deep breath, he turned his attention to the garden below.

A smattering of brightly plumed birds clustered around feeders, eager for seeds before spending their day weaving between the thick forest surrounding the city. Blue fluffy movement caught Laurent's eye as Sparrow, still in that delectable robe, refilled each feeder, crooning to the birds and the plants surrounding her.

Laurent couldn't take his eyes off her—the way her golden hair, mussed from sleep, framed her angular face, the curve of her hips, the golden legs that ended in little gem encrusted silk slippers. He knew he wasn't her only option. That the gargoyle he considered his best friend also showed interest in Sparrow.

At this point, the ball was in Sparrow's court. He'd respect her decision if she chose Merrick to take to bed over himself.

But...

Last night, over that final glass of wine, she opened up to him about her past. And he had listened, his heart hurting for hers. She told him about her youth—a story filled with death and despair, loneliness and isolation. Sparrow told Laurent of how she came to the Opal Palace with her parents, how she established such a tight-knit friendship with Esmeray, how Esmeray had been her one true friend.

It painted a different version of Esmeray to Laurent, one he knew Merrick must have been privy to at the waterfall as he fought alongside the Queen. A version that the Kingdoms of Irridessen hadn't smeared with the labels *traitor* and *murderer*.

And when Sparrow's words became softer, her voice huskier, when she finally started dozing on her purple couch, Laurent gently scooped her into his arms and carried Sparrow to her bedroom, laying her down gently on pink pastel sheets, before closing the door and walking down the hall to his own room.

He wondered if she knew he carried her to bed.

As if she could hear his brooding down in the garden, Sparrow turned, beamed at him, and waved enthusiastically. Laurent smiled tightly and awkwardly waved back, ripping his mind from how soft her skin felt against his hands. A flash of green light and Sparrow was standing next to him on the patio.

"Good morning." Her sweet voice sounded like a hundred silver bells as she appeared next to him, taking a sip out of her coffee mug. "I believe I have you to thank for getting me in bed last night."

Laurent inclined his head towards hers. "Sleeping on that couch didn't seem right when all of your guests have their own bedrooms." Around Sparrow, his worries melted away, making him feel lighter than he had in a long time.

Was it only a few days ago he'd been crammed in that tiny house in Spinella, sapping out his energy to build a portal?

Was it that recently that he slept on rocks in the Pyritee Pass–utterly burnt out after pushing through that portal?

She laughed, her aqua-blue eyes twinkling as she squeezed his arm. "You are such a wonderful male." Sparrow clinked her mug to his as Merrick came into view, cresting the top of the stairs. Laurent felt his jaw clench in annoyance–Merrick was *shirtless*. Laurent sliced his eyes at Sparrow, who had raised her mug to her lips, where it was frozen, as she took in Merrick and every single one of his bronzed abs. Laurent softly cleared his throat, snapping her out of whatever trance she'd been in. Sniffing delicately, Sparrow took a long slug of coffee, the tips of her pointed ears burning red.

"Mornin'." Merrick smirked, before taking in both of their coffee mugs. "Damn, I didn't grab a cup." He frowned for a second but then shot Laurent a sneaky look. "Let's see if this works." Merrick rubbed his golden ring and Laurent touched his, wondering what Merrick was up to. Merrick sent a thought down the connection. *"Esmeray, can you please bring me up a cup of coffee to the patio?"*

Laurent grinned. "She's probably pissed she can't talk back to tell you to get fucked."

And Laurent was right. Esmeray appeared a couple moments later, her black hair tousled, strands caught in the curl of her horns like she just pulled herself out of bed. She wore a black silk shirt with matching shorts and atrociously bright pink slippers. But she held two coffee mugs in her hands, passing one to Merrick with a scowl. "Get fucked, and get it yourself next time," she hissed–making the two males burst out laughing.

"Love the shoes, Meer." Merrick saluted her with his mug.

"I couldn't find my black ones," Esmeray grumbled, "and *who* told you about calling me '*Meer*'?"

Sparrow grinned sheepishly, her golden hair blowing gently in the early morning breeze. "Whoops–that was me."

"Great," Esmeray said darkly but her green eyes sparkled with mirth. "Is Lenna awake yet?"

Sparrow shook her head. "Not yet, but let her sleep a little longer. I'm sure these next couple weeks will take a toll on us all. Just...let her rest while she can."

Esmeray conceded with minimal huffing, slumping dramatically onto one of the patio chairs, stretching her wings behind her to catch the first warmth of the new day. Patience did not seem to be a strong talent of the fearsome Queen, and Laurent's lips quirked into a smile at the thought. Keerian was the most patient male in the world, so seeing his mate practically buzzing with the need to do *something* other than sitting still made Laurent miss his friend with a fierceness.

"We need her diving into the Prism right away. I don't want to wait any longer and allow Adara more time to figure out what we're up to. And I don't know what *she* already knows, and that in itself is dangerous."

Laurent spoke up. "I can help with that. I've dealt with magical objects before–maybe some of my past knowledge can be beneficial. If we get started today, hopefully we can gather some answers and figure out a plan."

"Sounds good to me," Esmeray yawned. "What are you up to today, Sparrow?"

Sparrow took the seat next to her friend, setting her coffee mug on the table between them. "I'm going into town to grab some groceries. I thought it would be nice to make dinner tonight at the house. And I want to see what the townsfolk are rumbling about. Florra may be a small town, but the beings here are perfectly nosy and always willing to gossip. Maybe it can give us some insight into Adara's movement. Plus, then we can have a nice meal while we unravel what our next steps should be."

Merrick and Laurent murmured their agreement, and Laurent choked back a groan of delight at the thought of Sparrow cooking. He loved to cook, though he rarely had the time, or a permanent enough place, to cook to his heart's desire.

Esmeray hummed as she took a sip of coffee. They were silent for a long while, taking in the sights and sounds of the morning. Birds chirped below in the garden, the sun shone warmly down on them, the smell of coffee and flowers filled the air. Sparrow smiled as she watched a few birds land at a feeder. Laurent couldn't take her eyes off her and reflected on what she told him last night. He understood now why she was so full of life, so in tune with nature—for a long time she'd been cut off from both.

And in the stillness, with the tranquil morning breaking around them, Laurent wondered how many more of these quiet, peaceful moments they would share.

Chapter Thirty-Seven
Lenna

The cheery singing of songbirds gently roused Lenna from sleep. As she came to her senses, the lilac walls of the bedroom greeted her, the smell of coffee making her realize that the rest of the house was already awake. She swallowed and sighed, her dry throat being the biggest push to get out from under the soft, floral sheets.

Lenna sat up, stretching legs that were still sore from the walking she'd done yesterday through Pyritee Pass. The delicate nightgown hugging her thick curves that Sparrow rustled up seemed too scandalous to trot around the house in, so Lenna crawled out of bed, grabbing a silky robe that hung on the door.

In the washroom, Lenna tried and failed to get her curls under control before giving up. They were frizzy, dry, and completely irritated with her lack of care towards them over the last few days. With a choice word to her hair's reflection in the mirror, Lenna padded barefoot out of the bedroom, making a beeline towards the beckoning aroma of coffee.

No one was in the whimsical kitchen as she entered, giving her a chance to look around at her leisure and take in Sparrow's decorating. Bright green cabinets, adorned with mismatched iron and porcelain knobs, covered one side of the kitchen, the other displaying a collection of intricately painted pottery sitting on narrow wooden shelves. The bright colors bounced off pristine, white marble countertops where an array of glass jars held an assortment of spices–but one larger jar contained some sort of swirling silver fog. Lenna peered closer, transfixed, until the undulating wisps seemed to notice her attention. It stopped moving immediately, transforming with a soft, indignant *puff*, into a white power that settled at the bottom of the container.

Lenna wondered if that went into any specific food or drink. Part of her wanted to ask Sparrow what it was out of curiosity, but another part seemed hesitant to know.

Lenna's search for a coffee mug was blissfully quick, since one already sat out by the coffee pot, the brew inside steaming. Pouring a generous amount into her cup, Lenna strained her ears to pick up any sounds that would point her in the direction of where the rest of the group was. A quick peek out the window to the front yard confirmed that Sparrow and her assortment of houseguests were probably on the rooftop patio. With a wince, Lenna moved towards the stairs, already anticipating the burning in her sore legs.

Cresting the last steps, her muscles groaning in protest, she did indeed find the group. Sparrow and Esmeray were reclined back on patio chairs, the latter's eyes closed, wings draped like a cloak on either side of her. Esmeray had an arm propped behind her horns, her dark hair knotted and askew, making Lenna feel better about her own frazzled curls. Sparrow looked much queenlier than the actual Queen sprawled out beside her. The fae's golden locks perfectly draped around her shoulders as she sat poised and proper, flipping through a book. And pointedly ignoring the two males that kept shooting glances in her direction.

As Lenna stood awkwardly at the mouth of the stairs, Esmeray cracked open one eye, noted Lenna's stiff posture, and flippantly waved her tattooed hand. A third chair appeared to Sparrow's right.

"Sit down and relax for a moment before we get started with the Prism." Esmeray's eye closed again and she went back to her sunning. Lenna crossed the patio, appraising the new chair, courtesy, she knew now, of Esmeray's illusion magic. With a tentative hand she touched the seat, half worried it would ripple and disappear. Finding it sturdy and solid, Lenna gently lowered herself down, gripping her mug a little tighter–just in case. Finding the chair extremely comfortable, Lenna nestled in a little deeper, relaxing enough to raise her coffee to her lips.

Merrick grinned at her from the opposite side of the patio where he and Laurent were engaged in serious conversation, their stern faces an almost comical difference from the two females lazing in the sun. Laurent inclined his head towards Lenna in a half bow. Lenna smiled as she took another sip of coffee.

She couldn't help herself as her gaze quickly dipped to take in Merrick's shirtless, chiseled torso. He stretched his arms above his head and flexed, eliciting a soft growl of irritation from Laurent.

Laurent was dressed more casually than Lenna had ever seen, in a loose, short sleeved tunic that revealed his muscular arms where, to Lenna's surprise, white tattooed swirls decorated both forearms up to his elbows. They were beautiful, making the powerful and handsome fae even more alluring.

Lenna looked from Laurent's tattoos, to Merrick's, before her eyes jumped to Sparrow's blacked out tattoo spanning the length from her fingertips to her elbow, and Esmeray's fully tattooed hand, the ink slipping up to cup her shoulder–so at odds with the moon-pale skin of the Queen's other arm.

In Doortan, tattoos were only done sparingly, and rarely ever on women. Seeing the artwork decorating the arms around her, she appreciated the beauty of each individual design.

"What's with the tattoos?" Lenna inquired, immediately drawing the attention of everyone on the patio. Esmeray fully opened her eyes, blinking and baring her teeth at the sun, Sparrow put her book down, and Merrick and Laurent paused their soft bickering to turn towards her.

"Merrick never told you?" Laurent gave an admonishing look to the gargoyle, a smug expression on his face. Lenna shook her head.

Merrick threw his hands up in exasperation. "Again, do you know how *hard* it is to explain every facet of our world to someone who has never even *heard* of us?"

Lenna mumbled an apology that was quickly waved away by Sparrow, who extended her tattooed arm towards Lenna to inspect. Lenna gingerly took the fae's hand, marveling at the deep black ink that wrapped around and filled her palm. "The tattoos appear once a being begins their descent into their individual power. It's our *acat*. There's no exact date or age, but usually around your twentieth year, the tattoos begin to manifest onto your skin. There is a correlation between the tattoos, the powers one receives, and for anyone with fae blood in them, the god or goddess that blessed you."

"Right." Laurent picked up where Sparrow was going. "The *acatis* also foreshadow how strong your gifts will be as you age. Even gargoyles, with no magic per se, are given gifts from Alke of strength, agility–"

"Stubbornness," Esmeray cut in, her light snark aimed towards Merrick, who took the rib in stride.

Merrick looked down at the multiple bands wrapping from his elbow down to the middle of his forearm. "Yeah, I got that band pretty quick.

And it's one of the thicker ones." He shot Esmeray a wicked grin, sharp canines peeking out of his full lips. The Queen rolled her eyes.

Sparrow interjected, "Like gargoyle horns travel down family lines—most of the time." She tipped her head towards Esmeray's curled horns. "A fae's magic usually travels down lineage as well. Once a god claims a bloodline, *typically*, the same sort of magic shows up in the children. And if a fae mates with another fae, the offspring gets blessed by one of the parent's lineage gods. The gods bestow their markings on you, and you receive the *acat*."

Esmeray bowed her head, and Lenna wondered if each of them knew the god or goddess that blessed them. "But," Sparrow continued, her voice softer as she rubbed her tattooed hand against her thigh, "sometimes, a different god takes an interest to a being and claims that individual as their own—with no regard for the family's lineage god."

Lenna cocked her head. "So, the more tattoos you have the more powerful you are?"

"For fae, or someone mixed with fae lineage, yes. And some fae have a sort of separate battle magic. You probably noticed Esmeray's battle magic presents as gold. Mine is blue—the blue flame." Laurent glanced down at his own arms, before clasping his hands behind his back. "For gargoyles—or gargoyle lineages, the more bands on your arm, the thicker they are, the stronger you and your Sentry are."

Lenna cut her eyes, wider now at the implication, looking from Laurent to Esmeray. Her fully tattooed arm seemed completely ostentatious against the rest of the *acatis* around her. If Lenna did the calculations right, the next most powerful being on the patio would be Laurent. But she didn't know exactly what Laurent or Sparrow's powers truly were.

"Esmeray *is* the strongest being here. By far," Merrick supplied. Esmeray scowled, as if the reminder was one she wasn't keen on acknowledging.

"But I don't know who my lineage god is," she added, crinkling her nose slightly at her tattooed hand, "my father's side, the fae side, have water magic. I obviously do not. My battle magic is gold, and my familial battle magic has always presented as water wielding."

Sparrow said, "I don't know my lineage god either. Meer and I both received different *acatis* than our parents."

The two females shot each other a smirk. "It's probably why we became such fast friends at court," Esmeray confessed, "Sparrow has always understood me more than Adara."

"Probably because you both have such a desire to be troublemakers," Laurent quipped unhelpfully, smiling wide as Esmeray and Sparrow playfully punched each other's tattooed arms.

"*Anyway.*" Esmeray shot Laurent a sarcastic grin before turning to face Lenna. Honey brown eyes met determined green. The Queen addressed the Oracle, and Lenna felt her cheeks flush as the rest of the group set their eyes upon her again. "Ready to use the Prism?"

CHAPTER THIRTY-EIGHT
THE PRISM

A STUNNING FEMALE WITH wings the color of fresh snow glided slowly along the pebbled path along the beautiful gardens. Her long, white hair was unbound, slipping down past her waist. Delicate, slim horns adorned the top of her head, no more than four inches long, and looked to be made of solid opal. Her pale hands were clasped in front of her, portraying the image of fragility and purity.

Next to her, a handsome gargoyle accompanied her walk. He was tall and burly-towering over the wispy female beside him by a foot. His wings shone metallic and golden in the light of the setting sun. Even the bone structure of his wings looked to have been crafted of the precious element, as did the thin membranes connecting the ligaments. Sleek gold horns curved up from his skull, solidifying the image of a godly warrior. Tight curls of rich brown hair were tied back into a knot at the nape of his neck. Dressed in a full regalia of white armor, the male walked slowly, his head turning on a swivel for any sign of danger.

The female led him through the winding garden, where hedges full of white roses snaked along the path, ever so often interrupted by a marble fountain, or an old, weeping willow with its branches swaying in the light breeze.

The gargoyle male listened politely as the beautiful female pointed out flowers and exotic trees, but his dark green eyes continued sweeping across the landscaping, alert to any outside intrusions. She seemed to be shoving down irritation as the male politely nodded—without really engaging in any of her commentary.

As sounds of metal clanging on metal broke the tranquility of the gardens, the gargoyle pricked his ears up in unease. The male raised a hand to quiet the female, his body tensing. With a hand on the hilt of a dagger strapped to his side, his eyes darted around, searching for the source of the noise. Silently, he stalked forward, gaze roving over the hidden grass plots behind the hedges. Next to him, the female had her mouth clamped down in a thin frown—as if the sounds that would typically be interpreted as danger were merely an interruption to her day. The gargoyle stopped in his tracks as he beheld the female over the hedges to their left with wings black as night.

Esmeray wore a white gown, splotches of mud and dirt marring the fabric. The bottom of the hem was jagged, as if it had been purposely and haphazardly cut. Fluffy skirts that had undoubtedly been shaping the flimsy material lay discarded and dirty on the ground. She didn't look up as the gargoyle with the golden wings paused—watching.

Esmeray's black hair whipped, free and loose, as she swung the sword in her hand. Around her, four guards wearing the same armor as the golden winged warrior parried and blocked her sword's thrusts.

The golden gargoyle smiled, his muscles relaxing. Behind him, the female scowled, white wings snapping close to her lithe body, her eyes shooting from the male to the dark-haired princess—her twin sister.

Adara watched as Esmeray whirled around, her sword clashing against the swords of two guards. The three weapons clanged together, catching—Esmeray's sword holding in the middle. With a leer, Esmeray spread her black wings wide, launching up and over the two guards, effectively dislodging her sword from the other two—and decapitated the guard on the left.

The male standing with Adara shouted, one hand thrown across Princess Adara in a protective stance, the other flying to the broadsword strapped down his back between his golden wings. Adara put a palm gently against the male's muscular forearm, shaking her head. She did not look the least bit affected by the sister who just beheaded a royal guard in the garden.

"My sister is blessed with the power of illusion. The guards are not real." Her voice was soft, but the words were short and curt, as she gave the male a tight smile. "Princess Esmeray has been prohibited from training with any real warriors by our father. In defiance, she makes her own. Flesh and blood yes—but nothing more than an illusion, Sir Keerian."

Keerian, mouth agape, hand frozen around the handle of the still-sheathed sword, darted his eyes from the beautiful Princess at his side, across the hedge to the beheaded guard. As Adara spoke, the beheaded guard—the illusion—stood and headlessly bowed towards them before disappearing in a flash of gold. The three other guards mimicked the bow before the light enveloped them as well.

The golden wave of magic faded, leaving a scowling Esmeray glaring at the pair across the hedge.

"What." Esmeray's eyes narrowed as the sword in her hand disappeared. She crossed her arms, sending a leveled look at her sister. "What are you doing, Adara? And why are you with Sir Keerian? Father will be pissed that you left your room."

Adara smoothed her hands down the front pleats of her pristine dress—as if the dirt on her sister would jump from her soiled gown to her own. "I asked Father if I could walk in the gardens. Sir Keerian volunteered to escort me since the threat of the rogue fae band has still not been resolved." Adara cocked her head, mirroring the look of irritation Esmeray shot at her, though the corners of her full lips turned up in a sneer. "Imagine Father's wrath when he realizes you left your room, with no escort, to sneak away and play with swords."

Esmeray's jaw clenched as she assessed Adara and Keerian, seemingly weighing her options. Then, the black winged Princess smiled, a smile that did not reach her eyes.

It was purely predatory, Esmeray all but baring her teeth at her twin.

The dark twin versus the twin of light.

Finally, Esmeray huffed, "Tell him. I don't care." She shrugged with feigned indifference, the smile fading to a grimace, the fabric of her ruined dress rippling against her thinly muscled body. The twins appraised each other with disdain, but it was Keerian that broke the rolling tension.

"Princess Esmeray, it is not safe for you to be out here alone. Please, let me escort you back to the Palace." He reached out for her, but Esmeray ignored him. Tossing her sheet of black hair over her shoulder, she turned away and waved her hand in the air. Six guards appeared, standing in perfect formation.

Keerian stepped back, his hand dropping listlessly to his side. Now, each guard created by Esmeray's illusion magic appeared perfectly in his likeness.

Esmeray shot a smirk over her shoulder before launching herself at the closest Keerian-illusion, black wings whipping around to impale the illusion's throat with the sharp talon at the apex of her wing. Keerian subconsciously placed his hand to his own neck, but couldn't stop a slow grin from spreading across his face.

Adara growled, whirling towards the Opal Palace in the background, bundling her skirts in her fisted hands as she stalked back to the entrance of the gardens alone.

Keerian stayed rooted to the spot, transfixed. Watching the warrior Princess as she fought against and easily took down the remaining five Keerian-illusions. As the last illusion disappeared, her eyes locked with his. They stood, silently watching each other, neither making a move to leave.

Chapter Thirty-Nine

Lenna

Lenna blinked furiously as reality came back into focus. Crammed on the couch in Sparrow's living room, knee-to-knee with Esmeray on one side of her, and Laurent on the other, the Prism's iridescent glow faded, leaving the faceted stone grey and cool in her hand.

Laurent blew out a rough breath as he gently pulled out of Lenna's clammy grip. Esmeray was the last to detach from Lenna, her fingers slowly relaxing from their position on Lenna's forearm. She opened her eyes, a pained expression hollowing her features. "I may have chosen this particular thread of memory just to see Keerian again. That was the day I realized he could be my mate. We just...felt drawn to each other."

They had decided together, an hour ago, that the first thread Lenna would dive into should be simple to find amongst the tangled web of the past. With both Laurent and Esmeray touching Lenna, it was easier to separate the strands of the past, helping her travel down into the Prism to the memory Esmeray chose. Since Esmeray and Laurent had memories of Keerian and Adara, they acted as anchors to direct Lenna's mind, making the path infinitely clearer. Esmeray had added that an untroubled memory would make Lenna feel comfortable with the Prism, but Lenna wondered if it was because the Queen was afraid of seeing her parents' murder, and needed a reminder of a happier time before digging into the agony once more.

The Prism and its workings were explained in detail before the memory had been chosen. As the Oracle, Lenna was the only one that could delve through the threads of the past and revisit memories. Anchoring herself to another being made the thread that being intertwined with glow brighter and stronger, like a beacon for her subconscious mind to follow.

A blessing and a curse, apparently.

Anchoring also allowed those other beings to *see* the past. Laurent warned Lenna of the dark side of this. Past Oracles had been taken and imprisoned so their captors could travel through memories. To *see* enemy armies gathering on a battlefield, to find advantages in war, to revisit the life of a dead loved one. Both Oracles and anchors had apparently gone mad rifling around the past too much.

Lenna balked at that, but Esmeray and Laurent gently urged her on, the latter explaining breathing exercises and mental tricks to help Lenna relax enough to keep her mind clear and steady. The former adding that the last Oracle in recorded history that went mad was apparently still a lovely being with an even lovelier collection of taxidermized animals. They had just been a little extra...eccentric.

Once Lenna got the hang of it, she'd be able to revisit any memory—with or without an anchor. It would just take practice. Lenna could tell by the shifting postures and anxious looks that learning to utilize the Prism to its full extent was of utmost priority and she swore to herself that she wouldn't fail her new friends.

They were her friends...right? Lenna absentmindedly chewed her lip as she stared at the sharp planes of the Prism. Her thoughts drifted to Marlo. Marlo had been her friend. Even Orla, after their conversation in the pantry, had been...friendly-*ish* considering the circumstance. Lenna wracked her brain.

Besides Diana, there were no lifelong friends that Lenna trusted. She snuck a peek from beneath her lashes at the beings around her and hoped she would not let them down.

Sparrow and Merrick had gone to the market to pick up ingredients for dinner, and were finishing up putting away their wares as the Prism dimmed. The mood in the living room was low, Esmeray and Laurent blankly staring at the stained glass window, lost in memories of their own, while Lenna fought to keep her nerves under control. The three startled when Sparrow breezed into the room and dropped two bulky parcels in Lenna's lap. Lenna, still unsteady from the Prism, looked quizzically at the fae, who bounced on the balls of her feet, gesturing to the wrapped packages. "I figured, since we went to town, that you needed a few things. So, I took the liberty of doing a bit of shopping for you." Sparrow beamed as Lenna blushed, suddenly feeling off-kilter for a very different reason.

The first parcel, the largest, contained a gorgeous, pale peach nightgown with a matching robe. Lenna gently ran her fingers over the luxuriously silky fabric, her throat tight with emotion. This gift...this gift, and the fae that gave it to her, soothed her wavering thoughts. She did have friends here. "Thank you, Sparrow, truly. This is beautiful." Sparrow waved away her gratitude, her smile wide as she wriggled with anticipation.

"Open the next one." The giddiness in her eyes drew a smile out of Lenna as she tore a little more enthusiastically into the second, smaller package.

Two bottles of hair products clinked together. Lenna peered into the sealed glass jar of the first, her eyes widening at the shiny cream inside. "It's magically formulated for beings with thick curls like yours. Just a little glob, brushed through your hair in the morning, and each curl will be perfect.

The shopkeep said the second bottle banishes flyaways and frizz. I've seen you glowering at your hair, so, I figured this would help." A curved comb was nestled between the jars, with three small rubies decorating the handle. "And that is just because all females deserve a pretty comb." Lenna threw her arms around Sparrow, who hugged her back fiercely.

"It's only a little something to get you feeling more acquainted with our world." Sparrow smiled, before clasping her hands together and standing, shooting Lenna a wink. "Okay. I'm going to get dinner started. I also bought eight more bottles of wine. I recommend anyone that wants a nap to go take one now. It's going to be a late night."

Esmeray rubbed her eyes and raised a hand. "I'll definitely take advantage of a short nap. Being in the Prism was...draining." Laurent, slumped next to Lenna, murmured in agreement through his half-lidded gaze.

The room emptied quickly. Sparrow headed back to Merrick in the kitchen, and Esmeray got up with a groan, reminding Sparrow to not let her nap for more than an hour. Laurent had his hands clasped against his chest, his head tipped against the back cushion of the couch. Lenna shot a glance towards the fae, keeping herself still until the sound of his deep breathing confirmed he was already asleep. Quietly, Lenna scooted from her seat, snatched up the Prism, and darted into her bedroom.

CHAPTER FORTY
LENNA

LENNA BLEW OUT A shaky breath as she quietly shut the bedroom door behind her. The faint clinking of pots, and the muffled voices of Sparrow and Merrick in the kitchen, were the only sounds in the house that she could hear over her rapidly beating heart. Lenna couldn't make out what they were saying, even as she pressed her ear to the door. But the curiosity over their conversation was short lived as an awkwardness washed over her, turning quickly to guilt for eavesdropping.

Forcing herself back to the situation at hand, a faint blush crept across her cheeks at the implication that she was being far too nosy. Lenna kicked off her shoes and readjusted the mound of pillows against the headboard, making a firm back rest for her to lean against.

She needed to learn to wield the Prism.

Quickly.

Lenna rolled the weight of the Prism between her palms, the cluster of grey quartz fracturing the light from her nightstand lamp. For so long, her desires had been pushed aside, her choices stifled, in favor of another's goals and dreams. She'd been deemed unimportant, merely property of her husband, her wishes and wants judged harshly if they didn't align with Doortan's society.

But in this, in using the Prism to get justice for the slain King and Queen of Irridessen, she could do a lot of good for the world. Her power was truth, her sword an oddly shaped rock, and her spoils the potential for a life in these lands.

Doortan felt a million miles away, as if years had passed, not days, since she wove down the dirt path back to the cold Manor, the heavy humidity making her wheeze, as she slogged through the muck, trying desperately to ignore the pounding in her head.

But here, in Irridessen...

Here, life felt vibrant, bright. *Hopeful.*

Lenna inhaled slowly as she coaxed her mind into the Prism, the stone beginning to glow, only half wondering if this was a terrible idea to do alone.

She sunk deep into the tangled web of memories. Without an anchor, Lenna could barely make out the slightly brighter thread against the rest—the thread to her own past and the intersecting and interwoven strands of lives she'd interacted with.

All around her threads knitted together, shooting off far into the distance, going all the way back to the origins of the Prism's creation. Closer to her lay a shorter path, though no less intricate, all bisecting into a pulsing gold orb. Esmeray had explained that the orb led to the present, and if Lenna pushed through that golden light, her subconscious would simply return to her body, pulling her safely out of the Prism.

It was an escape hatch, Laurent forewarned, in case an Oracle got so lost in the past that their minds couldn't discern how to get back out. Lenna tentatively glanced again at the orb, reassuring herself that she would use it if she couldn't get out herself, before rising over the threads, debating where to start.

Gently, and ever so carefully, Lenna latched her mind onto the thread of her own past, concentrating on finding the point in time where she was waving goodbye to Marlo and Orla as they escaped from Doortan's clutches and began their travels to a new life.

Lenna found the memory easily, pride bursting through her, as she once again watched the ship sail away from port and out to sea. The threads unraveled as the vision faded, shooting out of the memory itself, coiling in multiple directions, some brightening, some dulling. Lenna eased her consciousness along the two threads that outshone the rest, guessing those connected to Marlo and Orla, and gradually wove her way down the length, trying to get closer to the present, to see where they were on their travels.

Right before the golden glow of the present forced her back to reality, Lenna sunk deep into the threads, thinking this would show her Marlo or Orla's previous morning. She dove into the memory, the anticipation of seeing Marlo again making her giddy. The light faded as she slipped through the thread.

Nothingness.

Only swirling, murky fog, so thick Lenna couldn't figure out up from down. The fog rolled around her, faster and faster. Lenna scrambled out, panic overtaking her, back from whence she came, away from the sheer density of the smoke.

Lenna dry heaved, jolting off the pillows, as her consciousness slammed back into her body. The Prism dulled. Lenna grappled to piece herself back together as a wave of nausea threatened.

She focused on her breathing first, until her lungs could take more than shallow, panting breaths. As her fear subsided, she stretched her feet, then fingers, working her way up her body, relaxing her tensed muscles, until the numbness and terror wore off, the buzzing in her head abated.

A sinking feeling in her stomach dulled the rest of her nerves. She failed. She had wanted to see them again, to hopefully follow that thread just a bit more to check on Marlo and Orla, make sure they were either already to the port in Bardon, or getting closer to their destination.

Doubt dug in its talons. Maybe she hadn't used the Prism properly, maybe she was too close to the present. Lenna mulled over the thought for a moment longer before deciding to try again. She had to master the Prism—she could figure this out without bothering anyone to anchor her.

She'd try a different memory. One that could build her confidence up and confirm that she was using the Prism correctly. Lenna decided to find Diana, to check on her old friend she hadn't heard from in years. Steeling herself against the small pit of dread that bloomed from the sensation of falling into that smoky nothingness, she dove down again, pushing that kernel of anxiousness away.

Lenna again traveled down the path of her past, searching through the web to find the last point in time her past crossed with Diana's. She started rifling through the years, her teeth clenching at the flashes of Leon that blipped across her mind's eye.

There.

A small thread, dull and thin, arched out from her own, weaving through a different path. Lenna speared for it, going deeper into the Prism. Her mind slowed, sluggish as she pushed through, slipping around Diana's thread for a recent memory of her dear friend. But another, brighter thread shot off of Lenna's past, wrapping around Diana's. From the positioning of the thread, its closeness to the orb of the present, Lenna sunk through the threads at their point of intersection, curious, since she hadn't seen Diana in years.

It was overcast and raining as the small procession stood atop a hill. Mourners dressed in their finest memorial attire gathered around a headstone. Though the storm around them raged, no one paid it any heed.

A numb shock rippled through those gathered. Lenna felt that uneasy pit in her stomach grow as her consciousness darted through the crowd to read the engraving on the slab of white marble.

But the moment she lay eyes on it, her mind stumbled back, away from the freshly filled grave, away from the group gathered to pay their respects. Away from the stone jutting from the soft earth that read, In Memory of Lady Diana Merle.

Dead.

Her oldest friend, her confidant that she had not spoken to in years, the friendship she allowed to stale and dissipate, resigned to a cold body given to the ground. Reeling, her heartbeat pounding in her physical chest, Lenna whirled around, desperate to rip herself from this memory, her gaze falling to the mourners gathered. And there, standing in the middle of those assembled, dressed in his finest black coat, stood Leon.

Lenna stared at her estranged husband for a moment, disbelief and rage warring inside of her, before she launched herself back into her body, a humming roar following her as she tore from the Prism.

The Prism's glow faded slowly, as if even the stone sympathized with Lenna's shock and betrayal.

Diana was dead.

And Leon had gone to the funeral without telling her, without any sort of notice to his wife that her friend passed. Lenna leaned against the headboard, staring, unseeing at the ceiling above, twisting her thin wedding band from a lifetime of lies ago around her shaky finger. Tears welled up, her breathing coming in uneven bursts. Crushing her lids closed, a single tear escaped, slipping down her cheek. *Where would Marlo and Orla go? Could she get a letter out to them?*

She didn't know.

Didn't know where they were, didn't know how to get word to them.

She had simply failed.

Again.

Blindly, Lenna threw herself back into the Prism's depths, the only escape from the troubled thoughts in her mind. She let the threads swallow her, wanting to get lost in them, fumbling through the dimmer strands to find something bright, something, anything, to dig into.

A brilliant thread near hers, only briefly intersecting, caught her eye. Without much thought, she flung into it, ripping through time so quickly that she couldn't make out the flashes of visions that flickered through her mind's eye. As her travels down the past's timeline began to slow, she dove.

Bright light streamed in from massive floor to ceiling windows, overlooking a beautiful courtyard. Shoes clipped abruptly against white marbled tiles. "Your Highness," a familiar female voice called out, "your sister was looking for you." Lenna turned, eyes wide as she beheld a young Sparrow dressed in what Lenna could only assume was Opal Palace fashion. A pale green gown fluttered around her ankles, cinched in at the waist with a braided belt. Small gems, arranged to look like flowers, twinkled with each swish of her skirt. She looked younger, as if she was only in her mid-twenties, the shining face of a wealthy female growing up in court. Her acat had already appeared, the harsh black ink so contrasted against the soft gown.

Lenna turned to see who Sparrow spoke to, as Adara stepped out from behind a large opal pillar. If Sparrow wore the attire of royals, Adara was dressed as if she, herself, was a goddess. A pearl white gown swept behind her with tiny diamonds threaded through the silky material. Adara looked to be around the same age as Sparrow, her face rosy and pink, her brilliant blue eyes vibrant, though they narrowed onto the fae. Adara raised a perfectly groomed brow. "What does Esmeray want?"

Sparrow shrugged a delicate shoulder. "She just told me she was looking for you, and to tell you she was heading up to your rooms."

Adara looked down her nose at Sparrow, drawing herself up straight, her immaculate white wings snapping shut behind her. "I do not have time for Esmeray's whims. Didn't you hear? I'm going to sit in a council meeting with my father." With a glare, Adara sidestepped Sparrow and proceeded down the hallway, past marble statues of Kings and Queens past. "Tell Esmeray if she deigned to act like a Princess for once, I'll see her in the council room."

With a prim sniff, Adara departed down the grand hall, throwing a mocking glance back towards Sparrow. Sparrow's lips thinned as she bowed her head to the Princess.

As Adara disappeared, her expression changed from innocence and piety to mischievous. She straightened, throwing a sneaky smirk over her shoulder, making her way to a set of double doors that opened to an intricately carved balcony. "She's gone," Sparrow chirped, leaning over the banister precariously, tilting her head up to whomever she addressed.

Lenna watched as a young Esmeray swept down from above, wearing leather pants and a baggy black tunic. "Gods, Adara is such a bore these days," Esmeray complained, hooking a booted foot onto the railing.

Crinkling her nose, Sparrow shot a glare at Esmeray. "Why do you smell like dragons?"

Esmeray feigned outrage, clutching a hand to her chest. "Sparrow, if my parents didn't want me hanging around the dragon lairs, they wouldn't have made the entrance to said dragon lairs so easily accessible." Esmeray tipped her chin to a marble statue of a Queen long dead across the hall. "If you want, I can show you. The hidden entrance is behind that statue." Esmeray *leaned closer to the fae and whispered conspiratorially, "There's a magic pathway that connects the Opal Palace to the Obsidian Palace. It's supposed to be super-secret. Only my parents and a few of the higher up council members know—so naturally, I like to sneak through and explore the catacombs beneath the Obsidian Palace whenever I fancy."*

"I have no interest in talking to beasties that want to eat me," Sparrow blanched, causing Esmeray to laugh, the bright sound tugging the corners of Sparrow's lips up into an uneasy smile.

"Well, fine. Did you get to chat with my boring sister?"

Sparrow grinned fully, canines flashing, eyes shining with mischief. "Adara's going to the council meeting, so we have a few hours to spare before anyone truly realizes we're gone."

"Let's go," Esmeray crowed, hopping onto the balcony. "I've been itching to get out of the Palace for days. I want to go wander around a different city. Ooh, let's go to Baubble—the barkeep there will let us drink at his tavern for free." No acat graced her arms, and Esmeray's skin looked so odd without it. Sparrow giggled, reaching her hand out to her friend. Esmeray gripped it, and the pair waned in a flash of green light.

Lenna eased out of the Prism, her thoughts still rattling incessantly though the raging, the screaming, had dimmed. With a heavy sigh, Lenna placed the Prism on the nightstand, burrowing down into the plush bed. Lost in swirling emotions and heavy grief, Lenna closed her eyes and succumbed to sleep.

CHAPTER FORTY-ONE
ESMERAY

THE NAP WAS MUCH needed after diving into the Prism, but my body and my heart still felt heavy. I searched through the drawers, finally finding the sweater I had been thinking about since resurfacing from the past.

It was old and well loved, the black knit stretched out at the hem. The back was open, roomy around my wings, with a strip of fabric that connected the base of the sweater to the nape of my neck. But the scent on the sweater was why I needed it. It still smelled like Keerian. I bundled the extra length of the too-long sleeves into my hands, bringing them up to my face to inhale his scent. Leather and dew-covered forests. I couldn't stop the tears blurring my vision.

Keerian's sweater came down to the middle of my thighs, so I added some soft black leggings underneath. My hair was a mess, the normally straight locks tangled. With some effort, I tamed the flyaway pieces from the curls of my horns and wrapped my hair into a bun on the top of my head.

The smells coming from the kitchen were divine, and I could hear Sparrow's lively chatter drifting into my room. I wiped away the tear that escaped before it made its way down my cheek. With a deep breath, I headed towards the motley of voices coming from the kitchen. It was time to begin planning. But I already knew what I had to do.

And it didn't involve risking the lives of any of the beings residing in Sparrow's home that I found myself growing closer and closer to.

"IT WOULD BE STUPID to all go in at once. Adara's probably waiting on us to do just that. It would be suicide without the proper precautions."

We sat at the yellow dining room table. Dinner had been consumed in its entirety an hour ago, and the talk had turned to next steps.

We couldn't be sure if Adara was aware that I had Merrick, Laurent, Sparrow, and the Oracle on my side. For the sake of the plan, we assumed. My uncle had seen me with them, and I knew his sniveling self would immediately crow that information back to Adara.

"Infiltrating the Opal Palace without knowing what spells Adara could have in place would be stupid." Merrick nodded his agreement to Laurent. Forgoing a wine glass entirely, the gargoyle was drinking straight from the bottle.

Brooding. It seemed to be his base emotion.

I swirled the contents of my own wine glass, listening to the two ex–King's Guards bicker back and forth on different battle strategies.

Merrick rubbed his beard. "I don't think we can trust anyone. We need to keep this between this table, and this table only."

"The first thing we need to do," I interrupted, not looking up from my wine glass, "is confirm my suspicion that Adara killed my parents."

Lenna, from the other side of the table, winced. "If I use you as an anchor, Esmeray, would that be the fastest way to find what we need?"

I nodded towards the Oracle, and she settled herself back in her chair, one hand resting against her stomach. We had all eaten seconds of the delicious pasta and fish that Sparrow whipped up. Merrick and Lenna had both opted for thirds–the pair now looking uncomfortably full. Sparrow directed her next question at Lenna. "Do you think you would be able to get that memory tonight? Let's get the confirmation that Adara is behind the murders of King Scottrell and Queen Elera and see if we can get any clarity on the spells or the book."

Lenna nodded, her face a bit pale, but she stood up and disappeared down the hall, coming back a few moments later with the Prism.

"I've been practicing." Her soft voice was laced with grief, her eyes never leaving the grey stone that she placed gently on the center of the table. "I had to check on some friends from the Slate Kingdom."

"And are they alright?" Sparrow inquired, kindly giving the Oracle her full attention. Lenna did have a life before she came here. I wondered if she left loved ones behind when Merrick took her to the Opal Kingdom. The thought made my stomach clench. I had never asked, too wrapped up in my own shit.

Lenna looked wistfully at the Prism. "No. Well, I don't know... I couldn't find their thread." Her voice shook, as if there was more she wasn't saying, but the Oracle didn't seem inclined to share.

Sparrow gently reached out her hand, grasping Lenna's forearm. Speaking low, she noted, "The past cannot be rewritten. Although that is normally seen as a relief, when the past doesn't lead to a future we hoped for, it can be difficult to understand. But you can always talk to us if you need anything."

I hated myself for pushing, adding this to the list of things I would need to beg forgiveness for at another time, but I said, "Let's look now. I want everyone to anchor–so all of you will also see what happened to my parents.

The more beings that know the truth, the better." I left out the part where it put them all at an elevated risk of being called traitors to the Crown.

I figured now was not the time to bring that up.

Around the table, Merrick, Laurent, Sparrow, Lenna, and I linked hands. Lenna inhaled deep and focused on the Prism. I sent a quick prayer skyward that this would work. I didn't call upon a specific god, though I felt a cool presence at my shoulder for a moment.

Lenna exhaled and her eyes fluttered shut.

On the table in front of us, the Prism began to glow.

CHAPTER FORTY-TWO
THE PRISM

"SHE IS OUR DAUGHTER, *Scottrell.*" *The harsh whisper came from the beautiful Queen. Her short, soft grey hair was curled away from her face, the first signs of aging showing in graceful lines around her eyes. Her wings, as white as Adara's, but with longer, spiked opal talons on the tips, snapped shut behind her as she paced the royal bedroom. Dressed in a simple pearl and silver gown, the Queen was ethereal, but the light from her green eyes was gone–replaced with grief and fear.*

The King sat in a lush red and gold armchair against the window, where the soft light of dusk was beginning to filter into the room. His dark hair was short, cropped close to his skull, a simple golden crown atop his head. He rubbed his face with his hands, both covered in intricate, wave-like tattoos that fluctuated with the movement. With a deep sigh, he slumped deeper into the chair and removed the crown, tossing it onto the low table beside him. His mate turned again and began pacing towards him, twisting the sleeves of her dress between her hands.

"Elera, I don't know what else to do. All these years we dismissed Adara's interest in spell books as an innocent curiosity. We should've paid closer attention." The King reached out a hand to the pacing Queen, beckoning her closer to the armchair he occupied.

The Queen gave her mate a droll, flat look, but closed the distance between them—just out of reach of his extended hand. "If Esmeray is right—and that is a big 'if' considering her track record—the spell book needs to be destroyed."

"It's a part of our ancient fae heritage," the King started, lowering his hand, his fingers curling into a loose fist. His blue eyes flashed. "It should be preserved for historians."

"Fuck your heritage," Queen Elera spat, her snow-white wings flaring out from her sides. "Those spells are killing *our daughter."*

"Then we take them away and lock them up someplace even Adara cannot find."

"What about Esmeray?" Queen Elera took a step closer to King Scottrell.

"What about her? She's soul tied to Commander Keerian whether we like it or not. Carra decided her fate as Queen on High. I say, we take away the book from Adara, and confine her to her room for tomorrow's celebration of Esmeray and Keerian. Once she's had time to come to terms with her new position, we will help her come to accept the title of Lesser Queen." King Scottrell stood and grabbed his mate's arm as she paced in front of him again. Pulling her close, he kissed her, deep and slow, until her wings relaxed, and she nestled into his broad arms.

"Fine," Queen Elera breathed, staring into the King's eyes, a small smile playing at the corner of her lips. "We will tell Esmeray tomorrow—that it's just a precaution."

"Adara cannot know that we are moving the spell book." The King looked down at his Queen, kissing the top of her head between her two dainty horns.

"Adara cannot know," the Queen agreed, as the King led his mate to the large bed behind them.

THE CANDLES IN THE Royal bedroom winked out one by one, bathing the entire room in night's murky darkness. The sleeping King and Queen did not stir as the bedroom doors creaked open.

Illuminated by the faint candlelight in the hallway, Adara stood, her hands balled into fists. Her expression brimmed with rage as she slunk into her parents' bedroom. As her skirts swept across the floor, bodies of the guards in the hallway became engulfed in silver edged flames–burning only them–before a ghost wind swept down the hallway, scattering their ashes.

Adara, her head cocked to the side, white-blonde hair spilling out of her tangled braid, stepped lightly towards her father, not even sparing a glance at her mother–her likeness. The Princess raised her hand where short, jagged nails grew longer, sharper. She whispered in an ancient tongue as her nails began to glow with the same unearthly silver as the fire that consumed the bodies of the two gargoyles that had been stationed at the door.

Her hand slashed down. The sickening sound of flesh tearing, followed by panic gurgling of the King choking on his own blood filled the room. Adara whipped her other hand towards the open door, where a translucent shield appeared, concealing the voice of the dying King from anyone with fae hearing outside.

The Queen, her mother, launched up, her eyes filled with fear and pain as she beheld her daughter. Blood slid down Adara's arm as she crooned, "It won't be long now."

The Queen's head whipped towards her mate, and she screamed, throwing herself over his convulsing body, as her own began to bow in pain–the soul tie ripping her life force out as the King's dimmed.

Adara began chanting in the same ancient language, silver light wreathing her hands, as King Scottrell died. His mate let out a low whimper as her life dwindled and extinguished.

The light disappeared as the Queen took her last, shuddered breath, and met her mate in the afterlife. Adara smiled, her blue eyes dull, as she leaned her head back and laughed, the maniacal sound breaking the quiet of death, before she turned on her heel, walked out of the bedroom, and waned.

CHAPTER FORTY-THREE
LENNA

LENNA SLUGGED THROUGH THE Prism as the images of the dead King and Queen faded, the quaint dining room coming back into focus. After what they had witnessed, the yellow table and the mismatched colorful chairs seemed too loud, too bright.

"Fuck." Merrick's ragged voice pulled Lenna's subconscious the remaining way back. Merrick's wings drooped at his sides, the grief on his handsome face palpable, as he slowly ran his hands through his shaggy brown hair. Laurent, across the table from the gargoyle, wordlessly poured a hefty glass of wine for himself and passed the rest of the bottle over to Merrick.

Tears streamed down Sparrow's cheeks, her face devoid of color. With shaking fingers, Sparrow reached across the table to Esmeray, who had not moved except to pull her hand out of Lenna's. Esmeray didn't meet her gaze.

The Queen's voice broke. "Adara framed me by murdering them the way I've trained to kill... The nails..." A single tear slid from her glassy eyes. A moment later, another followed, then another.

"What do you mean?" Sparrow asked gently, taking her friend's hand, squeezing lightly.

Merrick answered, since Esmeray just continued to stare wordlessly at her wine glass. "Esmeray slashed the throats of some of the gargoyles that came for us at the waterfall. If Adara knew how Esmeray would fight, it would be easier to frame her for the murders. Adara must've watched you train to figure out your tactics."

Esmeray frowned. "Adara shouldn't have that magic. The bare bones of it is that I can make my nails sharp with illusions. Adara only has water magic."

"She must have used a spell to somehow recreate your *acat*." Laurent shuffled some papers around the table, finding a blank piece before picking up a quill, dipping it into ink and starting to write. "Or she's been hiding another gift this whole time. Royals hiding rare fae abilities is an annoying part of court life that I've uncovered many times during my days as Spy Master."

Lenna peered over his scribbling arm. The words made no sense, but Lenna worked through the pronunciation silently.

"That's what Adara was saying. It's a spell." Lenna said quietly.

Sparrow and Merrick craned their heads to take in the writing.

Finally, Esmeray moved. Snatching up her glass, she swallowed the remaining wine, growled and poured another. "We need someone to translate what the words mean. And we need to know what other spells Adara knows."

Sparrow looked at Lenna, before standing and taking the remaining full bottles of wine to the kitchen, announcing they were all cut off, they needed to sober up, and that she was making coffee.

Lenna stretched her legs out under the table. Using the Prism for hours today made her dizzy, and seeing the carnage of the dying King and Queen made her nauseated, especially after finding out Diana was dead. All she wanted to do was curl up in bed and sleep for two full days.

In her temples, the first beat of a headache thrummed, in perfect sync with her heartbeat. The throbbing amped up, until Lenna squeezed her eyes shut against the crushing onslaught of pain.

She inhaled deep, exhaled slow, relaxed the muscles in her face. The agony let up–slightly. She took another breath, and another, the spasms lessening.

One minute.

She could close her eyes, breathe deep and slow for one minute before anyone would notice.

The low voices around her faded.

All Lenna could hear was her breathing and her heartbeat as the pain slowly released its talons from her head.

Chapter Forty-Four
ESMERAY

I watched Lenna inhale and exhale, low and controlled. I knew the enormous strain she was under, especially since she admitted to using the Prism herself while closed off in her bedroom. Next to me, Laurent was droning on about different dialects of the fae and how the words scrawled on the paper were purely phonetic and spoken like languages that went extinct long ago.

Unfortunately, none of us could confirm any other tidbits of information, and all admitted a translator would be necessary to even start in the right direction.

Lenna began trembling next to me, shaking so hard that the fork in front of her started rattling. I grabbed her hand–it was cold as ice. I gasped. Merrick shouted for Sparrow, who came running out of the kitchen.

Lenna's eyes flew open–but her gaze was unfocused, dazed.

"The light will swallow up the darkness. Forgetting darkness absorbs light every night.

When the moon is full, the darkness will feast, and the beasts will rejoice and rally over the coming blood."

I shook her by the shoulders, shouting her name, but she didn't come to. Lenna swayed in her chair, her head slowly turning to look through me.

"The darkness absorbs the light. Black wings conceal the moon. The blood runs below the veil."

Lenna smiled, the hazy grin lopsided, before her entire body pitched forward. I caught her head in my hands before she could smash against the wooden table.

My heart raced, Laurent furiously repeated and wrote down what Lenna had said.

Fuck. Seer indeed.

Sparrow knelt next to Lenna's chair, placing a large glass of ice water in front of her as Lenna let out a garbled moan, squeezed her eyes shut, and slowly picked her head up from the table. As she slumped back, rubbing her eyes and blinking furiously, she startled, darting her head around the table, as if she just realized we were all staring at her.

"It–it happened again...didn't it?" Lenna asked, her voice no more than a rough whisper. Merrick huffed a confirmation, his face grim. I looked over Lenna's curly hair, meeting Sparrow's hard eyes. She nodded once and angled her head towards the kitchen, requesting a private conversation. I gently rubbed Lenna's back before standing. Merrick and Laurent, sensing the shift in Sparrow and my demeanors, stood as well. Merrick claimed my seat, Laurent slid into the empty chair at the head of the table. Lenna looked from one to the other, confusion causing the thin lines on her forehead to crinkle further. Laurent began reading back to Lenna the words she spoke, the Oracle growing more and more pale.

I followed Sparrow into the kitchen, throwing a golden light against the door so the others in the dining room couldn't hear.

"She needs to stop using the Prism so much," Sparrow snapped half-heartedly, busying herself by pouring the now steaming coffee into various mugs.

I leaned against the cabinets, rubbing my horns, the swirl comforting and familiar, the ridges along the sides tactical and soothing. "I agree, but what the fuck was that prophecy about?"

Sparrow shrugged as she placed each mug on a circular tray. "It could be anything–something that will happen tomorrow, or something that'll occur years from now. We need to focus on containing Adara and getting Keerian back, the prophecy can wait."

"What if its connected?" I pushed, flaring out a wing to cut Sparrow off from the kitchen door.

She threw me a withering look before nudging my wing with the tray in her hands. "What if it isn't, and we get tripped up in the semantics? I have an idea on who can potentially translate the spell. You, me, and Lenna need to go to town tomorrow morning. Keeping her hidden is not helping anymore."

"What about the rest of the spells?" I hated myself the second the words came out. Lenna was tapped–another dive into the Prism could put her dangerously close to a burn out. The last thing we needed was for our Seer-Oracle to spend the next week unconscious while her magic replenished.

Sparrow glared at me. "Lenna needs to rest. I know how serious this is with Adara, but Lenna is our *only* way to get the information we need. Let her sleep tonight, and we will bring the spells we know to town tomorrow. And *if* Lenna seems rested in the morning, then *I* will anchor her and search for the rest of them. You have *got* to sit some of this out–let us help you. You are no use to Keerian if you are burnt out as well."

I put my hands up in mock surrender. I truly didn't want anything to happen to Lenna. I'd only met her a few days ago, and already felt a fierce need to protect her. I waved my hand and the golden barrier disappeared.

Sparrow stepped back into the dining room, immediately fussing over Lenna, and placing mugs at every seat–except mine.

I smiled. She knew me so well.

I stood in the doorway for a long moment, taking in the comradery, the soft words to Lenna. The closeness that, only days ago, had been nonexistent, now bloomed and grew like the thick, strong vines wrapping around Sparrow's garden. I took one more moment to watch, before I waned in a flash of golden light.

CHAPTER FORTY-FIVE
MERRICK

"Where's Esmeray going?" Merrick directed gruffly to Sparrow once the gold light winked out. Sparrow hummed a non-answer, settling against the lavender chair across from him. "What did you talk about?" His eyes narrowed, taking in the fae female slowly sipping her coffee, her eyes never leaving Merrick's in a silent challenge.

"If Esmeray wanted you to know, she would've announced it to the whole room," Sparrow replied simply, setting her mug down on the table. She smiled sweetly at Merrick, resting her chin in her hands. "Don't question your Queen's actions." The tone was gentle, but Sparrow's words were edged with venom. "I mean, she *is* your Queen, right?"

Merrick snapped his teeth together but didn't push further. Sparrow was loyal to a fault, but she had a good head on her shoulders. If she wasn't concerned, Merrick decided he shouldn't be either.

"Lenna, dear, why don't you go get some rest? I know a being in town that might be able to help us translate the spell Laurent wrote down, and I'd like you to join Esmeray and I tomorrow." Sparrow's kindness did not go unnoticed by Merrick. He also noted the purplish under eyes and colorless skin on the Oracle, and had recommended the same before Sparrow returned. Lenna nodded, finally standing up on shaky legs.

The Oracle's hand reached out to the Prism, but Sparrow gently lay her own atop Lenna's. "Why don't you leave that here for now? Focus on getting some rest, okay?" It wasn't a question. Merrick could tell Sparrow knew exactly what she was doing. They needed to keep Lenna out of the Prism so that she didn't burn out diving into whatever she was looking for in the past. Merrick did not understand the draw—going in and out of the Prism had left him nauseated from the drag and pull of consciousness. Somehow, it was worse than waning.

Lenna's brows furrowed for a split second, but she murmured her agreement and wished the table good night.

Merrick stared down Sparrow, Laurent doing the same once they heard the door to Lenna's bedroom close. The beautiful fae ignored both of them as she collected the papers Laurent had written the spell from Adara on. Without looking up, she cleared her throat. "Esmeray and I decided that the seer prophecies are not necessarily about saving Keerian. For the time being, we will tread carefully, but won't be wasting time trying to find some semblance of commonality between the prophecies and our goals."

Laurent pursed his lips.

Merrick bit out, "And you both decided that without asking us? Or Lenna?"

Sparrow's blue eyes narrowed on him. "Esmeray and I have been unravelling truth from lie, tracking down potential sources of information, focusing on saving Keerian, and exposing Adara for much longer than you have. I am *very* thankful that you are both trusting Esmeray *now*, but some things will take time to catch you up on—things that do not involve you, and things that will take too long to explain."

Merrick threw his hands up. "So, we're supposed to sit here and give you our blind faith?"

"Isn't that what you gave Adara before Esmeray revealed the truth to you?" Sparrow snapped. The words cut deep, but she wasn't wrong. Merrick and Laurent exchanged a look, the latter blowing out a long breath.

"Can we exchange this coffee back for wine now?" Laurent changed the subject expertly, dimming the unease in the room. Merrick could tell he was trying to breeze over the power struggle going on between Sparrow and himself. Part of Merrick wanted to demand answers. And the other part wanted to see Sparrow carefree, wine drunk, and happy.

Sparrow, seemingly picking up on the subtle messaging, smiled brightly at Laurent. "Why don't we take a few bottles up to the roof? It's a nice night." Nothing else about Esmeray's whereabouts was provided, besides alluding to her being back in time to go to town tomorrow.

He wondered what the Queen was up to. She was Keerian's mate. He worried for a moment that she could endanger herself, but thought back to how unhinged and violent Esmeray fought at the waterfall, coming to the conclusion that if anyone could defend themselves, it was her.

Forcing a pleasant look on his face, Merrick helped Sparrow pick up the remaining cutlery and mugs from the table. At least, with Esmeray gone to gods-knew-where for the night, he could get a few hours of flirting in with Sparrow.

Laurent, following behind them with his own hands full, seemed to have the same idea. The thought made Merrick's blood race.

He loved competitions.

But he hated losing.

THE NIGHT AIR WAS chilly, but the small fire Laurent conjured to float in the center of the patio gave off a nice, radiant, warmth.

Sparrow was back in that fluffy blue robe, killing Merrick slowly with those golden legs on display. She had taken up residence on one of the chairs they carried up from the house, her legs crossed at the ankles, golden hair spilling around her shoulders as she sipped delicately from her long-stemmed wine glass.

Laurent was engaged in conversation with her, his eyes politely never leaving Sparrow's face. Merrick prayed Sparrow wouldn't notice the war raging inside of him. He was so drawn to her. Her wild lease on life, her sharp mind, those curves, that golden hair.

Sparrow's musical laughter snapped Merrick back to the present, his eyes darting to Laurent.

Had Laurent cracked one of his rare *jokes*?

Merrick clenched his jaw, easing a languid smile on his face—trying to appear as if he was listening to the conversation, not imagining Sparrow's body under his own.

Sparrow grinned at Laurent, her dainty hand reaching out to grip his forearm. Merrick's pulse jumped, wishing that hand was wrapped around his—

"What's going on in that mind of yours, Merrick?" Sparrow asked, again interrupting Merrick's thoughts.

Merrick opened his mouth, closed it, and tried, unsuccessfully, to think of a single word to say.

Her laugh rang out again as her other hand reached out and stroked his arm. She squeezed both lightly before releasing them, picking her glass back up from the ground by her chair. "You do know I can tell you're both flirting with me...right?" Her blue eyes revealed a wicked gleam Merrick had not been privy to before.

Laurent swallowed thickly. Merrick sat up straighter, hoping something witty and devastatingly charming would spill forth from his gaping jaw. "I–we–uhm..." *Fuck*. Merrick didn't know what to do with his hands, his mouth. He cleared his throat and began chugging his wine.

"Have you ever been with a female together?" Sparrow's question clanged through Merrick, causing him to choke on his drink. He couldn't bring himself to even look over at Laurent.

"Ah–I... No." Merrick felt his face heat. Fucks sake, he was one hundred and twelve years old, a fierce, battle-hardened warrior, part of the Opal Palace's elite. And he was completely and utterly speechless in front of this female. Laurent, on Sparrow's other side, seemed to be faring just as well–if not worse.

Sparrow gave them both a wolfish grin, her sharp canines gleaming in the soft firelight. "No pressure, but my bed is big enough for three–wings included."

With that, she stood in a fluid motion, blew the two males a kiss and traipsed slowly down the stairs and out of sight, that damned blue robe swaying with the movement.

"I...think we may have gotten this all wrong." Laurent finally broke the silence after Sparrow disappeared down the steps. "While we were both hunting for her affections...this entire time...we may have been *her* prey."

Merrick grunted, trying not to mull over her proposition–or bed size. Or the male sitting across the fire from him. Without a word, Merrick grabbed the rest of the bottle of wine that Sparrow left behind and took a long swallow.

CHAPTER FORTY-SIX
ESMERAY

I DIDN'T TELL ANYONE where I went last night, and Merrick's half-hearted questioning the next morning led me to believe Sparrow told him to leave me alone. Not that it mattered anyway. My main idea had fallen short, a fool's shot in the dark. But at least I was now the proud owner of magic nullifying cuffs and chains, courtesy of the Obsidian Palace's treasure troves, that we could use to contain Adara if needed. A contingency plan that Sparrow had thought of and I executed.

I shook my head, clearing out the intrusive doubts, as Lenna, Sparrow and I wandered down the streets of the shopping hub in Florra. Sparrow was chattering excitedly to Lenna about the shops we passed–what they sold, who they were owned by–every detail. Lenna hung onto each word, throwing more than one longing look into storefronts.

Keeping Lenna under wraps had been the original plan, but Sparrow swore Florra wouldn't sell us out to Adara, and argued that Lenna should be able to see *some* of the charms of Irridessen so that she knew why we fought so dearly to protect it.

Our destination was rather inconspicuous for a being that could translate dangerous and illegal ancient spells, but I trusted Sparrow's lead. That female could start off talking to you about the weather, and before you knew it, you were spilling your deepest, darkest secrets to her.

A quaint bakery came into view as we rounded the corner, a bright lavender building nestled between an apothecary and a butcher's shop. The cheery lettering painted in a sweet looking mint green above the door read "Hale's Bakery." But the colorful entrance was nothing compared to the smells permeating into the street. I closed my eyes, inhaling deeply. I hated to admit that I'd be leaving with something warm and chocolatey after we talked to this magical spell translator.

Sparrow opened the door, a small bell tinkering as we crossed over the threshold. Lenna let out an appreciative sigh beside me as she beheld the rows and rows of baked goods sitting on wide, erratically painted shelves. Magic kept everything in here fresh, the loaves of bread sitting out in the open, still steaming as if they just left the oven. Delectable desserts filled every inch of countertop space and stacked neatly on the tops of round, wooden tables. As the chiming sound from the entry bell faded, a paisley curtain that separated the back kitchens from the storefront fluttered.

A stocky male with sable skin and a big, bushy beard appeared. His shoulder-length, black hair was spun into locs and decorated with small turquoise and amethyst gems. He had no wings, no horns, and was only a few inches taller than me.

Human?

Sparrow knew a *human* that could translate ancient fae spells? I swept my eyes toward her, questioning, but she dutifully ignored me.

"Hale!" Sparrow rushed forward, the skirts of her creamy blue dress rustling as she embraced the male into a tight hug. "It's so good to see you." Her enthusiasm made me swallow my trepidation and plaster a smile on my face. The male hugged her back fiercely before taking in myself and Lenna. His amber eyes widened in fear as he noticed me.

"My Queen." Hale bowed so deep that his nose almost touched his knees. I shot Sparrow a look that hopefully conveyed "*I changed my mind, this is a bad idea.*" Sparrow narrowed her eyes at me. As Hale straightened, Sparrow gave him a beaming smile.

"You don't have to do all of that, Hale. Esmeray is a dear friend of mine." Sparrow gestured to me. I gave him a small, totally not feral, smile, which did absolutely nothing to relax him. *Shit.*

"And Lenna!" Sparrow grabbed Lenna's hand, pulling her closer to Hale to see if that introduction could calm down the male that looked as if I just threatened to burn down his bakery with him inside. "This is the Oracle I was telling you about, Hale."

Hale had looked at me with fear, but he stared at Lenna as if she was the most delicious dessert he'd ever seen. To my surprise, Lenna blushed wildly and gave him a massive grin, her honey-brown eyes twinkling as she shook his hand. They exchanged greetings, which I quietly stepped away from. I tightened my wings closer to my sides, trying to look as non-threatening as I could for being dubbed the Queen of Nothing. I felt suffocated. Keerian was so much better at pleasantries than I was. He embodied that same calming presence that Sparrow did—able to make someone feel safe just by being near them.

I did not.

Sparrow, mission accomplished, reached out and steered me back towards Hale.

Second attempt.

"Now Hale, we talked about this. Esmeray is *innocent*, remember?" I had no idea Sparrow was so close with the baker, but it seems to have paid off as her words registered.

"Ah, yes, I know, Sparrow. It's just a bit intimidating for our Queen to be visiting me in my bakery, is all." His voice was deep, gruff as he ran his fingers down the length of his beard. I immediately liked him, even though the vote was still out on if he liked *me*. I reached forward and shook his hand.

"Thank you, so much, for allowing us to interrupt your workday," I started, "Your shop is lovely, and everything smells fantastic."

That seemed to work. His amber eyes immediately sparkled as his full lips cracked into a bright smile, revealing perfect teeth with slightly sharpened canines. *Half fae, half human?* I couldn't tell for sure.

Sparrow, it seemed, looped Hale in prior to our meeting of our big ask for his assistance translating the spells Laurent wrote down from the Prism, and my own recollection from the one time I peeked at a spell written down on parchment from Adara's book. After a quick tour of the bakery, with some free tastings that made my mouth water for more, Hale ushered us through the curtain and into the back of the shop.

Quickly winding through the kitchen, weaving around multiple ovens merrily churning out loaves of sweet-smelling cookies and bread, we ducked through another curtain, this one dotted with bright hues of pink and green, depositing us at the base of a narrow staircase. The walls seemed to groan and warp to accommodate Hale's full figure as he climbed, gesturing for us to follow.

This was...weird.

I kept my *acat* rallied right under my veins–just in case. Hale huffed as we neared the top, where a single door came into view. An odd thrum of power seeped from the other side.

The door opened with a croak, as if the hinges themselves told us to tread carefully. Dust and soot marred every inch of the cluttered room. A rectangular table littered with half-melted candles, jars of bones and dirt, and some glowing green substances even I couldn't identify, took up most of the space. Shelves crammed with heaps of scrolls, scraps of parchment, and books of every size bordered each wall, expanding from the creaky floor to the cobwebs branching out from the ceiling. There were skulls of various shapes and sizes dispersed amongst the tomes, and I realized with an uncanny chill that there was a *gargoyle* skull, with short brown horns, being used as a bookend. I shot Sparrow a warning glance, but she only squinted, shushing me, as Hale ushered us in with a buoyant chuckle.

We clustered around the table, Lenna and Sparrow more at ease than me. Hale gave Lenna a shy smile as he shut the door, and she positively *beamed* at him in return. I felt like I climbed up a staircase to a completely alternate realm. Taking up a quill, Hale began scrawling furiously on a piece of parchment, presenting the writing to Sparrow. "Are these the words Adara spoke?"

Sparrow scanned the writing before nodding, pulling out our own notes to compare. Hale bowed his head over the scribbles again, his bushy eyebrows knitted in concentration. Absentmindedly, he picked up a jar of bones and shook them, the sharp sound making Lenna jump. "The spells would be written in runic form in the book, but with the pronunciation from your notes, compared to these runes you saw, my best guess is that this spell book came from the Larimar Islands originally."

"How did you learn to read runic spells?" I asked, my curiosity finally getting the better of me.

Hale smiled, gently placing the jar of bone fragments back down onto the table. "My ancestors come from a very ancient lineage of fae called the M'ghoen. They were dubbed throughout history as the 'Spell Weaver Fae.' My father's direct lineage can be traced back to the M'ghoen who used to live in the Larimar Islands. My mother was human, she came over from the Slate Kingdom when she was young–meeting my father when they were both in their thirties. I came along quickly after Carra confirmed their soul tie." His hearty laugh made Lenna grin up at him. "The M'ghoen have been gone for thousands of years, but their history has been verbally passed down through the ages. My father was a scholar, and he made it his life's work to travel to the Larimar Islands and learn as much as he could about the fae tribe that lived there. He never published any of his findings, since the laws here state that spell work is forbidden, but he used to tell me stories, and through the years, he began teaching me how to translate spells and read ancient languages."

"How would my sister have gotten her hands on a book of spells potentially from an entirely different Kingdom?" I wracked my brain to figure out how this even made sense, coming up short with any feasible answers.

There were seven Kingdoms in all, each ruled by a different royal family, and rarely interacted with any type of warmth or friendliness. The Obsidian and Opal Kingdoms were the only Kingdoms where one royal family ruled the entire continent–Irridessen. The Slate Kingdom was directly south of Irridessen, mostly unaware of the existence of magic, and was not considered during times of war as an ally or an enemy. With the large amount of humans living there, the Slate Kingdom was never seen as a real threat to any Kingdom where magic was prevalent.

The Larimar Kingdom, usually called the Larimar Islands, sprawled off the coast of the Opal Kingdom, an archipelago that intertwined its own rich history with a motley of varying cultures. There was a steady peace between Irridessen and the Larimar Islands–but that was moreso a formality due to the closeness of their borders. To the west of the Obsidian Kingdom, separated by the wild seas, Ingotheria loomed. The biggest continent consisted of three separate Kingdoms. The Ruby Kingdom lay imposingly off the coast of the Slate Kingdom and allied closely with the Topaz Kingdom. With those two empires hosting the largest standing armies, ruled under the iron wills of their royal families, most diplomatic talks with Irridessen ended in all-out brawls. The Jade Kingdom kept to themselves, self-governed by four deadly Witch Covens, and better off left alone.

For some type of artifact to be given to the Opal Kingdom from the Larimar Islands was odd, but at least we weren't dealing with witches. My blood chilled at the thought.

"The book may have been given as a sly threat or a gift to a Kingdom that would never be able to translate the dark secrets it held. Or the book may have been discovered in the Larimar Kingdom and taken to the Opal Palace as a piece of antiquated history." Hale shrugged, picking at a piece of soot on the wooden tabletop. "This spell is written in a very old dialect if these runes are correct, and is the same spell that you heard spoken. Unfortunately, it's one that I hoped would never see the light of day. It's a mirroring spell."

I looked at Sparrow, alarm registering on her face. "That's how Adara was able to use your illusion magic to create daggers out of her nails."

"How would she be able to do that?" I directed my question at Hale.

"If she's able to pull that magnitude of spell off without killing herself in the process, it would be relatively easy. All she would need is some hair or blood from the being whose power she wanted to mirror." The next words out of Hale's mouth made my skin crawl. "But since you are twins, she wouldn't need anything from you. Lineage-wise, the same blood that runs through your veins, runs through hers—making the spell much more volatile, yet much more serious."

"With that spell, could she transfer something like...a soul tie?" My voice was barely louder than a whisper, my heartbeat pumping in my ears.

Hale considered the question for a long time, rubbing his stubby fingers over the jawbone of some sort of dead animal. "With that single mirroring spell? It would come down to the gritty technicalities over actual spell work yet... If she was strong enough, it's a possibility. But there would be other factors to consider based off the elements of the soul tie in question."

Lenna took the quill and ink from the table, sliding the parchment over before fixing Hale with a determined stare. "Like what?"

Hale hemmed and hawed for a minute, before replying, "The spell would need a significant amount of power to replicate Carra's magic. She would most likely need the blood of the being soul tied to you, maybe an additional sacrifice for a boost of power, and I would hazard a guess that it would need to be a special full moon. One with infinitely more power than a regular, monthly moon. From there, she could *potentially* use the spell to mirror a shadow of the soul tie from you to her. But if it didn't work, both you and your mate would be killed in the process."

"A shadow?" Sparrow repeated, as Lenna transcribed the information on the parchment. Hale silently pushed the ink bottle closer to her.

"A shadow," he confirmed. "Alike in every way except the way that truly matters, that Carra did not bestow the soul tie to Adara. Meaning to try and replicate it to complete the transfer... It could potentially kill all three of you if Adara isn't powerful enough."

Pieces started clicking into place in my brain. Adara had been relatively quiet since I was exiled a year ago, and there hadn't been anything momentous about the last few full moons. But the next moon...

I hissed, the realization dawning on me as dread settled into my throat, "Adara's been biding her time waiting on the next full moon—the Soul Moon. If she tried to complete the spell with the Soul Moon, would she have enough power to pull it off?

"I hate to be the one to say this, my Queen, but...it would give her power an edge." Hale said quietly, not meeting my eyes.

Each month's full moon honored a different god or goddess, on top of celebrating Carra and her gift of soul ties. But only one month a year was the moon venerated as fervently as the impending Soul Moon. The moon for the month Carra herself was born.

The most powerful moon of the year.

The moon where the majority of soul ties bloomed.

Sparrow paled, her tattooed hand covering her mouth, as she calculated the date. "Meer, the Soul Moon's in three days."

My chest constricted as, suddenly, time seemed to speed up, my thoughts zinging around my mind, shrieking. I couldn't get a full breath down.

Adara was going to attempt to transfer my soul tie in three days.

I felt sick, I felt hot.

I felt...*rage*.

Pushing down the panic, as I was so adept at doing these days, I waited for the familiar numbness to envelope my senses. It didn't come. It left the rage and fear, and I felt it twist and build in my soul.

We said a hasty goodbye and thanked Hale—Lenna even promised to come visit him in the future. He smiled broadly at that before sending us home with more baked goods than we could carry. As he escorted us to the front door, Hale wished me well, and told me he hoped one day soon, Keerian and I would walk through his bakery door. I extended my hand to shake his, but he grabbed me and pulled me close, hugging me tight.

"Don't let anyone stand in your way," Hale said gruffly as he let go.

With a flash of golden light, I waned the three of us home. We had a fight to prepare for, and a lot less time than we anticipated. Hale's words echoed in my head, and I knew, in my soul, I would burn this realm to ash if it meant I got Keerian back.

CHAPTER FORTY-SEVEN
LAURENT

"THREE FUCKING DAYS IS *not* enough time, Esmeray," Merrick snapped, earning a growl from the Queen facing off with him in Sparrow's living room. With both gargoyles posturing, wings out, legs braced, snarling at each other, the already small living room felt much more cramped.

Laurent stayed quiet, presiding warily from the purple couch, making sure this fight did not get any more physical than it was already escalating towards.

"I can do this *without you*," Esmeray sneered, baring her teeth at Merrick.

Sparrow stomped her foot, shouting over their raised voices. "*Enough*, both of you."

She shoved herself between their wings, jabbing a finger into Merrick's chest. Laurent liked that. After Sparrow's announcement that both males were welcome in her bed together, Laurent and Merrick had barely been able to look each other in the eye. Laurent was not opposed to the idea–as long as some very clear rules were drawn. But this was not the time or place to bring that up while Keerian's fate hung in the balance.

Laurent spoke once the arguing died down. "We need to get into the Opal Palace. I can build a portal past the wards that kicked Esmeray out, but I need to start now if we're all going." Laurent directed the statement at Lenna—she was so fragile compared to them. Part of him wanted to urge her to stay here, but she was so integral, needing to activate the Prism and show the Opal Palace's court what really happened to their King and Queen.

If word got out there, it would travel fast.

Esmeray nodded grimly, shoving Merrick with a wing as she turned towards Laurent. "That works. If you can start the portal now, that would be a huge help."

Laurent bowed his head, easing off the couch. "Consider it done. We will be ready to depart in three days, and will make it to the Opal Palace before the full moon hits its apex."

Lenna stepped gingerly towards Esmeray from where she'd been hovering at the doorway while the fighting had gone on, biting her lip between her bottom teeth. "So, I just need to show the same memory that we saw? But without an anchor?"

"Yes." Esmeray crossed the room, taking the spot Laurent vacated on the couch. "If any of us anchor to you, our consciousness goes into the Prism as well, and we can't protect you from Adara inevitably trying to attack you. You'll need to push the memory out of the Prism, and project it into the minds of the assembled court. Sparrow and Laurent are going to help you learn how to do that." Patting the couch, Esmeray waited until Lenna sat down before she took Lenna's hands into her own. "I cannot thank you enough for everything you're doing to help me." Gratitude flooded Esmeray's face as she looked around at the rest of them. "All of you—thank you."

Sparrow waved her off. "Thank us after Keerian is back here, safe and sound, and Adara is locked up tight."

"Come on then, Lenna, Sparrow." Laurent smoothed out the wrinkles of his lilac-colored robe. If he had to teach Lenna how to project memories *and* build a portal strong enough to slip past wards, he would need every second he could get.

Lenna squeezed the Queen's hands once more before following Laurent and Sparrow into the dining room. The last words Laurent heard before closing the door were a harsh, "Don't you *dare*-" from Merrick before Esmeray disappeared into a flash of golden light.

CHAPTER FORTY-EIGHT
MERRICK

MERRICK PACED THE LIVING room, muttering under his breath. Esmeray had disappeared again and he was sick of her coming and going as she pleased without any of them knowing her whereabouts. If something happened to her, they could all just kiss their lives goodbye. Adara would spit roast the lot of them.

And the audacity she had to flip him off before waning—gods, how did Keerian put up with her attitude?

He huffed, rubbing a hand through his rapidly growing beard. From the dining room, he could hear Sparrow's soft voice instructing and praising Lenna as she worked to project a memory from the Prism into their minds. A twinge of frustration spiked in his blood. Of course, Laurent was there with Sparrow, bonding over helping Lenna. At this point, the only way Merrick felt he may even be blessed to take Sparrow to bed was if Laurent would be there, too. The thought, supposed to irk him, rang hollow. *Would* he be interested in Sparrow's offer?

Merrick growled, storming over to the couch and plopping down, his wings rustling as irritation wracked up his spine. Maybe it wouldn't even matter. The odds of them all coming out of the confrontation with Adara alive were slim to none.

Should he take Sparrow up on her offer now? Would this be his only chance? He teetered on the edge, his thoughts growing darker and darker. Offering himself to Sparrow, knowing Laurent had to build a portal over the next three days, was selfish. *Fuck. Was* he willing to take Sparrow up on her offer?

The blast of golden light flaring through the room pulled Merrick out of his brooding. Esmeray appeared, panting heavily with that frustratingly wild gleam in her eye. Her light tan breeches were covered in blood, and her nails were rapidly shrinking from razor sharp daggers back to normal, less deadly, points.

"Fun night?" Merrick asked dryly, as Esmeray doubled over, wheezing. "How many beings did you kill?"

"Fuck you–four." She slashed Merrick a wicked grin before reaching into her pocket of space to pull out a full bottle of red wine.

"You seem more out of breath than you were at the waterfall," Merrick challenged, crossing a leg over his knee, earning a sarcastic eye roll from the Queen.

"They were all very highly trained fae warriors from Adara's private circle," Esmeray admitted, pulling the cork out with her teeth and spitting the stopper onto the table. "It wasn't a fair fight. They all attacked at the same time. It was good practice though."

Merrick narrowed his eyes. "If you were fighting Adara's warriors...I hazard to guess you just strolled into the Opal Kingdom, horns and all, to make a statement?"

"I had to pick up a package from an old acquaintance in Baubble," Esmeray innocently corrected as she drank deeply from the bottle. With a half swallow, half cough, she passed the bottle to Merrick. "I wasn't *in* the Palace. And I used an illusion of well, *you* actually, to pick it up. Oh, and do I have news."

Esmeray filled Merrick in quickly as they passed the bottle back and forth. Adara was indeed up to something sinister for the full moon celebration. The townsfolk were confined to their homes unless they had royal blood. Those who did had been forcibly ushered to the Opal Palace to stay until after the Soul Moon.

Queen Adara dispatched her entire standing army to patrol the closest towns, with a strict lockdown in place. Apparently, Adara was no longer hiding her power, and the beings living in the towns surrounding the Palace were either terrified and trying to escape, or extremely thankful to have such a fearsome and powerful Queen Absolute. There had been no mention of spell work from what Esmeray gleaned–the townsfolk were under the impression Adara feared Esmeray would try to usurp her rule on the night of Carra's holy celebration. And that the armies and lockdown were to protect the surrounding towns from the murderous Queen of Nothing.

"The ones that are scared–those could be allies." Merrick pondered the new information, swirling the wine in the half-full bottle. Esmeray hadn't been keen on sharing the information with only him first, but he threatened to tell Sparrow that Esmeray got blood on the living room rug. So, she begrudgingly relented.

Esmeray rolled her shoulders and rubbed her neck, her black horns glimmering with the light from the stained-glass lamp propped next to her on a thick stack of books. Merrick glanced quickly at her horns again. He had never seen horns like hers before. The curled horns with the deadly points never came up during any of his gargoyle lineage studies, but the beauty and cruelty that they embodied was mesmerizing. The pointed ears in the center of the curl were especially individual. While half fae, half gargoyle beings were not uncommon, they usually had a much smaller set of horns.

"Potential allies–or they think Adara and I are both evil, cut from the same cloth. And they're trying to stay out of both our warpaths."

She had snuck to her room and changed into clothes that were thankfully blood free, but Merrick could tell she was still riding the high of killing Adara's loyal guards. "How did Adara's warriors find you?" Merrick asked.

"I had just picked up a package from an old friend, and apparently, the neighbor of the fae male I visited decided to rat me out after he saw me cast an illusion. He found those four dipshits getting drunk at the nearby tavern and thought his loyalty would be rewarded if he told them I was in town."

"I'm assuming it wasn't."

"No," Esmeray scoffed, "the guards killed him immediately. They feared the consequences of Adara finding out that I slipped into town without her knowledge. Those bumblefucks came to find me... But I found them first. Two of the guards were stronger than I anticipated–fire magic–but they were still no match for me. Got my blood pumping though. I hate being burned. Even with my fast healing abilities, the new skin *itches*." Esmeray leaned further into the couch, her black wings draped at her sides like a royal cape.

"You are bat shit crazy." Merrick shook his head. "What was so important that you decided to wane to the Opal Kingdom?"

Esmeray, grinning like a fiend, reached into her pocket of space. With care, she pulled out a soft drawstring pouch. A small clinking sound made Merrick's ears perk up as she shook the bag tantalizingly before opening it.

Six thin, gold bands, with six evenly spaced gems fell into her open palm. "I figured we all needed an upgrade," she announced, plucking one ring up to pass to Merrick. Wide eyed, Merrick twisted the ring around the tip of his finger. The six gems–a black onyx stone, a bright green emerald, a shiny ruby, a gold gem, a grey stone, and a purple amethyst were embedded into the band, each twinkling in their own snug casing.

"These are mind speak rings." Merrick's voice filled with wonder, thumbing the band between his fingers. Esmeray gave him a mischievous grin in return.

"I figured this would be easier than us all talking through the same ring. I am so tired of hearing you and Laurent silently bicker through yours. And you both do it so frequently, I think I have a burn mark on my chest from the damn thing heating up every two minutes." She pulled Keerian's ring out from the bodice of her white sweater, the ring zipping along the chain. "Each gem is magically linked to one person. So, if you want to talk to Laurent only, touch the amethyst and only he will hear you."

"Woah." Merrick whistled low, thoroughly impressed. The rings Laurent, Keerian, and himself had cost each of their yearly salaries. These rings, with the ability to mind speak directly to one being or all of them through a system of jewels… The price would have been astronomical.

"I'm a Queen with no Kingdom, literally a Queen of Nothing. If I can't spend my money on my friends, what should I spend it on? There's only so many bottles of wine I can drink." Esmeray shuffled through the pile of rings in her hand before finding the one that was made for her finger.

Merrick grinned, slipping his old ring off and his new one on. The bright gems sparkled. "Adara isn't going to know what hit her."

Esmeray chuckled, the sound both cruel and divine. "That, my friend, is the whole idea."

Chapter Forty-Nine
ESMERAY

Sparrow, Lenna, and Laurent rejoined us after an hour. Lenna was positively beaming with pride as she confirmed the mind projection worked, and she felt confident enough to do it on a larger scale.

Merrick had forgiven me for slipping off, although I think it had more to do with the fancy new jewelry adorning his finger. I presented Sparrow, Laurent, and Lenna with theirs, the latter titillated that one had been made for her. I watched as she slid it onto her finger, next to a gold wedding band that seemed to draw a scowl to her lips for a beat. For the next hour, we tested out the rings' capabilities, memorizing what gem got through to whose mind. If I got any solid sleep tonight between my Adara problems and Sparrow's incessant tapping of my golden gem on her ring, I would fully consider it a miracle.

Now, Laurent stood in the center of the living room, crafting the portal that would take us to the Opal Palace. I had only ever heard rumors of his magic, and was intrigued to see a portal's creation. The give and take process of the fae feeding out bits of his *acat* to weave into the bobbing and twisting smoke was breathtaking.

Sparrow kept one eye on the back of Laurent's head, while engaging in conversation with Merrick, who stretched out his legs next to her and lazily rested his arm above Sparrow's shoulders against the back of the couch. I knew my friend well. If she'd convinced them both to come to bed with her, I wouldn't have been surprised. But the awkwardness Merrick exuded, even though I could tell he was trying to be *so* smooth, made me believe the offer had been given, but the two males were still thinking it over.

Sparrow didn't have a mate, but that never stopped her from taking home her fair share of partners—usually rotating between a couple of them at a time. I asked her once why she never chose one sole partner and settled down, and the answer I thought I would get was not the one she supplied. *It's difficult to choose—like there are two parts of me that each needs different things,* she'd confessed.

I hoped to be far away whenever she got it on with Merrick and Laurent.

Lenna, to my left, was deep in the Prism, slack jawed and dazed as she practiced filtering back to the memory of my parents' murder in anticipation of finding it quickly when the time was right to project it to the court. Adara set us up nicely for that part, unbeknownst to her, by forcing so many beings to attend her farce of a full moon celebration. Instead of just snagging the minds of the assembled court, Lenna would be able to push the memory into the minds of the court *and* all families with a titled bloodline in the Opal Kingdom.

Couldn't get more of a credible witness pool than that.

I sent a prayer to Carra, asking her to watch over Keerian in these last couple days before I would see him again. Going this long without him had pushed me past my breaking point, fracturing and reforming me all over again, casing my heart in rough stone that wouldn't crack until I was once again in his arms. I could tell by the ease I killed Adara's warriors that I was ready to wreak havoc on anyone who dared to keep us apart.

Interrupting my contemplative silence, Sparrow asked quietly, as if the words were too heavy to speak out loud, "Have you decided what to do about Adara?"

Keeping my eyes focused on the portal, I found myself unable to take in Sparrow's expression. I kept quiet.

"You *are* going to kill her... Right?" Merrick tuned in on our conversation. "She's too dangerous to keep alive."

Flicking my eyes up to Merrick, I gave him a slight nod, which Sparrow spied immediately. "No," she snapped, "if you kill Adara, how are you any better than she is? Killing and taking over the throne?"

I inhaled sharply through my teeth as my temper slammed its horns deep within my flesh. "I'm already better than her," I growled at Sparrow. She glared at me, the rage in her blue eyes cutting me to my core, before she rose in a fluid movement, storming out of the house. Merrick frowned, brow furrowing, torn between following her or staying in the living room. I jerked my head towards the front door and silently, he strode after Sparrow.

Brooding, I sipped my drink, not tasting the bitterness of the red wine.

"It's none of my business," Laurent said lightly, causing me to startle. Not taking his eyes off the portal he continued, "but you will never be able to please everyone when you take the throne."

"I'm beginning to notice that," I mumbled, leaning my head against the back of the couch. Defeat swirled around me, threatening to hang its heaviness around my neck as I pushed it away, burying it deep beneath my hardened heart.

The portal started hissing and sizzling, the white and grey smoke turning a viscous, poisonous green. Laurent's hands trembled with the strain of controlling his magic. The mist turned into a sludge–sticking to itself and slowing down. Laurent's face screwed up in a snarl, his teeth flashing as he grunted, the soft blue magic at his fingertips pulsing at a furious rate as he drained himself.

I was on the edge of my seat, hovering, worried and unsure how to help until Laurent huffed, "I'm fine. This was expected." Sweat dripped down his face, soaking the neck of his pale orange robe. "I must build the portal past Adara's wards, and there's a lot of them. Seems she found a trick or two in that spell book to make it near impossible to break through."

The toxic color must have been visible out the front window, because Merrick rushed back into the room, Sparrow close on his heels. Her eyes were wide with fear as Laurent calmly explained what he was doing and the complex wards. Sparrow gently touched Lenna, and the Oracle gasped, her eyes rolling back into her head as she arose from the Prism's depths, quickly assessing the scene around her.

I heard Sparrow quietly filling Lenna in as vivid green light bathed the room in a venomous glow.

"Impossible?" Lenna blurted out, eyes wide as she gripped onto my arm, shooting her gaze to the thrumming portal.

"*Near* impossible," Laurent chuckled, the sound falling flat as he winced with pain, a silent curse appearing against his curled lips. His hands shook more, the thick green smoke bucking and fighting against the command of his power. The plant pots on the bookshelf behind the portal began rattling. Books thumped off the shelves. My magic rose in my veins, ready to attack an invisible foe. With a strained growl, Laurent slashed his hands at the portal and....

The smoke sped up, and the poisonous hue dissipated, leaving only white light behind.

"Whew," Merrick breathed, plunking back down by Sparrow on one of the poufs. "That was intense."

"We're through the wards. The ride may be a bit rough to get there, though." Laurent's concerned eyes met Sparrow's, and she fluttered her eyelashes at him in return.

"Nothing we can't handle. Rough is fine," she said innocently. Laurent audibly swallowed. Merrick glowered. I assumed him trailing off after Sparrow hadn't gained him any favor with her.

I cleared my throat, the apology I owed Sparrow anxious to come out. Sensing my intentions, Sparrow stepped forward, interrupting me. Her eyes were soft as she looked at me, and somehow that hurt worse. She already forgave me, and I hated that the pity reflected in her eyes was directed at me. "I have news."

"You were on the front porch with Merrick for ten minutes, how did you *get news*?" Laurent asked, his eyebrows notched with confusion as he looked from fae to gargoyle.

Sparrow flicked her eyes to me. I knew how she got information, but if she wanted to keep her powers a secret, I wouldn't rat her out.

"Through the grapevine," she hedged, shifting her weight from one foot to the other, before taking up residence on the arm of the couch. Her blue eyes were solemn, immediately putting me on high alert. "Townsfolk in the Opal Kingdom are disappearing."

"What do you mean...disappearing? What townsfolk?" I questioned, a hollowness filling my chest.

"Here and there, a few at a time. But those numbers are adding up to a glaring issue. Beings are being taken. By something."

"My guess is by Adara," I clarified, feeling my magic thrashing under my skin.

Merrick hissed low. Next to him, Lenna looked petrified, clutching the Prism tightly to her body.

"We don't *know* if it's Adara," Sparrow corrected.

"I'm not ruling her out," I replied abruptly, the bite in my words meant for my twin, though Sparrow cringed, immediately making me feel like the shittiest friend ever. I needed to get out of this house, needed to expel this pent-up frustration. Every time I turned around, something was altered—*wrong*. Just this morning, Sparrow mentioned Adara closed the borders of Irridessen to diplomats from the Larimar Islands to *"focus on strengthening our own lands,"* and I had almost thrown my coffee mug against the wall.

I frowned at my nails as they grew back into daggers, now fashioned out of black diamond. Infinitely stronger—and much sharper. Cupping my tattooed hand, I willed a ball of golden light into my palm, the power pumping and whining to be unleashed. I squeezed my hand into a fist, and it disappeared.

Soon.

Soon these nails would be wrapped around Adara's pale throat.

And it would take all my concentration to not rip it out.

Without meeting anyone's eyes, I acquiesced, "I will not kill Adara until we know for certain there are no catastrophic spells in play to be triggered upon her death. The dungeons underneath the Obsidian Palace are where I'll put her. For now. Until we learn more."

Sparrow inclined her head towards me, as if my words were more apology than information. Which—they were. She knew me better than anyone. For Lenna's benefit, Sparrow added, "The first ruler of the Obsidian Kingdom was the Witch Queen, Queen Minerva. This was, of course, *long* before the fall of the Witch Covens. But while in power, Queen Minerva ordered her Coven to etch runes into the caverns below the Obsidian Palace. Though the witches have been banished from these lands, the runes remain. They nullify all fae magic, making them an excellent way to imprison beings with powerful *acatis*."

"If we imprison Adara there, it will give us time to figure out *what* she's been up to this past year. If she has anything to do with the missing beings, we can decide what to do with her...long term." I picked at my nails as inklings of a solid plan formed in my mind.

Merrick grunted *his* opinion of what I should do, miming a knife sliding across his throat and silently pretending to gag and slump over, dead. Sparrow shot him a look that would have faltered the gods themselves, though the gargoyle only smirked and shot her a wink.

If Adara had been capturing beings for some nefarious purpose, I did need her alive to question her. I felt restless without the backing of a court, of a Kingdom–adrift. There was nothing I could do to protect Irridessen except survive until I could rip Adara from the throne that I never wanted.

Until now.

Pivoting to the Oracle, I pulled out two daggers I unearthed from my bedroom in Sparrow's house, items that Keerian had left behind when we returned to the Opal Palace. Swallowing against the lump in my throat, I tapped each blade against my horn–the *tink* they made confirmed they were deadly and perfectly sharpened. Lenna looked at me in shock as I presented them to her. "You're going to want these." I pushed the hilts into her palms, avoiding looking at the daggers themselves, one of the only material things I still had of my mate's. *Keerian would've made the same decision if the roles were reversed,* I reminded myself. *He would never send someone into battle unarmed.*

"I've never used a dagger before. I've used a bow and arrow hunting but that's...about it." Her face blanched as she eyed the blades.

"Hopefully, you won't need to use them at all. Between the lot of us, you only need to draw these if we're all dead but... I don't want you to go in unarmed. If it comes down to it, aim for the throat."

Lenna let out a hoarse whimper as I demonstrated a few slashing and parrying moves that she could practice. I prayed she would never need to use them. I prayed our plan would go off without a hitch.

I prayed Keerian knew I was coming for him.

I was doing way more praying these days than I had in my entire life. And it made me feel completely helpless. If these damn gods were any good at their jobs, I wouldn't be in this mess to begin with.

CHAPTER FIFTY
LENNA

THE PORTAL WAS READY as the sun set in Florra. Laurent had barely left its side these past few days, stating the finesse it took to transport five beings while also keeping most of his magic intact was the reason for being so protective of it. Apparently, making a portal where the exit wouldn't appear until precisely when they went through it was something even Laurent and his expertise had admitted he wasn't masterful at.

Lenna and Sparrow snuck peeks at the portal once or twice, but were shooed away each time by Laurent. He wouldn't let anyone except Merrick into the living room until it was done.

Esmeray had been in and out of the house, citing she had a few avenues to explore to make sure she was prepared to take on Adara. Sparrow hadn't asked, and when Lenna had, Sparrow told her that was just *"Meer being Meer,"* and to leave it at that. Sometimes the Queen came back dejected, slamming the door shut to her bedroom. Sometimes she came back covered in blood. If that was the case, Sparrow would give her a pointed look–but ultimately sigh and wave a hand, the sound of the tub in Esmeray's room filling with water a compromise in itself.

Finally, Lenna had gone to Esmeray directly, feeling slightly guilty for going behind Sparrow. When she asked Esmeray where she was going,

Esmeray sighed softly and admitted she was trying to find any information on the missing beings to see if anyone could pinpoint who had been taken, or if there were any leads. Esmeray said she was using illusions to infiltrate cities and ask questions, listen, and to try to gather any tidbits or details that could be useful. From the drawn look on Esmeray's face, Lenna came to the conclusion there was no new direction–the search was coming up empty. And the Queen was taking it hard and personally.

Lenna had come to care for cocky, sarcastic Esmeray. Lenna became used to the smirk and the sass and was in awe of the ease and confidence the Queen exuded. Lenna even considered Esmeray a dear friend, and they had spent the last day while Laurent finished the portal telling stories of their pasts to each other whenever they had a moment to sit down. The glittering green eyes and the swishing curtain of black hair leaving a room was as familiar to Lenna now as her own red curls. Black wings launching off the patio was a normal sight, and Lenna found herself watching Esmeray as she flew off, hoping and praying her friend would make it back safely.

The silent, soulless, bloodthirsty Esmeray that stormed out of the bedroom this morning was not the being Lenna was familiar with–the haunted look in Esmeray's eyes put Lenna on edge. That look scared her more than stepping foot in the Opal Palace, or projecting the Prism's memory to an entire court. Lenna hoped the Esmeray that came back from the Opal Palace still had her soul intact.

But she pushed it down. The portal was ready. Laurent had given them an hour warning telling them to get dressed and to make it quick.

Now, Lenna stood in the hall by the kitchen, swallowing trepidation as she chanced a look at herself in the mirror Sparrow hung to make the hallway seem wider than it was. In Lenna's small bathroom mirror, she had only taken a quick glance at herself before losing her nerve and scooting out of the room.

But here, now, the reflection staring back was a different sort of stranger than the reflection that haunted her in Doortan.

She was dressed in soft black armor, the heavy leather material specifically designed for her curves. Flexible panels of golden metal protected her shins and her stomach, and harnesses strapped around her thick thighs, cradling the daggers Esmeray had given her. Lenna twisted and turned in the mirror. A hum began to roil through her blood, as if even her very bones said, *look, look at you*–this *is you*. The knowledge that she was *needed* and *integral* to this plan made her heart swell. She felt more important this past week than she had in thirty years.

Esmeray and Sparrow strode out of fae female's bedroom simultaneously. Lenna took one look at the pair and knew blood would be spilled tonight.

Sparrow was dressed simply, but lethally. The leather she wore was white, with the same flexible golden armor Lenna wore. Sparrow's top came up to her throat, down to her hands, held in place with thin loops that hooked to her middle fingers. Her hair was pinned back, out of her face, showcasing her pointed ears. A sword was strapped down her back, keeping her hands free for whatever gifts she would utilize. Lenna realized with a start that she hadn't seen Sparrow use much magic besides making flowers bloom. Lenna wasn't sure what Sparrow kept hidden but the blacked-out tattoo that covered half her arm alluded to some deadly surprises.

One look at Esmeray, and Lenna's heart stuttered.

Esmeray was dressed in black leathers as Lenna, but without any armor protecting vital organs. Her top was designed as a harness, wrapping around the back of her slim neck and buckling at the side, leaving her arms and wings exposed. The black leather pressed against her breasts, pushing them up, the tight black breeches curving around her muscled thighs.

Her wings and horns complimented the picture she portrayed of death itself. Either from illusion magic or if Esmeray had sharpened them, the talons gleaming atop the apex of her wings and at the bottom junctures of the black membranes were wickedly pointed and looked ready to slash into unfortunate souls blocking her warpath.

But it was the crown that sat atop her head, perfectly formed to wrap around the base of her horns, that made Lenna pause. The golden crown displayed a huge black diamond held in the center by two entwined golden serpents. The Queen of Nothing was about to make an entire Kingdom bow. Without knowing exactly why, Lenna did just that, bowing down onto one knee.

Before *her* Queen.

Lenna felt a hand on her shoulder, and looked up to see Esmeray kneeling before her, a soft smile illuminating her face. "Rise, Oracle," Esmeray murmured softly, curling a finger under Lenna's chin. The Queen's dagger nails were gentle against her skin as she guided Lenna up.

"You look...*badass.*" Esmeray grinned wide, her fangs peeking out as she took in Lenna's armor. Lenna blushed and crinkled her nose sheepishly at the compliment but was relieved to see some of Esmeray's normal demeanor peeking out.

The three stood in the hallway for a moment, before Merrick appeared from the living room, dressed in flexible grey armor with many scuffs marring the leather. His dark brown eyes were somber, the assortment of daggers and swords strapped and belted to his body alluding to his proficiency in battle. Lenna couldn't count how many weapons the gargoyle carried.

"It's time," he rasped, his tone commanding and curt. The voice of a lethal King's Guard. Lenna felt sweat begin beading on her body as she trailed after them into the living room. The portal stood, thrumming with impatience, before Laurent. The swirls of smoke were gone, leaving only pure white light in its wake. The power radiating from it was palpable, making Lenna's chest heavy with pressure.

The portal Lenna traveled through from Doortan had been half the size of the one currently pulsing in Sparrow's living room.

Laurent turned to take them all in, dressed in his usual styled robe, but these were matte black with golden threading woven through the seams.

"No goodbyes," Sparrow said quietly. "We go in together, we come out together with Keerian."

"No goodbyes," Esmeray repeated firmly, as she looked from Merrick and Laurent to Sparrow and Lenna.

They gripped each other's hands, faces grim. Everything on the other side of this portal was unknown. The only thing Lenna knew for certain was that her soul would never be the same after this.

Chapter Fifty-One
Keerian

He hated her.

Keerian seethed with quiet rage as he sat upon the white marble throne next to Queen Adara, unable to speak due to some godsforsaken spell from Adara's book that rendered him completely mute.

If he could use his voice, Keerian would roar for the court assembled to run. They were here under the guise of a special celebration for Carra's Soul Moon, unaware they were sheep being led to their slaughter.

This was *so fucked*. His thoughts were a garbled mess. The False Queen at his side was portraying them as a pair, a *couple*. But really, Keerian was bound with invisible chains upon the throne the late King Scottrell had ruled from. It felt wrong, dirty, to sit on this throne–like he tainted the image of the great fae king that he had sworn his life to serve and protect. Even if sitting here wasn't his choice.

But the King was dead, the Queen was dead, and Esmeray, his love, his mate, had disappeared into the night kissed wind.

Up to gods only knew what.

Esmeray had been silent, barely more than smoke and whispers, over the last year. The only way he got any information about his mate's where-abouts was through the bits of gossip he overheard from the Opal Palace's guards stationed outside the small room where Keerian had been held. The guards tended to disregard Keerian completely while he was imprisoned, unless they were bored–then they goaded and mocked him, trying to get him to smash against the invisible barrier keeping him contained. Keerian patiently watched, listened, and waited, identifying each guard by their individual scent, and made a mental note to seek bloody retribution on every single one.

Okay, he was male enough to admit that *patient* may be a strong word, but he only allowed the digs to get under his skin once, and when he had bounced against the barrier, his nose broken and bleeding, he vowed to keep a much tighter leash on his temper.

For Esmeray.

If he ever got out of this predicament. Adara had locked him in a tower, outfitted with a single barred window, warded so thoroughly that even Keerian, with no magic besides what he had been blessed with as a gargoyle, could feel the wards sapping his strength.

Queen Adara sat next to him now, poised on her own throne, her pure white wings clasped tightly behind her back. Keerian threw a seething glare to the False Queen besmirching the name and throne of the late Queen Elera.

Adara was dressed in an elaborate yet modest gown of snow-white lace, the material hugging every inch of her too-thin body. A crown of silver and white diamonds circled her head, and her horns peeked out from her unbound hair. She would have looked beautiful, demure, if the monster lurking under her pale skin hadn't stained her soul.

Queen Adara visited his room, his private dungeon, daily, disappearing quickly when she found him not inclined to play nice. When he had been chained, gagged, and ushered to the throne room this evening, he knew something dark was going down–that Adara's fucked up soul tie plan was in effect.

Keerian struggled fruitlessly against the invisible shackles that encircled his wrists, keeping his hands planted firmly on the arms of the throne, earning a soft hiss from the Queen. The bonds tightened.

"If you fight it, I will put an invisible chain around your throat." Queen Adara breathed, her voice lilting and soft, sounding as if she innocently asked if he was enjoying the party, not threatening to choke him.

He directed his fuming instead towards the intricately carved opal pillars that framed massive windows overlooking acres of royal gardens. To the untrained eye, it seemed elegant, ethereal. Keerian knew it was nothing more than a well decorated cage.

The court milled about the giant throne room, enjoying drinks and food, chatting with each other, none the wiser that, come midnight, a large portion of them would be dead.

Every thought screamed at him to fight, his gargoyle instincts–his Sentry–howling, thrashing, against her magical hold on him. Keerian had miscalculated Adara's cunning and played right into her claws. Every time she darkened the doorway of his prison, they played a game, where he would ask where her spell book was hidden, she would refuse to answer, and he would taunt her, trying to get her angry enough to slip up, to cross the threshold of wards and trap herself in that small room with him so he could snap her scrawny neck. But she never did, and all he'd gleaned was that the book was hidden from sight. He had no idea where.

Keerian hadn't cared about being locked up. He had no qualms for his own well-being, only that of his beautiful mate. Every morsel of information he heard regarding Esmeray was his sustenance, his nourishment, more so than any meal the guards forced him to consume.

And Adara, at the apex of the full moon, would rip his sacred soul tie from Esmeray and transfer it to herself. Binding Keerian's soul to hers for eternity.

Death sounded better.

Adara had gloated, mere hours ago, about her plans. Which was why he was currently sitting mute, her magic a nasty metallic tang against his tongue.

The power needed for the spell would be obtained through a drop of his blood, a drop of Adara's blood, and the life blood of twenty pureblooded gargoyles and fae. Forty beings would die in an instant, and a spell was already snaking through the room, unseen, choosing the beings that smelled of the purest blood, marking them for death. Keerian could catch the silver glimmer as it twisted between beings, but if he hadn't known what to look for, the spell would've gone completely unnoticed.

And it was currently going unnoticed amongst the revelers in the throne room.

If his death didn't mean the death of Esmeray as well, he would've taken many more reckless liberties during his confinement.

It was too late now.

Keerian stared down the False Queen, sitting so annoyingly proper and regal next to him, and mouthed the filthiest curses he knew at her. Adara didn't even spare a glance in his direction.

He hated her.

Queen Adara stood, clapping her hands twice. The court quieted, all faces turned towards their Queen Absolute. Keerian noted who looked afraid, and who looked at the Queen with delight. He made his own marks of death.

"My dear court." Adara raised her hands, her dull blue eyes stopping to take in each face as the silvery shimmer of her spell coiled around her, whispering the names of the ones chosen for her sacrifice. Her smile turned serpentine. "I am so blessed to have you all gathered today to witness a miracle of our time." Poisonous words wrapped in beauty. *Miracle.* "Our Goddess, Carra, has admitted to me that Sir Keerian was soul tied to the wrong Queen." Whispers began though the room, some faces nodding along with Adara, enraptured with her beauty, her presence. A few royals looked disgusted, and Keerian guessed those were the beings Adara had her Queen's Guard personally round up and force here.

Adara continued, raising her arms wide, her slim white wings fanning out. "Carra has given me the power to correct this...*unfortunate* situation. My traitorous sister used her illusion magic to steal a soul tie that was rightfully mine, and tonight, I will take it back."

Keerian narrowed his eyes, hate simmering in his face. He felt help-less–he had been caught by a powerful spider and she was not letting him out of her web anytime soon.

And the Queen wasn't stupid, even mentioning the word *'spell'* would cause panic and the reaction of disgust to grow throughout the assembled court. If only they knew the Queen was using a highly forbidden form of magic. He tried his voice again–still nothing.

Tilting his head to the side as much as he dared, he glanced out one of the large windows, his heart darting into his throat. The full moon was almost at the height of its journey through the night sky.

He had run out of time.

The transfer would happen any minute now. He prayed Esmeray would survive. Somehow, he would find her again–if not in this life, the afterlife.

Next to him, Adara pulled in a sharp breath, bringing him out of his too short prayer.

A group of beings closest to the entrance doors screamed as a flash of golden light barreled through the throne room.

Chapter Fifty-Two
MERRICK

THE HEAVY WOODEN DOORS, carved out of the ancient white birch trees that grew throughout the Opal Kingdom, exploded open with a wave of Esmeray's tattooed hand, and blinding golden light flashed through the massive throne room.

Gargoyles and fae alike screamed in terror as the light dazzled their senses. Merrick–unaffected since he had ducked his head at Esmeray's warning–watched as a second wisp of gold blitzed up the opal steps of the dais, pouncing on a silvery, smoky vapor, and smothering it completely.

An anticipatory heaviness gathered as Esmeray held her head high and took her first step towards the dais. With each thud of her black leather boots, beings shrank back from the Queen of Nothing–only a handful were brave or stupid enough to hiss insults as she passed. Esmeray paid them no mind. Her focus was on the two beings atop the dais.

Adara stood at the top of the steps, and Merrick felt his throat constrict as he beheld Esmeray's twin. Adara's normally beautiful face–the face her father had joked would bring any male to his knees–was now lined with shallow wrinkles creasing around her mouth and eyes. Her face twisted in anger, but there was a hollowness to her that Merrick had never seen before. Her hair was limp, lifelessly hanging around her shoulders like a heavy cloak. Even the small opal horns atop her head seemed muted. Adara's wings were tucked close to her sides, the thin structure of them suggesting she rarely, if ever, flew.

Her light blue eyes were dull, the irises more grey-ish and full of hatred. Esmeray and Adara shared the same pale skin tone, but where Esmeray was curvy, lithe, and muscular due to independently training for decades, Adara looked bony and bloodless.

The spells that she so coveted were sucking the life out of her. Leaving a husk in their malicious aftermath.

But it was the gargoyle with the golden wings atop the second throne that made Merrick's heart leap. Keerian sat upon the large marble throne–face frozen in pure shock from watching his mate break down the doors with ease and waltz up the aisle. His curly hair was pulled back in a bun, and his normally close-cropped beard had grown out past his chin, the red and brown curls thick. He wore a simple, long-sleeved tunic with silver buckles at the throat, and loose satin pants, both pure white to match Adara's lace dress. But Merrick noted he looked unharmed. A little haggard and his beard was much too burly, but no injuries marred his body.

Adara's eyes narrowed onto her sister, flicking up to the crown Esmeray wore as a challenge and a promise. Noting the murderous look in Adara's eyes, Merrick stepped in front of Lenna, his grey wings opening wide, blocking the Oracle from any magic that was inevitably about to be unleashed.

As Esmeray approached the marble steps leading to the dais, the court around them started to panic once more. A handful of fae had tried to wane, only to realize they were trapped here. Esmeray had, once again, blanketed a throne room with wards–forcing everyone gathered to stay.

So the Oracle could project the truth.

Frenzied voices began ringing out as some beings screamed, others began pushing and shoving each other out of the way. Merrick saw the glint of steel being passed between gowned bodies, the ulterior motives unclear.

Were these allies?

Or foes?

Sparrow seemed to note the same, and a soft green sheen of light began sparkling around each of the Oracle's footsteps, swathing her in a muted glow of protection magic. Merrick thanked the gods for Sparrow's quick thinking. If anything happened to Lenna, they were fucked.

Merrick felt his ring heat up on his finger, Laurent's steady voice welcoming.

"Keep an eye on Lenna. I don't like how the court is behaving. This could get nasty real quick."

The two curved daggers at his belt were easily within reach, and Merrick brushed the hilt of one lightly with his fingers to keep himself grounded. Focused. He glanced back at his commander, still seated on the marble throne.

Keerian seemed to struggle, trying to get off the throne he occupied, unsuccessfully. His bright, moss green eyes were filled with fear as he witnessed Esmeray stop in the middle of the room and reach into that special pocket of space to slowly pull out her golden staff. Merrick had asked Esmeray back at Sparrow's house where she got the weapon. She had cut her eyes to him mischievously before stating she found it, and its name was Goldriel.

Esmeray tilted her head to the side and smiled. "Hello, sister."

Adara took one step closer to the edge of the dais, ignoring her twin to address the chaotic court. "The Queen of Nothing has come to interrupt us on this holy night with her nefarious intentions." The beings quieted. The mayhem and disarray abruptly changed throughout the room to a heavy tension. The court seemed to await the next words with bated breath. Adara finally addressed Esmeray, her voice lowering as she spat, "How dare you show your face here, you *bitch.*"

"That is no way to speak to your True Queen Absolute," Esmeray replied, loud enough for the whole throne room to hear, black wings spreading wide as she stopped short, Goldriel tapping the ground lightly. "I thought you'd learned your manners over the past century. Or, at least, the way Irridessen's succession magic works."

Merrick started, staring incredulously at her. He knew what Esmeray had done the second she called herself the True Queen Absolute. The magic saturated into the very ground of Irridessen had named her Queen on High with the current succession orders from her parents, and only Esmeray had the authority to change any future royal titles. And she was. Now. In front of everyone.

Even as she spoke the words, a sheen of glittering magic filled the air and collected around her, Irridessen itself acknowledging her authority.

Esmeray wasn't here only to save Keerian and defeat Adara, she was here to take *everything*.

By discrediting Adara's claim to *either* throne, and banishing the titles of Queen on High and Lesser Queen.

There was now only one True Queen of Irridessen.

One.

And it was Queen Absolute Esmeray.

Sparrow stepped lightly to Esmeray's side, shooting a glance in Lenna's direction.

"Now," Laurent whispered to Merrick's left, "Lenna show the court now—while Esmeray has Adara distracted."

With trembling hands, Lenna reached into her pocket and pulled out the Prism. A few beings closest to Lenna gasped as they lay eyes on the coveted cluster of quartz, whispers spreading like wildfire. *The Oracle. The Oracle has come. The new Oracle has been activated by Moirai. Gods Bless the Oracle of Terramere.* She closed her eyes, hurling her consciousness into the Prism. The grey stone began to faintly glow. Laurent shifted himself in front of Lenna, cutting off Adara's view of her and the Prism. Merrick prayed to Moirai that those whispers that the Oracle had come to the Opal Palace would not reach Adara's ears, that Esmeray would keep her too distracted to notice what was happening.

Lenna succeeded quickly. As Merrick watched, the beings closest to him twitched and flinched as the memory from the Prism began playing in their minds. Slowly, the entire court succumbed as Lenna pushed the memory of the King and Queen's brutal murder at the hands of Adara into their minds.

With a smug smile, Merrick turned his attention back to Esmeray. She was pacing, clacking her staff against the white tiles on the floor, keeping Adara's focus away from the Oracle's actions and the now fully dazed and unfocused court. The memory was continuing to play. Merrick glanced at Lenna. Her face was ghostly pale, eyes screwed closed, brows scrunched in concentration, as she shoved the memory from the Prism into the minds of the assembled court and held the connection open. Tiny beads of sweat formed on her brow, but she pressed on.

"I'm offended. Really sister...I never received my invite to this party," Esmeray pouted, the clicks of the staff in her hands a rhythmic beat as she continued to pace.

Adara shot Esmeray an acidic smile. "You were always too little, too late, dear sister. The full moon is already at its apex, and Carra has blessed me with the power to reverse this abominable soul tie."

"You mean that little *spell* you had slithering around here?" Esmeray finally stopped pacing, and began inspecting her sharp black nails, completely unruffled. Adara stiffened. Esmeray slid her eyes up, a wicked grin flashing across her face. "Did you fail to notice your little silvery snake disappeared? That *was* the first step of your spell—right?"

Merrick and Laurent exchanged a look of confusion.

"How did Esmeray know about any of the spells Adara cast tonight?" Merrick touched his ring, throwing the question through all of the gemstones.

And a deep, rich, baritone—one he hadn't heard for a year, but that he knew as well as his own—answered, *"Because I told her."*

"Keerian?" Laurent's voice barreled down the connection, jolting Merrick out of his initial shock.

Merrick's gaze darted back towards Keerian. And there, sitting on his best friend's left hand, sat a thin, gold ring with six stones embedded in the band.

CHAPTER FIFTY-THREE
ESMERAY

KEERIAN HAD NOT TAKEN his eyes off me since my abrupt arrival to this fucked up little party Adara had thrown. It emboldened me. It centered me. I could feel our soul tie strengthen and bloom bright and fast now that we were finally reunited. Or at least close enough to being reunited.

"Hello, finally, my love," I purred to Keerian, directly through that black onyx embedded in our rings. The direct link to my mate's mind. Sparrow had waned the second we stepped through the portal, slipping the ring onto Keerian's finger without Adara noticing, since I was busy blinding the room with golden magic, hiding her own burst of green to appear back at my side. Then I activated wards to restrict the court from waning. Keerian's voice had immediately filled my mind, roaring at me to kill the spell that was weaving around the throne room, and my second burst of magic stifled it completely.

Adara had muted our connection with those *almost* impervious wards. After we slipped past the barricade using Laurent's brilliant portal, I felt our soul tie clear and sing out to me.

My mate, *my mate*, he was here.

My heart had felt heavy, foggy, until I took that first step out of the portal and into this throne room. Now, my heart felt light, beating in rhythm with Keerian's own.

I had never felt more powerful, as if my *acat* grew stronger within me. As if it had also been leaden and slumbering in Keerian's absence.

Nothing would stop me from being reunited with him. I just needed to deal with my twin first. Changing the succession to myself so publically had been a gamble, and I'd hidden my surprise when I felt Irridessen's own magic swell around me, marking me so quickly as the one True Queen Absolute. Now, I needed to tear this traitor off my throne.

Sparrow's body was half-hidden behind my wings, and I noticed the sheer shimmer of her own gifts projecting translucent shields of protection around the assembled court to keep them safe in case Adara realized they were all under Lenna's influence. And to keep them contained in the throne room until the memory finished.

No magic in, no magic out.

I kept pacing, diverting Adara's full attention to me as my own illusions pushed, unseen, against the spell she used to hold Keerian to that throne. Sparrow's and my magic searched for any kinks in the cast spell. Thinking of what Hale told us about Adara mirroring my power, I reversed my methods, using my own illusions to mimic the essence of the spell, aiming to release the hold she had on Keerian.

"What's the plan here, my love?" Keerian's husky voice filled my mind, eliciting a thrill down my spine. I fought the urge to look at him, my eyes only on Adara, luring her into a false sense of security. So far, Adara hadn't noticed the Oracle, or Sparrow's shields around the assembled court.

"I'm working on it." I shot back down our connection. *"You just hang tight until you feel that hold on you loosen."*

"So, sister, what exactly were you trying to accomplish with this theatric?" I asked my twin. "Because we both know the outcome. You aren't strong enough to kill me. Even with your spells."

The baiting worked. Maybe a tad too well. The air in the room began to hollow out and thin, rallying into Adara's spell enhanced battle magic. Feeding her power. Silver tendrils slipped from underneath her lace dress, rearing their eyeless heads, readying to attack.

Adara bared her teeth in a snarl. Her nails began growing long and jagged, glowing that unearthly silver. I braced myself, rallying my *acat* around me, golden light flaring from Goldriel. Ready to block and dissipate the impending attack. Sparrow's green battle magic formed out of the corner of my eye, snaking out of her hands like vines. I crouched–

"Murderer," the faint voice whispered behind me. I blinked, losing my focus. My power winked out at the same moment Adara's did.

"*Murderer!*" Another voice shouted, as the court assembled began coming out of the Prism's thrall, their renewed anger centered on Adara. Hate filled their eyes, hate that I had become so accustomed to, now rightfully focused onto their False Queen.

Adara flicked her eyes from me to Merrick, finally noticing Lenna, hidden behind him. Her eyes dropped to the Prism, still faintly glowing in Lenna's white-knuckled grasp.

"Oracle," she breathed, her eyes glowing silver, "*you* are an unexpected nuisance."

And then Adara struck.

Faster than a viper, silver power snapped from her hands, barreling directly toward Lenna–a kill shot.

"NO!" Merrick shoved Lenna out of the way with his wing, throwing himself into the full path of the blow. Lenna tumbled to the ground and rolled, hastily snatching up the Prism that flew out of her hands before scrambling back.

The breath left my lungs as Adara's magic hit Merrick directly in the chest, ricocheting him into the base of an opal pillar near the throne room's doors. Merrick hit the marble tile with a sickening *thud*. Blood trickled down his face, red rivulets flowing into his beard before pooling onto the floor. His grey wings crumpled around him at an unnatural angle as he slumped over.

And went still.

Sparrow screamed, launching herself at Merrick's limp body, throwing herself atop him. She slammed her palm down on his unmoving chest. Bright green light flashed and dissipated. With a cry, she hit Merrick in the chest again, harder, green light flaring brighter, enveloping them both. I threw out my hand, Goldriel flaring bright as golden power wrapped them in a shield a split second before another sharp burst of silver streaked across the throne room.

It hit the shield and exploded against the pillar, raining chunks of opal down. Sparrow ducked, but my shield held, the rubble bouncing off and rolling onto the floor.

Laurent ran over to Lenna, scooping her up and pushing the Oracle through my protection magic with Sparrow and Merrick. Lenna immediately fell to Merrick's side with panic etched into her features. Whirling around, black robe billowing, Laurent bolted towards me as bright blue and white flames curled around his fists.

Rage clouded my vision.

I only saw her.

Standing on the dais.

The disgust on her face as she watched Sparrow's green light flash again.

Goldriel hummed with power in my hand. I slashed the staff across my body, magic shooting out, hitting an invisible shield around Adara. She didn't even flinch. Her gaze landed back on me. But it was like she was looking *into* my soul. Not me.

In my mind, Keerian opened up our ring connection, roaring at Laurent and Sparrow to assure him that Merrick was alive. Neither answered. He thrashed against the invisible hold binding him in place, as if strength alone would break their nefarious grasp.

I whipped my staff again, hearing a satisfying *crack* as Adara's shield weakened against my onslaught of rage-edged power. Laurent jumped skyward, raining fire down atop Adara's barricade, resulting in a sheen of silver appearing around her. Her shield was weakening. He landed at the base of the stairs, readying himself to strike again.

"Laurent, stay there," I shouted the words into his mind, Keerian still bellowing at Sparrow to tell him if Merrick, if his best friend, was alive. *"If we rush her, Adara could wane Keerian out of here to complete the spell. We cannot lose them. My wards will not hold her here if she has a spell to break through them."*

I could feel Laurent's anger palpating from him. The flames around his fists grew.

"Go. But, if this looks like it is going sideways, I am roasting her," he growled back.

I pumped my wings, flying up the marble stairs at breakneck speed, hitting Adara's shield head on. My horns absorbed the brunt of the impact, and Adara staggered as her shield flickered and died out. Blood ran down my nose, filling my mouth at the hit, and I spat it out as I landed–almost hitting the hem of her dress.

My twin. No more.

I took two steps up the stairs. Adara stood still, though dull blue eyes tracking my every move. Her silence made this all the more dangerous. She was acting like a wary, caged beast as I approached. *How much of her soul had she given over to the spell book?*

And that brought me to a crushing realization.

I couldn't kill her *at all* if she was under the influence of that spell book. If she wasn't in control of herself. If somehow, Adara had gotten entangled into this accidentally, if she had killed and murdered under the duress of the spells in the book... Her planned imprisonment and execution was potentially a rescue mission instead.

"Yield," I snarled, pointing Goldriel directly in her face.

"Do you *know* what I uncovered in my research?" Adara whispered, taking a step away from me as I moved up the remaining stairs. She completely ignored the deadly weapon aimed at her face.

"Enlighten me. When you yield."

Adara smiled, her thin, colorless lips curling into a smirk. She waved a hand and the beings still behind Sparrow's barricades began screaming in pain. Two fae females close to the dais began clawing at their eyes as blood poured forth–before slumping over, dead.

"Sparrow, drop the shields now!" I screamed down our mind connection. The shield she had created–effective against regular magic–was useless against Adara's ancient spell magic. Something neither Sparrow nor I anticipated. We had inadvertently trapped the court, leaving them defenseless. My mind eddied out as panic threatened to overtake me. I whirled Goldriel away from Adara, aiming at and breaking the wards I put in place with a bolt of gold, allowing beings to wane once more.

Sparrow twisted her body towards the commotion, her face paling as she saw the two dead fae. Other beings, a female gargoyle closer to the doors, and a fae male began roaring in pain as invisible gashes appeared across their bodies, their blood now staining the white marble tiles. The fae looked down in shock, his hands unsuccessfully trying to hold his life blood inside, before collapsing.

The shields disappeared. Sparrow shouted to those assembled, pointing to the open throne room doors, her hands still faintly glowing green, "Get out now! Wane, take every being you can–*run.*" Fae began waning out of the room, grabbing as many beings they could possibly carry with them. Gargoyles and fae that could not wane, rushed towards safety, pulling their companions along. A few brave fae waned back in to carry more out.

Adara's grim smile remained as another being dropped dead, a male gargoyle that looked as if his throat had been slashed by the sharpest blade.

"Adara, stop." I took another step up the stairs.

"My spell should work with or without the necessary sacrifice," she murmured, mere feet in front of me. Her dim eyes fixated on the chaos below, though I saw the kernel of uncertainty flicker in the depths of her expression. Three steps and I could take her out. But with Keerian so close... If she tried to harm him...

She cocked her head, as if she could hear my thoughts, coolly looking me over before turning her head ever so slowly to take in Sparrow, still healing Merrick.

"Does she know the god that blessed her?" Adara asked me, completely catching me off guard.

"I–No. She doesn't know. Why," I deadpanned, slowly creeping up the next step as Adara continued watching Sparrow's attempts to heal Merrick with blatant curiosity. I prayed he was alive. My gut knew from the silence through our mind connection that it was grim.

"The spells...work in wondrous ways," Adara said simply, tearing her gaze away from Sparrow as a silver dagger appeared in her pale hands. She rolled her shoulders back. "They showed me how to mirror your illusion magic by telling me exactly which god blessed you with your *acat*. From there...I could build *anything. Create* anything–even a soul tie." The dagger was plain but deadly, with a long blade wrapped in a white marble handle. I flicked my eyes from it to Keerian. He was still bound to the throne, my magic frantically beating against Adara's own. His green eyes widened as he looked from Adara, to the blade, to me.

My heart cracked.

Adara gently wrapped her fingers around the hilt of the dagger, inspecting it as if she was nothing more than a customer at a sword shop. "Mother and Father... They never told anyone which god blessed you. I inherited Father's water magic. Decidedly from Beyos, himself. But it's a pathetic skill, really. I'm not even that good with it. My power was always a disappointment. Father could command the tides, and I could barely conjure enough water to fill a bath." The dagger gleamed in the light from the hundreds of candles nestled in the chandelier overhead. "But you...you came out different than me. I always knew when we were children... And when we both received our *acatis*...your entire arm was tattooed while I only got small, easily unnoticed tattoos on my shoulder. It hurt."

"You sound like us as children now, Adara," I snapped, pushing Goldriel into my pocket of space where I could keep it close. At this distance, my nails could attack more effectively than the long staff. "Do you know how upset I was when only you got our father's water magic? The magic that we used to whisper about when we were young? How we planned to build waterfalls around every side of the castle? How we wanted to create a giant pool for a kraken in the gardens when we *both* inherited his power? I used to try and try for *hours* to conjure up water like you could."

"But then you did. With your illusions," Adara hissed. "Don't leave out that part. How thrilled Father was when he saw you conjure up more water than I ever could. When you created a waterfall down the very stairs you now stand upon." Adara took a sidestep. It was small, I would have missed it if I hadn't been carefully watching her. A step closer to Keerian. "But then he realized it was an illusion–it wasn't his gift. And he was angry. But more than that–he was afraid. Do you know which goddess can create illusions? There have only been whispers of your brand of magic through the telling of time. And I bet you didn't know that your lineage god has the *exact* same horns as you."

"No one knows what the gods and goddesses truly looked like, Adara. How can you know what goddess I got my fucking horns from?"

Adara merely gave me a smug smile.

I became aware of a thudding in my ears, as if my breaking heart already knew what Adara would say. The goddess whose stories of bloody conquest were turned into an old wives' tale to scare misbehaving children. Which goddess was so reverently feared and spoken of only in whispers.

Which goddess had gone down in history revealing that death itself was the grandest illusion of all.

"The goddess that blessed you, dear sister, is the Goddess of Death. Phades."

CHAPTER FIFTY-FOUR
ESMERAY

"That's impossible," I whispered, "Phades has never blessed an *acat.*"

Phades was the monster in the shadows. Not a single being spoke her name louder than a reverent whisper as an acknowledgement of her immense prowess. Both her twin, the Goddess of Life, Faune, and herself had been cast from the god realm, Aurramere, together at the beginning of Terramere's creation. Legend said Phades and Faune did everything together, intertwined in all their decisions–until a disagreement between life and death. Phades had stated that even death itself was an illusion–that it was only a ripple between this world and the next. Faune disagreed, stating that death was a finite end, since beings in the afterlife could not come back to the living realm. My mother had always tamed down our bedtime stories and the final argument that had separated Phades and Faune, but once I was old enough to read, I found a very different ending to their story–one with way more peril and bloodshed.

Faune and Phades had fought, but ultimately never came to an agreement. There was never a reconciliation, never a moral to the story of compromise outside of the stories told to me as a bedtime tale. Faune stayed in the lands of the living, creating and coaxing the life of all beings into a gentle existence. Phades disappeared between the veils of the world to live in endless death in Minmere, where she ruled over the souls that passed on.

Finally, Faune had returned to Aurramere, and Phades...disappeared from history, rumored to be in Minmere to this day. No one had ever been favored by Phades. Until apparently...

Me.

Adara turned, a dismissive gesture in itself, and took a seat on the throne next to Keerian, balancing the dagger on its tip against the marble armrest. She twirled it with her fingers, the blade dancing to a song of bloodshed to come. "Did you know, Esmeray, that our parents *knew* you were blessed by Phades—but didn't tell you?" She laughed, the sound hollow and false. "After that, I think Father realized my gifts were decent after all."

I snapped and lashed out at Adara, catching her off guard. My nails sank into the soft flesh of her cheek before a blast of silver threw me back down the stairs.

"You stole from me," Adara hissed, that quicksilver leaping into her eyes. She touched her cheek, pulling away fingers covered in blood.

"I didn't steal *anything* from you." I flew up towards the ceiling before clasping my wings behind me, freefalling to land on the dais between Adara and Keerian. "Keerian is my mate. Our soul tie was blessed by Carra. I love him, Adara." Adara was delusional. It was time to get her into a nice, completely-not-cozy cell and see if the effects of the spells faded.

Faintly, in the back of my mind, Sparrow's voice whispered wearily, *"Alive—he's alive. Merrick is alright."*

"You don't deserve the crown." Adara began shaking, her whiplash of emotion so unlike the proper and sensible sister I thought I knew. We'd bickered in the past, but I never truly believed we'd fight to the death over a throne. She had been cool and detached moments ago, and now she was frenzied, out of control. She gripped the dagger in one hand, pointing it at my face. My hand twitched, magic beginning to crackle between my fingertips. I refused to back down. "Keerian was *mine,* until he saw *you* in the garden. The soul tie was supposed to be *mine,* the title of Queen on High was my *destiny!*" Adara screeched in rage, "You never even *wanted* to rule."

"This is *enough,* Adara," I snarled, conjuring up the manacles and chains from the Obsidian Palace that nullified magic. A shadow of doubt flitted across my mind that they may not work against spells since the barriers had not–but if we could wane Adara quickly to the holding cell we chose in the Obsidian Palace... She wouldn't have time to fight back.

"No!" Adara shrieked as she took in the thick chains draped across my forearms, her voice morphing into...into...a deep rumble. "You cannot control me–you cannot *contain me. I* am Queen Absolute, and *you* are the Queen of *Nothing.*" The last word came out as a roar as Adara spread her wings wide, launching off the dais and landing on the white tiled floor below. The bodies from Adara's sacrificial spell still lay in the spots they fell, though blood stopped weeping from their wounds, pools of red now staining the once pristine floors.

Adara shifted.

Her white wings grew, and visible, opalescent fissures began forming along their boning. I reared back as her spine arched, and a heavily spiked tail lashed against the steps. Slim hands turned into leathery pads, turned into claws, as Adara shifted into her Sentry. I took another step back, my eyes darting to the rest of my new family spread around the throne room. I'd *never* seen Adara shift. She always complained that our Sentry form was archaic and beastly, and she was too prim and delicate to turn into a monster.

The Sentry Adara revealed was everything that snaked from my nightmares as the huge white gargoyle lifted her head and bellowed a song of death, shaking the chandeliers and opal pillars. More debris began falling as the filigree beams branching across the ceiling cracked. It felt as if the whole room shifted around her.

Laurent, Sparrow, and a limping, but alive, Merrick, stood between Adara and the throne room doors. Lenna was nowhere to be found. Most likely waned out by Sparrow or told to run the second Adara began shifting. Laurent's hands were wreathed in blue-white flames, his eyes reflecting his molten power as he beheld the gargoyle before him.

Sparrow slowly unsheathed her sword from her back, green light pulsing from her palms. Her battle magic flared, pushing up the thin blade, until the entire length was engulfed in tendrils of green. Merrick looked steady enough, fisting two short, curved swords. His wings were snapped shut, one still bent at an odd angle towards his thigh, but the warrior seemed to not notice as he took a step towards Adara.

They looked so small, so fragile, standing in front of Adara's Sentry. I fumbled through the surface level fae magic inside of myself, finding that inky black strand connecting to my own Sentry. I drew in a sharp breath as I shifted, the familiar icy burn zipping through my muscles, my blood, as I rolled my shoulders, wings elongating, thickening the bones themselves. My horns lengthened, the spiral protecting the sides of my throat.

Adara's Sentry was easily twice the size of mine. I pushed down the uncertainty that I may not have an easy fight as I launched off the dais, landing on four solid paws, black talons digging into the marble tiles as my wings snapped open. Opening my maw, I roared my own defiance, my spiked tail thrashing between Adara and my family.

Holding the line.

I lowered my head, a growl reverberating along my throat as I paced in front of her, baring razor-sharp black fangs.

Whatever spells Adara was performing had changed her Sentry from a gargoyle to a monster. Silver cracks marred her leathery hide from her talons to her throat, a consequence of the spell that had gained her the considerable size advantage.

Merrick gritted his teeth. Through my slitted pupils, I saw him pushing to Sentry–with no success. His body was still healing, and if he forced into a shift, he could do irrevocable damage to himself. I needed to draw Adara away from the idea that Merrick would be easy to finish off.

A guttural snarl formed low in my belly as I bared my teeth at my twin. Adara screeched again before her maw darted out, aiming right for me–only to be caught by the throat at the last second by a radiant golden Sentry.

Keerian had broken through Adara's bonds and shifted, his Sentry one of pure majesty. His golden wings beat hard as sharp, solid gold teeth and talons ripped into the soft flesh on Adara's throat.

Adara shook him off, throwing him to the ground with ferocity. I roared my mate's name as I launched towards him–only to be kicked in the flank by Adara's skin shredding claws. Bright red blood spouted down my black, scaled hide as I rolled, landing upright. The coppery sting shook me to my core, but I shoved the pain deep. Next to me, Laurent began shooting dark blue will-o-wisps at Adara, and she yelped in pain at the impact before whipping her tail around, hitting Laurent in the chest and sending him careening into a pillar. Laurent missed being impaled on one of her opal tail spikes by inches. He staggered upright with considerable effort, rallying flame around him once more, before continuing his barrage of power directly at Adara's monstrous face.

Sparrow and Merrick, to my left, launched into action simultaneously, driving Adara back with their combined forces. Sparrow wrapped vines of green magic around one of Adara's legs, anchoring her to the floor and causing her to stumble onto a knee. Merrick's sword slashed down, cutting into Adara's considerably thick hide on her leg as Adara snapped at Sparrow, who darted out of the way just in time to avoid getting mauled by sharp teeth.

Thundering down the aisle into a leap, I landed on Adara's wide back, shooting golden power into her wing, trying to tear the membranes and keep her grounded.

I got in three solid hits before Adara broke Sparrow's magical hold and bucked, sending me flying into the staircase.

Keerian scrambled up the stairs to me, his talons pulling chunks of opal out of the dais. He gently nudged me with his gold snout. I'd knocked my head when crash landing, and had to shake the daze from my vision. He nudged me again, more urgently, and I groaned in response.

"Meer, are you alright?" His expression was one of worry and trepidation–but his entire focus was on me.

I screeched out a warning, shoving him away just as Adara's tail came smashing down between us, cracking the staircase itself. Keerian roared, soaring into the air, sinking his fangs and claws into any piece of Adara he could connect with between her thrashing wings, tail and teeth.

Around me, Sparrow, Merrick, Keerian and Laurent fought and fought, gaining a step, before losing it again. Even with all of us, Adara still held a considerable advantage. Silver sparks erupted around her, revealing a bird cage that snapped closed around Sparrow and Merrick, trapping them in Adara's mimicked illusion magic.

Laurent dodged the attack but stumbled–caught in time by Keerian. My throat felt dry. My heart pounded. These beings were my family–and Adara was aiming to kill us all. I felt disembodied, the thudding in my ears drowning out all other sounds as I took in the wreckage of the room, the valiant, combined efforts of Keerian and Laurent–the Golden Gargoyle and the Spy Master. Reunited at last.

Sparrow and Merrick banged against the bars of their cage, trying to break free. Laurent, his fire burning him up, had gone from a blue and white inferno to trickling plumes of orange–a bad sign that he was coming close to burning out his supply. And Keerian, my mate, my love, snarled at Adara in anger, trying to close the gap between them to do more damage. Even if the cost was to himself.

To us.

In that moment, I knew what I needed to do.

I sprung up from the crumbling stairs and slammed the tips of my horn into Adara, right as my jaws closed around the juncture between her wing and side. With a flash of bright gold light, I waned my twin and I out of the throne room.

CHAPTER FIFTY-FIVE
LENNA

Outside the throne room, the Great Hall had descended into pure panic. Disorder and turmoil flooded the space, spilling out onto the balconies, down to the courtyards below. Lenna darted past the thickest part of the fighting, cries of pain echoing in her ears, as she dodged flashes of magic and the clashing of swords.

Lenna was shoved to the side as a fae female ran by, screaming at someone to help her, to get a healer, as she dragged a moaning gargoyle towards the center of the hall, blood leaking from his thigh, painting the white tiles an unnervingly deep red.

Queen's Guards, and those loyal to Adara, battled against the tide of beings who directed their anger at being tricked onto her closest supporters, pops of magic and the gurgles of the dying a quieter sound than the ringing of steel on steel, the shouts of betrayal and rage.

Heart hammering in her chest, Lenna backed away from the clamor, holding the Prism so tightly to her chest that her palm ached and the sharp planes of the stone cut into her fingers. Unsheathing one of the daggers Esmeray had given her with her other hand, she shrank back into the shadows along the wall, her grasp around the hilt so clammy that she almost dropped it. Behind the throne room doors, a roar shook the foundation of the Palace, answered almost immediately by a screeching bellow.

Sparrow had taken one look at the monster Adara shifted into and waned Lenna out of the throne room under the orders to hide until this was over. Or run–if the battle waged did not result in Esmeray winning the throne.

Lenna scrambled away, ducking behind a marble statue of a long-dead royal a split second before a blast of magic whizzed past, ripping away half the statue's face.

Pulling her knees to her chest, Lenna panted, her mind bleating in terror. Curled up in a ball, she felt so utterly alone. Battles raged around her, and yet Lenna was frozen to the spot, petrified. She was not a warrior, not a battle-hardened gargoyle, nor a powerful fae.

She was just...Lenna.

Human, powerless, way too mortal to be involved in this fighting.

As tears spilled down her cheeks, a sharp poke to her stomach gave her pause. The Prism dug painfully into the soft fold of her belly. Grimly, she brought the Prism up to her eyes, wondering who would be activated upon her death. At least she hadn't failed to project the memory of the King and Queen's murder. At least she could be proud of herself for completing her task–even though she was no help after, and would probably die here, afraid and alone.

"Esmeray waned Adara out of the throne room, and we don't know where she went." Laurent's voice broke in her head as her mind speak ring heated on her finger. *"Where are you?"*

"I'm in the Great Hall, hidden away from the fighting," Lenna whispered back into Laurent's mind, embarrassment heating her cheeks at the implication that she hadn't been helpful after projecting the memory while others fought.

The Great Hall. Lenna jolted.

It looked...familiar.

Suddenly, Keerian's voice began shouting through the ring, open to all six of them. *"Esmeray! WHERE are you? Please, please, gods, tell me where you went."* Over and over, Keerian roared down the ring for his mate. It ripped into Lenna's heart–his pleas for Esmeray to answer, the deafening silence as the Queen did not.

"We'll come get you, stay where you are," Merrick's weary voice rumbled through her head. Lenna didn't respond as she stared at the Prism in her hands.

Throwing herself into the Prism, Lenna flung herself down the thread of her past, searching for the strand that connected to Esmeray, barreling down its length to the Queen's most recent memory–as close as Lenna dared to the glowing golden orb that would shove her back to reality. Right at the cusp, Lenna dove into Esmeray's thread.

A soft flurry of snow, so white it was almost blinding, came into view. Esmeray, back in her normal form, was panting and bleeding in front of temple ruins half-buried in snow.

Lenna blanched as she realized this was the setting of the nightmare she had in Doortan, of the monstrous black gargoyle hunting her. But through this lens, the black gargoyle was Esmeray, in dire need of help, as the huge white Sentry stalked the perimeter, trying to locate the Queen. Lenna's eyes darted around, trying to discern any sort of landmark that could help locate Esmeray.

Lenna launched her mind higher, higher, towards the clouds.
There.

The black spires of the Obsidian Palace. Esmeray had waned Adara to the mountains above the Obsidian Palace for her final stand.

Yanking her mind out from the Prism, Lenna moved to touch the ring on her finger, to tell the others she located Esmeray. But what could they do? Esmeray had waned to the Obsidian Palace, away from them, to keep the bloodshed between her and her sister. It begged the question–did Esmeray want them to come? Or was she getting Adara away from the throne room to finish the fight herself, without further endangering Merrick, Laurent, and Sparrow?

As another burst of magic fizzed by, Lenna flinched, stilling as she took in the destroyed face of the statue in front of her.

The hidden entrance to the dragon lairs are behind the marble statue of a Queen long dead.

The Hall *was* familiar–from the memory of young Esmeray and Sparrow. It all came flooding back. She'd been so numb after finding out Diana passed, had been so worried about Marlo and Orla, that the memory of Sparrow and Esmeray as children seemed trivial.

But she had thrown herself into the Prism, not really looking for anything particular, and wound up seeing that memory. As if Moirai had steered her there, knowing she'd need the knowledge for the future.

For this moment.

She was not only the Oracle of Terramere, but a seer as well. What if Moirai had nudged her to the memory of Sparrow and Esmeray, using the past to give her information helpful for this fight?

Lenna quickly got to her knees, running her hands against the curved wall behind her.

Adara was big.

But not as big as Resso.

If Lenna could get to the dragon lair...could she beg the dragon to help Esmeray take on Adara above the Palace?

Her fingers snagged on a small knot beneath the wall. Her breath hitched.

Tentatively, Lenna pressed her finger against it, the wall shivering before turning translucent. Lenna slipped through without a second thought, praying she wouldn't be stuck down here. But she had come to care for the beings in the throne room fighting for the truth that *she* revealed. She could do this.

Jagged black rock walls and a narrow stone walkway that turned into steep stairs greeted her–the air musty and cold. The moment she passed through the magic, only silence greeted her–all noise from the battle in the Great Hall cut off. Sliding the Prism snugly between her breasts, Lenna palmed the second dagger and began the descent, the stagnant heaviness pressing into her nerves as the temperature dropped rapidly. With a huff, Lenna followed the path the God of Sight sent her on.

Down, down, the air growing thinner as she wheezed, taking the tight, winding staircase as quickly as she dared, praying she wouldn't trip. A roiling black wall of smoke blocked her path, but she pushed through without a moment's hesitation, her steps hurrying as the iciness of the barricade rubbed over her.

The staircase ended abruptly at a ledge, opening into an airy cavern. Lenna craned her head up, spotting the glimmering glass floor of the Obsidian Palace's throne room high above her.

The magical barricade was a portal that connected the two Palaces together. She faintly remembered the vision-Esmeray saying something about that, but a whoosh of air was her only warning as Resso rose from the shadows below, his maw snaking out towards her curiously.

Hovering in place, his huge wings keeping him airborne, Resso appraised Lenna. His nostrils flared as if he was scenting her, and a spark of intrigue flickered in the dragon's moon-colored eyes.

Lenna's hands shook as she laid both daggers on the stone floor, keeping her eyes locked on the mighty dragon in front of her. She didn't want Resso to consider her a threat–or dinner.

Resso growled. Lenna backed up, her spine colliding with the icy rock wall. Hands still trembling with fear, Lenna reached down her bodice, presenting the Prism to the ancient beast.

"I am the Oracle of Terramere," Lenna whispered quietly, holding the Prism above her head, her curls buffeted in the bursts of wind coming off Resso's wings. "And I need your help."

She had no idea if the dragon remembered her from the throne room above, or if he even cared that she was the Oracle. Her feet sidestepped towards the entrance to the stairs. If Resso decided he wanted to eat her, she could escape up the staircase, run back through the weird portal, and pray that he didn't unleash a torrent of fire to turn her to ash.

Resso cocked his head, staying level with the ledge.

Lenna wished her Oracle prowess included being able to mind speak with dragons.

"Queen Esmeray is in the mountains above this Palace, taking on Adara for the throne. Adara killed King Scottrell and Queen Elera."

Resso's slitted eyes seemed to widen. Queen Elera had ruled from the throne here. Lenna prayed the dragon liked the gargoyle Queen enough to care who her murderer was.

"I think I can show you, with the Prism, if you don't believe me," Lenna added, her voice cracking with fear. In response, the dragon snorted, white smoke curling out of his nostrils.

Then, without warning, Resso let out an ear-splitting screech and shot up, up, to the glass floor that trembled and shone as he disappeared through it. Lenna sent a prayer to whatever gods would listen from down here that Resso was on his way to aid Esmeray.

Lenna stayed rooted to the spot for a moment, until another roar shook the caverns. Remembering then that Resso was not the only cave dragon down here, Lenna bolted, swiping both daggers up with one hand. Gripping the Prism tightly in the other, she turned and ran back up the stone staircase, back through the magical portal, back into the Opal Palace.

She was not only Lenna. She was the Oracle of Terramere, and she would face whatever evil came for her and her friends. Even if that put her in league with the beasts from her nightmares.

CHAPTER FIFTY-SIX
LAURENT

THE RINGING IN HIS ears from the immediate and utter silence was deafening as the gold light flashed and the two Queens disappeared.

"Where did Esmeray go?" Keerian yelled as he shifted back into his original form. His white tunic immediately became stained with blood from where Adara's talons had sliced into his Sentry's hide, but the bleeding was ebbing quickly, his gargoyle healing abilities already clotting the wound. "Where is *my mate?*"

The Golden Gargoyle bellowed Esmeray's name, over and over, until his voice cracked under the weight of Esmeray's decision. Laurent's own heart felt as if it was ripping in two as Keerian's panic smothered the room in anxious energy.

"Esmeray waned them out—but why?" With Adara gone, the cage holding Sparrow and Merrick disappeared, the former keeping a sharp eye on the latter. "Why would Meer do that?"

Keerian buried his face in his hands, groaning, "Because she realized we were losing. So, she made the choice to finish it herself." He blew out a deep breath, and Laurent knew the fearsome Commander was making his own peace with death in case Esmeray fell against Adara and the soul tie yanked him to Minmere. "She didn't want to put you in any more danger."

"We were here supporting her–supporting her claim," Sparrow shot back.

Keerian shook his head in grim acknowledgement. "She would've fought death itself if one of you met your end."

Merrick paled, looking over at Sparrow. "One of us did," he admitted too quietly.

"What?" Laurent crossed his arms, eyes narrowing, as Sparrow swallowed and looked down, scuffing her leather boots against a dried blood stain on the floor.

Merrick inhaled slowly before answering. "The kill shot Adara aimed at Lenna... It stopped my heart. I *did* die for a few minutes." He reached his arm out, wrapping it around Sparrow's slim waist. "Sparrow bought me back."

Laurent resisted the urge to remove Merrick's hand from Sparrow. Now was not the time. Not with the fate of the continent resting in the resolution of a battle none of them were involved in. Even before everything started, this had ultimately always been Esmeray's fight.

"How?" Keerian crossed his arms, wincing slightly from his injuries, and surveyed Merrick up and down as if he couldn't accept the utter nonsense Merrick spouted. Merrick threw him a droll look in return. "Then you weren't dead. No one can bring a soul back from Minmere."

"But I did," Sparrow whispered hollowly, not meeting the Golden Gargoyle's eyes. Instead, she stared at her hands, her brows pinching. "My *acat*... I didn't even know if it would work but...I use it to bring flowers back when they begin to die. I built on that, and in my panic...my magic intensified. I touched Merrick's chest, saw his soul floating in pure darkness, and I pulled it back into his body."

The four of them, somber-faced, stared at each other. Sparrow suffered minor injuries, a few cuts and bruises, but that was all. Laurent sustained slashes to his arms and back, the material of his robe ripped and hanging. He was pretty positive his hand was broken, but with his accelerated healing, he knew he'd be back to full health in a few hours. He was more worried about the scrapes on Sparrow.

Merrick looked great for a male allegedly back from the dead. His bronzed skin stayed a little pale as he recounted his out of body experience, and his left wing still hung at an unsettling angle, but he assured everyone multiple times that he would go to a healer to make sure his broken wing was set correctly to avoid permanent damage.

Keerian still shouted down his mind connection to Esmeray but there was no answer from the other side of their ring. Sparrow, Merrick, and Laurent also tried, and failed.

"We need to find Esmeray," Keerian ordered, his metallic wings rustling with impatience. "We couldn't take Adara in her Sentry form all together—what is Esmeray going to do that we couldn't?" He began pacing, those golden wings catching the light of the full moon now well past its apex. "If we can somehow track her, if we can narrow down where she went, we could bring in reinforcements from the Palace. I just got Esmeray back. I will *not* fucking lose her again."

Sparrow moved away from Merrick to grip Keerian's hand in hers gently. "You know Esmeray best. She wouldn't do what she did without reason. Keep faith in her."

Laurent opened his connection to Esmeray again. There was nothing but deafening silence on the other end of the ring.

"Where are you?" Laurent shot down his ring to Lenna. If Lenna peered into the Prism, she could track the Queen's most recent memory and see if they could glean any information.

There was no answer from Lenna's ring either.

"Well, Esmeray isn't dead," Merrick noted dryly, nodding towards Keerian. "You're still standing." With a glance at Sparrow and Laurent, Merrick continued, almost sheepish, "And...something else happened–"

Sparrow shot him a look that conveyed the message of *"shut the fuck up."* Laurent winced, inclined to agree with Sparrow's decision. Now was not the time.

Before Merrick could say anything else, the throne room doors creaked open and Lenna's curly red hair appeared. Laurent sagged in relief. Sparrow, whirling towards the doors, cried out and ran to the Oracle, wrapping her in a tight embrace.

Sparrow had waned her out once Adara began shifting, and Lenna, thankfully, had taken one look at Adara's lengthening teeth and practically jumped into Sparrow's outstretched arms.

The battle that waged in the Great Hall had dissipated once word of Adara's disappearance spread. It seemed the beings forced to participate in the bullshit full moon celebration had ruthlessly beaten back any of Adara's remaining supporters, and now healers slowly wove through the injured, helping who they could.

With a tight frown on her otherwise bloodless face, hands palming the dull grey Prism, Lenna announced, "I know where Esmeray went."

Chapter Fifty-Seven
ESMERAY

The hard snow broke my fall as I landed, claws digging into the frozen earth, skidding to a stop against the broken columns surrounding the ruins of the temple. Still in Sentry, my ragged breath left behind plumes of hot air as I scrambled my way up and over one of the half-buried pillars, trying to steady my breathing as I dove into a small recess that hid me from view.

Adara stalked around the ring of the ruins, growling deep in her throat, her massive head shaking off snow drifts from our crash landing. Her tail steadily bashed against the temple, breaking huge chunks of rock off the pillars surrounding me. I had gotten a lucky hit in the moment we appeared high above the mountains of the Obsidian Palace and I freefell down into the ruins themselves, where the haphazard rubble granted me a little coverage.

"Where are you, little sister?" Adara hissed venomously as she blasted through a large wall of the ruins with a burst of spell enhanced silver magic. It shattered to the ground, much too close for comfort.

I shifted back into my normal body to fit under the broken pillar easier. My entire being hurt. Now, in this form, without the bonus of thicker skin, I shivered against the cold wind that stirred up snow flurries all around us.

Crawling on my stomach, I surveyed the battlefield from my vantage point, the moonlight gilding everything silver.

We were way above the highest spires of the Obsidian Palace, on the mountaintop itself, where the air was achingly thin and the temperature dropped dangerously low at night. Even though the stars illuminated the mountain brightly, a hundred yards down the mountain, dark shadows of a tree line stood tall and bare, defiantly growing in the harsh conditions. Snow blanketed the ground up here year-round, and the deserted ruins were rarely, if ever, visited. Sometimes Sentries would come up here for training, but I doubted I would get lucky enough for a pack of elite gargoyle warriors to find me.

Not that I wanted them to. Adara's wing was bleeding profusely where I'd bitten her, the blood dripping down her side and bouncing off the snow. If I could get her to shift, I could get her subdued. Slowly, I reached into my pocket of space and pulled out Goldriel.

She wasn't healing fast.

But I didn't know if that was a side effect of whatever spells she cast or because her magic was burning out. I prayed it was the latter. Her nostrils flared, trying and failing to scent me as the wind thrashed through the jagged ruins, scattering Adara's hope of detecting me easily.

I waited for that wind to blow past again, and the moment the swirling and eddying gusts snapped through the barren ruins, I slammed the tip of Goldriel through the frozen layers of ice, activating the wards I'd placed along the rim of this very temple as a contingency plan in case everything went to shit, and I needed to finish this alone. The containment wards flared to life as I forced my depleting magic into them.

Merrick always complained when I disappeared for hours, since I never told him what I was up to. But now, seeing Adara irrevocable trapped in the ring of wards I'd placed here a few days ago, I felt a small slice of relief that at least this plan was working.

Gingerly, keeping my wings tight to my sides, I stepped into her line of sight. "Adara–" but like a wild beast caged, she lunged at me, my wards forcing her back. She was good and trapped now. "Adara, you need to shift back. We can figure this all out, but I cannot talk to you like this." I raised my hands as a show of good faith, Goldriel disappearing. Really, I couldn't get the damn manacles around her if she was the size of Sparrow's house.

"You planned this." Adara pushed her front paws against the wards, her white wings pumping hard in an attempt to fracture them. They held her in. "All because you wanted my throne."

I blinked in surprise. "I *never* wanted the throne, until *you* killed our parents."

"I did what was necessary," she grunted, turning to lash her spiked tail into the wards. "You received the first soul tie. *You* were going to take the Opal Palace, the one thing I wanted my entire life. Ninety-eight *years*, Esmeray. I went to all the diplomatic meetings, I built all of the connections, I engaged with every single boring suitor Father deemed appropriate. And yet it wasn't enough. Why?" With those bitterly spat words, she stopped fighting the wards, pinning me in place with one, dull, blue-grey eye. "Why did you get everything and I got nothing?"

"You would have gotten the Obsidian Kingdom," I said quietly, taking a step closer, trying to keep my demeanor calm. "You could've found your mate while you ruled from the Obsidian Palace, and we could have been the sisters I always wanted us to be."

"You never saw me as a sister," Adara stated flatly. "You were too busy training, or sneaking out of the Palace with Sparrow. If I ruled from Obsidian, you would've pitted your court against me, taken it all anyway. You considered me your rival from the moment your *acat* manifested."

"Do not play the fucking victim, Adara," I sneered, my wings flaring out at my sides as my hold on my attitude slipped.

Hale told us once Adara was separated from the spell book, she wouldn't be able to enact any spells. By waning her this far, depleting my magic in the process, she should not be able to feel its effects. But she continued acting frenzied, twisted and furious, just as she had in the Opal Palace's throne room. Was she even under the influence of the book? Or was this my sister all along–a beast under that beautiful skin, finally revealing her true self.

My mind churned, thoughts muddled from the pain that continued radiating through my body.

She had silver battle magic now, and hadn't wielded a drop of water during the fighting. But we came from a strong lineage of fae on our Father's side. Maybe she couldn't manipulate a lot of water because she had that second form of battle magic hidden away all along? Or was the silver hued power purely a gift from the spell book? I wracked my fuddled brain to try and remember what magic she showed in our youth, but I didn't remember her power ever presenting as silver.

Adara wouldn't be the first to keep a deadly gift under wraps and out of sight. Growing up in court, I'd learned just how cunning fae could be. And after hitting my head hard on the dais steps, everything was processing a bit too slow. I blinked back the fog in my brain, trying desperately to straighten out my line of thinking.

Adara sighed, stretching, and settling on her haunches, one giant paw resting against the wards. "Do you know the only regret I have in this life?" She cocked her head to me. Lost in thought, I didn't see it coming.

"What?"

"My only regret in this life is that I couldn't find you on the night I murdered our parents," Adara said smoothly. "I wish I could've killed you too. Even if that meant killing Keerian in the process."

And with that, Adara hurled forward, breaking through my wards with a mighty *bang* that shook the mountain top itself.

CHAPTER FIFTY-EIGHT

ESMERAY

ADARA LUNGED TOWARDS ME, my body moving out of instinct. I waned, but my magic was burning out quick. I only managed to make it fifty feet to her left. Breaking into a sprint, I aimed for the tree line I could make out in the distance. This clearing would be my end unless I darted into the taiga, where she couldn't fit in Sentry form. Under the cover of the dense trees, I could get a reprieve from her attacks to formulate a new plan.

I heard her bellow in frustration, breaking out into a thundering gallop after me, her long strides shrinking the distance between us much too quickly. I wouldn't make it to the tree line. With a split-second to decide, I snapped open my wings, the icy wind bolstering my flight towards a rocky outcropping off the mountain instead. Aiming wildly, I threw a hand behind me, flinging as much magic that I dared muster towards her. She easily deflected as I slid the last fifteen feet to the crevice, landing and rolling, my wing clipping a sharp edge of rock as I dove into the meager cover. Blinding pain shot from wing tip to fingertip, but I clawed and wriggled my way deeper into the narrow space between two slabs of stone, a heartbeat before talons longer than my arm smashed into the hard shelf above me.

Debris rained down, sharp shards peppering my already injured wings with fresh cuts as I covered my head. Pushing down any thoughts of my mortality, I rallied all my remaining fae magic. If I had enough for one last attack, I would make it fucking count.

For my mate, for my friends, for my Kingdom. I would take the shot.

For retribution, for revenge, for the hurt and anger I felt over the last year, I would enjoy it.

Grabbing Goldriel, I centralized my power to the still intact rock in front of me. If I blasted the wall outward and hit Adara, it would bring this entire outcropping down on her. The staff in my hands trembled as I drained all my remaining magic into it. I couldn't wane, couldn't even make a fucking illusion of a teacup right now. I'd never been this deep into my power, and knowing that I was tapped out after this, bolstered me enough to drain everything I had into Goldriel, the golden moonstone nestled at the tip glowing brilliantly–as if it knew.

With one shot left, I aimed to kill.

The moment I felt my magic quiver, the sign I was almost out of power, I slashed Goldriel across my chest, directly at the wall of stone separating me from Adara. Gold light exploded outwards, slamming into the rock just as Adara leapt, trying to use her considerable weight to collapse the small nook I found to bury me under the mountain's unforgiving mass.

My magic burrowed into the cracks forming above me from Adara's barrage. I held Goldriel steady, pouring more and more golden power into the slab of mountain. Sweat and blood trickled down my brow, freezing almost immediately, a scream tearing from my throat as I continued dredging up every drop of my *acat*, forcing it to bend to my will, focusing on those rocks. New cracks spiderwebbed out, groaning under the assault of Adara slamming her body into it on one side, and the wobbling stream of magic, still holding and swelling, at its underbelly.

The alcove began trembling, and I gritted my teeth until I tasted blood. I felt the shift in the earth at last and slammed that final, feeble strand of magic into the epicenter of those glorious cracks, right as Adara's talons raked through the surface, a hair's breath from my face.

With a deafening explosion, splintered shards of mountain crashed directly into Adara's open maw. Gold light flared outwards, blasting Adara backwards as she howled in pain, hitting one of the few pillars that still stood from the temple of a Witch Queen long dead. The pillar rocked and swayed before toppling over, crushing Adara beneath its weight. I ducked my head as rock rained down all around me, destroying the face of the alcove and opening it to the elements.

My entire body shook as I managed to limp the few feet and peer out. Warm blood ran in rivulets down my neck and chest, my *acat* so depleted even healing was not happening anytime soon.

I made it out of the rubble before collapsing into the searingly cold snow.

Numb.

Every inch of me felt numb, shrill ringing in my ears scrambling any coherent thought. I tried to shut it out, pressing an icy hand against my sensitive ear. Wincing at the pain and sensation, I pulled it away, only to see blood covering my palm from a burst eardrum.

I could barely move. That last bit of magic drained me of everything. My head spun. Blood from a cut on my forehead dripped into my eye, clouding my vision before I wiped it away, surveying the aftermath. Almost the entire temple was now reduced to nothing more than haphazard piles of slate. Adara lay, still in Sentry form, half buried under rock, the wing that had already been mangled now snapped completely, hanging limp at her side.

I tried and failed to get to my feet. Using Goldriel as a crutch, I managed to stand, the staff supporting most of my weight. I staggered away from my twin. She had been knocked unconscious and if Sparrow was here, I knew she could force Adara to shift back. It wasn't magic I had, but I knew from experience Sparrow did. And now that Adara was out cold, it would be easier for Sparrow's complex magic to take the time it needed to shift her.

I managed to half drag myself towards the tree line as I touched the black onyx on my ring. The screeching in my ears thudded in beat with my heart, drowning out every other sound except my ragged breathing, the cold air burning my lungs.

"Keerian," Gods even the voice in my mind was barely above a whisper. *"She's unconscious, I need Sparrow to come shift her back. I'm above–"*

The pain hit me before I realized what happened. Adara lashed her tail out, striking me full force. My staff flew out of my hand as I smashed into a thick tree trunk.

"Seems your luck has run out," Adara mused, stalking towards me. Blood covered her white hide, but she was alert, her teeth flashing into a savage grin as she took in my rapidly deteriorating condition. I collapsed on my side, wings trapped under me. My horns protected my head from the full brunt of the impact, but other than that, I felt very broken.

"How…" I asked weakly, my entire body screaming in pain. Feeling my end was near, I looked up to the beautiful full moon, blinking blood out of my vision, desperate to see it clearly one last time.

The crushing realization hit me that I was going to die. I took a deep breath, staring up at that moon, at Carra, my mind on Keerian. His striking green eyes, his quick wit and sharp laughter. *"When all seems lost, and the darkness closes in, illuminate your own path."* He had told me that once, under a blanket of stars atop a waterfall in Florra. I asked him, *"But what if no one follows?"* And Keerian had feathered kisses down my horns before replying, *"Lead anyway."*

I used to joke, in those early days of our soul tie, asking him if he actually, truly, loved me—almost disbelieving that this incredible, kind, supportive male was my mate. He'd laugh and assure me, *"I love you—horns and all."* The moon blurred as tears threatened. *He* was going to die.

"I learned another trick from you, and since you are only a few seconds from death, I'll humor you." Adara picked up a paw and swiped at the air between us, a rip opening in space to display a thick, black and gold book on a short, opal pedestal, the air itself splitting and crinkling back, the edges burning quicksilver.

"Your staff is never far from you, so I decided to take a lesson out of your book—" Adara murmured proudly, the power-hungry lust on her face slackening her jaw as she gazed upon the spell book, "—to always keep mine close."

An unearthly hum filled my bones as I laid eyes on the actual book for the very first time. And even with my blurred vision, even with my magic burnt up in my blood, an ancient whisper slipped down my exposed skin, curling gently and invisible, around my throat, brushing over my wings, threading through the curls of my horns. Strange magic—warm and inviting, cold and detached, limitless and finite thrummed in the air. The breath wooshed out of my lungs as Adara's shimmering rip in space taunted me, the spell book its captive inside.

My mind quieted.

And I realized how I could defeat my sister after all.

I closed my eyes, wanting Adara to think the defeat was devouring me whole. Adara had the spell book with her the entire time. Hidden away in the same manner I used to store my staff. Her own pocket in space. She had mirrored my magic to always keep her book of spells close.

But now I knew why I'd never seen the book in person, why the spells I'd seen were written on parchment. Adara did not want anyone finding out that it wasn't the spells *written* in the book that gave her more power–but the book *itself*.

Because the book contained its own well of magic.

I let out a dry chuckle, the sound escaping through my split lip. "I should have known," I sniffed, a few tears tracking down my cheek as I directed my sharpening vision to the white beast before me. "You were never very original. Always had to imitate me."

"Fuck you," Adara spat, as she took the bait.

She lunged and I rolled, her talons slamming into the snow where my chest had been a split second before. I threw my body towards that rip in space, desperately flinging my hand out–

My fingers closed around the spine of the ancient book.

Even the wind on the mountain seemed to pause.

Power barreled into me so hot and fast that I gasped, archaic and other-worldly magic flooding into my veins.

I breathed deeply through the thrum of energy that roiled through my blood, a dam breaking–the book's magic unending.

I could feel it all.

I could feel everything and nothing.

And I stood tall, no longer needing Goldriel to support my weight as I raised my head at Adara. My wing was definitely broken, but the pain was secondary to the dizzying high of power that settled deep in my soul. She hissed, a shadow of doubt flitting through her slitted pupils.

I smiled and dropped the spell book into the snow, immediately feeling the connection to its magic sever. But I had taken enough, bolstering my own *acat* as Adara had done–not to cast a spell, but to fill up the well of my depleted magic.

To stand on my own to finish this.

"Yield," I commanded, as golden battle magic formed at my fingertips, sparking and whipping around me on that silent, snowy mountain top.

Adara only snarled and advanced a step.

I smirked. "I hoped you'd say that."

And I unleashed every ounce of magic from that spell book upon my twin.

Adara screeched as brilliant gold erupted from my palms and engulfed her, the force of an ancient and terrible power that she had tried to warp and control exacting its own retribution onto her.

I squeezed my fists shut. And where a massive beast had stood just moments before, a slim figure appeared crumpled on the ground through the dimming golden light. The magic had knocked her back into the thick trunks of the tree, and she shifted back to her regular form, unconscious.

The second that last glimmer of gold faded, so did the strength of the spell book's magic. I sank into the snow, utterly spent, all of the wounds I had felt before tapping into the spell book's magic slamming back into me full force. Crawling on my hands and knees, I slipped my hand into my pocket of space, unearthing the nullifying cuffs. I slowly affixed them to Adara's wrists, then each ankle, the metal flaring green as they clicked and locked, nullifying Adara's fae magic, and restricting her shifting abilities.

My eyelids grew heavier, my bruised and battered body shutting down. I just needed a few more seconds.

I growled, pushing my body away from the brink of unconsciousness, my vision swimming, my head thudding and unnaturally light.

I reopened my pocket of space, picking up Goldriel with one hand, my other sinking into a snow drift. I didn't feel the cold.

Using the moon stoned tip of Goldriel, I pushed the spell book into my pocket of space. I didn't want to touch it, wary over the amount of power it held, and the consequences I would already face using its magic. I didn't want to hold some foreign power in my veins after seeing what happened when Adara used it.

Was I already corrupted?

I didn't feel corrupted.

But I also couldn't feel the tips of my fingers or anything below my knees, so this probably wasn't the time to ponder that. I needed to get it to Hale, have him look at the book. And then it needed to be destroyed. That much magic in the wrong hands, well, Adara was bad enough.

The spell book disappeared, and I could have sworn the damned thing seemed disgruntled as I shoved it into thin air. I gently fisted my palm, locking it in my own pocket of space. With the edges of my vision blacking, I tried crawling back toward the tree line, towards Adara, my twin reduced to little more than a shallowly breathing mound in the snow. My broken wing threatened to pitch me forward.

I needed to get off this mountain, acutely aware that my *acat* was so thoroughly depleted that I was no longer healing at all. I was very much in danger of death, though dying from the cold was a little too anti-climactic for me.

I needed to tell Keerian where I was. My frostbitten fingers fumbled to touch my ring.

I needed...to tell him something.

What was I telling him?

I needed...

I closed my eyes.

BRIGHT LIGHT FLASHED THROUGH my eyelids, bringing me back to consciousness. I cracked my eyes open in time to see black wings blot out the full moon. A whistling shriek pierced the quiet.

The great black dragon landed in the snow with enough force to shake the mountain. He roared, the sound of promise and devotion, as his wings spread wide, opening his maw and shooting silvery fire high above the tree line.

"Resso?"

Either my fuckled mind was now conjuring hallucinations, or the cranky cave dragon was really standing before me.

I was bone cold, so cold that I could no longer even shiver. The dragon, who, only days ago, had curled up around his horde and told me he did not interfere with the wars of royals, let out a rumbling whine and gently nudged me with his nose.

I groaned, trying and failing to get up off the snowy ground. Craning my neck, I saw Adara stir and open her eyes, a soft whimper escaping as she beheld the shackles adorning her wrists and ankles. I glared at her.

She didn't meet my eyes as I stared her down.

My sister. My twin. My parents' murderer. My mate's captor.

Turning my attention to the impatiently chuffing dragon I gave him a small smile, the motion pulling my split lip open again. The pooling blood dripped down my chin.

It was warm. That was nice.

"You came," I said to Resso.

He only grumbled a response, smoke shooting from his nostrils.

"Can you please get us out of here?" I asked the black dragon as he appraised me with a flat, unamused stare.

"First I must obey your Oracle, and now you want a ride?" He blinked slowly at me as I laughed, the sound rough against my raw throat. I hadn't the faintest clue what he meant, but I was damn happy to see him and confirm he was actually real. Tears threatened to consume me as Resso wrapped a chained Adara in his massive claw. She had the good sense to look mortified and stay silent.

Resso huffed again, as close to chuckling as a dragon could get, his wing flattening towards the ground. It took a few attempts to move my stiff, frozen body, and to half crawl, half clamber up Resso's side. It was a considerable effort, more warm blood trickling out as my wounds reopened.

I finally seated myself behind massive black spikes at the nape of his neck. I patted him as he stood, his powerful haunches launching us into the sky, gliding down the mountain to the Obsidian Palace.

CHAPTER FIFTY-NINE
LENNA

WITHIN MINUTES OF LENNA'S proclamation, Sparrow had waned them to the throne room of the Obsidian Palace, where, upon arrival of the notorious Golden Gargoyle, now King Consort of Irridessen, Lord Magnamus was placed in chains and hauled to the dungeons deep within the mountains to wait on Esmeray to decide his fate.

The Regent hadn't put up a fight, only sighed his displeasure, as Keerian landed against the glass floor with enough force that the skeletal hands lining the wall of the throne room gripped their torches tighter. Keerian pointed a sword at the fae's throat and bared his teeth. The disgraced Regent had yielded quickly.

Keerian now paced at the base of the dais, one of Merrick's borrowed short swords in his hands. Sparrow, Merrick, and Laurent kept shooting each other increasingly odd looks across the throne room that Lenna was too tired to try and decipher. She sat alone at one of the stone pews that curved around the room, focusing on keeping her trembling hands clasped and her teeth set to stop them clattering together. She took deep breaths, working to calm herself after the events of the night.

They had arrived to find the Obsidian Palace in complete chaos. Apparently, the Palace had not been as remote and forgotten as Adara and Lord

Magnamus bet on since those still standing after the battles at the Opal Palace waned here after Lenna confirmed Esmeray's location. The Opal Palace's court immediately spread the news of the Prism's memory to the Obsidian Palace's assembled court. All beings from the guards and servants to the housed royals had begun a bloody rebellion against Lord Magnamus and any of Adara's loyal supporters. It had only quelled when Keerian, Merrick and Laurent arrived, the three Elite Warriors quickly getting the situation under control.

None of them were surprised to hear that the Regent was not very well liked.

Anyone who continued supporting Adara had been hauled to the dungeon. Those who fought, died quickly. Sparrow had even gotten in the fray–making sure any being who found themselves sympathizing with the wrong side of events was handled.

Now, the throne room was empty, per Keerian's request. The court was busy enough outside the throne room doors where healers were assisting with the wounded, and guards stood at attention, making sure their group inside was not bothered. Lenna had taken the few moments of slight peace to clear her mind and get her breathing under control. Resso had found the Queen, and Esmeray relayed to them through their rings that she would land in the throne room of the Obsidian Palace.

As they waited, Lenna thought of the bakery in Florra and the sweet scents that enveloped her there. She thought of those nights they sat atop Sparrow's patio, drinking in the views from the surrounding forests and city lights. She thought of the handsome baker that smiled at her in a way she had not been smiled at in years. She thought of her friends that surrounded her now, and how dear they were to her heart, a missing piece clicking into place. She thought of the fierce Queen that assured her mate, just moments ago through their rings, that she was okay. Lenna found herself, for the first time in decades, excited for the future.

Keerian blew out a breath and plopped down next to her on the bench, folding his glorious wings behind him. He nodded at her, his green eyes bright. "We haven't had a chance to properly be introduced," Keerian chuckled, extending his hand.

Lenna unfolded her trembling fists, grasping Keerian's palm in her own. His fingers wrapped all the way around hers, but his grip was gentle. Introductions were exchanged and Lenna immediately felt drawn to Keerian as if they were old friends. "Esmeray talks so highly of you, I feel like I already know you." She blushed, realizing she was speaking so informally to the new King Consort.

Keerian laughed, the sound bright against such a dark night. "Good. That will make what I ask next hopefully much easier." He reached over and clasped her other hand in his. "Lenna, what you did for my mate and me was so brave, so incredible, that I could never repay you for your help. You uncovered the truth and didn't back down from it. You revealed that truth to the world." Keerian smiled. "And Esmeray *may* have ratted you out about your trip to the dragon lair. Resso told her."

Lenna's blush grew furiously underneath the warm grin from the handsome male. "But to start, I want to offer you a home with us at the Opal Palace–or the Obsidian Palace. Honestly, wherever Meer decides she wants to live as Queen. But you will always have a place with us. Or, if you want a house anywhere in Irridessen, consider it done. I'm sure Sparrow would love to help you decorate."

Lenna felt the shock register on her face as she stared at the King. Keerian beamed as her mouth fell open. "Did you think we would just leave you high and dry? Ship you back to the Slate Kingdom? Sparrow told me how integral you are to this family–and the absolute least I can do is make sure you never want for anything ever."

She was so overwhelmed with emotion, all Lenna could do was nod rapidly.

A home.

She could put down roots here, or at the Opal Palace, or anywhere she wanted. This kind male offered her the one thing she felt she'd been searching for–that feeling that she was home.

Tears threatened to fall, and Lenna managed a croaky, *"Thank you,"* before throwing her arms around the King, hugging him tight. He laughed again, his gold wings and strong arms hugging her as she cried and cried against Keerian's shoulder.

The floor behind the dais began shimmering like a pool of the purest water.

Merrick, Sparrow, Laurent and Keerian snapped their attention to the glass. Lenna stood on shaky legs, still reeling from Keerian's offer.

The massive black dragon flew up from the floor, landing in front of the dais and the group. Adara was trapped in his talons, the manacles around her wrists pulsing with dull light. Sparrow shouted out a particularly foul curse word, storming towards Adara, before Laurent snagged her by the upper arm, reeling her back to hold her against his body as Sparrow struggled to tear into Adara, her teeth bared and green magic coiling around her hands. Adara locked eyes with Sparrow, her frown curling into a full sneer as Merrick rushed to the doors of the throne room, calling in four guards that proceeded to drag Adara to her cell.

But it was the sight of the bloodied, dark haired Queen, slumped over Resso's neck, that held Lenna's attention.

Esmeray gave the group a lopsided grin, her eyes half closed and her wings limp at her sides. Keerian soared up to where his mate sat, gathering her gently in his arms, careful not to jostle her torn and broken wings. Laurent called for a healer, and a thin fae female with short copper hair came rushing in from the hall, giving the great dragon a wide berth as Keerian lay Esmeray against the stone pew. Keerian held onto his love the entire time the healer worked. Slowly, Esmeray's wings reformed to their original shape, the rips in the thin membranes repairing before Lenna's eyes. The cuts and scrapes had gone from open and bleeding to the small, pinkish marring of new skin.

The healer worked in silence, not stopping until Esmeray held up her tattooed hand. "Thank you," she said, her voice stronger and her face beginning to show signs of life again. Color flushed back into her cheeks, and her eyes became clearer, more focused.

The healer nodded, her short hair swaying in the faint candlelight. "No flying for a few days, my Queen," the healer stated with a pointed look. "I don't want to come back, reset your wings again, and reprimand you." Esmeray rolled her eyes, giving the healer a wicked grin. "I'll see what I can do. Again, thank you, Collette."

Collette stood, bowing slightly to Keerian and Esmeray before waning out of the throne room in a burst of yellow light.

Resso nudged Esmeray with his snout. Lenna watched as Esmeray placed her small hand against the giant nose of the dragon. Silent words were exchanged before Resso chuffed, his tail flicking–not unlike a house cat–and he ambled over to the rippling floor, disappearing to the caverns below.

Esmeray swayed slightly as she stood, apprehensively locking eyes with the Golden Gargoyle who looked at her as if she was the force his whole world orbited. A beat of silence followed.

Esmeray's eyes began filling with tears, and she let out a shaky sob, taking a stumbling step to her mate. Keerian let out a hoarse, strangled growl, closing the distance between them in two long strides. He grabbed the nape of Esmeray's neck, twirling her around to crush his lips against hers. Merrick whooped and clapped, the sentiment mirrored by Sparrow's cheer and Laurent's amused expression. Lenna felt her cheeks heat as Esmeray seemed to melt into her mate's arms, her nails, back to their original, less deadly shape, digging into Keerian's already torn and bloody shirt. Their mouths clashed, deepening the kiss, their wings wrapping around each other, shielding them from view.

After a long moment, they broke apart, Keerian holding onto Esmeray's hands as they stared deep into each other's eyes. There was so much love, so much understanding, passing between them. Lenna was sure they were communicating silently down the rings—a million things they needed to catch each other up on from the horrible year they were forced to spend apart.

Esmeray rested her head against Keerian's chest, their horns glinting in the candlelight. The dark black of Esmeray's seemed to absorb and refract the shining light from Keerian's golden pair. Lenna looked away to give them some semblance of privacy, and she could've sworn she saw Sparrow drop Laurent's hand. But it was so quick, out of the corner of her eye, that Lenna thought she may have been seeing things.

Laurent cleared his throat, directing his question to the room. "So...what do we do now?" he asked, tucking his hands into the pockets of his ruined robe, his long fingers sticking out the bottom from a rip through the material. He moaned dramatically, pulling the material up to inspect the damage.

Esmeray laughed, the sound light, as she squeezed Keerian's hand. "Well, as the Queen Absolute, I'll figure it out, but first, let's go back to Florra."

CHAPTER SIXTY
ESMERAY

Sparrow flat out refused to let me wane. I was still a bit breathless from the kiss Keerian and I shared, and still aching in my bones and soul from the fight, so I relented with only a tiny bit of bickering.

As we prepared to head back to Florra, Laurent asked if I wanted to see Adara before we left. The question clanged through me, but I shook my head and he dropped the subject.

Now wasn't the time. Mentally, physically, and emotionally, I needed to sort out my thoughts. After I spoke with Hale and could confirm I wasn't corrupted by using the spell book's magic, then...

Then I would begin interrogating my twin on the details of her year-long reign.

"Let her sulk in a dirty, freezing cell for a few days. It'll make her more than ready to answer my questions." As I talked, I could feel *it*—the book's unnatural power thrumming tantalizingly in my pocket of space. It wanted to be let out. I could feel the pressure of that otherworldly presence bearing down behind my magic, and I hoped Hale could provide some insight on why the damned thing seemed so...sentient.

"We can't stay in Florra long," Keerian murmured to me as he wrapped his arm around my shoulder. "You have two Kingdoms to rule now. Or at least one, and to put a new Regent in the other." He surveyed me again, head to toe–his eyes landing on the little cuts still healing across my cheek. "Are you feeling alright?"

No. I thought to myself, though I gave him a big smile, telling myself I'd open up to him once we were alone. "I'm fine, my love," I said aloud.

No, I think I'm the sole being favored by the Goddess of Death, and I don't know where to begin unpacking that.

"I just need a good night's sleep, and we can figure out the politics tomorrow."

I didn't want to take the throne of even one Kingdom, and now I have an entire continent to rule. Gods.

Keerian nodded, but the look he gave me let me know he was not convinced on the state of my well-being. I could never lie to him. He always saw right through me, anyway.

"I'll tell you later," I promised my mate through our personal connection on our rings. *"But, do you think Laurent and Merrick are acting weird or is it just me?"* I shot a glance over to them, half to change the topic of conversation, and half because the two males were acting awkward as fuck around each other.

"Definitely weird," he agreed. *"Sparrow too. But did you know Merrick died and Sparrow used her magic to bring him back to life? Maybe that's why it's weird between them."*

"Wait, Merrick, you *died*?" I whirled around, grabbing the grey winged gargoyle by the shoulder. "Why do you look so...alive? And why did no one tell me?"

Merrick groaned, swatting me away. "Oh, here we go. Thanks, Keerian, buddy." Rolling his eyes at me, Merrick amended, "I didn't like...die *all* the way–Sparrow bought me back."

"How?" I asked Sparrow. Out of all the fae I knew, I never really understood Sparrow's *acat* to begin with–I don't think she even understood it that well. Her battle magic was green light, which was rare in fae, but not unheard of. Even Sparrow always said she wasn't sure what god or goddess favored her, but she was content with her gifts and mused it must have been a long forgotten "*plant god*" that took a liking to her soul.

"*Plant god*" my ass if she bought Merrick back from Minmere.

Sparrow shrugged. Out of all of us, she seemed the most unfazed by the actual death Merrick had come back from. "I don't really know. I tried healing him like I heal plants, and I think in my panic, my magic connected me with his life force. I saw him falling into the darkness of death and I–I pulled him out."

With a sideways look at Merrick, causing Laurent next to her to stiffen, Sparrow added, "So, he must not have been *all* the way dead to begin with." Ducking her head, she smoothed her hands down the bodice of her top, before pivoting to Lenna, fussing over the Oracle and wanting to know how Lenna fared in the dragon dens.

Sparrow wasn't a healer–her family came from a long line of healers, always holding it against her that she didn't inherit the same gifts. The most healing Sparrow had ever done was for a plant that wasn't happy in its new pot and the leaves withered. Sparrow had poured magic into it, curing whatever ailment the plant had, until each leaf was back to its original, shiny green self.

I added that to the long list of shit I needed to figure out when I had the energy to. I sighed, giving myself the mental permission to deal with this all tomorrow, turning towards the dais and the new, opal-carved monstrosity of a throne sitting there. With a nonchalant wave of my hand, the throne exploded, turning to ash and blowing away on a phantom wind I illusioned to breeze through the room.

"Why'd you do that?" Keerian asked, a grin threatening to form on his handsome, rugged face.

Laurent chuckled, answering for me. "Lord Magnamus never sat on a throne large enough for beings with wings. This is the second throne of his that she's destroyed."

My reward was a dazzling smile from my mate, who let out a rough chuckle, rubbing his beard as he stared at me. "You are crazy, but I love you. Horns and all."

I laughed, giving my mate a quick kiss on his cheek. "Well, I offered Regency to someone with wings, I was just accommodating them."

"Who did you place as Regent?" Keerian questioned curiously, crossing his arms. "I thought you were holding off on politics until tomorrow."

"It's a *temporary* Regency," I explained with a coy smile as the floor began to ripple again. "I had to wait until the new Regent of the Obsidian Palace could go speak with his subjects and explain the situation."

Resso's large black snout appeared out of the floor, and he glided through the throne room to perch at the top of the now-empty dais. Those large silver eyes blinked and his rumbling voice filled my mind. I knew he projected to Keerian and Merrick as well. *"I was asked to keep an eye on things for our Queen Absolute."* He huffed as steam swirled out of his mouth. *"Temporarily. I need to go take a long nap around my treasures, Queen Esmeray."*

I gave the mighty dragon a bow. *"I will be back tomorrow, my scaly lord,"* I said dramatically and Resso grumbled, the throne room echoing the noise.

The group stared at me, Lenna keeping one eye on the dragon sitting on its mighty haunches above her. "What?" I asked, amusement filling my voice. "Resso can keep this Palace in line for a day. Who's going to try and argue with a *dragon*?"

Keerian tipped his head back, cackling, and even Merrick shook his head, a bemused expression on his face. Laurent, filling in the pieces as they were offered since he couldn't hear Resso's voice, gave me a tight-lipped smile. "Well, I know for a fact all the fae will behave." His smile widened, flashing sharp canines. "After a day with a dragon ruler, the Kingdoms will be *so* ready to crown you Queen Absolute."

I shot them a grin as Sparrow stepped forward with Lenna, reaching her hand out to Laurent. Laurent clasped her hand, and they locked eyes, Sparrow giving him a shy smile before turning and reaching out for Merrick's hand. Merrick gave her a look of something extremely heated. Keerian, oblivious to what I saw, grasped Merrick's other hand before pulling me tight into his body. I wrapped my free arm around Lenna as she linked hands with Laurent.

With a flash of green light, the six of us waned back to Florra.

CHAPTER SIXTY-ONE
LENNA

Lenna barely saw Esmeray and Keerian during the long days following. A week had passed since the showdown at the Opal Palace, and the new normal that followed took some time to get used to.

Adara resided in the dungeons deep below the Obsidian Palace, locked in a cell that nullified all magic—thanks to the runes and handiwork of witches who ruled from the Obsidian Palace long ago. Esmeray had only visited her twin once, to question her on the disappearance of the beings they had still not found, and even though reports of beings going missing had ceased, Adara yielded nothing.

Much to Esmeray's mounting frustration.

Merrick and Laurent both volunteered to reside at the Obsidian and Opal Palaces respectively, handling any chaos or disorder that cropped up from Adara's imprisonment and Esmeray's coronation as Queen Absolute. Lenna offered to help with whatever Esmeray needed, but Sparrow put her foot down, begging Lenna to stay at her house and keep her company while everyone else was away.

Lenna enjoyed the first week of relaxation. She slept deeply, with no troubling nightmares. She helped Sparrow work in the garden, clean the house top to bottom, and spent the mornings sipping coffee on the patio with Esmeray. The evenings consisted of Sparrow and Lenna reading in the living room while splitting a bottle of wine, while Esmeray and Keerian waned off to the waterfalls to—as Sparrow called it—*"fuck each other's brains out."*

The new routine felt peaceful, and Lenna reveled in the slower pace. It was the first time since arriving in Irridessen that she could truly sit back and not worry about anyone trying to murder her. Plus, staying in the same house as the King and Queen had its perks. One being the crowns.

Esmeray had more crowns than Lenna could fathom. Apparently, after taking up the throne, Esmeray joyfully waned down to the dragon lair and raided their trove, choosing her fill, as Resso snored in his cave, aware of the Queen's presence, but too tired from a single day of "ruling" to ultimately be bothered.

Esmeray had nudged Lenna playfully, asking if she wanted to join. Lenna did not. Her feet still got a little sweaty as she recalled the dragon's cavern, the sheer drop into darkness, those little ledges, and the huge beasts that Lenna was still not convinced wouldn't try to eat her.

But every morning, a new crown sat atop the Queen's head—some golden with dark stones, some with uncut gems and filigreed metal, some were heavy looking, with thick bands and fat, precious stones that cost more than Lenna's entire Estate in Doortan. And a few were thin, with dainty pearls and diamonds cresting between Esmeray's curled horns.

Those were Lenna's favorite. The diamonds were so sparkly in the morning sun as Esmeray trudged up the stairs in varying dresses to have coffee with her and Sparrow before waning Keerian to either the Obsidian or Opal Palace to bicker with royals all day—as Esmeray put it. Apparently, multiple advisors, Dukes, and Lords were jonesing for the Regency position, but none of them were up to par for the Queen Absolute.

Esmeray and Keerian would get back to Florra each night and Esmeray would toss the crown off her head onto the closest surface–much to Sparrow's dismay. There were crowns in the kitchen, crowns atop lampshades in the living room. Lenna even found a crown with an emerald the size of her fist hanging off the outside handle of Sparrow's pink door.

It was early morning on the eighth day, when Esmeray stepped off the staircase and onto the patio, that Lenna noted no crown adorned the Queen's head, and the usual dress of the week had been replaced with loose fitting black linen pants and an oversized sweater.

"No crown today?" Lenna asked flippantly as Esmeray let out a deep sigh before sprawling onto the reclining chair on the patio. Her midnight black hair was tied into a top knot resting between her horns. It was much more "normal Esmeray" than any of the finery she'd worn all week.

"Even Queens need a damn day off," she muttered, tipping the coffee cup to her lips.

Sparrow sent her friend a feline grin before turning to Lenna. "Esmeray mentioned going to see Hale today. Want to come?"

Lenna felt the blush creep into her cheeks and Esmeray laughed. "Hale is a good male, Lenna. You know, as Queen, I *can* grant divorces–Merrick told us you have a pretty shit husband in the Slate Kingdom."

"Really?" Lenna squeaked. Her hands trembled, and she squeezed them together around her coffee mug. Divorce was unheard of in the Slate Lands–and there were only a rare few that even went through the exhaustive steps to try and get one. Typically, women who requested divorce were shunned and exiled from most social standings.

Lenna felt a weight lift from her shoulders as she considered.

If Irridessen had taught her anything, it was the importance of facing the truth–no matter how difficult. And Lenna knew the truth of her marriage now, and knew what she deserved. She deserved more than the feeling of being a burden, of being unloved. Because she *was* loved by her new family.

And Leon–he was her past, something that she had grown stronger than. She could stand on her own two feet, stand in the light, no longer cast aside in the shadows.

She was the Oracle of Terramere. And a seer. Which was pretty neat when she thought about it.

"I could also just kill him," Esmeray offered, her eyes glimmering green with malicious intent.

Lenna cocked her head, pretending to ponder her options. "Hmm, as tempting as that is...I think I'll take the divorce," she said quickly, laughing as Esmeray feigned disappointment. The happy memories of the beginning of her marriage had finally faded away, leaving the ugly stains behind. Exposed for what they truly were. *Her* past.

Esmeray nodded. "I'll have one of my priestesses draw up the paperwork, and we can have it sent out quickly."

"But Leon has no clue you exist here... He knows nothing about magic. He only knows there are Kingdoms outside of the Slate Kingdom, but I don't think he really gives them much thought. How will he know it's a legitimate divorce?" Lenna questioned, realizing now just how isolated from the rest of the world she had been.

"I was thinking about that," Esmeray said, spreading her wings and tilting her head back to take in the bright blue sky above her. "I think it's about time we stopped being so isolated from the Slate Kingdom."

CHAPTER SIXTY-TWO
ESMERAY

"You cannot be serious." Sparrow looked at me with wide eyes, her expression curious as she considered my statement.

"I'm deadly serious," I replied, pouring a second cup of steaming coffee from the pot I waned down to the kitchen to retrieve and bring back up to the patio. "There are humans in the Slate Kingdom that know lands of magic exist on other continents. Their King knows. He's been a representative for the humans since he came to power in his early twenties. He's almost eighty now–King Dalen."

Lenna nodded, her honey eyes bright as I watched the information clicking together in the Oracle's mind. "King Dalen has always been a kind ruler. His son, Prince Feydor, is set to inherit the throne upon his death."

I continued, between sips of coffee, "King Dalen has traveled to the Opal Palace–of course when he was much younger. But he has always been an ally for humans and has visited a couple other Kingdoms on diplomatic trips to advocate for his land. The fact that other lands have magic just isn't widely declared. And maybe it's time that changed. Other Kingdoms trade with the Slate Kingdom, but no one has ever offered a true alliance to King Dalen before. He may be a good friend to help bridge the gap between our worlds."

Lenna sipped from her own mug before placing it on the small table next to her chair as she thought over my words.

I pushed against my *acat*, feeling it's comforting pressure through my body. The damn spell book seemed to notice my attention, purring seductively to be let out of my pocket of space. I ignored it until the presence resorted to sulking.

Sparrow sat up in her chair, kicking off her pink fluffy slippers and pulling *my* blanket from *my* legs to cover her own. Conjuring up fluffy pillows and thin blankets to make the patio comfier while we relaxed and drank our morning coffee had become a ritual for us, as did her thievery whenever my blanket was *supposedly* bigger. I gave her an incredulous look, screeching with outrage. She crinkled her nose and hissed at me good-naturedly as she snuggled deeper into the stolen blanket, and I threw my hands up in mock surrender before using my magic to create a new, softer blanket for myself.

The minutes trickled by in a comfortable camaraderie as the sun rose over a beautiful morning in Florra. Finishing my coffee, I stood, stretching my wings out. I hadn't flown for more than a few minutes over the last few days, per healers' orders, but I could feel the cloudless sky calling out to me. I wanted to get closer to the warm sun that shone down on the peaceful town surrounding us.

As if he could read my mind—which in retrospect, I realized he kind of could, Keerian appeared at the top of the stairs, shirtless, with low hung, loose, grey pants that made my mouth water. Gods, my mate was hot. Coffee mug in hand, he crossed the patio and captured my mouth in a kiss.

"Want to fly to the waterfalls?" I asked him, stretching my wings out to their full span. They felt sturdy, and no aches danced down the boning or through the delicate muscles connected to my back.

With expert eyes, my mate gave my wings a once over before teasingly flicking the talon at the apex. "As long as you feel no pain, yes. It's been a week since you flew, and its a gorgeous day."

I grinned, hopping from one foot to the other, flexing and flapping my wings with anticipation. Keerian chuckled, holding up a finger as he drained his last dregs of coffee from him mug. "Lead the way–" he started, but before he could finish his sentence, I was off, launching into the air with a mighty push, soaring in circles around the patio.

I let out a cry of glee as I felt the weight I shouldered this past year finally melt free. A moment later, Keerian jumped off the roof, his golden wings the most beautiful I'd ever seen.

My mate, finally back at my side.

"We will be back in an hour to go to the bakery." I shot down the ring to Lenna and Sparrow who watched us with warm smiles as Keerian aimed for the forests on the outskirts of Florra.

"Have fun, Meer." Lenna replied, waving us off as she chuckled. Sparrow hooted as I banked past the patio again, and with that, I turned, speeding off to follow Keerian to the waterfalls.

My mate, my love, my King.

Chapter Sixty-Three
ESMERAY

The forest floor gleamed in the morning light as Keerian and I touched down atop the furthest waterfall from town. Because royal duties were overwhelmingly a pain in my ass, we'd made it our personal and fun mission to have sex atop each of the twelve waterfalls that surrounded Florra, and on this last waterfall, our distance from town meant no one else would be out here this early.

Keerian's wings shone as we walked along the waterfall's edge hand in hand, the silence between us brimming with desire. My wings rustled with impatience. I felt giddy, being back here with my mate. Truthfully, we had hardly been able to keep our hands off each other since being reunited. Now was no different.

The noise of the powerful waterfall drowned out most of the sounds around us, but even still, I swore I could hear Keerian's heartbeat drumming in tune with my own. Stopping in front of the tree line, I leaned back against a sturdy sycamore tree, tugging Keerian towards me. He gave me a smug grin as he leaned down.

There was no hesitation as his mouth captured mine, kissing me slow and languid as if we had all the time in the world. I moaned, my hands traveling up his broad, shirtless chest, until I could feel the rhythmic beating of his heart under my palm. Keerian deepened our kiss, his arm banding around my waist and cupping my ass to pull me tighter to him. I could feel his torso bunch and coil, practically vibrating under his tightly wound control. He'd been gentle with me as my wing finished healing, and from the way he pressed an achingly tender kiss to the corner of my lips before pulling away, I knew he wanted to handle me as if I were made of glass, worshipping me throughly yet never allowing his control to snap.

But I was already a hot, panting mess, and I wanted him to fuck me like the beasts we were. I knew how explosive and passionate we were together from when our soul tie newly bloomed, and as much as I adored making love to my mate under the stars, after a week of taking it easy, I was ready for him to devour me.

I needed Keerian's control to snap.

My core clenched at the thought, and I let out a breathy growl, nipping his full bottom lip with my teeth.

"Esmeray," Keerian murmured, the warning in his tone clear, "we need to take it easy until you're fully healed. I don't want to accidentally hurt you, my love."

I arched into him with a dramatic sigh, digging my fingers into the curls at the nape of his neck while pointedly extending and retracting my wings with ease. "My wing is perfectly healed. I flew here, didn't I?"

My free hand wandered south, trailing between our bodies. Never breaking eye contact, I gave him an innocent smile and cocked my horns, watching as he opened his mouth to argue.

His retort cut off the moment I wrapped my fingers around the head of his thick cock through those soft grey pants.

That tight control of his started slipping as I gave him a languid stroke once, twice, through the flimsy material.

Keerian groaned, tipping his head back, those glorious golden horns shining under the soft streams of morning light. "Esmeray," my name was half hiss, half prayer on his lips as my fingers slid under his waistband. I gave him a wicked grin as his hazel gaze darkened, knowing he was so close to taking me just the way I wanted.

"I need you, Keerian. Now." My breath hitched as he let out a rumble, his palms spanning my waist as he backed me up two steps until I was fully pinned against the sycamore at my back, my wings splayed on either side of the trunk.

"If you want me to stop–"

"Don't be gentle," I rose up to my tip toes, peppering kisses up his throat. "That's an order from your Queen Absolute."

A wicked gleam flashed across his face as Keerian grinned, his hands tightening against my hips. "An order," he mused darkly, "well then..."

One moment I was in control, teasing him with languid strokes of my hand down his shaft, and the next Keerian whipped me around to face the trees, a palm between my shoulder blades bending me over in front of him. I choked on a thrilled gasp, my pussy instantly soaked, and threw my hands in front of myself to catch myself against the trunk of the sycamore. He leaned over me to whisper, "As my Queen commands, so be it."

I squeaked in surprise as he swiftly shoved my linen pants to my ankles, his thigh pushing my legs apart to accomodate his massive stature. "So pretty and wet for me," my mate crooned, sliding a finger through my bare slickness to rub my clit with the exact touch that made my legs tremble. I felt as if I could combust with those feather-light touches and his desire-soaked words alone. "My pretty, wicked Queen. So insanely perfect for me in every way."

"Please, Keerian," I panted. My body was on fire under his touch, from the way he knew intrinsically what I needed.

He unfurled my hair from the bun between my horns, collecting the silky strands and twisting them once around his fist as he ground his cock against my backside, eliciting another husky mewl from my throat. "I love you," I said breathlessly as he positioned me exactly where he wanted me. My wings draped down my sides as I gave over complete control to my mate.

"Horns and all, my love," he replied roughly as he lined up with my entrance and shoved home, my pussy spasming around his girth in exquisite pleasure. I moaned at the sheer size of him, my nails growing into black daggers that I sank into the sycamore's trunk, holding tight as Keerian pulled out and slammed in again, our pleasure mingling with the roar of the waterfall behind us.

With one hand digging into the flesh on my hip, adding another layer to this glorious moment, Keerian's other slid up my sweater, kneading my breast and tearing another garbled gasp from me. I melted under his expert grasp, meeting him thrust for thrust as his body demanded more and more from me, my eyes squeezed shut, my nails creating deeep gouge marks down the sycamore.

My core clenched around him. Keerian let out a string of praise and curses as he fucked me harder, faster, bringing us both towards the promise of absolute bliss.

Our breathing grew ragged as we chased that high, until the most powerful orgasm I'd ever experienced crashed through me. I cried out, every muscle in my body seizing, as Keerian bellowed, following me over the edge and spilling inside of me.

If my nails hadn't been anchored snug into the tree, I would have fallen to my knees, but between my magic and my mate, my shaking limbs were supported well enough so I could catch my breath, coming down from the most incredible sensation of bliss. Keerian was half draped over me, one palm splayed across my belly, the other braced against the trunk over my head between my own hands until he was in control enough to gingerly straighten and pull out of me.

I felt the loss of his immediately. I opened my mouth to protest, but my wonderful mate had already tucked himself away and was kneeling behind me to scatter a line of kisses up the backs of my thighs as he drew my own pants back up to my waist.

I finally staggered upright, tugging my nails out of the tree, willing my magic to revert them back to their regular length.

Keerian pressed up against my back once more, his arm extending past me to run down the sycamore's trunk, tracing the gashes left from my nails. He chuckled, looking down at me appreciatively before kissing me again and wrapping me in his arms. "Have I pleased you, my Queen?" Keerian asked cheekily, his lazy smirk telling me he already knew the answer to that question.

I laughed, turning in his embrace to wrap my arms around his waist. "I must say, my King, you absolutely did. I'll require you to do that again this evening."

And after returning to Sparrow's home and visiting the bakery with Lenna, Keerian made good on my demand. As the moon shot beams of shiny light through the trees, we were atop the waterfall closest to Florra, and I thanked the gods for my perfect mate. Horns and all.

CHAPTER SIXTY-FOUR
LENNA

LENNA WAS IMPRESSED AT the speed in which magical mail was delivered from the Opal Palace to the Slate Kingdom. She was less than impressed with the "fuck you" Leon had sent back in bold letters written across the decree to divorce.

Now, here she was–standing atop one of the mighty ships from Esmeray's considerable armada, off the coast of Doortan, right outside the invisible, magic nullifying dome that surrounded the Slate Kingdom.

Esmeray, Laurent, and Lenna watched as the ships anchored in the Doortan port bobbed gently against the docks. Sailors were too busy loading and unloading crates, barrels, and freight to even notice the lone ship outside of the narrow inlet, its white sails displaying Esmeray's crest–two curved horns with a golden staff in its center.

If they didn't notice the ship, they were also completely unaware of its intentions.

Keerian flew down, shifting from his Sentry as he crossed the invisible barrier from the non-magic land to the sea.

"Leon's definitely down there," the Golden Gargoyle said as he shook his hair out, tying it neatly into a ponytail at the nape of his neck. Lenna used the Prism that morning to show them what Leon looked like. "His ships are the four dark oak ones with the blue banners. They must've just loaded up the season's trade goods–the holds are full of lumber, but there's no humans aboard."

"That's why he's there," Lenna replied, feeling her rage build. Her voice was low, emotionless. No more would she play subservient wife to that man. Lenna had thought Leon a monster before she had come face to face with real monsters–and survived. Now, Lenna saw her soon to be ex-husband as nothing more than a weak man. "Leon's paying the captains to begin their sail down the coast to sell the lumber."

Damn him. After he dismissed the letter Lenna had sent him with the divorce papers included, Lenna sent another–this one with a handwritten note telling him she was not coming back to Doortan and that he needed to sign the papers and break apart their loveless marriage.

At Keerian's recommendation, Lenna added that she would not take anything in the divorce, since the royal coffers were open to her for the rest of her life. If that was what Leon worried about, Lenna assuaged those fears saying all she wanted was out of the marriage. Nothing more from him.

Leon had written back two days later. A nasty letter demanding that she needed to stop the delusions of being someone who mattered, and to come back immediately to continue her wifely duties she had promised in her wedding vows. The divorce papers came back ripped clean in half.

Upset and needing to vent, Lenna showed Esmeray, and asked, albeit embarrassed, if she could put together one more letter with divorce papers. Esmeray decided a different course of action would be a better idea.

Atop the forecastle deck, Esmeray stood impossibly still, head cocked, her dark hair whipping down her back in a gust of wind. With disdain, she surveyed the four boats that would bring more riches to Leon once they delivered their precious cargo down south.

Laurent stood beside the Queen Absolute, resplendent in a white robe adorned with bright green vines embroidered down its sleeves. On Esmeray's other side, Keerian stood in soft armor made from flexible black leather, his golden wings shining in the afternoon sun.

Lenna opted for a lighter dress, a soft lilac smock cinched around the waist with a brilliant silver chain. Blue amethysts studded the belt, offsetting her free-flowing red-gold curls. The belt had been a gift from Hale, who Lenna had been visiting often at his bakery–without the escort of Sparrow and Esmeray.

It felt fitting to wear it today.

Lenna's eyes narrowed as Leon came into view. Her heart thudded, and her palms turned clammy at the sight of the balding, wiry man striding down the wooden planked dock. She balled her hands into fists, reminding herself that she was powerful, strong, smart, and loved by her true family. This poor excuse for a man was her past–and certainly did not have a spot in her future.

"Ew." Esmeray crinkled her nose as Lenna pointed out Leon. "You can do *so* much better." Keerian echoed the sentiment to Lenna, before leaning his head down to kiss his mate on top of a curled black horn.

As Leon stopped in front of the gangway of the first ship, Laurent stepped forward, blue flames dancing merrily at the tips of his fingers. He looked at Lenna. Lenna gave him a single, curt nod.

"Laurent," Esmeray commanded, a serpentine smile gracing her face, "burn the boats."

Laurent grinned as he shot two balls of flame high up into the sky, and they arched neatly before crashing onto the ship furthest down the dock. Fire exploded upon impact with the deck. The irony was not lost to Lenna. The lumber Leon made all his coveted profits on was the perfect kindling for the flames that enveloped the entire hull and mast within seconds. A tingle of thrill slithered up her spine at the crackling sounds of the fire raging and roaring.

Panicked shouts rang out from the harbor. Leon whirled around, his face mottled in anger, running towards the burning ship. Laurent had a delighted look on his face as he launched more balls of fire towards the next ship.

And the next.

And the next.

Within minutes, the four ships belonging solely to Leon were engulfed in flames, their cargo reduced to cinders. The profits gone. Esmeray wrapped Lenna in a hug. "Let's see if he decides to sign the papers now," the Queen laughed as a giant black crow hopped onto the narrow wooden railing in front of them.

The crow was double the size of the ones Lenna used to see in Doortan, its dark eyes fixated on Esmeray. The crow's blue-black wings shimmered in the sun, and a band of white feathers formed a crescent moon atop its head. Esmeray handed the crow an envelope simply addressed in bold black letters, "*Leon.*" The beastie took it gently in its sharp beak, before Esmeray directed the bird on who to deliver the letter to. With a nod of its feathered head, which completely bewildered Lenna, the crow hopped along the railing before flying towards the harbor, expertly weaving between the pillars of smoke curling off Leon's burning boats.

"First fire chickens and dragons, now giant crows." Lenna muttered to herself, "What's next?"

Esmeray laughed, her fae hearing impeccable. "I'm buying you a fire chick when you find a house to move into."

Lenna wasn't opposed.

The group silently observed the crow as it landed on a wooden chest in front of a purple-faced, screaming Leon. Leon startled at the larger-than-normal bird before gingerly reaching out to take the envelope from its beak. He tore it open, reading a letter Lenna knew she had not written, before bellowing at someone to bring him a quill and ink. He scribbled furiously before throwing papers back towards the crow, who screeched with indignation before collecting each piece of parchment in its beak and launching off the chest, soaring back towards their ship.

Lenna knew the exact moment Leon saw her. His face blanched, taking in the two winged beings, the massive crest flapping in the sea breeze–and Lenna. Fear wracked his features as he stumbled backwards, narrowly avoiding tripping over stacked crates behind him. Lenna burst out laughing as he turned tail and bolted down the dock, disappearing into the shadows of the town beyond.

"Okay," Lenna giggled, "*Who* wrote the letter and what *exactly* did it say?"

Esmeray beamed. "I did. I told him if he didn't sign those divorce papers, burning ships would be the least of his worries. And...well... I maybe threatened his life?"

"I added to it," Keerian chimed up, ultimately very pleased with Esmeray and his contribution. "I told him that alcohol is very flammable and one little spark and that nice Estate of his would go the way of his boats."

Lenna shook her head in amazement, her smile widening. "You two are very violent."

Keerian squeezed his mate affectionately, their wings tucked in between each other. "We just love you, that's all."

The crow landed with a triumphant air about it, bobbing its beak–and the signed divorce papers.

It was done.

Lenna was freed from the marriage that dimmed her very soul. Throwing her arms around Esmeray, she laid a smacking kiss to the Queen's cheek before turning to hug Keerian with the same ferocity.

The mighty ship turned, guided by fae magic, sailing swiftly away from the Slate Kingdom and back to Irridessen. As soon as Doortan faded into the horizon, Lenna slipped the wedding band off her finger, tossing it into the depths of the churning water below. As it sunk down into the dark waves, Esmeray waned them from the ship. In a quick flash of gold, Lenna found herself standing in front of a very colorful bakery in the heart of Florra. Esmeray winked before waning away with her mate and Laurent.

The afternoon sun warmed her face as she stepped lightly towards the bakery's door. Without a doubt, Lenna knew she was home.

EPILOGUE

Gulls screamed overhead as the body washed up onto the black sand beach. Lashed haphazardly to a broken barrel with a length of twine, sodden and still, none of the sea birds dared to get closer until they were convinced this was not a new threat to them. One gull, bolder and bigger than the rest, with a smattering of bright cobalt feathers down its back, was the first curious enough to investigate.

With a brave hop, the beastie landed atop the barrel, its gnarled feet perched against the metal rim of the wood, peering at the prone figure. A quick jab of its beak into sunburnt flesh, and a low moan emitted from the body. Squawking in fear, the gull launched itself back into the sky, its sea-blue feathers glinting in the harsh sun's rays.

The sounds of the fleeing birds and the soft lapping of waves was punctuated with a groan of pain that turned into a panicked rasp.

Coughing up sea water, her hands scrambling for purchase against the soft sand, Orla opened her eyes.

Her voice was gone, leaving only a raw roughness behind, as she retched up another belly full of salt water. Orla's mind bellowed at her, terror like she'd never known before sinking in, as she tried to stand. The waterlogged barrel yanked her back down, its sharp edges leaving a smattering of splinters against her palms as she pitched forward.

Dazed, Orla felt her muscles go limp, exhaustion tugging at her very bones. She inhaled the fresh air of the beach, her lungs wheezing as another flash of nausea gripped her.

With jerky movements, her fingers trembling, Orla finally managed to untie the twine that wrapped around her torso and leg, freeing her from the barrel. She fell to her hands and knees, gasping, until her stomach calmed. As another gull shrieked, Orla raised her head enough to survey her surroundings, squinting against the bright sun.

Black sand greeted her, stretching miles into the distance, broken up only by bits of debris that littered the coastline. White capped waves tugged and pushed more broken boards and destroyed barrels toward the land. Odd, fluttering strips of cloth floated on the surface of the bright blue water.

Her mind was foggy, bleating at her in alarm, yet she couldn't form a single, coherent thought. The sharp tang of salt filled her nose as she rolled onto her back, sitting up gingerly, fighting against the raging panic that caused her heart to hammer in her chest.

Where was she?

The last thing she remembered was getting onto a ship. Leaving Doortan.

Marlo had been there.

Dollin had been there, too.

Where were they now?

Shaking her head to clear her confusion, Orla pulled herself up, using the busted barrel for support. She tried taking a step, biting down a hiss of pain as the hot sand sizzled against her bare feet. Her legs wouldn't cooperate. Muddleheaded and swaying, she looked down at her torn pants and immediately collapsed to the ground as she eyed the huge, bleeding gash traveling from her hip down her thigh.

A loud creak brought Orla's attention to the edge of the beach, and she let out a hoarse screech as half of a ship's mast burst from the sea, sending a wave of cold water towards her that billowed softly over the burned soles of her feet, taking some of the sting away, before receding back. Drawing her gaze up to the top of the mast, Orla let out a strangled gasp. The ship's flags were torn and, and...charred along the edges. Her eyes widened as she beheld the bodies of two sailors tied to the heavy wood that had not survived, their limp corpses bloated from their time under the rough waves.

Bile rose in her gut at the sight of the dead and Orla heaved, half staggering, half crawling away from the water. It was instinct alone that guided her, wanting to be far from the drowned men, that pushed her to crest a hulking dune.

As she clawed up the sloping side, the sun beat down on her exposed skin, and disorienting swells of pain threatened to drag her into unconsciousness again. Orla's vision tunneled as an agonizingly sharp heat began trickling through her blood, filling her veins and choking out her breath.

Dragons.

It was the last conscious thought Orla had before she passed out, her body rolling back down the dune to rest on the black sand beach below.

ACKNOWLEDGEMENTS

When I first began working on Queens of Spells and Stone, all I had was the desire to write out this idea that had rattled around my head for ten years and fear of failure. But watching this story grow, take shape, and slowly become a book was more rewarding that I could have imagined in my wildest dreams.

Writing, traditionally publishing, and then making the decision to *republish* this book independently has been healing, thrilling, terrifying and ultimately life changing in the best way. I learned more about myself than I ever thought possible. But with that being said, my new indie career would not have been possible without the below people who cheered me on every step of the way.

Firstly, this story would have never even gotten finished if not for the unending support I received from my husband. Randall, it is a testament to our own epic love story that I found the security, the peace, and the passion to write this book. Thank you for being my blueprint for every written romantic moment and for being the other half of my soul. An additional thank you for coaxing me out of my writing cave nightly with extremely delicious food. This life is ours. This book is ours.

Secondly, the woman I am today is because of my wonderful parents. Mom and Dad–I'm sure this book comes at no surprise to you since my childhood was spent devouring every fantasy book I could get my hands on. Thank you for encouraging me to read and rooting for me when I began writing my own story. For taking me to midnight releases in bookstores, and for not chastising me too hard when I stayed up all night with my nose buried in a new book. And finally, thank you for always being there to give me advice. You are my role models and my sounding board for life and I am so grateful for you both.

Which brings me to the most wonderful sister I could ever have–Carly. No matter how many books I write, you will always be cooler than me and I appreciate that about you. Keep following your dreams and Facetiming me in the middle of the night.

Thank you Tori, for being the closest thing to an older sister that I have. You inspired one of my favorite characters through your amazing friendship, and I couldn't do this life without you. I appreciate you for keeping me (mostly) level-headed, and for turning me into a Taylor Swift fan.

Amanda, you are my personal book bestie and another sister in my life–thank you for reading an early version of this book when it was just a 400 page word document with a lot of typos and immediately demanding I finish writing Book 2. Thank you for believing in me and also for giving me the best godson I could ever ask for.

Cameron and Spencer–Thank you for your unwavering support and for being excited when I admitted that you both inspired characters. I am so lucky to have friends as awesome as you.

To Heather, Jess, and the rest of the Rattle the Stars PR team–Republishing this book with you has been the easiest release ever. Thank you for all of your editing support, PR support, and unhinged comments added while editing. I adore you all.

To Michelle–Thank you for taking my written out character descriptions and turning them into amazing portraits. I am in awe of your gift.

To Tina–Thank you for creating this gorgeous cover on such a wild timeline. You were a complete joy to work with and I am so grateful Instagram connected us.

A million THANK YOU's to my wonderful team of ARC readers for shouting their love for Queens of Spells and Stone from the rooftops (and through social media). I appreciate you all forever and ever.

To each and every reader who picked up this book, read it, and loved it, a major thank you times a billion! Moving into the indie space feels like coming home, and I am so grateful for your messages, your reviews, and your kind words. They are forever imprinted into my heart. I am so blessed to be able to share my stories and my love of writing with you all. Queens of Spells and Stone wouldn't be the book it is today without you, and I cannot wait to bring more books to your hearts and shelves.

And finally, to the three best puppies around–Mellow, Indie, and Pig–Thank you for the snuggles and love.

If you loved Queens of Spells and Stone, it would mean the world to me as an indie author for you to leave reviews on Amazon. Or on Instagram. Or GoodReads. Or other online book trackers. Or if you feel so inclined, send your fastest carrier pigeon to your friends and tell them you think they should read this book. Whatever works. (But if you do go the carrier pigeon route...I want pictures of said pigeon.)

About the Author

Katerina Stevens is a dark fantasy author who loves writing morally grey characters, creating friendly-*ish* beastie companions for said morally grey characters, and drinking coffee with wild abandon. She currently resides in Florida with her incredible husband, three spoiled dogs, two chunky cats, and a grumpy bearded dragon. She graduated from the University of North Florida after taking pretty much every creative writing class offered. Though she started off as a business major, she quickly discovered that math is hard, which led to her getting a bachelor's degree in Sociology. Outside of being an author, Katerina is a devout Capricorn, a tattoo collector, a Canva lover, and a OneNote enthusiast.